M000197853

Love
Handles

BOOKS BY GRETCHEN GALWAY

THE OAKLAND HILLS SERIES

Book 1: Love Handles
Book 2: This Time Next Door
Book 3: Not Quite Perfect
Book 4: This Changes Everything

Short Story 1: Can't Stop Wanting You
Short Story 2: Just Can't Forget You
Short Story 3: Can You Love Me Now?

RESORT TO LOVE SERIES:

Book 1: The Supermodel's Best Friend
Book 2: Diving In

Love Handles

Gretchen Galway

ETON FIELD

LOVE HANDLES

Copyright © 2011 Gretchen Galway

All rights reserved.

Eton Field
ISBN-13: **978-1-939872-01-2**

Cover design by Gretchen Galway

All rights reserved. Except for use in any review, no part of this book may be reproduced or transmitted in any form or by any means, electronic or mechanical, including photocopying, recording, or any information storage and retrieval system, without prior written permission of the Author.

All characters in this book are fictitious. Any resemblance to actual persons, living or dead, is purely coincidental.

www.gretchengalway.com

Chapter 1

THE FUNERAL WAS more fun than this, Bev thought, waiting in the lobby of her late grandfather's fitnesswear company. The young receptionist was on the phone and had been deliberately ignoring her since she came in. *Maybe she can tell I got my suit at Ross Dress For Less.*

Bev glanced around the dim lobby, shifting her weight from one foot to the other, surprised Fite Fitness looked more like the waiting room for a used car dealership than an upscale fashion manufacturer. It even smelled stale, like yesterday's lunch.

"That piece of shit car," the receptionist said. She wore a lopsided cordless headset over her skinny blond braids but was speaking into a cell phone she had slipped under the earpiece. "I hate San Francisco. I just replaced those brakes like last year, and the prick's like, 'Oh it's your fault for braking too much.' Like I should just crash into everybody. Stupid hills."

She doesn't look old enough to drive, Bev thought, feeling ancient at thirty. She checked her watch again. Only a few hours until her flight home to LAX. "Excuse me," she said, smiling broadly. "I'm Beverly Lewis."

The receptionist held up one hand, index finger erect, and kept talking.

"I have an appointment with Richard," Bev continued. "The CFO. It's kind of—"

The girl spun her chair around so that Bev was staring at the tangle of braids on the back of her head.

"—important." Her mother had warned her the fashion business was filled with self-absorbed, emotional people, but Bev was an expert—she worked with demanding four-year-olds every day. She just had to think strategy.

Next to the desk, racks of clothes were lined up like the under-staffed dressing room of a department store. Curious, Bev stepped to the other side, slid the hangers apart, and ran her hands over the smooth Lycra and polyester. Track suits. T-shirts, yoga pants, running shorts. Cropped tanks with built-in bras.

Poor man must have been senile, leaving his company to me. She was a preschool teacher with no muscle tone—which her grandfather would have known, if he'd ever met her. Shaking her head, Bev pulled out her cell phone and scrolled down to the number she'd got from the lawyer.

The desk phone trilled. The receptionist let out a loud sigh, set down her cell, and realigned her headset. "Fite Fitness, this is Carrie."

"Hi Carrie, this is Beverly Lewis, right next to you. I'm here to see Richard, the CFO."

Carrie jerked her head around and stared at Bev holding her phone.

Bev smiled, trying not to laugh at the look on her face. "Ed Roche was my grandfather," she said into the phone, since Carrie seemed to process better through it. "Could you please tell Richard I'm here?"

The woman's eyes widened. She nodded and swung back to the phone to dial. She mumbled something, dialed, mumbled again, then hung up.

"Thanks," Bev said, this time without the phone.

"He didn't pick up, but I left a message. You should have told me who you were."

"Sorry. Richard didn't answer?"

"I'm sure he'll come out and get you. It's kind of hard to find his office." Carrie pinched her lips together again, this time with an apologetic look. "I'd get you something to drink, but we don't have anything like that anymore."

"That's okay, I've got my water bottle." Bev pulled it out of her shoulder bag, waved at Carrie, and walked over to a lint-colored chair that may have been white when it was manufactured in the 1980s. She thought about the word Carrie had used—*anymore*—and wondered if business was as bad as it looked.

Not her problem. Her aunt Ellen could figure out what to do with it; Bev's life was hundreds of miles away.

She sat down next to a dusty ficus, noticing the brown leaves littering the floor beneath it. She lifted her hand and caressed a crispy leaf with her thumb. "Poor thing. When's the last time you had a drink?"

She got up onto her knees and leaned over the back of the chair, pouring her Calistoga into the pot. Clouds of dust motes rose up around her head, glimmering in the shafts of light coming in from the street. She sneezed.

"Did you lose something?"

The man's low voice made her flip around in surprise, hand over her mouth, fighting back another sneeze. Right behind her stood a muscular blond man in a tank top and shorts.

She tilted her head up to gaze into his face, suddenly wishing she'd spent a little more on her outfit for the day. With a face that would impress even her Hollywood executive relatives, the man was well over six feet tall, broad at the shoulder, narrow in the middle, and glistening all over—her classic nightmare.

She realized she'd seen him at the funeral, though not dressed like this.

"Thank you." She maneuvered herself off her knees and onto her feet, trying to look graceful. He must have just had a lovely view of her big butt. Her face burning, she extended a hand. "I'm Beverly Lewis. Are you Richard?"

His cheerfully sun-kissed hair didn't suit the gloom of the rest of him. His workout clothes were slick and black, his mouth was a hard line, and his penetrating dark eyes made her feel as though he could see through her retinas into the soft, jiggly underbelly of her soul. Not to mention the rest of her.

Why is he staring at me like that?

"I'm Liam Johnson. Executive Vice President," he said.

He took her hand in his, enveloping it completely. Unlike many men shaking a woman's hand, he exerted genuine pressure —as though he expected she was strong enough to take it, or didn't care if she wasn't. She squeezed back as hard as she could, secretly disappointed he didn't flinch.

He must have skipped the gathering at Ellen's house, just as Bev and her mother had. To go running, apparently, from the looks of him—unlike Bev, who'd been eating a cheeseburger.

"So, you're the granddaughter," he said. "Our new owner. What a pleasure to finally meet you."

The sarcasm in his voice made her stand up to her full five-foot-ten. She hadn't expected a warm welcome, but the depth of hostility was a surprise. He was probably one her aunt's allies. "I didn't know about his will until the day before yesterday."

"But you knew you had a grandfather. Funny I never saw you before now."

Her lips were tight over her teeth, holding up the smile she didn't feel. "Perhaps you could help me find Richard so I can get on my way. I have a flight in a few hours."

That surprised him. He frowned. "Today? Where are you going?"

"Orange County. I need to get home."

For a long moment he just stared. Then a corner of his mouth twisted. "Of course. Death can be such an inconvenience."

A chill settled over her. She studied him closer, trying to remember more of what she'd heard from her aunt that morning about the staff at the company. He must be the guy who grew up next door to her grandfather in Oakland. The protégé. Her grandfather's death must have been a shock to him. "You're the swimmer, aren't you? He hired you right after the Olympics."

"I'm surprised you would know anything about what he did."

Ah. That was it. "It's true we weren't close," she said. "But you were, weren't you?"

His jaw hardened. He shrugged.

"I'd love to hear anything about him you might like to share," she said. "Our branch of the family has been kind of estranged for a while."

"Oh?" A lot of unforgiving ice packed into one word.

"Since before I was born," she added. *So lay off, dude.*

"Your loss."

Bev looked past him to one of the doors along the far wall, nodding in agreement. She'd done her best to chat with her infamous aunt Ellen over the past couple of days, but her mother still wasn't talking to her—her only sibling—after thirty years. Not even at the funeral. It wasn't right.

"Perhaps we could continue this inside." She looked down at his exercise clothes with a raised eyebrow. "Unless you're too busy," she added.

Smoothing the tank top over his chest, the thin fabric clinging to sweat and muscle like synthetic skin, he began to walk towards a doorway. "The administrative offices are back here."

"Great. Thank you." She waved at the receptionist, but the young woman sat petrified and stared at Liam without blinking. No doubt the sporty ice cube was a difficult boss.

He led her down a narrow, carpeted passageway with offices on one side, most of them empty. The shabby carpeting was brown with tan stripes worn down the middle from the tread of human feet. Pausing in a doorway, he looked over his shoulder at her. "I mistook you for Ellen at first. I thought she might have dropped her phone behind the chair."

Bev walked faster to catch up. "Some people say I look like her, but I think it's just the black hair." Aunt Ellen had the same pale skin too, but their features were nothing alike. Ellen had a cold beauty Bev was happy to live without. It put people on edge, demanded attention, caused trouble.

He ushered her into a dark room, slapping the wall to turn on the lights. She was trapped inside with him. His gaze fell down her body. "You're right. I don't know what I was thinking."

She was annoyed with herself for feeling insulted. She lifted her chin and looked past him into the windowless office, noting floor-to-ceiling metal grids bolted to the walls holding up clothes and white foam presentation boards, sketches, magazines. "This isn't Richard's office, is it?"

"It's mine." He crossed his arms over his chest, the sheen of perspiration still visible on his skin.

"I need to talk to Richard."

"He's not nearly as important around here as I am." He walked over to his desk and sat behind it. "Talk to me."

She snorted. "I'm sure you are very important, Liam. Nevertheless—"

"You don't understand. Richard is just an accountant."

"And you don't understand. He has papers for me to sign."

Liam froze. His eyes flickered with an emotion she couldn't read. "Papers." His voice dropped. "What papers?"

Uncomfortable with the visible clenching of his classic jaw, she considered fleeing back to the lobby, but as a top executive he probably deserved to hear it from her. She sank down to the edge of a chair and crossed her arms over her chest. "Ellen had them prepare some legal stuff to cut me loose. Right now you guys need my permission for everything."

"Cut loose? You can't possibly sign anything so soon."

"Don't worry, I'm not making any changes. I'm handing it over to Ellen. They just need my signature."

"Not Ellen. You don't understand. You can't."

"Everyone knew she would inherit the business. She should." Though her mother had liked the idea of Ellen being disappointed for once, after years of being the favorite daughter, the one who got all of Daddy's love, attention, and money.

"Your grandfather left it to you." He leaned forward. "You have to keep it."

She smiled. Another four-year-old. "You'll be just fine. Sometimes we take things a little too seriously, don't you think?"

He tilted his head and regarded her, silent for so long Bev was afraid she'd offended him. Suddenly he leaned back in his chair, propped his elbows on the arms and regarded her over his steepled fingers. "You're perfect."

A nervous laugh caught in her throat. "Why, thank you, Liam."

"I'm not letting you out of this room."

She did laugh then. Maybe he was too accustomed to people bowing down to him. She got up and gave him a sad smile. "As of this week, I own this room."

He nodded. "And I'm going to keep it that way."

"Nice meeting you, Liam, but Richard is waiting for me."

With athletic grace, he was out of his chair and leaning over the desk towards her. "Hold on. Hear me out."

"No time."

"Tell you what." He pointed at her. "I'll call Richard for you. I'm sure his flight isn't as early as he made it sound. I—I'm sorry. You just surprised me. I know why your grandfather didn't leave the company to your aunt. And why you can't either." His brown eyes softened. "Please."

She froze mid-way to her feet, caught in the photogenic tractor beam of his face. "He was just confused. A mistake."

"Ed Roche was many things. Confused was not one of them, not even at the end." He picked up the phone, held her gaze. "I loved him, you know," he said softly.

Like a saltine crushed in a chubby fist, Bev's resistance crumbled. She sagged back down into the chair and said, "Okay. If it's all right with Richard, and you promise to walk me to his office."

With his gaze never leaving her, he stepped around the desk, dragging the phone with him, and got between her and the door. "Richard, I've got Beverly Lewis here. She's going to be about a half hour late. Can you stick around?"

While he was looking away she took the opportunity to study him more closely. Even in sweaty workout clothes, he was imposing. She had never been the insecure type, but she envied the effortless confidence he exuded like carbon dioxide out of his lungs, just the waste product of his existence.

He brought the phone back to his desk. "He can wait. He's flying out of Oakland and was just worried about getting over the bridge. But he's got a little time."

"All right. So, tell me—"

"First, let me get you some coffee or something." He strode to the door.

"No, really, I don't need—"

"And I can change out of these clothes."

"All right, but I have my own flight out of SFO—"

"I'll be right back." He stepped out into the hallway and closed the door.

Bev let out a breath, kicking off her left shoe to rub her aching toes. She could have gone straight to the airport and dealt with this over the phone, but then she would have been as bad as her mom, grieving with remote control.

The room was interesting—cluttered, but interesting. She glanced at the door and shoved her foot back into the shoe she vowed never to wear again. With a limp, she made her way over to a presentation board hanging on the wall. About three feet wide, each board displayed a parade of paper dolls—flat, simple sketches, filled with computer-generated colors and patterns. Fabric swatches with pinked edges were glued in a line at the bottom, though the bright colors had been ripped off and reattached with Scotch tape. Yellow Post-Its were scattered here and there, with "yes" or "X", or in one case, "NFW."

She noticed a thick binder open on Liam's desk. With another glance at the closed door and one at her watch, she edged closer and flipped through the pages. The men's line, from the looks of it. More sketches, lots of spreadsheets, actual buttons and zippers and fabric swatches taped to the paperwork. Fascinated, but curious about the fun stuff—women's—she peeked around his office until she found a bookcase with more binders. She dragged a heavy one labeled FALL into her arms and dropped it onto a table.

Ah, that was more like it. Some color. She smiled, imagining herself in the skin-tight yellow short-shorts. My God, the wedgie she would have.

"Glad you found something to do," Liam said from the door.

She swung around, annoyed at the wait, yet disarmed to see he'd changed into khakis and an olive button-down shirt that brought out the golden flecks in his eyes. His damp hair was combed back, emphasizing the strong bones of his face.

She pulled her eyes away and focused on the cup he held out to her. Long, tanned fingers curled around it. She took the cup without letting herself touch him.

It was natural to go full girly around a man who looked like him, just biology at work. And now he was bringing her something to put in her mouth. She wrapped both hands around the cup and went back to her chair.

He sat down behind his desk and watched her take a sip, saying nothing.

"So," she said, grimacing at the taste of the coffee. It tasted like something scraped off the bottom of the oven. "You were in the Olympics?"

He hesitated. "I swam backstroke in the relay. Though just in the heats."

"But you were on the team that got the gold?"

He turned his attention to his computer, put his hand over the mouse. "Impressed?"

"Sure." Bev loathed hard-core athletes. People who devoted themselves so intently to their own bodies were seldom concerned about anyone else's. "Go ahead and tell me what you wanted to tell me. We've run out of time."

He didn't turn away from the computer. "Just a minute."

She took a deep breath. At school, she had a responsibility to redirect children to polite behavior, and she knew a delaying tactic when she saw one. "You don't know why he left it to me any more than anybody else." She got to her feet, put the cup on his desk. "Whatever problem you have with my aunt, you'll have to take it up with her directly."

"It's not my problem with Ellen. It's everyone's problem."

"Look, I've heard she can be difficult. Believe me, I've heard stories. But there's nothing I can do."

"'Nothing' is exactly what you should do. Don't sign anything."

"She said the whole building has come to a halt since my grandfather died. Nobody has the authority to do anything."

"What she means is they're not letting her fire people anymore."

She studied him. "Like you?"

His eyes flickered with surprise. He picked up a pen and flicked the cap off. "Not just me."

"But she would if she could?"

"Oh, I imagine she would."

She propped her hands on her hips and looked down at him. "I think I see."

He scowled. "No, you don't. Please. Sit down. This isn't about me."

She stayed on her feet. "So, the big secret is that my aunt is difficult to work with so my grandfather left it to me. Is that right?"

"He began to doubt your aunt's long-term commitment to the company. She was looking to sell out."

Bev shook her head and looked around the office. "Well, given she's worked here for thirty years, she has the right. Listen, could you call me a cab? As soon as I sign those papers I'm off to the airport myself."

He got to his feet and was now the one looking down on her. "What's she offering you?" The corner of his mouth curled up. "Come on—how much?"

She felt guilty for even considering the fifty thousand dollars Ellen promised, but her mother thought she was being taken. "None of your business."

He snorted. "Thought so. Everyone has a price."

Her face flooded with heat. She blinked at him, struggled to stay polite. "You are totally off base. I might not even take it."

"*Might?* Your lawyers don't have a problem with that?"

"No lawyers. This family doesn't need a legal battle on top of everything else. If she wants to offer me money, I'm happy to consider accepting it."

"Happy?" He gaped at her. "Just like that?"

"Call me Switzerland. The rest of my family loves to fight. I don't." Giving the company to Ellen might help mend a few rifts, but if not at least her hands would be clean.

"Some things are worth fighting for. Some people are worth fighting."

"I'm a preschool teacher. We teach peace." She looked at her watch, suddenly angry she'd given him any time at all. "It's late. First you're going to show me where a bathroom is. Then Richard's office."

He stared at her silently for a moment, then stood up. "Well, can't say I didn't try."

Without another word, he led her out of the office down another drab hallway and into the factory proper. "The bathrooms are around the corner. I'll wait here."

She walked past a dark storage area filled with a row of racks stuffed with clothes, through a creaky door that was labeled with a hand-drawn sign. The bathroom was a tiny space with two stalls, one occupied. The air was thick with cigarette smoke and perfume and Pine Sol.

When Bev finished and was washing her hands, she heard a sniffle from the other stall, then a stifled sob that triggered every overdeveloped nurturing bone in Bev's body. After another sob, she gave in and asked, "Are you okay?"

The sobbing quieted. Bev felt bad for intruding and turned on the water. When she was reaching for a paper towel, the woman in the stall cleared her throat and said, "I just needed a minute." She sniffed loudly, and Bev remembered something her aunt had complained about at the funeral, how everyone at Fite acted like babies.

Perhaps her aunt responded to babies differently than she did. Bev unzipped her purse and dug through for something, anything, to offer. She took out a half-unraveled green roll. "Would you like a Lifesaver?"

The woman blew her nose. "The candy, right? Not drugs or something?"

Bev bit down a laugh. "Candy." She tore the wrapper apart in a spiral. "Wintergreen."

A long, delicate hand with chipped red fingernails appeared over the top of the stall. "You must be visiting."

Bev handed her the entire package in case she didn't want Bev's skin touching the candy itself. Some of her preschoolers would turn down a cupcake if they couldn't pluck it out of the plastic box themselves. "Yes. Just visiting."

She snorted. "Thought so. Nobody here would give a shit."

Her hand appeared over the door to return the package, and she muttered thanks again before falling silent. When it was obvious she could do nothing more, Bev went back out into the cluttered storage area.

Liam leaned against the wall, long legs crossed at the ankles. He pointed to a glass doorway past a drinking fountain. "The finance guys are through there. Think you can find Richard yourself?"

She was surprised he was letting her go. "Sure."

"I've got to get upstairs for a meeting."

"Of course."

He stood there, more relaxed than he'd been, then drew a card out of his pocket. "Here. If you need to reach me."

She just stared at him, disturbed by the faint smile growing in the corner of his mouth, the smile of a German shepherd.

"I won't—" she started to say, but he tucked it into her jacket pocket himself and strode away. "Hey!"

He was gone. Something about him disturbed her more than the cup of caffeinated sludge he'd given her. She reached into her pocket to feel the card but didn't take it out. It didn't matter how he made her feel. She wouldn't be back.

She walked through a swinging door into a carpeted, air-conditioned corridor, past the row of cubicles to the large glass-walled office at the end with the CFO's gold nameplate on the door.

It was dark. Closed. Empty. And affixed at eye-level, a folded-over yellow Post-It note with her name in all caps. She peeled it off and unfolded it.

Richard the CFO had left for the airport after waiting until one-thirty and wouldn't be back until Friday.

Bev frowned at it, confused, then groaned.

Liam.

She wrote an apologetic note to Richard on the Post-It and stuck it back on the door. Then she took Liam's business card out of her pocket, crumpled it in her fist, and threw it into the blue recycling bin near the copy machine.

She'd have to come back, just like he wanted. And worse for her, she'd have to delay it past Friday, since she couldn't call in sick at her job like corporate people. She'd already used up all her limited personal time on the funeral, helping her mother cope, visiting the lawyer. The next available time she would have was over a week away when the school was closed for the summer.

Liam Johnson thought she'd be easy to push around, just like her mother, her aunt, infant receptionists—everyone.

I will take the money, Bev thought, striding through the dark corridors, past Liam's empty office, out to the lobby.

She would call Ellen, reassure her the deal was still on. She'd convince her mother to reconcile with her sister now, the best chance in decades to get talking again. And she'd use that fifty grand to jump-start her career at the school.

One thing she wouldn't do was let one grouchy, sweaty jock get in her way.

Chapter 2

"SIGN IT." LIAM slipped a single sheet of paper onto Ellen's desk. "You made your point. HR won't let us keep Wendi on unless you revise this stupid performance review."

Ellen didn't look away from her computer. "I gave her the scores she deserved."

"You put down negative numbers. It's on a scale of one to five. It's not a thermometer. You're not allowed to go below zero."

Ellen glanced over without moving her head. "Not allowed?"

Tactical error. Liam shrugged and sat down. "Why the blood lust?"

"She totaled my Lexus."

"That's it? She scratched the bumper driving it to get your dry cleaning," he said. "You got off lucky. Wendi doesn't even have a license. She could have sued the company for pressuring her."

"What kind of loser doesn't know how to drive?"

"She grew up in the city. She takes MUNI everywhere."

Ellen, whose idea of public transportation was Southwest Airlines, scowled at him. "She's a loser."

"Sign it. This will get HR off your back. And me."

She gave him a disgusted look. "She's the worst assistant I ever had."

"You say that about all of them."

"And always true. A downward spiral."

He leaned forward and picked up her pen. "Well, now she works for Darrin. Not your problem."

"Everything here is my problem." But she took the pen, made a face at the column of threes he'd typed up under Wendi's name, and signed her ornate signature with its E filling half the page before shoving it back to him. "Tell her not to get too comfortable. The new people might have higher standards."

He forced himself to give her threat a lazy, unconcerned smile. *The new people.* So she did intend to sell. "I hear your niece wasn't able to sign those papers the other day."

Her eyes narrowing, Ellen hauled up her orange, metal-studded, moose-sized purse and dumped it on the desk. "Richard didn't wait for her. The girl just inherited his ass and he didn't bother to stick around, the dumbshit."

"She coming back soon?"

Apparently not considering Liam might have a different opinion on the matter, she exhaled loudly and pulled out a lipstick. "God, I hope not. We just FedEx'ed the papers down to her. But she has to find a notary and, quite frankly, it seems clear she is just as lazy as her mother. My big sister got pregnant at seventeen just to avoid homework, then made a career out of marrying for money." She exaggerated the "marrying" with air quotes.

Liam knew better than to swallow Ellen's character judgments, but he felt a surge of panic at the thought of one selfish stranger's signature standing between Fite and disaster.

"Wendi set the line meeting at one." He kept his tone neutral.

She jerked the cap off a tube and twisted the bottom until a stump of her signature crimson lipstick appeared. "Meetings should never be so close to lunch. You thought you were nice rehiring that loser, but it just hurts the rest of us."

"You're going out?"

"Hitting the stores, but maybe I'll make it back in time."

If she did, she'd just confuse everyone and push out the deadlines—revising and deleting and chasing new ideas—then contradicting herself next week. Most of the team could withstand her withering contempt for their choice of footwear, but her unstable, inconsistent management was torture. "All right, maybe we'll see you."

Ellen disappeared behind the swing-arm mirror clamped to her desk and lifted the lipstick to her grimacing mouth. Familiar with her method of dismissal, Liam left her and went to find Wendi.

He found her with the men's sample patternmakers holding up a bolt of thin, black stretchy fabric that, to his alarm, she was instructing be cut into shorts. "Liam! Check out this sick sample yardage. It's got 3D stretch or something, totally new."

He nodded hello at the patternmakers, who drew back in fear and got busy at the opposite ends of the table, and took Wendi's arm in one hand and the fabric in the other, guiding her out of earshot. Ignoring her disappointment, Liam shoved the roll back onto a storage rack.

"Too shiny," he said. "Our Fite guy can't look like he's running down the street in Victoria's Secret." If Darrin, her new boss, saw what she was doing, Liam would never be able to convince him to keep her.

He strode past the cutting tables, nodding but not speaking to the staff. "Move the Spring meeting to eleven," he called over his shoulder, knowing she had followed. "I want everyone there with whatever they've got so far. We'll be quick so it doesn't spill into lunch."

At five-foot-barely, Wendi was having to jog to keep up with his six-three stride. "But you said one."

"Now I'm saying eleven. Just whatever they've got. I realize it's a surprise."

Wendi's brown eyes widened under her Tina Fey glasses, her mouth dropping open. He watched her struggle to hold back her whining that the designers and their assistants were certainly not ready, had planned on cramming through the lunch hour, and would tear her apart when she delivered the summons. "That's in fifteen minutes," she choked out. "And Ellen just went out for lunch, and she's usually gone for hours."

Liam raised an eyebrow and looked at her.

"Oh. Right." Finally understanding him, she broke into a full run in her kitten heels and tore off past the patternmaker's tables on the far side of the floor. She threw open the door and clattered down the stairwell.

Design assistants couldn't afford to wait for the elevator. An irony, given the ridiculous shoes they liked to wear. Even at a fitnesswear company, the young fashion graduates teetered around in sexy stilettos or whatever they thought was sophisticated and hot, no matter how impractical for a person who was going to be doing thinly disguised manual labor for ten hours a day.

If Ed hadn't liked looking at the young pretty legs so much, he would have let Liam outlaw the heels. Everyone should wear athletic shoes or something they could move around in. They were a fitness company, for God's sake, not a New York cut-and-sew house. They stood for something.

But he wasn't quite in charge, was he? Not then, and not now. No, he was just responsible for the final result. Everyone came to him and he told them what to do, but ultimately it had been Ed behind every policy, every rule, every hire in the building.

And now it would never change. Ed had died and left the company to his spoiled descendants who would finally sell out Fite, take the cash, and leave Liam at the whims of whatever transnational holding company swallowed them up.

Just because Ed had wanted to leave it to a blood relation. As if Liam hadn't loved him more than his family ever had.

"Liam!"

He turned to see Wayne Woo, the men's new production patternmaker, waving at him from behind a rolling rack. Liam kept walking. "Can't stop. Late for a meeting." Which almost cheered him up, knowing how desperate the designers would be for him to be very, very late. It was cruel of him to move up a big meeting like that, but he was pissed off. At Ed, at the company, at himself.

But Wayne didn't give up so easily, chasing him down near the row of humming sewing machines outside the stairwell. "I've been working on this all night." Wayne shoved something on a hanger at him. "I resolved the chafing problem in the Fite the Man shorts. And the seams are flat along the hem, though we can't press these goods too hard or they'll shine—"

"Wayne." Liam gave him his coldest glare. "Not now."

The young man in the bicep-baring tank top didn't seem to hear him. He continued to hold the shorts out to him. "And if we change the reflective embroidered logo to a screen print, we can afford an iPod pocket—"

"Wayne!" Sally, a senior patternmaker in a Tinkerbell sweatshirt, ran over to rescue Liam. Or Wayne, really, since Liam was glaring at the well-built young guy, silently questioning Ed's hiring judgment again. Ed had loved the good-looking talkers, male or female and regardless of their talent. Though at least this guy looked like he knew the difference between a squat and a deadlift.

"Sorry, Liam. He won't bother you again." Sally pulled the guy away and whispered furiously into his ear.

Liam nodded and kept going, satisfied but wondering when he'd become the type of boss who couldn't bear to have the little people talk to him directly.

Wayne continued complaining to Sally. "But Darrin won't listen to anything I have to say either. He told me thinking is above my pay grade. Well, duh de dum, how fucking boring is that?"

She shushed him. "Not now!"

Liam turned around and saw Wayne shaking his head with the deflating enthusiasm of a new employee who'd just begun to realize Fite wasn't as cool as its ads. "Wayne, hold on. Come back."

The young guy lit up and hurried over. "Yeah?"

"Show me." Liam held out his hand, and Wayne thrust the shorts at him. With a practiced touch, Liam unclipped the hanger and ran his fingers along the inside seams, judged the fit of the waistband and studied the small inside pocket. "Darrin wouldn't look at it?"

"Just told me to save a couple bucks on the make so it could retail under thirty," he said. "But going cheap on the stitching makes it chafe, and taking out both pockets doesn't give you any place to stick your keys or music when you go out for a run."

"And what'd he say to that?"

"He said our customer isn't going out for a run. That he just wears the shorts to lie on the couch stuffing his face, and doesn't need a pocket for his remote control."

Biting back fury, Liam looked away and ran his hand through

his hair to stay calm. "He said that?" That snotty weasel.

"When I argued with him, he threatened to go to you." Wayne smiled, exaggerating the silver stud through his lower lip. "But I figured I'd save him the trouble."

"You weren't afraid of him?"

"I know his type. All bitch and no bite."

Liam snorted and put his hand on the guy's shoulder. He had to be a foot shorter than Liam but didn't cower like some of the employees did, and he liked that. "He's bitch and bite, I'm afraid. But thanks for telling me. Next time you see him, tell him I made you show me what you were working on and insisted you do it your way."

Wayne beamed. "Excellent."

"All right." Liam made a run for it before the guy thought they were friends now or something. He couldn't afford to be anybody's friend at Fite.

He went downstairs to the second floor conference room and stopped outside the door to give them every possible minute. He could hear the frantic, sniping conversation, chairs rolling around the table, the clatter of design boards and samples being hung on the metal-gridded walls. In spite of his foul mood, he drank in the familiar thrill from the creative process and reminded himself to try to go easy on them. Losing Mr. Roche had been a shock for everybody. And at some point, each one of them had gone into this business with enthusiasm, optimism, even love. And though reality had crushed most of the youthful fantasies within the first six weeks on the job, every once in a while he saw a hint of glee in somebody's face that she hadn't listened to her parents.

He walked in. "Hello, everyone."

All movement stopped for a split second while they glanced his way to measure his mood. None look reassured.

The product development conference room was like a going-out-of-business sale at a department store. Racks of clothes clogged the doorway. Boxes of sample buttons and other trim sprawled over a long, white table that filled the middle of the room. Old design boards hung by pant hangers on the floor-to-ceiling metal grids covering each wall. More metal rolling racks on wheels blocked the windows.

Darrin Kipper, the men's designer, sat at the opposite end of the table wearing an orange—salmon, Darrin would say—Armani suit, trying hide his indignation with presenting his line two hours earlier than he'd expected. *Mr. Roche never would have moved up a meeting*, his eyes said.

Liam looked around the room at the insecure, resentful faces. "There's no reason to be revising everything at the last minute," he said quietly. "For years we've worked right up until the deadline as though finishing early implied you didn't know what you were doing. Well, not any more. If you aren't able to show me our line a little earlier than you expected, there's something wrong with your ideas. You should have been done yesterday. The day before yesterday. Last week. Nothing has changed, only the bad habits in this building that have everyone running around with their heads cut off for the maximum amount of time possible. As though that were a virtue."

With that, he sat down, the creak of the office chair the only sound in the room. "All right," he said finally, leaning back and crossing his arms. "Show me what you've got."

The ten men and women around the table broke out of their paralysis. The designers mouthed furiously to their assistants to finish putting up the boards, and the assistants—all female—jumped up with their scissors and glue sticks and swatches and tear sheets and tried to look fashionably invincible while everyone stared at their thin, athletic backsides in action.

Darrin, angling for Liam's job like he always did, pretended not to care; he licked a skinny finger and flipped through the pages in *Men's Fitness*.

Jennifer, the designer for women's, stood up and straightened one of the boards. She spent most of her days defending herself from Ellen's critical oversight, and the strain had begun to make her look closer to forty than the thirty she probably was.

"Green!" She said suddenly, slapping her hand on the board dangling behind her. Everyone jumped. "American native plants, mostly from California. The color story is gold and lupine blue, with lots of small embroideries throughout evoking wildflowers and the natural earth—"

Jennifer continued to rattle on about environmental populism while Liam scanned her presentation board for the new sketches he'd asked for. Satisfied, he tuned out the rest of her speech.

He felt old. It wasn't his body. He was fitter, stronger, faster than he'd ever been—well, maybe not ever, but he was in damn good shape for thirty-three, and didn't stay up late partying anymore. He was disciplined, but his runs and his lifts were accomplishments of sheer will; he had to drag himself out of bed in the morning and push himself outside in the evenings, as though it just wasn't fun anymore.

"Liam?" Jennifer sounded terrified, and he realized he was scowling again.

He looked down at his hands to rewind the small part of his brain that had been listening to her. "Green is getting old. But it doesn't matter. I've never believed these themes do anything for our bottom line. I know Ed loved the marketing sociology but I don't. From now on, cut the bullshit. Show me the bodies you're cutting and the fabric you're buying and tell me why some woman at Macy's is going to pull Fite off the rack and hand over her plastic."

Jennifer sat down and propped her hands on the table in front of her, biting her lip. "Because they want something fresh, because they love the idea—"

"To hell with the idea," Liam said. "People can't afford just an idea anymore. What will we actually give them that they want? The only idea they like right now is not being separated from their money."

"I think we should rework the fit," Wendi said, and Jennifer's lip curled.

"The fit is perfect," Jennifer said to Liam. "I can't wear anything else."

Liam raised an eyebrow. Jennifer looked like she could crush ice between the cheeks of her ass. An undoctored picture of her abs was on the Fite webpage. Her shapely arms could lift Liam over her pretty head and throw him across the San Francisco Bay.

"There have been some complaints—" Wendi began, then drew back when Jennifer snorted. It was good Wendi didn't work with her anymore.

"From her mother." Jennifer threw up her hands and shared a smirk with a merchandising assistant. "Wendi's idea of market research is to take her sixty-year old mom to Target."

"She's fifty," Wendi said, "and what's that got to do with anything?"

"She's not our customer," Jennifer said.

"She'd like to be."

Jennifer glanced at the ceiling and sighed. "She's fat."

All eyes were on Wendi's face, now flooded with color and looking dangerously close to saying something fatal in reply. Liam had already saved her job once today; he couldn't rescue her again without sticking a bull's-eye on her ass. He held up a hand. "Stop. You're wasting our time." He pointed at Darrin. "Your turn."

Unusually relaxed, and not just in his typically affected way, Darrin smiled and slowly got to his feet. "Personally, I like ideas. Ed and I were always on the same page on that one."

Liam didn't let his surprise show on his face. Darrin didn't usually contradict him directly, preferring to skulk about in secret with his many complaints. For him to suddenly claim kinship with the late Ed Roche, whom he loathed with a passion, could only mean one thing.

He thought Liam wasn't worth sucking up to anymore.

"Bring a board, Darrin?" Liam asked. "Or are your ideas too brilliant to actually move into the third dimension?"

"You know what I'm wondering?" Darrin traced his finger along the stack of overlapping boards hanging on the wall. "If Ed wanted Liam to take over, why didn't he go ahead and leave the company to him outright?" And then he smiled at everyone sitting around the table like he was their best friend. A phony, back-stabbing friend with perfect teeth.

The only sound in the room was the rattle of the furnace vent.

Liam cultivated a tired look on his face and crossed his legs. "Didn't finish the board in time again, Darrin?"

Darrin continued to smirk.

"That wasn't a rhetorical question," Liam said. "Have you got it ready or not?"

Shrugging, Darrin sat down. "You can see it in two hours as planned."

All eyes darted back and forth between the two of them at either end of the table, waiting to see what Liam would do, which pissed him off more than he was already. He slowly got to his feet.

It was past time to make an example of the troublesome prick. And it might make Liam feel better. "Just as well. It'll be easier to look at without you around."

Darrin's smile got tight. "Without me around?"

"You'll be on your way to New York. Remember?"

Now off-balance, Darrin tried to share a snotty grin with Jennifer without losing control of the conversation. "Remind me."

"Your choice," Liam said. "You were missing Manhattan so much you decided to accept a transfer to the showroom."

"The showroom? With the sales guys?"

"It was hard to accept at first," Liam said, "but then you realized any job was better than none. Especially in this economy."

"But—but—you can't do that," Darrin said. "Mr. Roche never would have—I'm a designer—"

"You're a human being, just like everybody else. At least, I'm pretty sure."

"But you can't."

"Of course I can, dude," Liam said. "I'm the executive vice president and I'm your boss. And you're wasting my time."

He could have just fired the asshole, but Darrin was a relatively harmless, useful asshole, the kind with a degree from FIT and a portfolio and old friends working as buyers in New York he could call up any time. He just needed to have a whip cracked every once in a while to remind him to reign in his bad manners.

One of the problems with Darrin and the other regular garmentos everywhere: they looked down on Liam for his non-fashion background. Unlike Darrin, Liam's oldest friends coached summer swim team and spent every free dime at REI, not MAC. He knew all their important buyers, of course, but he wasn't anyone's shopping buddy. He didn't have a fashion—or any—

degree, and now that Ed was gone, the snide comments that he was just the over-promoted adopted son of a lonely old man would grow, and whoever bought Fite out from the family would be looking for any excuse to shove him out.

Ed had promised him it wouldn't happen. He'd been a cranky old man, but he'd never hurt him. At least until the end, when he'd grinned at Liam and told him it was all up to him now, him and his pretty face. Then gave him a picture of his granddaughter, a woman who looked just like Ellen, a woman he despised.

All the years of giving Fite everything he had were coming to an end, and he would have nothing to show for it.

Nothing.

"So, Darrin." He was eager to get far away from all of them before he made an example of someone who didn't deserve it as much as Darrin. "If you've changed your mind about the move to New York, ask your guy Wayne in Engineering how to save your job. He's got a great new short body that's just what we need and you should tell him that, or you'll be telling it to the Bloomingdale's buyer this fall. Jennifer, call up Wendi's mom and ask her why she doesn't like the fit. Be nice about it. Take her to lunch or something—without commenting on her physique." Then he got up, shoved his chair under the table, and strode out of the room.

There was only one way he was going to get what he deserved out of this nightmare, and she was playing around with fingerpaint in some Disneyland nursery school.

Taking the stairs two at a time, Liam ran to his office, his phone out of his pocket and his thumb hovering over Ed's lawyer's number. He'd stopped Bev once. He could do it again, and not by using his goddamn good looks. With an incentive to hold on to her ownership indefinitely, he could maintain his control.

Improve it. From the looks of her—and he tried not to remember how disturbing that had been, to be attracted to an Ellen clone, just like Ed had wanted—she was in serious need of money.

And unlike the sharks he knew were already circling, she would be easy to manage.

Chapter 3

THE BOY WORE a princess tiara and Batman cape.

"Cover your sneeze, please," Bev told him. "And then what are you going to do?"

"Wash my hands." He stuck a finger in his nose and galloped into the sandbox.

Cathy, the other teacher working that morning at the preschool, came by with a mug of tea. "Year went by fast, huh?" She handed it to Bev. "How're you doing?"

Bev smiled. "I'm fine, thanks. I never knew my grandfather." A boy ran past with a ball of yarn, one end tied to the tree, and she went over to untangle him. "Couldn't miss today, could I?" The second Tuesday in June, worst day of the year.

"Hilda asked me to check up on you. You always take graduation so hard."

"She did?" Bev swallowed her irritation. The director of the preschool liked to spy on her through her colleagues. "Well, tell her I'm fine."

"At least this year you can say it was the death in your family that upset you. You know, extenuating circumstances."

Bev kept her eyes on the sandbox. The handful of children outside with them were completely occupied with a garden hose, enjoying a school policy of child-directed play and obliviousness to water conservation. Kennedy, a freckled five-year-old girl with curly brown hair, stood off to the side, drawing on a rock with a black marker.

"The worst part is, I won't miss all of them."

Cathy smiled. "I know."

"But some of them, I miss so much—"

"Not now, Bev. I shouldn't have come over. You were fine before I came over. Hey, did you hear about the afternoon program?"

Bev looked up at her.

"You did," Cathy said, lighting up.

"Oh, yeah." The school's waiting list had grown to triple digits, and rumor was Hilda needed an experienced teacher to direct an afternoon class in the fall, largely independent of Hilda. Bev was going to make her an even better offer and buy into the school itself, finally giving Hilda the chance to retire in a few years—and gain Bev some independence.

Cathy checked over her shoulder and lowered her voice. "I bet she'll give it to you."

Bev bit back a grin. She thought so too. She was the most senior teacher and got along with everyone, kids and adults. "It's not that I mind working in a team. But I'd love to be in charge of my own program. Hilda is so . . ."

"Anal?"

They rolled their eyes in unison. Cathy glanced over her shoulder again. "I can't believe how hard she came down on you for that Valentine's Day project."

"The girls begged me. They really, really wanted hearts. I don't think it's fair to deny them their fun just because Hallmark gets out of hand." Hilda was passionately opposed to the commercialization of childhood.

"Maybe if you hadn't cut the hearts out for them."

"They begged me! It's hard for little fingers and round scissors to make that corner, there at the top where the heart dips in the middle. They were crying and pleading, and I mean really, what's the big deal? It's not like I shoved them out of the way and took over. I was following their direction." Bev gulped her tea. "She made it sound like I was trying to be Santa and they were my elves."

Cathy giggled. "Shhh."

Bev sucked in a deep breath, set down her tea on a windowsill next to the bubble machine, gazed at her kids. In less than an hour they wouldn't be hers anymore, and she was too grieved at the thought of never seeing them again to enjoy the anticipated changes she would make.

"Bef?" Kennedy, the rock-drawing girl, tugged on her jeans. Her cheeks were smeared with black marker, freckles, and dried yogurt, and Bev knew if she kneeled down to give her the usual hug she would lose it completely.

"Hey, friend." Bev rumpled her hair. "What are you up to today?"

"Feeling sad," Kennedy said. "Very, very sad."

Validate her feelings. "You feel sad."

"I lost Big Blue." Kennedy didn't just have pet rocks. She had friend rocks. "In the sandbox."

"Oh, it'll turn—" But it was Kennedy's last day, and if it turned up, she would be gone. Off to kindergarten, where they took away your rocks and gave you worksheets to drill for standardized tests. "I'll look for it."

"Don't bother. It's gone forever." Kennedy had an Eeyore streak they'd been working on narrowing, to no effect. She bit her little lip.

"Come on, let's look."

"Too late," Kennedy said. "It's circle time, see?"

Sure enough, Hilda was ringing the bell. Bev led the group today and couldn't be late; Hilda had just published an article in *Parenting* about the importance of routine in preschool-aged children's development.

"I'll look for it after circle," Bev said.

"It's okay." Kennedy's eyes filled with tears. "It likes the sandbox. It didn't want to go to kindergarten."

"Oh, honey." Bev dropped to her knees and opened her arms for a hug. "I know you're sad, and that's okay, but it will get better. Kindergarten is awesome."

But Kennedy jumped into her arms and began to cry. Not a temper-tantrum I-want-it cry, but the deep, mournful cry of an old soul staring into the abyss. *Now I'm done for,* Bev thought. She would have been fine with any of the other kids, one who cried every day, one who didn't name her rocks and give them rides on the tire swing, but not with Kennedy. Kennedy had only cried once, when Ethan had punctured her index finger with a staple right through the nail and then yanked it out with his teeth.

So Bev held on to her and let her sob, and kept most of her own tears from spilling over. Most.

"Kennedy." Hilda stood over them, wiping paint off her hands with a checkered dish towel. "Circle time!"

Kennedy drew back and looked into Bev's face with wide, anguished eyes. "Are you coming?"

"Ms. Cathy is doing circle today," Hilda said. "She needs you to pick out the story. It's your job today, Kennedy!"

"Okay." Kennedy wiped her nose on her arm. "Mommy has a job, too."

"That's right." Hilda extracted her from Bev and took her hand. "We all have jobs to do."

Thanks for not looking at me, Hilda. Bev turned away and wiped her own face and trotted after. "I'll do circle. I couldn't just leave—"

Hilda nudged Kennedy through the door into the classroom and gave Bev a cold look over her shoulder. "Later." She pulled the door shut between them, leaving Bev outside. Cathy's voice called for attention above the chatter.

The teacher not doing circle time had potty duty. *Damn it.*

She stormed off to the bathroom and grabbed the cleaning supplies, trying to think happy thoughts about Kennedy's bright future, about her becoming a peppy geologist with lots and lots of friends. Who would never have a boss who was a chronically dissatisfied egotist—

Bev's gloved fingers holding the non-toxic sanitizer bottle shook over the miniature toilet bowl. She was a nice person, but she hated doing what people told her to do. Especially impossible ones.

She flushed the suds away, snapped off the rubber gloves, and bent down to wash her hands in the tiny sink. *Get over it.* Next year, managing her own class, would be better. Working with Hilda—not *for* her—would be tolerable.

Hilda appeared in the doorway. "Let's take a minute in my office."

Bev put a spring in her step and a smile on her face and followed her into the alcove around the corner. "Maybe I should just sit this day out next year."

Hilda, a sixty-year-old battleax with silver hair and a big bosom, pulled her into a quick hug. "That's for the other children. Now, cleansing breath. Cathy will look out for Kennedy until her mother gets here."

Surprised by the embrace, Hilda stumbled back a step. "I'd never heard her cry like that before. I couldn't leave her."

"Reflection," Hilda said. "You were feeding off each other."

"It wasn't like that. It really wasn't."

Hilda pursed her lips and stared at her over her glasses.

The butterflies in Bev's stomach flapped their wings, but she managed a professional face, anticipating her coup when Hilda offered the PM job and Bev was able to offer a partnership. "It's just the last day," Bev said with a smile and a shrug. "Having to say goodbye."

"We had this exact conversation last year," Hilda said. "You promised you could keep it together this year."

Bev's smile tightened. "She needed me."

"You were getting emotional."

"Of course I was getting emotional. Kennedy's wonderful. They're all wonderful. And now we're saying goodbye."

Hilda dropped her head into her hand. "This is what I'm talking about. It's just too much for the kids to manage their own feelings and yours."

"I know, I know. But wouldn't it be hurtful if I acted like I didn't care? We spend all year loving them, to just shove them out the gate and wave and look happy about it—"

"We do not spend all year loving them," Hilda said. "That's your mistake. We spend all year teaching them. Or better yet, providing a safe space for them to teach themselves."

Bev bit the inside of her lip. "You know, love is a good thing."

"Not at school. It confuses them."

"They're so little."

"And you're not." She turned to her desk and picked up a piece of paper. "At least, I didn't think you were when I hired you."

The room fell silent. "It's not just the emotional stuff that's bothering you, is it?"

Hilda shook her head and took a deep breath, filling her lungs for an elaborate run-down, then bit her lip and shook her head as though there was just too much to say.

Bev's mind raced. Against the school's child-centered philosophy, Bev liked to direct the kids in organized projects, making group banners and costumes and murals and music and plays under her direction, instead of putting out all the toys and letting them do whatever they wanted. Hilda had halted the projects more than once and dragged her into the office for a chat. If the California public schools hadn't cut most of their elementary school arts programs, Bev might have looked into building a career there. "So you're not offering me the PM job."

Hilda drew back. "Oh, no." She held up her hands, palms out, as though bracing for a collision.

"Even though I'm the best candidate."

"You're not suited to it. I'm sure you can see that."

"No, I don't."

Bev frowned. "You can do better."

"Better?"

"Somewhere else."

Bev froze in her chair. "Somewhere else?"

"Head Start is more hands-on. And the city rec programs. I'm sure you can find something."

She was firing her? "You hate those programs."

Hilda shrugged. "Maybe you won't."

"They pay almost nothing. And the benefits are horrible, and the turnover—"

"I am sorry, Bev, but that's my decision." She swiveled sideways in her chair to the desk. "I've written you a recommendation. I only mention our philosophical differences, nothing about the inappropriate bonding. That might be hard to explain away."

Shaking, Bev got to her feet. "*Inappropriate bonding?* Yes, if you put it that way."

Hilda held up the paper, wiggled it around.

Cathy stuck her head in the room. "Excuse me. I need help out here."

Bev glared at Hilda and imagined yanking out her puffy gray hair with her fists like little Ethan had done last week.

"I'll be right there," Hilda said.

"Actually," Cathy said, smiling, "they're asking for Bev."

Hilda's eyes flashed. "We'll both be there."

Cathy glanced at Bev, eyebrows raised in concern, then fled. Bev grabbed the printed recommendation out of Hilda's hand and strode to the doorway, fuming, then spun around. "You know what I think? I think you're jealous. Of me. Of the love."

Hilda's mouth dropped open, and for a split-second something soft and uneasy flickered in her eyes. Then it hardened into naked contempt. "You don't want to be a teacher." She sat up bolt upright. "You want to be a mommy. Young women like you say you want to devote your lives to other people's children. It's a lie. You're lying to me, you're lying to the children, and you're lying to yourself. Now that you've hit thirty you'll realize you want your own baby and walk away. It's written all over you."

"*You* never had children."

Hilda shook her head in disgust. "You're not me. You want children you can manage. Line up and show off. Just like Jacob's mother last year, getting him head shots, taking him to auditions. At three years of age!"

"So I'm like a stage mom? Because I helped the kids make

valentines?"

"Two words," she said. "Annabelle Tucker."

Bev sucked in her breath. So that's what this was about. Not her job performance, not the affection the children held for her, not the meddling in art projects—Hilda nursed a grudge about a child Bev had first met in the university child care center over a decade ago. Bev had been a student teacher, getting her degree. Later, she had babysat Annabelle for years to help pay the bills. Last year, Annabelle, then fifteen, had asked Bev for an introduction to her father, a Hollywood exec. Now the girl had her own show on the Disney Channel.

"It wasn't my idea, but it seemed the nice thing to do," Bev said. "I didn't feel it was my place to make any career decisions for her."

Hilda shrugged. "Like I said, you'd be better someplace else."

Molars clenched together, Bev took a step backwards, then another, out through the door until Hilda's face and its smug disapproval went out of focus. She kept moving until all she could see was the frame around the door and the rows of cubbies on the wall, then she turned away from the office and wandered through the playroom. She paused to tidy up a pile of foam blocks, willing her hands to stop shaking.

When she reached the backyard, chest heaving with the effort to breathe, the kids presented her with a farewell bucketful of roly-polies, and for once, their Ms. Bef was too angry to cry when she said goodbye.

છે.

The apartment building was surprisingly shabby.

Liam frowned at the chipped concrete structure in the middle of the modest southern Californian street, double-checking the address on his phone. He could even hear the roar of I-5 from inside his car, her street not seeming to have the clout to extend the concrete sound barrier from its wealthier neighbors.

Maybe he'd made a mistake while inputting the number he got from the lawyer. The ranch houses on the rest of the street, though, were too small to be broken into apartments, and hers was definitely 2B, as in "to be." He remembered that part in particular.

She must live in the big shithole then, the one with the rusty dial-up box outside the propped-open security gate and gravel lawn and the dead shrubs lined up in geometrical precision along the sidewalk.

He wondered if she gave them bottled water.

He'd be in a better bargaining position from inside the building, not begging for an audience through an intercom with a gate between them. Even an open one. Smoothing down his dress shirt, straightening his tie, he decided to appeal to the mercenary spirit Ed had bemoaned all these years as the only unifying family trait.

Liam frowned at the useless security gate as he walked into the building. The elevator had a Post-It note over the call button declaring "Broke" so he found the stairs. At least it didn't smell like piss. The idea of her living where random thugs off the street could hide out in the stairwell bothered him.

Why did Ed's granddaughter live in such a dump? He pulled open the fire door—surprisingly functional—and strode down the hallway, looking at door numbers. Beverly Lewis's was in the middle on the left, not even the end unit. She had neighbors on all three sides and a kidney-shaped brown stain on the carpet in front of her apartment.

He wrinkled his nose and knocked on her front door, his knuckles making a hollow, tapping sound in the cheap wood.

Music turned off, and footsteps approached the door.

"Hello?" Eyes red and pale skin splotchy, Bev peered out at him through a foot-wide crack.

"Hi. It's Liam Johnson. From Fite. I'm sorry to barge in on you like this, but I couldn't risk the wait."

"Liam Johnson?" Her sad face lit up with rage. "You! What are you doing here? You're in my building."

"Unfortunately." He glanced over his shoulder. "At least I don't have to live here."

"What?"

"Sorry. May I come in?"

"You came all this way to insult me?"

"Not at all. I'm here to point out that you don't have to live here either." He glanced over her shoulder and gestured inside. "May I?"

She didn't move. "You have no idea how badly you screwed up my life. And now you just barge into my home and insult me. What's the matter with people? Couldn't you have been decent and respectful and used the phone? Didn't I deserve at least that courtesy?"

Taking in her tears and the illogical rant she'd flown off into, Liam concluded Bev was upset about something other than his sudden arrival. "I apologize. Would you have answered?"

She hesitated, her face conflicted. "Maybe."

"Hear me out." He rested his forearm on the doorframe, leaned closer, and smiled into her suspicious face. "I have a deal for you. I think you're going to like it."

Chapter 4

ACROSS THE HALL, a door opened and a young male face appeared. "You all right, Mary Poppins?"

Bev stopped glaring at Liam and took a deep breath. "I'm fine, Arturo. It's nothing."

"You want me to call my brother?" He looked Liam up and down and his eyes widened. "Or the cops?"

"No, no. This guy's just a suit. Thanks, but I'm fine. He and I will talk inside." With a tight smile at her neighbor, she stepped back for Liam to enter, shooting angry sideways looks at him.

Just a suit?

He stepped inside and felt as though he'd been magically transported to a high-end SOMA condo. Like his. Somehow, she'd managed to make the hard angles of the institutional '50s apartment building look cool. Not a single shabby chic, cozy thrift-store item in sight—everything was sleek, simple, and modern. She didn't even seem to have—ah, there it was. A white, long-haired cat, comatose on a black rug and looking like a fluffy plus-sized slug.

For a moment, he forgot why he'd come. He ran his fingers over a triangular lamp shade. "Is that a Winzler?"

"IKEA," she said. "Winzler's not quite in my budget."

He nodded, turned, pointed at the low-backed leather sofa. "You like red?" Other than white, black, and stainless steel, red was the only color in the room.

"Yes." With quick, rough jerks, she combed her fingers through her dark hair and pulled it back into a ponytail, sending little peachy ears on each side of her head into high relief.

He jerked his attention away. *Remember, she's nothing special —just a younger version of Ellen.* "You've got a talent for design."

"Oh, thank you so much," she said. "What do you want? As if I don't know."

Shrugging, he smoothed his hand down his shirt and fought down the absurd urge to tuck a loose strand of hair on her cheek behind her ear. "Ellen mentioned she had mailed the contract to you."

"I've already signed it. You're wasting your time."

His stomach dropped. "You mailed it?"

She closed her eyes, hesitating, and he felt the breath seep back into his lungs. There was still a chance.

"There's nothing you can say to change my mind," she said, then walked over to the door and pulled it open for him. "You might as well go."

"I'll pay you more."

She paused, pulled the door open wider. "I'm sure you could. That's not the point."

"It's not?"

"Ellen deserves it. It's time for my family to move on."

"Ellen? Deserves?" He was confused. Buying time, he went over and reached above her head to push the door shut again, inadvertently getting close enough to smell a hint of lemon. Nothing bottled or distilled, just nice. He stepped back away from her, even more confused by the rushing of his blood.

"I need a drink," she said. "Stay, go, whatever. I don't care."

Glad she moved away from the door and out of scent range, Liam walked into the living room and sat on the red leather couch. The cat didn't move.

"No thanks, I drove here," he said when she returned with a highboy.

"It's Diet Coke."

He glanced down at it.

"Let me guess, you don't drink Diet Coke?" she said.

"It's fine." He brought it to his lips and watched her over the rim.

"Liar."

He sipped. "Mmmm."

To his satisfaction, her scowl melted away. She was trying to bite back a smile. "Cut it out. I'll get you something else."

"Don't bother—"

"I bet you're the Brita pitcher type," she continued, "so you're in luck. My brother got me one for Christmas, and I even set it up."

As soon as she was out of sight, Liam set the soda on a bamboo coaster, irritated with himself for not hiding his tastes better. He didn't want to give her any reason to turn away from him until she'd agreed to his deal.

"Drinking water is a type?" he asked when she returned.

"Admit it. You have a special pitcher and you change the filters in it every month instead of every two, just in case."

"You're supposed to change them more frequently depending on rate of use."

She laughed, triumphant, and he was momentarily stunned by the transformation in her face. *Nothing special*, he repeated to himself. Ellen had the same supernatural complexion, the impossibly blue eyes. But Ellen never glowed like that, like she was filled with something bright and warm.

"Well, drink up with confidence, then," she said. "My rate of use is low."

He drank, willing himself to hide any disgust with the stale taste. But the water was fine. "Your brother works in Hollywood, right?"

"And my father." She set her drink down and leaned over to pick up the cat. Limp and unresponsive, the animal sagged in Bev's arms and didn't complain when she sat down across from Liam and pulled it tight against her chest like a fur breastplate.

"Nice cat," Liam said.

She snorted. "Nice try, Speedo."

He squeezed the drink in his hand. "Don't call me that."

She shrugged, pulled the cat closer. "All right. Liam." She sagged back into the sofa and closed her eyes, sighing. "Go ahead. Say what you came to say."

Displeased by how vulnerable she looked, Liam took a sip of his water and thought strategy. It would help to know why she had been crying before he arrived. "Bad day?"

"Very."

He waited. Took another sip.

"I don't want to talk about it," she said.

"All right."

Frowning, she buried her face in the cat. "I was fired this morning."

Hello. "I'm sorry to hear that."

"Sure you are."

"No, really." His mind raced with possibilities. Even shitholes charged rent, and she wouldn't be living here if she'd had any surplus. No wonder she'd signed the papers already. "It was a surprise?"

"Totally." She sank deeper into the sofa. "I'd planned—well. Never mind."

"That's a lot to deal with, all at once. Your grandfather, Fite, now this."

Not nearly as suspicious as she should have been, she glanced up at him. Grateful. "I feel bad for complaining. My mother's going through worse."

He doubted that. From what Ed had told him, Gail Roche-Lewis-Torres was a spoiled, selfish woman with no sense of family. But he said, "I'm sure it's hard on her. Just in a different way."

Over a horizon of white fur, she gazed at him with softening eyes. "Thanks."

Something inside him struggled against its rusty restraints. His conscience. When she tilted her head to stroke her cheek slowly along the cat's back, he suddenly imagined her doing the same to him, in bed.

He turned his head away so quickly he sloshed the water into his lap.

"Oh," she said. "Let me get you a towel."

"No, it's fine—"

But she was already up and heading for the kitchen, her round ass swaying out of sight. Thank God.

"Don't worry," he said when she returned. "It didn't get on the leather." Just on his best pants. He scowled at the dark spot.

The interruption had broken the spell, and she didn't sit down again. "You might as well go, Liam. Whatever you wanted, you'll have to talk to Ellen about now."

"You're probably right." He got to his feet. "But humor me. Are you hungry? Let me take you out to dinner. My dime." In her apartment, she looked entirely too cocooned to take risks.

She hesitated. "I've already eaten."

"A drink, then. Coffee, tea, beer, whatever you want."

"What I want is to be alone." She leaned over and stroked her cat, now a fuzzy ball in the corner of the sofa. He wondered if it was real. "It's been a long day."

How could he make his offer in a way that would appeal to her financial needs as well as her family loyalty? Which, surprisingly, she seemed to have. "I have a better deal for you than Ellen—"

"Her deal is plenty."

He held up his hand, "—and it's not just a wad of cash." His brain struggled for the magic word. "It's security."

"Wads of cash can provide quite a bit of security."

"For now, maybe," he said. "But they have a nasty habit of shrinking. Really quickly."

"I'm not extravagant."

He glanced around her apartment. "No, but you'd like to be, wouldn't you?" He stepped closer to her and noticed how tall she was. "You've obviously got great taste. Wouldn't it be nice to use it properly?"

Eyes narrowing, she stepped back. "You've got the wrong idea about me."

"Instead of a single payout, I'm offering you a salary, a share in the profits, a future." He smiled as warmly as he could. "Which is what your grandfather wanted, I'm sure."

"Everyone has a theory about that. One that's convenient for them." She waved her hand. "Besides, the company's on the rocks. My little visit was enough to see that. A share in zero profits is zero."

That was what he'd expected to hear from the start, so he was prepared. "Fite has hit rock bottom, but we're still here, and can only get stronger with Ellen out of the way. Ed exaggerated the company's problems to keep the staff from spending his money or expecting raises, bonuses, special treatment."

"Like functional lighting?"

"Exactly. He liked the psychological effect. Felt it kept everyone on their toes."

"Jesus. My mother was right. What a miser."

He gritted his teeth, offended she'd insulted a man he had loved, the one who had just left her his life's work. "I've been Ed's EVP for years now and have the perspective you lack. Give it some time. I was going to suggest you keep your current job, but since that sudden change in circumstance, I'll just say that you now have the leisure to find another one that suits you best. Without any time pressure."

"You'd pay me a salary even if I had another job? Hundreds of miles away?"

"Not me—Fite," he said, encouraged. "And as owner, you'd have your hands on the profits, too. Not just now, but for years to come—and I assure you, there will be profits. Perhaps not this year, but soon. You're young now, but someday you're going to want to retire and have—"

"Hold on," she said. "All this, for doing nothing?"

"Not for nothing. For the company."

Her face was blank. "Just because you don't want Ellen in charge. Is that right?"

"Your aunt may have wonderful qualities," he said, though unable to think of any, "but managing a business is not one of them. I don't think she'll be able to hold on to the company for more than six months, even if she wanted to."

"Unlike you?"

"Or many, many other people."

"How about me?" A hard gleam came into her eyes. "You're happy enough to have me at the top."

He had to be careful here. "Your grandfather must've left it to you for a reason."

"And you think that had to be so you could remain in control, right? Because a stupid little preschool teacher would be easy to push around?"

"I have no opinion whatsoever about your intelligence," he said, then paused to regret how unflattering that sounded, "or about your career. But let's be realistic. You need the money, and Fite needs . . . to not have Ellen in charge—"

"You almost said, 'Fite needs me.' That's what you mean, all of this. You're the big important guy and without you, the company will burst into flames and everyone will be out of a job—"

"No." His own temper flared in response to hers. "This is not about me. It's about Fite."

"Please." She stalked over to the door and jerked it open. "Get out. It's been a long, horrible day and you are now leaving."

"Beverly—"

"Get out of my home."

She'd never listen to him while she was so angry, so he moved over to the door and stopped just before he was out in the hallway. "I'm sorry for whatever I said that offended you. But what you're doing is not in either of our best interests. Or Fite's. The company is filled with real people who are going to suffer if Ellen—"

"Out." She placed her palm in the center of his chest and began to push. "She's not that bad."

He was momentarily distracted by the pressure of her hand through his shirt. "All she knows how to do is fire people. She keeps a hit list in her desk—"

One unexpectedly powerful shove, and he was in the hallway.

"Goodbye, Liam Johnson," she said. "If I were in charge I'd be tempted to fire you, too."

And then she was gone.

He glared at the closed door, heard the clicks and thumps of multiple dead bolts, and cursed himself for screwing that up so badly, not even sure what had set off her temper. Just like her aunt after all, all short-sighted emotion. If she just took a moment to think about what he's said instead of just flying off the handle, she would see he was right.

Damn. Not that it mattered now. She'd signed the papers. It was just a matter of days.

He'd better get back up to San Francisco tonight to start warning the staff.

❧

Bev carried her tray with its taco and tiny plastic cups from the salsa bar to a table near the front window. She chose an outward-facing seat so she could admire the strip mall parking lot with her getaway car while her father got a burrito.

Although Anderson Lewis was a marketing executive in Hollywood, he avoided trendy restaurants. Except when he was with Andy, of course—her older brother. He had followed in their dad's footsteps so completely, working ten times as hard as was healthy and earning twenty times as much as Bev, so that if he made time to eat, it damn well wouldn't be El Cheapo Taqueria off I-5 in Buena Park. And Anderson Sr. wouldn't expect him to.

She sucked iced tea through a straw and fought back despair. No job, no hope of one for six or more months, and that arrogant jock had made her feel unclean about taking money from Fite. *Stay out of the way, little girlie. Here's a cookie. Sit over there and don't interrupt.*

Liam's patronizing attitude had inflamed the hunger she'd

been feeling to make something bigger of herself. To be in charge, making decisions and taking risks.

If anyone would understand that hunger it would be her father. Worried about her future, disgusted with her poverty, he'd been after her to get an MBA for years. A real job. Use her brains for evil, he liked to say, only half-joking.

He walked over to her, humming to himself and carrying his tray with one hand while he returned his wallet to the back pocket of his dark-wash jeans. He was tall and big-boned, like Bev, but with the sinewy physique of a fifty-year-old man who never watched TV unless he was on a treadmill.

"Since when don't you return your own father's calls?" he asked. "You'd think I was trying to sell you an indie picture about skin disease in a third world country."

"Sorry, Dad. It's been crazy."

"Crazy." He snorted and frowned at the foil-wrapped log on his plate. "Crazy is this thing on my plate. It's bigger than your head."

If Bev ever argued with her father, she would have pointed out the restaurant was his idea. "Do you want to switch?" She offered him her taco.

"That the pollo or the carne?"

"Carne."

"Can't," he said, brow furrowed. His third wife, Tia, was in charge of what he was allowed to eat, a moving target of restrictions and obscure supplements that only she could remember. "Is it good?"

"Don't know yet." She took a bite and couldn't resist smiling. "It is. You sure you can't—"

His face stretched longer. "No, I promised. That's what you get for marrying somebody from Santa Monica."

And somebody a third his age, she wanted to add. "So, you heard about my grandfather."

"Of course I heard about him. Both your brother and sister called me to complain about it as soon as they heard." He pierced his burrito with a plastic knife and began to saw. "You're still sulking about Tia."

She stopped chewing. "I'm what?"

"You never liked her. I'm supposed to say, that's your prerogative, give agency to your pain or some bullshit, but I won't. She's part of the family now, so get over it."

Bev put down the taco. Anderson had been married three times. Twice in the past ten years, both to women in their early twenties. His second wife had lasted three years, the marriage ending when she got pregnant by an anesthesiologist from Las Vegas. Tia, his new wife, already had two children of her own from two previous relationships, neither of their fathers lasting more than the gestation period, and loved to talk about when she and Anderson would finally have children of "their own."

Given her father's terrible taste in women, Bev was understandably prejudiced against anyone he liked. But this time, her reluctance to talk to him had nothing to do about his love life. "I didn't get back to you because I didn't want to argue."

"I never argue."

She snorted. "I knew what you would say, and I'd already made my decision. But now I'm not so sure."

He stuck the fork in his mouth. "I don't know what you're talking about."

"About the company. Taking the money instead of moving up there."

"You think I'd want you to move to San Francisco?" He stared at her, his cheeks bulging with burrito. "You mean, to work in the fashion business?"

She hesitated. "You never did think much of my chosen career
—"

"Career? Oh, you mean the little kid thing?"

"See?" She tried to roll her taco back together. "You've always wanted me to go corporate. Devote myself to making money."

"Nothing wrong with making a living," he said. "Which is why you shouldn't try to rescue a struggling business you know nothing about."

She gave up on the taco and put her hands in her lap. "I thought you'd pressure me to give it a shot."

"Hardly. But that doesn't mean you're stuck being an underpaid babysitter for the rest of your life. I don't think you like kids as much as you think you do," he said. "At least, not other people's kids. Maybe you'll change your mind when you have kids of your own, I don't know. How the fuck—excuse me—how the hell would I know. I'm not a goddamn shrink."

His face always got red when he was upset, which was much of the time, one of the reason's Bev avoided him. Nothing she said seemed to prevent an argument. Her thoughts scrambled back over his words. "You don't think I could do it."

"Don't tell me you're considering it?" He wiped a stream of salsa off his chin. "Listen, Bev, Ed Roche was one class-A manipulative jerk. Pardon me speaking ill of the dead, but he was. If he left his company to you, it wasn't for anyone's benefit but his own. He had no reason to benefit you in particular, so you can be sure it's something you'd be better off without."

She lifted her iced tea. "Why wouldn't he have any reason to benefit me in particular?" She tried not to be offended to hear him say nearly the exact same thing she'd told Liam.

He looked at her in surprise. "You think he got sentimental in his old age." He gave a dismissive snort and lifted his drink. "You know what he did the day your brother was born? His first grandchild?"

She shook her head.

"Nothing," he said. "Nothing at all."

"Look, Dad, I'm not saying he was some big, loving guy—"

"And then you were born. The great man sent a card," he said. "For your birthday, two *and a half* years later."

"I'm not defending him," she said, though she was. "People change. Especially in their old age."

He grimaced. Anderson Lewis was hostile to reminders of his own mortality. "You might think that's no big deal now since you don't have children of your own. But some day you will—" She opened her mouth and he waved his hand between them. "—And if you don't, it'll be a damn waste."

She smiled. "Thanks, Dad."

He raised one white eyebrow and shoved a large bite into his mouth. "My point is, your grandfather did have children, which should have triggered some human feeling. But no. The year before your mother and I started, uh, dating," he said, "your grandmother died. He'd never been much of a father, working all the time, but it got worse. I'm sure that's what drove your mother to chase after some poor dope who didn't even know she was in high school." He flicked his temple with an index finger. "Then she got pregnant. Barely seventeen, her mother recently dead, and Daddy kicks her out of the house. Of course I had to take care of her. And then two kids. She never forgave him."

It was never easy to hear the same, bitter story. Too young and poor to start a family, her parents had divorced before Bev was in preschool.

"What happened with Ellen? Everyone talks about her like

she's pure evil or something, but she was even younger than Mom."

"Took her father's side. Called Gail a slut, hid in her room, didn't unlock the front door."

"But she was just a teenager," Bev said.

Her father shrugged. "Whole family loves to nurse a grudge."

Sadly, it was true. Bev didn't understand it—why fight with the only family you'd ever have? "He left me a picture of my grandmother, through the lawyer."

"Sounded like a nice lady," Anderson said. "I bet he didn't appreciate her any more than he appreciated your mother, or you and Andy."

Or Kate, she thought, though Anderson didn't know Bev's half-sister very well. "But he did leave her the house. And, of course, left me the company."

He dropped the remains of his burrito on the plate. "And for Andy? The one who could actually do something with a business? No, Bev. He was just stirring up trouble, probably to teach Ellen a lesson. Make her work for it a little harder. If he could have figured out a way to prevent you from profiting in the end, he would have."

Bev looked away, out to the parking lot where a woman was strapping a pug into an infant car seat. "Why do you think I couldn't do it?"

"Know what? I'm getting Andy on the phone." He pulled out his cell and slid his thumb over the screen. "First you're mad because you think I want you to go into business, and now you're mad I don't."

"I just wonder why you think I can't. Like it's totally impossible or something."

He wasn't listening. "Sorry to bother you, son. Got Bev here.

She's having delusions of grandeur. Fashion executive. Yeah, I know—" he paused, listening, and raised his eyebrows at Bev. "She's sitting right in front of me." He held out the phone.

Frowning, Bev didn't move. "I didn't say that."

Anderson jabbed the phone at her. "Listen to your brother."

Listen, not talk. She took it. "Hi Andy." A couple years older, Andy had grown up cheerfully protecting her from all the insults and disappointments of life. She'd been quiet and sensitive; he'd been loud and tough. They were a balanced pair. Sometimes it had worked too well, locking them into habits with each other that were hard to change.

"Hey," Andy said. "Are you nuts?"

"Dad's got it all wrong," she said. "I was only talking about my options."

"One of those being nuts?"

"Andy," she said, then raised her voice to be heard over the yelling she heard on her brother's end of the line. "You sound busy. Dad shouldn't have bothered you."

"I thought you liked teaching."

"Of course I like teaching," she said. "Dad shouldn't have bothered you."

"The fashion industry isn't as glamorous as it sounds, you know. I know how you love clothes, but apparently it's not so fun making a living at it."

"Actually, Andy," she said, "I've been there. Just last week, actually."

"I heard. I thought you sold out to Ellen."

She hesitated. "I am—I was—oh, Andy, I don't know. Some of those people seemed so . . . eager to have an outsider come in." She turned her thoughts away from one eager person in particular.

Andy snorted. "So you are considering it."

"I'm not delusional." She glared at her father on the other side of the table. "I feel guilty. Not about Grandfather, but about everyone in that company. It's not the happiest place in the world. And you've heard the stories about Aunt Ellen."

He exhaled into the phone. "You're running away from something. What happened?"

"Nothing." She listened to her brother's silent disbelief for three long seconds, then got to her feet and walked out of the restaurant. Out on the sidewalk, with her back to her father inside, she said, "Dad shouldn't have called you."

"I know you, Bev. Something happened, and now you're running away from it. Boyfriend problems? Mean boss?"

"That is not it." She wandered away from her father's gaze to stand in front of a manicurist next door. "Actually, I need to find a new job."

"Aha," he said.

"I was fired."

"And now you doubt yourself and want to throw away your entire career at the first setback."

"I'm not throwing anything away." It was she who'd been chucked. "It's too late for me to find a permanent teaching position for the fall anyway. Like it or not, I am available to deal with Fite, and they just might need me."

"You can't do what other people need. You have to do what's right for you." His voice softened. "You love teaching. You've stood up to Dad's bitching about it for years, which was great. I always backed you up there."

"Maybe this is what I need." Bev took a deep breath. "Did you know I made more money typing W-2's into a computer last summer as a temp than I did educating children? Hilda paid more than most, but it was probably still less than you pay your secretary—administrative assistant—whatever."

"Some cardiologists make less than Gwen does. And she deserves it."

"Point is, if I ever want to buy my own home, quit the summer jobs, upgrade my car, save for my retirement, I'm going to have to figure something out."

"Figure what out? You'll get a fortune when you sell Fite." He paused. "Right?"

She didn't want to tell him how little she'd agreed to take from Ellen. "I refuse to bankrupt her. She's family."

"Not going to—Bev. How much?"

"You don't understand. None of you understand. Fifty thousand is a fortune to me, and to her, I'm sure—"

"That's it? For the entire company? Oh, Bev. This is a perfect example of how you're too damn nice. Really, it's pathological. Give the phone to Dad. He's going to tie you up until I get over there. Are you at that taco truck in Santa Ana?"

She gritted her teeth. "Will you listen to me? I am not being nice." How she hated that word. "And besides, maybe I won't sell it at all. I have a chance here to do something different."

"Even if it's all wrong for you."

"Exactly," she said, then closed her eyes while he crowed into the phone.

"Run, baby, run."

"Oh, be quiet." She looked up at the hazy platinum sky above the strip mall. Her brother was rich, successful, crafty, and insufferable. "I'm just looking at all my options."

"I don't think taking on that company right now would be a good option for anyone, Bev. Except as a tax write-off."

"You haven't been there. It's a little rough around the edges at the moment, but there's a real history you can feel, people with passion—"

"Grandfather was Fite's heart and soul. I read that in his obituary in the *Times*."

"There are other people there with heart and soul. I felt it." She heard him snort. "And don't rag on my feelings, you dork. If it doesn't work out I'll just get another teaching job. Any money I get"—earn, she added silently—"from Fite will help me be sure this time. I'll approach a school as an investor, not as some underling."

"Find another teaching job now," he said. "No need to pretend you're something you're not."

"Pretend?" She squeezed the phone. "I'm not pretending. I'm exploring. Grandfather left this company to me, and nobody really knows why. He must 've wanted—"

"No offense, but if Grandfather wanted somebody to actually take over, he would have left it to me. Mom says he was just trying to piss off Ellen."

"No offense? I'm not in first grade anymore, Andy. I didn't get an MBA, but my GPA and SAT's kicked your ass. Managing children takes a hell of a lot of quick thinking, guts, and creativity."

"Okay, okay, I'm sorry. Of course you're smarter than I am, you always were. But you're too nice. You're a preschool teacher, not an asshole. From what everybody says, Grandfather was. Not to brag, but look at me. And Dad. To succeed in business, you have to be. Look what Grandfather built all by himself, from nothing. He wouldn't have given Fite to the nicest person in the family if he thought she'd actually be crazy enough to keep it."

Bev looked at her father through the glass as he picked at the black beans on his plate with his fingers. "Nicest person in the family?"

"You're a chronic do-gooder," Andy said, laughing. "I can just imagine you in management, going around trying to make everybody feel good about themselves. Nobody would get any work done. They'd walk all over you, Bev."

She swung away from the restaurant so her father couldn't see how angry she was. "Maybe Grandfather did leave Fite to me for a reason," she said in the voice she would use with the most difficult, ignorant, obstinate five-year-old. "Maybe it wasn't just to teach Ellen a lesson. Maybe he wanted me to get in there and change the whole feel of the place. Me, the stupid nice one. Why is that impossible?"

"Because it contradicts absolutely everything we know about him?"

"They need me." She took a deep breath. "You know, when I visited, there was a grown woman crying in the bathroom?"

"Better than at her desk," Andy replied.

"See? That's why he didn't leave it to you. What kind of attitude is that?"

"A realistic one," he said. "You have no idea how hard it is to manage people. Real people, not miniature ones."

"Do the people who work for you cry in the bathroom?"

"How the hell would I know? So long as they don't take too long, it's none of my business."

"But it is," she said. "They'll work better if they're happy."

"Oh yeah? You've got studies to prove that?"

She glared at a parked SUV. "I bet there are."

"So you think you're up for that?" he said. "Completely transform a corporate culture? One devoted to fitness, you crazy person? This from a girl who forged a doctor's note to get out of P.E. in fifth grade. What, kickball was too hard?"

That was the only time she'd ever been caught. "You try

running the six-hundred-yard dash with brand-new C-cup breasts and no bra."

"You could have asked Mom for one."

"None of the other fifth graders wore bras back then," she said. "I would have been teased even more than I was already."

He snorted. "You won't be able to wave around a doctor's note when you're the boss. Everyone depends on you."

"I know all about that, believe me. You think little kids take care of themselves?"

"It's different, Bev. How would you feel if I told you I thought I could be a better preschool teacher than you, tomorrow, without any training or experience?"

She closed her eyes and rubbed her thumb along the edge of the cell phone. "Maybe you could," she muttered, feeling in her heart the little-sister worship she'd struggled with all her life.

"No, Bev, I couldn't. I'd suck at it. And you'd suck at managing. You know why? Because you hate conflict. You've been avoiding me since last year, ever since you found out I broke up with Julie. And I'm your brother—you think I didn't notice? You think I was too busy to notice my little sister didn't reply to my emails?"

She flinched. "I just couldn't believe it. She was so cool. And she really loved you."

"You can't avoid people when you're the boss. Especially over crap like that."

Bev let her mind drift away, past her view of the L.A. glare, far from the stink of the manicurist's acetone wafting out through the doorway. Inside the restaurant her father was probably getting restless, eager to return to his new wife who wanted to produce more satisfying offspring. "I'd better get back to Dad. I kind of abandoned him."

The phone was quiet for a moment. "Letting Ellen or outside management take over is the nicest thing you can do for everyone there," he said. "From what I hear, they need expert help. Not you."

But she barely heard him. Her thoughts had fled north. "Thanks for the advice, asshole."

He let out a short laugh. "We done here?"

"Please. Get back to work."

They clicked off. Bev wandered slowly back inside to where her father was scowling at the chaos of tortilla, aluminum foil, and rice on his plate.

Anderson took the phone from her. "He knock some sense into you?"

Bev sat down, reached for her cup, then froze. "Not exactly," she said, realization growing. Her gut knew it first, and her heart swelled, filling her chest with pressure. She looked up into her father's concerned scowl, surprised with herself, and felt a grin spread across her face.

All these people—from her family to her ex-boss to the damnably imperious Liam Johnson—thought so little of her.

Well, to hell with them.

"I'm driving up to San Francisco tomorrow," she said.

Chapter 5

BEV SAT IN the hard chair across from Ellen's empty desk and inhaled slowly through her nose, telling herself she had nothing to be afraid of. She looked at her watch. Exhaled slowly out of her mouth.

Two minutes, she'd said. Almost thirty minutes ago. The drive up from Orange County had taken seven hours, two more than expected, and she'd come directly to the Fite office in San Francisco eager to get her conversation with Ellen over with. Her nerves were intermingled with exhaustion and hunger and thirst. She should have stopped for an early meal first, and the thought of a tall glass of iced tea was driving her mad.

Should she get up and go look for her aunt? She lifted her bag to her lap and confirmed her water bottle was still empty. She organized the gum, pen, cell phone, and notebook again. Took out the cell, scrolled through her contacts, glanced over her shoulder at the door, reaffirmed her ringtone and backdrop settings, put it back in the bag next to the wrinkled pack of spearmint sugarless. She had already eaten off her lipstick seven times and worked a thread loose on the hem of her blouse.

There was no reason to be afraid of her mother's sister. Ellen wouldn't be happy to hear the deal was off, but she'd adjust. And in time, the family would have the opportunity to develop a closeness they hadn't had in Bev's lifetime.

Ellen strode into the room and dropped a binder the size of a late-model microwave oven on the desk.

No big deal.

"Please tell me," Ellen said, clipping the ends of her words as she eased herself into her chair, "that I misunderstood your little message." She fixed Bev with a laser gaze.

Bev tried to keep her posture casual, but her long, awkward legs twitched like a gazelle, ready to bolt across the urban savanna out to her RAV4. "I am sorry, Ellen. I know you must be very disappointed."

Ellen held up her hand, the white tips of each French-manicured finger reminding Bev of Elmer's glue. "Sorry? Please," she said. "You went back to your boring little life and starting thinking this one would be more exciting. Right?"

"That's not—"

"You got to dreaming of yourself as someone glamorous and special," she continued. "Your own fashion company! Wow! What a bomb!"

Bev's anxiety turned cold. "That is not it."

Ellen made a disgusted noise in her throat. "I don't have time for this." She shoved a paper towards her. "Here's my final offer. Take it, or I walk."

"You what?" She flinched inwardly at the anger in Ellen's smooth, beautiful face, then slowly reached for the paper.

"Look at that. All itemized. I tried to keep it simple." Ellen flipped open her laptop screen. "This is your last chance to get anything out of a confused old man."

Bev glanced down at the sheet in her hands with two bullet-pointed paragraphs. One listed a promise of a lump-sum cash payment of a hundred thousand dollars. The second was titled "Cabin In Tahoe" and noted an address, website, and appraisal value of nine hundred and sixty thousand.

She gave up on the relaxed breathing and gaped at her. "I couldn't take this. You don't have to give me anything. I just want to work here."

Ellen turned a wild gaze on her. "I can make some very talented people interested in this company, pros from real companies. In New York, a real city. I want to get Fite into the big leagues too much to let Ugly Betty come in here and mess it up for fun."

Bev sat up taller, her pride stinging. "I'm not going to mess anything up."

"Exactly." Ellen handed over another paper. "Here's where you sign."

Bev smoothed the first paper over her lap with her palms, making no move to take the contract Ellen shoved towards her. Two weeks ago, she'd been happy to give Ellen whatever she wanted, but now she knew she'd been too hasty. She met her eyes. "I'm not signing anything. I'm sorry."

Ellen looked at her watch. "If you don't sign that within the next five minutes, I'm going to hand over my resignation, effective immediately. Without me or my father, an over-promoted, color-blind jock will be the only person with any executive experience in the company." She leaned back in her chair, giving Bev a flat-eyed smile. "On an average day I work thirteen hours, but compared to my father I was a part-timer. An hour from now, an email will go out forwarding all calls and complaints to you. If they can't find you, they'll page you over the PA—which is even wired into the bathrooms. Which is good, because that's where you'll be hiding."

Bev's palms were damp; she wiped them on the sides of her

thighs. Maybe she was fooling herself—seduced by a fantasy, of false glamor, of being the boss—but she hadn't driven all the way up from L.A. just to give up in the first five minutes. Besides, Ellen had to be bluffing. "What about Richard? The CFO?"

"He hasn't been allowed back in the building since our first little negotiation."

Bev felt a surge of guilt. And anger. She doubted Liam even felt guilty about that. "I see."

"Take it." Ellen stood up to glide the paper over to her. "You can't possibly expect me to offer you anything more."

"If you really think I'm that bad for Fite, why leave? Why not stay and protect it from me?"

Sinking back down into her chair, Ellen's hard face twisted into a half-smile. "You'll learn your lesson soon enough," she said. "And I'll get Fite then."

"You think I'll give up and sell to you anyway."

"Not sell. Give," she said. "Three minutes."

Bev looked down at the paper in her lap, studied the numbers, the address in Meeks Bay. *I bet it's beautiful.*

Ellen smiled.

"You just have this kind of money lying around?" Bev asked. Having had a salary of less than thirty thousand a year, Bev couldn't conceive of what it would be like to have so much all at once.

"Daddy may not have been clear-headed at the end, but before that he knew which one of us really loved him. He was understandably generous."

Bev shook her head, dispelled the fantasy. She would never be able to live with herself. The last thing she wanted were deeper divisions in her family. "If you let me work alongside you, Fite would pay my salary. You wouldn't have to give up anything."

"Just everything that matters," Ellen said. She clicked the end of a pen, flicked it across the desk like a spear.

"I can't take this," Bev said.

"Two minutes."

"Ellen, please reconsider. I'm not going to mess anything up. I'm an organized, intelligent person, I work hard, I—"

Ellen blew her nose loudly into a tissue and walked across the room to an open file box. With her back to Bev, she lifted an ornate ceramic vase filled with peacock feathers off a shelf and began wrapping it in newspaper.

Jesus, what a bitch. Her mother had given up on her only sister thirty years ago. Even now, after the funeral of their father, she expressed no regrets about their cold war. Bev stared at Ellen's narrow, rigid back and thought, *I can see why.*

So maybe a family reunion was unlikely. But Ellen had to be bluffing about quitting. After a lifetime of working at Fite, she couldn't just walk away—

"Sixty seconds." Ellen dropped the box on the floor with a thud.

"I'm not going to sign it like this." Bev struggled to think fast enough. She fell back on what she knew best. "How about I get us a snack, and we can talk about it—"

"Last chance, Betty." She strode over to her. She'd slung a large bag over her shoulder and held the box in her arms, the peacock feathers curving up behind her left ear like green and purple iridescent antlers.

Bev glanced at the papers in her lap and got to her feet. "I can't, Ellen. Surely you can wait—"

"Just sign it." Eyes fixed off into space, Ellen waited, unmoving.

Bev studied her cold, bored profile. She sat back down. "No," she said softly. "Not like this."

Alarm flickered across Ellen's forehead, then vanished. Without meeting Bev's eyes she bent at the knees, plucked the paper out of Bev's grasp, and strode out of the room holding her box.

Bev sat in the empty office, the chaos of unfinished designs— bolts of fabric leaning in corners, sketches and photos on presentation boards, samples piled up on racks and conference tables—scattered around the room like abandoned children. The phone rang, and off behind her she heard the PA echo through the hall asking for somebody whose name she didn't recognize.

"Whoops," Bev whispered.

&

It was time. To everything there was a season, et cetera et cetera. Liam lifted the overflowing box under his desk and hauled it to the door.

You're a sentimental dork. He was done with this business, thanks to Ed, yet he was carrying home mementos like an eighth-grade girl.

He looked down into the box at the sketches and tear sheets —a Macy's ad for the first pair of Fite the Man shorts he'd designed on top of the pile—and reassured himself he could hardly leave behind the evidence of his Achilles heel. Ellen would probably move into his office before lunchtime and comb over every inch, mocking and taking and destroying like a ravenous, sarcastic locust.

Better off taking it all home and recycling it at the condo. Nobody knew him there, nobody knew Fite or Ed Roche or his damn descendants, and nobody cared.

Nobody.

With the edge of the box digging into his ribs, Liam paused

near the door and turned around to look around the office, where he'd spent most of his adult life. Right after the Olympics, with Dad finally in his grave and nothing more for Liam to do but maintain a pulse for his mother and brother and sister, Ed had offered him the job at Fite and saved him from God knows what. Law school, probably. He wished he had the brains for engineering, but he didn't. Other jocks went into broadcasting, but he knew he didn't have the charm or patience for that bullshit, though his old friends did very nicely every four years when another Olympics rolled around.

He might have to consider that after all. His salary at Fite had been good, but hardly enough to retire on. To stay in the Bay Area, which was a given, he'd be taking a pay cut—if he could find a company to take him in. He wasn't a fashion guy, he was a jock —an asset at Fite Fitness, but not at Levi's or BeBe or any of the other apparel companies in town. And though it was common knowledge he didn't have an MBA, only Ed had known the worst of it—that he'd never finished his BA, either.

"Damn." He dumped the box on the floor where he stood and thought of Rachel, Jennifer, even Darrin. Wayne, George at the back door, Alfred in the grading room. Sure, he was short on options, but any one of the lower staff people would hurt more than him with the sudden loss of a paycheck.

He bent over and rested his forehead against the door, cursing Ed for leaving him without the tools he needed to get the job done. He remembered the gleam in Ed's eye, telling him about his granddaughter. Well, the tools he was willing to use, anyway.

"Damn." He couldn't bring himself to walk away. Maybe he wasn't the warmest boss in the world, and most of the people at Fite probably thought he was a bastard, but he wasn't going to screw them over the way Ed had screwed him. He had to stick around as long as he could, if just to write stealth recommendations for Ellen's casualties.

He banged his head against the door and gazed down at his new Nikes, absently calculating their make and reverse-engineering the midfoot overlay. Just as he was about to bend over and take one off to bring to the shoe merchandiser, he heard a knock.

If he hadn't been inches from the door, he wouldn't have heard it at all. Just a tap, then a pause, then another tap. A chill tickled down his spine, and he stood up straight, the midfoot overlay forgotten. "Yes?" he barked out, not as irritated as he sounded. Nobody at Fite would knock on his door. Nobody would dare.

Silence. He thought he heard the sudden exhalation of breath and, impossibly, he imagined the scent of lemon blossoms. Vowing his next job would be for a publicly held corporation with thousands of employees and absolutely no family ties amid staff whatsoever, he flung open the door. "You."

Her face, with its impossibly clear complexion, so similar to Ellen's but without the severity of expensive makeup, peered up at him. "You, yourself."

He turned away, shoving aside his curiosity about the woman, wondering how he—even with his acute senses—could have possibly smelled her through the door. She must have doused herself in Lemon Pledge that morning. Yet he couldn't resist inhaling the scent deep into his lungs before striding over to his desk, surprised she'd come by to see him in person. Ellen had walked over too, of course, but she liked to gloat, and his impression of Bev Lewis had been that she'd avoid conflict.

Which is why he knew she wouldn't withstand Ellen's final offer.

"Stop in to say goodbye?" He lounged back in his chair and propped his feet up on the desk.

She lingered in the doorway, tilted her head, and said nothing. His attention dropped to the cheap suit she wore, the same ugly one from her previous visit with faded black jacket that didn't match the darker black pants. His professional eye took in the poor, baggy fit at the waist that hid whatever body she had underneath—tall but soft and obviously nonathletic. A before picture. The woman off the street.

Not their customer.

"You should drop by some of the SOMA showrooms while you're here," he said. "Pick up some new pieces for your apartment. Your new apartment. Or house, perhaps?"

"What are you talking about?"

"Furniture. Home furnishings. That kind of thing. San Francisco has some cutting-edge designers."

She was still frowning. "You think I'm here to go shopping?"

"Let's not waste each other's time." He turned to his computer, where he'd been copying over his personal files to a thumb drive. When they'd accidentally loaded Illustrator on his PC, nobody thought he'd actually use it. Nobody but Ed knew he had, or that he'd loaded the custom sketching software too, and flown to Denver for a private tutorial to learn it as well as anyone. Better. "Ellen's new offer was probably a fair one. You obviously needed the money." He realized now that was what Ed must have intended all along; Ellen learns her lesson, and his lazy but wholesome granddaughter gets the windfall.

"What the fuck are you talking about?" the wholesome granddaughter asked. Her blue eyes flashed down at him over the desk, and he lost his train of thought. Up close, under the fluorescents, they were turquoise. A best-selling color for the summer line, the last delivery before the big fall assortments when the colors went dark and muted and natural again. A bright, happy, energetic color that stood out starkly against her pale cheeks and thick, black lashes.

Perhaps she wore colored contacts. Nobody really had eyes like that.

She blinked, growing visibly uneasy with his gaze, but still angry. "You seem to think you know something. But I don't think you know what you think you know."

He broke the spell by looking down at her ugly suit. A less flattering garment could not have been designed for her, but he realized why she'd chosen something so baggy around her waist when he looked at her chest, now at eye-level. She had to be a D cup, at least. Nothing off the rack would fit her well, with breasts like that—

"Hello." She waved and sat down. "You can stop making snide comments about me going shopping. I didn't sell the company."

He leaned back and the chair creaked. "Not yet."

"I'm not going to."

"You just haven't seen Ellen yet," he said. "She's waiting for you."

"Yes, I did, and no she's not, and I wish you would believe me. I've refused Ellen's final offer, and she's decided to—" She stopped and glanced away. "To wait for me to change my mind." Then she took a deep breath, nodded, and looked back at him. "We'll call it a leave of absence."

Hope began flopping around in his heart like a Golden Retriever puppy. With years of practice he threw a thick, suffocating blanket over it. "Leave of absence?"

"She said she quit, but I can't believe she would do that. I'll call her tonight. The last thing I wanted was more bad blood."

He looked at her. "What exactly did she say?"

"I'm sure she'll cool down. She packed up a box and left when I refused to sign, saying she was just going to wait for me to drive Fite into the ground so she can pick up the pieces."

The puppy stuck his nose out from under the blanket. Without glancing at his own pile of belongings behind her, he asked, "She packed up a box?"

"I'm sure she's waiting for me to call her any second. She expects me to break under the pressure."

So did he. He tried not to smile. Reminded himself he'd have to be very, very careful negotiating between the two disasters Ed had dumped on him. Just enough of the granddaughter would keep the aunt away, but not so much that he went insane or the company went under with her clumsy oversight. He reached for his coffee, sipped, met her eyes. Now he understood the hysterical edge lingering there. "Ellen had an exaggerated view of her own importance. Fite is better off without her."

"She says the same about you."

"Sadly for you, that is not true. This place revolves around me."

She raised an eyebrow. "You have a high opinion of yourself."

"I'm the executive vice president. I have a high opinion of the job."

"My aunt was a vice president—"

"Of shopping." He forced a tight smile. The expense reports for that woman had dwarfed her salary.

Bev shook her head, but her eyes grew wary. "You said 'sadly.' Why 'sadly?'"

Biting his lip as though he was trying to hide something, he let his eyes drift away from her and over to the box near the door. Then he inhaled deeply and didn't meet her gaze.

She took the bait. Twisting around to look behind her, she asked, "What?"

He shrugged, pushed himself slowly to his feet. In a panic now, Bev took it all in at once—the stripped shelves, the bare wall racks, the empty desk. She gaped at him with her mouth in an O.

"I know when I'm not wanted." He was proud of himself for sounding sincere.

"You're leaving?" She shot to her feet. "You, too? Oh, Christ. No. You can't. You just can't."

He opened his eyes wider and said nothing.

Gripping her head with two soft-looking hands, she made a pitiful moaning sound in the back of her throat that was disturbingly erotic. "Oh, God," she said, and he tried not to think of what she would sound like in bed. Because he was pretty sure he'd just heard it.

He strode over to the door. "You've made it clear you don't want me. As did Ellen. No sense delaying the inevitable."

"Wait!"

He was slow to turn around, careful to look unhappy about it. "Sorry, Beverly. It's really for the best."

"Please." She was holding a hand out to him, palm up, eyes wide.

Slowly, very slowly, shaking his head and sighing, he took a few steps back towards his desk and crossed his arms, enjoying the way her gaze raked over his body. He knew he was tall and built and imposing, and maybe this time it was all right to use it to his advantage.

She was definitely eyeing him in a daze, taking a step back and licking her lips.

"All right," she said. "What do you want?"

Chapter 6

"I'LL MAKE YOU a deal." Liam sat back down behind his desk. "Don't call your aunt. Let her quit. She's never done it before, so you should consider the possibility that she's quite serious about abandoning you here to fail."

Bev's stomach lurched. "I'm not going to let the company fall to pieces."

"Of course you're not. Because you're going to stay out of my way."

She did not like the way he stared at her. How did he always get the upper hand? "From what I hear, Fite is barely floating now. Why should I think you can do anything better than what you have been doing?"

"Bev." He shook his head. "Fite's current problems are not of my making."

"Of course not," she said. "How could they be? You being senior VP and whatnot."

"Executive Vice President, please."

"'Please', yourself," she said, her voice rising. "Make your case. Why should I believe you should be in charge?"

"You don't have any choice but to believe me." He pointed a finger at her. "You may have hidden talents, but unless your preschool had a side business merchandising fitness apparel for the mass market, your lack of experience is going to kill this company and the livelihoods of everyone working here."

"All unless I hand over everything to you."

"I'm sick of watching nepotism destroy this company. You may be a blood relation—and as you've admitted, little else—but you have no genuine claim to tell anyone what to do here. Least of all me."

Her head was pounding. Ellen had left. The CFO was gone. How the hell could she let this guy leave too? Her brother was right; she was here on a whim, avoiding her troubles at home, trying to prove she was just as important as any corporate Hollywood type.

"I thought I could bring my mom and Ellen back together," she muttered.

His jaw hardened. "Perhaps a multimillion-dollar apparel manufacturer isn't the place for family therapy."

"Damn." She ducked her head and stared at her hands, conflicted. Was she being selfish to want to stay? She looked up at him. "Tell me what you do for Fite that's so special."

"No."

"Excuse me?"

"I've already proven myself. You're the one who hasn't."

She gritted her teeth. Stood up. Sat back down. They stared at each other over his empty desk. She was reminded of one of her first days working in the university child center, when a tot still in diapers refused to get off the swing. After three hours on it. He'd filled his pull-ups and desperately needed a change—which was why he kept his death-grip on the swing chains—but nothing Bev said could convince him to get off. Bribes, threats, demands—nothing. Finally the professor strode over, pried him off with impersonal strength, and comforted the boy while he cried.

Bev was stuck cleaning his diaper. And hosing down the mess.

Taking a deep breath, she had to admit she wouldn't be able to overpower Liam Johnson with that kind of approach. He was entirely too big.

"All right," she said. "You can continue as you were. I'll just have to learn on the fly."

He nodded. "No meddling."

"No. That's too vague. I can't promise to do nothing if you're terrible at your job."

He barked out a hard laugh, his eyes not smiling. "Then promise you'll do nothing if I'm not terrible."

"I can't promise to do nothing. Come on, be reasonable."

He strummed his fingers on the desk. A single strand of loose blond hair fell down over his eyes and tossed his head to clear his vision, never breaking his gaze on her. "We'll approach your time here as an executive trainee," he said. "Involved, but—declawed."

"Is there an executive training program here?"

He snorted, then recovered. "Sure. We don't call it that, but sure. Of course."

"All right then. We'll start there, and discuss more later. It is my first day, after all."

He shifted in his seat and started working on his computer. "And apparently, not my last. So I need to get back to work."

She was dismissed.

۶

"If I didn't need this guy so much, I'd kill him," Bev said to her mother from her cell, sitting in her car outside her grandfather's empty house in the Oakland Hills. The driveway was half the usual length, under ten feet, allowing room for the squat glass-and-steel building to cling to the steep slope. The June sun was only now setting behind the fogged-in Golden Gate Bridge to the west, a postcard view. A multimillion-dollar postcard. "I had to beg him to stay."

"How much?" Her mother, Gail, sounded like she was doing her nightly Pilates. Lots of grunting.

"For as long as Fite needs him, I guess—"

"No, Bev. How much money did you give him?"

"Oh, he didn't ask for any money. He just wanted me to promise to stay out of his way."

"*Promise?* That's it?"

"I refused to sign anything. That's my one management technique so far. Don't sign anything. So far it's working."

Gail sighed. "You're over your head, honey. If he's survived this long, he's a snake. Don't trust him."

"It can't be good business for everyone to be so hateful and miserable and mean to one another."

"Daddy made his fortune at it," Gail said. "And Ellen, of course. If business is bad, it's probably because he got soft in his old age. That Liam character and the other ladder-climbers probably took advantage of that."

That didn't sound right to Bev, but she needed more time to be sure. "I actually feel guilty about Ellen resigning. I hope she cools off and can come to some kind of compromise." She propped her elbow on the steering wheel, rubbed the bridge of her nose, tried to massage away the tension.

"Don't be fooled. She always gets what she wants in the end."

"She's your sister. You can't live the rest of your life hating each other."

"Why not?"

Bev tried to think of a new tactic. "It's bad for your health."

"Oh, health advice from you. That's priceless."

"I like health!"

"You will some day, when it's too late," Gail said. "How's the house look? I paid a fortune to get it cleaned out. I suppose it's good one of us is up there to do some quality control."

Bev sighed. "I haven't been inside yet, but it looks fine. Quite a view. It must be worth a fortune."

"At least my mother had a heart, though I'm amazed my father didn't find a way around her will and leave it to Ellen or the Raiders or something. Hateful man."

Still waiting for the death to trigger a mellowing of the bitterness her mother had been drowning in for years, Bev popped open the car door. "I'm going in now."

"At least you thought to call me. The lawyer said that key I gave you is only for the side entrance, down the hill. The rest of the keys should be on the counter. Think you can handle it?"

"Yes, Mother."

"If the place is a mess, call the number I gave you and raise a stink. Don't be a wimp."

"I'm sure it's fine. Talk to you soon. It's been a long day." Her head pounded and her contacts were dry on her eyeballs.

"Watch out for Ellen. She'll probably show up for work tomorrow like nothing happened."

"I wish she would."

Her mom paused and made deep breathing noises. "Why he didn't leave it to Kate or Andy, I'll never understand. It's like he wanted Fite to go under."

"Good night, Mom," Bev said, hanging up. What tiny nurturing bone Gail had in her body was only exercised on her older brother and younger half-sister. She should have been used to it, but it still made her want to scream.

She had screamed once, as a teenager. Her mother brought

her to the pediatrician. But it wasn't like in the old days when people had a family doctor she might have known since she was a baby. Her mother took her to some random young guy who had a dozen patients—most of them in diapers—crying in the waiting room. The nurse took her blood pressure, weighed her on the scale decorated with cartoon stickers, and the harried doctor handed her mother a psych referral on a scrap of paper.

Bev decided it was easier to move out, go to college, and live her own life as she pleased. Which she had, and would continue to do. You couldn't change people. You had to learn how to work around them.

She made her way down a path of flagstones around the left, past the large front entryway and a manicured Japanese maple to the side door. The key was taped to an index card with the lawyer's note—"Alondra," the name of the street. She peeled it off, worked it into the top lock and tried to turn it.

Maybe it was the doorknob key. She jerked it out of the deadbolt and pushed it into the doorknob. No luck. She tried jiggling and twisting, then attempted the other lock again, all with no success.

Her mother must have had it wrong. Or Bev heard it wrong.

She found a second path, this one winding down the right side of the house. The sun had dipped out of sight and the long shadows were fading to a uniform dark gray. The cold wind cut through the gaps in her jacket. This side of the house was less trafficked and didn't have any flagstones to smooth the sloping dirt. Her dress shoes had no tread, and at a sudden dip in the hard earth, she lost her footing and slid down, *whap*, onto her butt.

She cried out, pushed her palm into dust, struggling back to her feet. A thorny stick came up with her and caught on her black pants. Though she worked it free as gently as she could the thorn made a hole in the rayon. She tossed the stick aside and slid down another few feet.

This doesn't feel right.

The only door she could find on this side of the house was behind a hedge of squat, sprawling lemon trees that had overgrown the original landscaping. She'd gone to the emergency room in third grade with a two inch citrus thorn imbedded in her heel—still had the scar and no interest in getting punctured again.

She hiked back up to the front door, regretting she hadn't tried that first. But the key didn't even fit into the lock, let alone turn, and she was left in the growing darkness with a pounding headache and an exhausted longing to get inside and sleep. Tomorrow was going to be even harder than today.

A short post-and-rail fence divided the house from the neighbor's, a big Craftsman lit up with outdoor and indoor lights, the house spilling over with the sounds of music and people. She crept over to the fence, peered over. If she walked on their side down the hill, she could get around the lemon trees to a landing in front of her grandfather's side door.

Eh, what the hell.

Grateful for her long legs, she swung one over the fence, then the other. Her heart pounded. Here she was, on some Oakland hillside in the dark, climbing into somebody's yard wearing torn pants. She kept her head up and strode down their side of the fence, not bare earth but mulch and ground cover, towards the lemon trees. Just a few more yards and she could climb back over.

Then the dogs came.

They weren't big, or angry, or even particularly fast. But they were many and they were loud, and heading straight for her like a swarm of yapping, ground-hugging bees. With an athleticism she never managed in normal life, Bev loped down the hill, shimmied over the rails to the other side and stumbled up to the patch of concrete outside her grandfather's side door. She pressed her back against the house and faced the dogs, struggling to get air back into her lungs.

The dogs yapped and yapped. Hands shaking, Bev took out her key and turned around to feel the door. Just get inside. But she couldn't find a lock. Her heart was flopping around in her throat and the dogs were getting louder and this was obviously not the door into the house.

While the dogs—there had to be twenty of them, none bigger than a loaf of bread—continued to yap, Bev rested her head against the door and wondered how she was going to get back up to her car. Vaguely she wondered why the dogs had stopped at the fence; the high posts were hardly an obstacle for such small animals.

A man's voice carried over the din. "What the hell's the matter with you guys?"

Bev stood up straight, smoothed her palms over her pants and tugged down her jacket, trying to look not like a woman who had just fallen in dirt and climbed over fences, but a decent, quiet neighbor lady just trying to get into her house after a long day.

"Somebody there?" the man called out. "Hello? Hey, you guys, easy!"

Bev pushed away from the door and stepped out from behind the lemon trees. The hill under the house sloped fast into a wild, rocky outcrop—she could never go around the house in that direction. She'd have to admit her situation.

"Sorry for disturbing you!" she called out. Eyes on the dogs, now lined up like miniature cavalry along the property line, Bev walked a few feet closer to the fence. The man was lit from behind, a tall and powerfully built silhouette that got larger as he approached.

A woman's voice called from the house. "Liam? What is it? Don't let them get into the raccoon den. The mother just had a litter. They can be vicious—"

"It's not a raccoon," the man said from fewer than ten feet away, while Bev imagined several ways she could kill herself. Did he recognize her?

"Liam, it's just me," Bev said, trying to feel relieved it wasn't a stranger who would need convincing not to call the police. "Bev Lewis. I'm trying to get into my grandfather's house."

He stopped walking and said nothing for a long moment. Then, to the dogs, "Quiet! Friend. Friend!"

"Who is it, Liam?" The woman came up behind him and bent down to the dogs. "Hush, now. Hush. Such tough guys."

Bev waved, at a disadvantage from the house's floodlights shining in her eyes. The woman who had joined him was tall, pear-shaped, but too hidden by the backlighting for Bev to make out her age or features. "I am so sorry to disturb you." Bev took one more step towards the dogs, which only set them off again. Drawing back against the house, she raised her voice over the din. "I'm Bev Lewis, Ed Roche's granddaughter. My key doesn't seem to work."

The woman bent over to calm the dogs. "But that's the closet for the water heater, isn't it Liam?"

"Indeed it is," he said.

Bev looked back at the door. *Crap.* She turned back to Liam and the woman. "I tried the other doors first but they didn't work either. I've never been here, you see—"

"Ed had a granddaughter?" the woman asked, sounding shocked. "I thought it was just Johnny, Ellen's son."

An unfamiliar ache struck Bev in the chest. "I'm Gail's

daughter. One of two."

"Gail?"

"Ellen's older sister. She left home really young," Bev said, wishing she'd taken her chances with the lemon tree.

"Mom," Liam said. "Beverly is the new owner of Fite Fitness. Beverly, this is my mother, Trixie Johnson."

With the conversation easing their minds, the dogs had broken ranks at the fence and regrouped around Trixie. She leaned over and picked one of them up, peering closer at Bev. "Nice to meet you. I had no idea you existed. We moved up here when it was just Ed. Were you at the funeral?"

A sense of loss struck Bev full in the chest, and she could only blink into the blinding light and try to keep her unexpected distress off of her face. *No idea you existed.* "I sat in the back."

"She'll be living next door for a little while," Liam said roughly, putting an arm around his mother to pull her away from the fence. "Go back inside. I'll take care of this."

"But how did she get down there?"

"It's none of our business," Liam said. "Ed's gone now."

"Just make sure none of those raccoons have snatched one of my tough guys." She moved away. "Nice to meet you, honey. Hope we didn't scare you."

When she was gone, Liam leaned his hip against the fence, crossed his arms, and waited.

"The key didn't work," Bev said.

"How did you get down there?"

"The same way I'm going to get back." Bev braced her hands on the fence post and threw a leg over.

"You're lucky my mom's got a thing for rat dogs, not Rottweilers."

"Actually they're kind of scarier. You don't expect the cute little things to attack. Like a doll in a horror movie." She ignored his stare and swung the other leg over. Unfortunately her physical prowess had waned, and she caught her toe on the rail and slumped forward, only to have Liam grab her by the arm and haul her upright on his side of the fence.

"Thanks," she said, breathless and mortified. "I'll be going now."

His fingers were tight around her arm. "To where?"

"A motel, I suppose." She pulled her arm free and began hiking back up the hill to her car.

He remained silent, back in the gloom along the fence line, and she was grateful for it. The last thing she wanted right now was more small talk with an employee who made her feel like a child. A female child.

But then he was at her side again, effortlessly matching her determined pace. "Come with me," he said, sounding annoyed. "We've got a set of keys that should work."

"You?"

"Neighborly backup."

She tripped. "You still live next door?" She'd assumed he was just visiting his mother.

He turned onto a brick path that led towards the large, bright house. "No. We've been—we were—friends with Ed since I was a kid. He was all alone, you know." She didn't say anything in defense, but he didn't seem to be trying to bait her, just stating a fact.

They reached a wide front porch and went up the steps, and Bev saw Liam and his mother were not alone. Vintage R.E.M. was blasting in the living room, and a twenty-something woman in a ripped t-shirt sat in a recliner reading *Organic Gardening* and drinking red wine next to a guy in head-to-toe black. His face was red and angry.

Liam turned to Bev. "My sister April and her boyfriend..." he trailed off, frowning, then shrugged. "Don't know his name."

The guy glanced up at them, brought a bottle of beer up to his lips, then returned to staring at April.

"Hey," April said in greeting, barely glancing at them. She went back to her magazine as if her boyfriend weren't there.

"The keys are in the kitchen," Liam said. "You can come with me or wait here."

The silent drama between April and her boyfriend made her uncomfortable, so Bev followed Liam down a hallway, looking down at her shoes, hoping she wasn't tracking dirt over the glossy oak floors. She picked a leaf off her jacket and tucked it in a pocket.

"Bev needs Ed's keys," Liam said, stepping into a sunshine-hued kitchen and heading straight for a baby-blue armoire in the corner. Trixie was stirring a pot on the stove, and looked up at Bev as she entered. "Otherwise she'll need to find a motel."

Curious to see Liam's mother in a well-lit kitchen, Bev noted her high cheekbones and white, pixie-cut hair. She wore a patchwork denim apron around her generous hips, hot-pink Crocs, and no makeup.

"A motel?" Trixie asked. "Why?"

"Never mind, here they are." Liam pulled a set of keys out of the armoire's front drawer and came back over to Bev. "But don't try the water heater door again. These are for the actual entrances."

She held out her hand and smiled tightly. "Thanks for the tip."

He stared at her, not handing over the keys, while Trixie came up behind him and rested a hand on his shoulder, facing Bev. "I shouldn't have said what I did about your poor mother. Or about you not existing. The kids come over and we open the wine and the next thing you know I'm a blathering idiot."

"Oh, please." Bev smiled at her. "I'm so sorry I disturbed you."

"I've been disturbed for years," Trixie said. "No need to take credit for it."

Liam raised his eyebrows and nodded, then Trixie noticed and swatted him on his butt with a wooden spoon.

He twisted around. "Hey, you got chili on my jeans."

Bev's gaze slipped down to the seat of Liam's jeans. Trixie just laughed, swatted him again, and went back to the stove. Bev dragged her attention back up to his face.

"Come back here if there's any problem with the keys," Trixie said. "I don't want to hear anything about a motel."

Bev shook her head. "No, really, it's fine—"

"Let's go," Liam said.

Trixie reached her hand out to him. "Let me see those first."

He frowned, looking suspicious, but handed them to her. She clutched them in her fist and addressed Bev. "Promise me you won't go looking for a motel," she said. "I've got five bedrooms here and four are empty because my children would rather live in an ugly high-rise in San Francisco rather than with their own widowed mother."

"Uh—" Bev said, absorbing the implied loss of Liam's father with the awkwardness of the invitation. "That's very kind of you —"

Liam reached over to take the keys away from her, but Trixie twisted away, hopped on a chair and lifted her arms and the keys over her head. "Promise." She towered over the room. "You wouldn't want to be the cause of an unfortunate family altercation."

"But—" Bev glanced at Liam.

"Mom," he said, voice calm. "She has a house next door. All she needs are the keys that you are, for some unknown, scary reason, not giving to her."

Bev was more smitten than scared. "Thanks for the invitation." She tilted her head back to address her. "But I'm sure I'll be fine."

Liam put his arms around his mother's waist and hauled her off the chair. "Honestly, Mom, I don't know why I don't have you locked up."

"Hah!" Trixie held her head high while he grunted and dropped her onto the floor. "As if California cared enough to have mental health care facilities for those in need."

"Perhaps a vacation to Utah, then," Liam said. "Keys."

Any foil to Liam was a friend of hers. "I promise not to go to a motel," she said. "Thank you."

"You're welcome, hon." Trixie smoothed down her apron and tossed the keys to Liam. "See you later." She turned back to the stove and began to hum and stir.

"Shall we?" Liam asked, hand extended towards the door. He made no move to give her the keys but she didn't want to argue in front of his mother. She followed him out past his sister and her unhappy boyfriend out into the night and over to her grandfather's front door.

"I like your mom," Bev said.

"Everyone does." He pulled out the ring of keys, selected one swiftly and fitted it into the lock. "But you have to be careful she doesn't take over. She adopts people." He twisted the key, pushed his shoulder against the door, and stopped.

Bev sucked in her breath.

"Huh," Liam said.

"You sure that was the one?"

He turned to face her. "Someone must have changed the locks."

"But the cleaning service didn't have any trouble getting in."

"When was that?"

"I'm not sure. Friday? Thursday?"

"My bet would be Thursday. That would've given Ellen all day Friday to have a locksmith over."

"You think Ellen—"

He was close to her, but she couldn't see his expression in the dark. "You've made a promise to my mother."

She peered at him, wishing for light. Was he laughing at her? "Why don't you check the other keys?"

He *was* laughing. She'd never seen him laugh before, and the creases in the corners of her eyes and the deep chuckle in his chest took her breath away. She stared.

"Sorry," he said, sobering. He tried the other two keys. No luck. "I don't suppose you have the garage door opener? She probably didn't have time to reprogram it."

"No garage door opener."

"Pity." He leaned his back against the door, crossed his arms over his chest, and said in a cheerful voice, another new side to him she found alarmingly human, "Would you like me to try the side door—the real one?"

"What is so funny?"

He ran his hand through his hair. "I don't know. Maybe just that your aunt has caused me a lot of grief over the years."

"So you're happy to see someone else suffer?"

"Just someone related to her."

Annoyed with how her heart melted like cheese to see a smile on his face, she held out her hand. "Let me try."

He nodded, still looking amused. "Of course." One of his

hands came up under hers and held it steady while the other pressed the hard keys into her palm. Then he folded her fingers around it and squeezed. "Be my guest."

Her heart jumped, just because of that one, quick touch of his hands. She jerked free and strode down the left side of the house, berating her body for reacting to him.

Her body was a bad listener. In college she'd learned not to trust her body's judgment, the way it got her in one relationship after another with guys who had no interest in the rest of her. And every time, her heart had gone where her body led, got naked with the rest of her, and then, too stupid to know everything is temporary, would break.

Damn. She was going to have to get out of Trixie Johnson's offer of hospitality gracefully. Because as she feared, none of the keys worked on the side door either, and Bev had to admit the likelihood that Ellen—through malice or misunderstanding—had changed the locks.

Liam was waiting for her up near her car when she returned. "The Claremont is the closest hotel," he said. "No reason for the heiress to stay in a dump."

The Claremont was a luxury spa—heiress or no—she could hardly afford. Without Ellen's payoff, Bev was as broke as ever. She'd have to figure out how to draw a salary, but had no interest in depending on Liam's advice.

"I'd better explain to your mother."

"No, don't bother. She'll be fine."

"I promised."

"Under duress."

"I promised."

They made their way back to his house. Back at his front door she waited for him to open it, but he just stood still behind her.

"Last chance," he said.

She opened the door herself and stepped into the living room just as Liam's sister pulled on a coat. The boyfriend was gone.

"Liam, I'll need to ride back with you," April said.

"Ah," was all he said in reply.

"Oh, don't you start, too. It's not like you've got any better taste than I do," April said, then noticed Bev. "Sorry. Present company excluded, of course."

"Oh, I'm not—"

"April, you are pathetic. As I told you five minutes ago, this is Beverly Lewis. Ed's granddaughter. She's trying to get into his house next door."

April waved off her brother's insult. "I should have known. You're way too normal-looking."

Not sure if that was a compliment, Bev checked Liam's face for a reaction just as April added, "Not like the supermodels Liam loves so much."

Bev plastered a smile on her face and didn't let herself brush any more dirt or leaves off her clothes.

"Bev is the new owner of Fite Fitness," Liam said. "I report to her now."

"Bummer," April said, but didn't specify for whom before flinging open the front door and stepping outside. "I'll wait in your car. Don't take too long, all right? I've got to note Billy's departure on my blog."

Bev shared an amused look with Liam just as Trixie came into the room. "No luck?"

"Apparently the locks have been changed," Bev said.

"And now Bev is going to use your computer to find a decent bed for the night," Liam said.

Bev said, "Oh, no, I can find—"

Trixie made a cheerful tisking sound. "You promised. Now you can help me eat all this leftover chili. Whatshisname was a vegetarian. Do you eat meat, Bev?"

"You are not going to make her eat too," Liam said.

"Not if she's a vegetarian. What do you think I am? Are you, Bev? A vegetarian?"

"No, but you don't have to feed me, really. I'm fine."

"You'll be doing me a favor. In exchange for the room. We'll be even. I can't possibly eat all this chili, and the freezer is full of my strawberries. They were so good this year. Do you garden?"

The smell of rich, spicy meats spilling out from the kitchen and the thought of fresh homegrown strawberries were triggering deep hunger pangs Bev had managed to ignore all afternoon.

Her longing must have appeared on her face because Trixie grinned and clapped her hands together. "Liam, pour your friend a glass of wine."

"Mother, she's only here because you're pressuring her."

"I have to be pushy so she knows I mean it. I'm not making some phony offer I hope she refuses." Trixie grinned at Bev—a big, toothy smile that reached her ears.

"No, you're making her accept an offer she'd rather refuse," he said. "All she wants is a calm, private room at the Claremont without some pushy crazy lady bothering her."

Annoyed by his assumption of what she wanted, Bev gave Trixie her warmest smile. "I would love to stay here tonight, Trixie. Thank you so much for the offer. Your house is beautiful and I hate hotels and your chili smells fantastic."

Trixie beamed at her. Then both she and Bev turned to Liam and gave him a daring look in unison.

Liam's mouth flattened and he stared back at them. After a long second, he said, "April's waiting in the car," and turned away to pull open the door. "See you at work, Beverly."

Trixie took her arm. "He's probably afraid I'll put you in his old room," she said, leading her deeper into the house. "Men are such little boys at heart."

Chapter 7

EARLY THE NEXT morning, Liam paced the perimeter of his office with a tennis ball in his hand, hurling it at the wall every few steps and trying to distract himself with the effort of catching it before it hit the ground.

Both of the offices next to his were empty; nobody wanted to be his neighbor for long.

He stopped his pacing and ball throwing long enough to grab the phone and dial the front desk. "Has she come in yet?"

"No," Carrie said.

"You didn't leave your desk since I came in? You're sure?"

"Yes."

He exhaled and hung up, cursing Ed's bad taste in hiring an antisocial teenager for reception, then called George at the back door. "Well?"

"Quit your nagging," George said. "I told you I'd call you. Not that I know what she looks like."

"Like Ellen, but . . . softer. Younger."

"'Younger' I get. But 'softer'—what the hell does that mean? Fat?"

Liam closed his eyes. The hip replacement hadn't improved George's disposition. "No. Not really. Just call me if there's a girl you don't recognize with black hair."

"Told you I would."

Liam hung up and hurled the ball at the back of the door as hard as he could. "Softer," he muttered in disgust. He should have used words George would have understood. Big tits. Big ass. He leapt up and caught the ball on its arc over his head. Big pain.

There was a thump at the door not of his making. He glanced over. "Yeah?"

The door swung open. Bev stood there, coffee in hand, wearing a dress that made him drop his tennis ball onto the floor. The garage sale suit was gone, replaced by some fitted, silky gray thing that wrapped tightly around her small waist, clung to her large breasts and hips and, he followed it down, over her long thighs to her long calves, ending at a pair of black clunky shoes that hinted at her real career. He dragged his gaze up to her face. "You're wearing a dress."

She looked worried. "Is that a problem?"

Hell, yeah. "You look very nice." He looked away and took a deep breath. "Like one of the design assistants."

She took his comment as an insult. "Damn. Maybe I should change." She ran her hands over her hips, drawing his attention with them. "I tried on seven outfits this morning."

"You look fine," he said, his eyes fixed back on her face. "The assistants come out of design school and see us old slobs and realize they're the only cool people here. Within two years they quit and move to New York."

Her eyes went wide with alarm. "That's not the message I'm going for."

He shrugged and slumped into a chair as though her appearance had no effect on a callous old pro such as himself. "Looking hot is an advantage in this business."

She looked down at herself and laughed. "Well, good. I think." She came closer and sat in a chair next to him. "So, I noticed nobody wears Fite to work."

"I wear it sometimes. But I'm just a dumb jock. Not a real garmento."

"Ah. Dumb. That must be why you're the senior executive."

"But see, that's just because Mr. Roche felt sorry for me." He traced the edge of his desk with a finger and forced a smile. "My father died, you see, right after the Olympics."

"Your mother told me. I'm so sorry."

He cringed inwardly at the thought of whatever else his mother had told her. "And of course, Stanford only took me because of the swimming."

"I know how you feel. UCLA only took me because of my grades."

He hesitated, having to bite back a laugh. He met her eyes. "Losers, both of us."

"Pathetic."

They looked at each other, each of them smiling, until Liam realized something and his face fell. "Hey, how did you get in here without anybody seeing you?"

"Carrie saw me," she said. "I gave her a muffin."

Liam looked over at his desk and saw the red light wasn't blinking on his phone. "She should have left a message."

"And I told her I'd tell you myself that I was here."

He bit back his outrage. "I told her to call me."

"Are you trying to spy on me?"

"Of course. You think I can just let you wander around on your own?"

She got a sly look on her face, eyes bright. "Your mother did."

His humor evaporated. Surely his mother hadn't broken out

the old photo albums. "You were nice to indulge her." He
struggled to keep his tone light. "But I'm sure you're eager not to
stay another night."

"It's a beautiful house. I slept in the Rose Room. And she
made me waffles."

He didn't see any hint of unearthed secrets, pity, or surprise.
Just a woman who'd spent one night in an unofficial bed-and-
breakfast. "With vanilla protein powder? Or the real kind?"

Her eyes went wide. "Ah, that's why they tasted a little funny."

"We're kind of creative about nutrition in our family," he said,
then regretted saying anything. They weren't friends, and
shouldn't be talking about his family. He got to his feet. "Come
on, I'll show you your grandfather's office. You can make the calls
from there."

"Calls?"

He gestured towards the door. "To the locksmith."

"I need a tour of the rest of the place too. Are you too busy? I
could ask Carrie—she and I have become buddies."

"Carrie?" He stared at her. "Front desk Carrie?"

"Did you know she spent two years traveling in Mexico,
studying silver jewelry?"

He shook his head.

"Nearly got married to some German guy with a cooking
show." He continued to stare. Bev added, "He was traveling
through Mexico, you see, and they met up."

"I had no idea she was able to conduct a conversation."

"Maybe you should try talking to people every once in a
while."

He snorted. "I'm curious to see what she would do if you
asked her for a tour, since I've never seen her get out of her chair.
I'm not convinced she has legs."

Bev laughed, but he kept a straight face, and she sighed. "Forget Carrie." She got up. "I want you to give me the tour. That will look better anyway. Some of your authority might rub off on me."

The thought of him rubbing any part of her was bad. He got to his feet and strode to the door. "I have time for a quick run-through. Then you can get comfortable in Ed's lair."

"Lair?"

"You'll see."

She followed him. "Is there a security badge or something I need to worry about?"

"Security badge? Like a sheriff?"

"No badge, then."

He shook his head. "We'll start at the back door. Where the magic begins."

She followed him down the tiled hallway, past the vault of old clothes, into a loading area that opened to the back alley. Old George in his Oakland A's cap sat perched on a stool, reading the paper and eating an apple.

"This is where our deliveries come in and out," Liam said. "Thanks to George here."

"Not like I do anything," George said. "Damn company should put us both out of my misery."

Bev bit her lip and glanced at Liam, who was hoping George would be his typical trollish self and knock some reality into Bev's head. With Ellen gone, all he needed was to show Bev how much happier she'd be owning Fite from the other end of the state.

"George, this is Beverly Lewis. Ed's granddaughter." Liam's eyes fell for a moment to her mouth, then were drawn down to her body for a quick peek before snapping back over to George. "She's the new owner."

George stopped mid-chew and stared. "No shit," he said, his mouth full.

"Nice to meet you, George." She smiled. "Yummy apple?"

That made George raise his white, untrimmed eyebrows and take another bite. He looked at Liam without moving his head. "You kiddin' me?"

Bev kept smiling as though George had welcomed her with open arms. "Let me know if there's anything I can do for you."

George's eyebrows stretched up even higher, suggesting there wasn't. "Never seen you around before, have I?"

"You will now," she said. "How long have you worked here, George?"

Crunch. Another bite, apple-spit drooling down his chin. "Too long."

She nodded, smiling, apparently oblivious to his hostility. "Then I bet you're an incredible resource for a newcomer like me," she said. "If you see me screwing up, you let me know."

George scowled at her, took another bite, and looked at Liam with a *What the fuck?* expression.

That was just the first dose; she couldn't maintain that good cheer forever. Liam pulled her away, past the morning delivery of white bunting rolls propped on their ends, each fuzzy cylinder five feet tall and three feet in diameter, to the freight elevator. "Moving on up." He punched the call button. "This is the easiest way up to the engineering floor."

After a couple of minutes the car appeared above them, visible through the grate, jerking and squealing. Liam waited for it to settle before he tugged the cage open. He stepped aside for her to get on first, then climbed in after her and banged the door closed. "Let's start at the top floor and work our way down." He held down another button and the elevator lurched and rose.

She tilted her head back to watch the floor above them approach, slowly become level with them, then sink below. He noticed her neck was long and pale and had a faint blue vein pulsing below her jaw. He leaned his shoulder against the car wall as the floors groaned past. "You must love kids, to teach preschool. Aren't you going to miss them?"

"It's not just about liking children, like I'm just some glorified babysitter who never wants to grow up."

He'd found a nerve. Filing that away for future use, he asked, "Who said that?"

She turned aside and watched the next floor appear through the gate. "The education of children, especially young ones, is not highly compensated. Some take this as evidence of its unimportance."

He tried to remember more about her branch of the family. Hollywood types, lots of money. Not the kind to live in a dumpy apartment like hers, or value her teaching career.

"The education of children is more important than anything," he said. "Certainly more important than exercise clothes."

Looking suspicious, she tried to catch his eye, but he focused on the elevator controls until the car reached their floor. The elevator jerked and he pulled the gate aside, then shoved the metal door open for her. They walked into a bright, white-walled corridor filled with a dozen women huddled over a row of sewing machines. The rattle and thrumming of their work echoed across the tile.

At the machine closest to the window, Shirley Hwang, the floor manager, held up a piece of black fabric.

"Mr. Liam." She wagged it at him, her red bifocals falling to the cord around her neck. "This new stuff. It keeps getting holes. Very crappy material."

Looking around for one of the assistants, he went over and took it from her. "Do you have the original roll?"

"Feng has it." She pointed down the hall.

Normally he would tell her to find an assistant to deal with it, but Bev was watching and could use the education. "I'll have Rachel check it out."

Shirley nodded her satisfaction and went back to her table as he and Bev walked where she had pointed.

"The cutters are down here, next to the patternmakers."

"I thought the sewing was contracted out," Bev said. "Like to China."

"Production is all over the world. But we need in-house staff for development." He found Feng and talked to him for a moment until he found the fabric he was looking for and hooked it under his arm. "Feng agrees it's no good. I'd introduce you," he said to Bev, pulling her away, "but he hates to be interrupted, and has lots of sharp blades. They've got Darrin breathing down everyone's ass this afternoon. FedEx goes out at three." Of course, Darrin was pushing them because Liam was pushing Darrin.

They continued walking.

"Do you still swim?" Then she looked away, blushing, as though regretting the question.

He raised an eyebrow and looked down at her. Had she been checking him out? "I hurt my shoulder and never quite recovered enough to compete again."

Her blue eyes filled with pity. "I'm sorry. That must have been hard."

Out of habit he didn't mention how much he'd loathed swimming. For some reason people found that remarkable. Dad had been dead for over a decade—no point dwelling on it now. "I do a lot of running these days."

She grimaced.

"Not a runner?" he asked.

She propped her hands on her hips. "Do I look like a runner?"

Not minding to have a reason to stare at her body, Liam let his gaze drift down over her breasts. "We make clothes that would help."

"Help?"

He kept his face blank. "With the bouncing."

Instead of being offended, or laughing, or looking embarrassed, she shrugged and said in a matter-of-fact tone, "I have other problems."

"Oh?"

"I lack physical coordination. Always have. The rest of my family is fine—jocks, all of them."

"You don't have to be a jock to move around."

She patted him on the arm. "Said by the Olympian."

"Exercise should be non-negotiable. For anyone."

"That's the kind of talk I can't stand. Who's negotiating? With whom? This is my body. Nobody else's."

"It's a pact you make with yourself. To be a complete, healthy human being. Basic maintenance, like brushing your teeth."

"No, it's a chore to look good to other people. If you're not into it—and I will never, ever be into it—you do it for the status. People don't talk about brushing their teeth like, 'Oh, sorry I'm late. I was brushing my teeth. I've been brushing my teeth so much lately and it's really wearing me out. I've been working with a dentist on how to brush my teeth more effectively.' And then their friends jump in, 'Oh, I can totally tell. They're so white! So strong!' and 'Who's your dentist?'"

He stared at her. Had Ed known this about her when he put her in the will? "You have just inherited a fitnesswear company."

"No shit. Thank God it's clothes, because if this was like a gym or something, I might be in trouble."

Momentarily speechless, Liam led her into a carpeted hallway away from the sounds of the sewing machines. Maybe her aversion to exercise would make it easier to keep her out of the way, which was a good thing.

He lifted the bolt of bad goods in his arms and strode past a short, fuzzy cubicle wall with a strip of two-inch wide gray facing material pinned across the entrance, like the yellow tape of a crime scene warning away intruders. Rachel resented anyone who had a real office.

"You have to get it lower," Rachel said into the phone. She wore a fitted white t-shirt, black slacks, and silver ballet flats—her typical uniform. Practical, like he was; Liam wished the other assistants would follow her example. "They're narrow goods. There's no way we can retail over thirty."

"Rachel." Liam shoved the fabric under the tape across the entrance. "Shirley says this stuff is crap. Keeps getting holes."

Rachel swung around in her chair, her phone to her ear under the angled bob of her reddish-brown hair. She gave Liam an unimpressed eyebrow lift, took the fabric without moving the phone away from her shoulder, and slid her gaze over to Bev. Surprise flickered in her bright blue eyes, then was gone; she threw the fabric down to the ground and swung back to her computer.

Liam gripped Bev's elbow and guided her down another hallway to the stairwell. "I would introduce you, but she's obviously busy." She'd have plenty of opportunities to meet Rachel later, like it or not. He grinned to himself in anticipation.

Bev looked around with a smile on her face, immune to the lip-curling looks of merchandising assistants around the walls of their cubicles, the way they stared at the car wreck of her black clogs and uneven black ponytail. "It's cool. I didn't realize the desk people would be right next to all the action."

When he got her into the stairway Liam stopped walking, eager to relieve her of any glamorous fantasy as soon as possible. "The desk people hate all the action. It's noisy and full of fumes and they get constantly interrupted."

"But it's exciting." She rubbed her hands together. "People are making things."

"Making each other insane, usually."

"You're just burned-out. When's the last time you had a vacation?"

"Me, burned-out." He laughed and shook his head. "Since your aunt quit, I'm the most senior non-exempt or non-union employee in the building. I do not burn out."

"Having been here for too long is evidence for my case, not against."

He leaned back on the stair railing and giving her a pointed look. "Careful. You just might convince me to take a really long sabbatical. Now, when you need me the most."

"Maybe not right now, but as soon as I can learn my way around." She smiled at him, eyes wide and innocent, adding, "Or once I can hire somebody to back you up."

"Like a replacement?"

"More of an understudy." She crossed her arms and studied him down to his feet and back up, a slow, pointed look that made him uncomfortably aware of how her pose propped up her deep cleavage. "You look healthy, but who knows—you might get hit by a bus."

Surprised, he pulled his gaze back up to her face. A strikingly familiar, hard, blue-eyed beauty stared back at him. But instead of the disgust her aunt's face usually inspired, he found himself uncomfortably turned on.

The preschool teacher had an edge.

Interesting.

"You aren't as nice as you pretend." His low voice reverberated against the concrete walls.

She stopped smirking and frowned. "Of course I'm nice. Too nice, everyone says."

"No, you're not."

"Just because I pick on people my own size—"

He pushed up to his full height. She was tall, but hardly as tall as him. "I think you're just as mean as anybody. Maybe more. Just spend a lot more effort hiding it."

For some reason he didn't understand, she flushed dark pink and started blinking her eyes. Another nerve.

"I am not mean," she said.

"And you're hardly Switzerland," he said. "'Doesn't like to fight', my ass. You just smile a lot and hope nobody notices you're telling them the exact opposite of what they want to hear."

She looked at the floor. The corner of her mouth curled up. "Child Development 101."

"Yes, well, I'm not five, so cut it out."

Her smile fell and she stared at him. He became aware of how dark the stairwell was. The only sound was the distant staccato of machinery. And then he smelled her lemon soap again, or whatever the hell she was bathing in.

She frowned. "Smiling is a good thing. You should try it." She lifted a finger and wagged it at him. "One of my reasons for coming here at all was to help improve the morale. There are too many miserable people. I don't care what you or my—what other people say, that's not good for business. Even my aunt admitted that morale was low."

"Bragged, more like." He wondered about Bev, the limits of her niceness or her ability to lie to herself.

Bev gestured down the stairs. "Think we could keep moving, or do you need more rest?"

He took a step down. "I needed a minute to reflect upon the discovery that you and your aunt share more than just your looks."

She snorted.

"Your grandfather's floor is the next one. One half of it is storage, though." He pulled open the fire door—marked AUTHORIZED VISITORS ONLY—and let her walk ahead of him. A long, well-lit hallway with wood floors and buff-colored walls stretched in either direction. Ed's office was off to the right, through a frosted glass door with CAPTAIN printed on it with gilt block lettering.

"Captain?"

"He thought of Fite as a ship," Liam said.

"Not very democratic, ships."

"No."

She walked towards the glass door. "Don't tell me there were floggings."

He stopped and gave her a hard look. "Listen, Bev. You can change a lot of things, but if you get rid of the flogging this place is going to fall apart."

She came to a halt and stared at him. Then whacked him hard on the arm. "I had to get the comedian."

He rubbed his stinging arm. "So much for not flogging."

"Executives deserve it. I just wish the rest of the company could have seen it. Good for morale." She walked over to the glass door and tried the handle, but Liam had to pull out his keys to let them in.

"At least these still work," he said under his breath. He had to get her tucked away where she wouldn't cause any trouble. My God, he'd almost been flirting with her.

More like a frat house lounge than an office, Ed Roche's private suite stretched along a wall of windows overlooking SOMA San Francisco. Gym equipment scattered around islands of modular furniture like lily pads: an elliptical trainer, a treadmill, a stationary bike, other bulky machines with pulleys and straps. Free weights stacked up with bars in racks along one wall, reflected in the wall-to-ceiling mirrors behind them. A jukebox huddled in the corner, powered-up and glowing.

"Lord," Bev said, squinting. "Is that an ice hockey table over there?"

"Vintage."

"It's very male, isn't it?"

Liam sighed in satisfaction. "It's awesome."

"Do people hang out in here?"

"Ellen and me and—are probably the only ones in the building today who've ever stepped foot in here." He'd almost said 'and Rachel' but that wasn't for him to say. All kinds of rumors floated around, most false.

"I'm sure they're grateful," she said. "I was thinking he made everyone exercise or something. As a condition of employment."

"They'd be lucky to be able to. Gyms are expensive."

She walked around the TV throne to a kitchen alcove. New stainless steel appliances, marble countertops. She went through a sliding door to Ed's bathroom and came out shaking her head.

"He could have lived in here."

With a grief he didn't try to hide, Liam said, "I think he did."

"What about the house in Oakland?"

Liam crossed his arms over his chest, disapproving of the

family that left an old, lonely man to fend for himself. "Usually empty."

"I barely knew him, you know."

Liam shrugged.

"What about Ellen?"

"Are you kidding?"

"But she loved him. Just not the rest of us. And she has a son, my cousin. Are you angry at him too, or just the females?"

"I'm not angry."

She gave him an annoyingly knowing look. "Sure you're not."

"Your grandfather was a great guy. Flawed, but who isn't? When I needed him, he was there, and I'm not the type to forget it. That's all I'm going to say." He pointed towards a side door. "His office space is back there. You can check it out after I show you Engineering. Purchasing is on second. HR and Finance are on first, back near Richard. Or rather, where Richard was. Then I have to get back to work."

"Did Ellen really fire Richard because of me?"

He began walking back to the stairs. "Who knows? She probably doesn't even know herself."

"But now we need a CFO."

"Hire him back."

"I can do that?" She hurried to catch up to him. "Of course I can. Hold on. Quit walking so fast."

Reluctantly, he slowed.

"My first act as owner is to instruct my executive vice president to rehire the CFO." She smiled. "It's your fault he got fired. So fix it."

He scowled to intimidate her, but she just smiled. "He wasn't very important. He didn't have the power his title implied."

"Not important to you maybe," she said, "but who knows?

Maybe he was the quiet little engine keeping this place running. Dotting all the i's and crossing the t's. Unrecognized hero."

"He was an accountant. They use numbers, not i's and t's."

Her smile hardened. "Do it."

After a second he decided this wasn't a fight he should waste his energies on. "All right."

She beamed. "Today?"

"Is that your wish, Your Mightiness?"

"Yup."

"All right. Then we better finish the tour so I can get right on that."

She nodded. "On with it, then."

He looked down at her, a sinking feeling in his stomach, and wondered for the first time if Ellen would have been a better alternative to this deceptively cheerful pain in the ass.

No. Bev might have a stubbornly optimistic streak, but it wouldn't be enough to keep her happy in a business that thrived on misery. He would have to accelerate her inevitable slide into disillusionment and get her back into a preschool where she belonged.

He'd be doing her a favor.

೨ഌ

Before the day was out, Bev had working keys to her grandfather's house in Oakland, knew which doors were real and which were water heater closets, and was relieved to be out from under her senior VP's family roof. Aside from the panoramic view of San Francisco Bay, the house on Alondra Avenue was remarkable only for its total lack of personality. The estate service had packed up most of her grandfather's things, putting them in storage until Bev's mother was ready to face it all, which Bev feared would be never.

The next morning, after a choppy night's sleep in an unfamiliar house, Bev walked through Fite's front door with a vase in her arms. "I brought in a few flowers to cheer up the place."

"Ooh, sweet peas!" Carrie popped up. She'd taken out her braids, leaving her hair in a kinky triangle that ended at her shoulders. "I love those!"

"They'd naturalized near my grandfather's house." Bev rearranged the long stems in the water. "I'm not sure how long they'll survive in a vase, but it was worth a shot."

"I'll take care of them." Carrie petted the soft curve of one petal with the tip of her finger. She bent close and sucked in a deep breath. "They smell like candy."

"More where that came from." Bev took one last sniff of the sweet flowers before heading for the elevator. Liam had insisted the stairs were the only way to her grandfather's executive suite, but there had to be some way of getting there via the elevator; the original building designers wouldn't have skipped a floor.

She stepped inside and frowned at the number plate. Sure enough, one of the middle buttons had been taped over with a square of scrap plastic. Shaking her head, she scraped it off with her fingernail and pushed it, happy to feel the car creak and rise, understanding her. She rolled up the plastic and tape and stuck it in her shoulder bag, feeling powerful as the doors opened into the gleaming wood floored hallway, right in front of the glass door to her grandfather's lair.

Lair. She needed to think of a name for the place. It was hardly an office, with all those toys in it. She pulled out the set of keys she'd acquired the day before—a fist-sized wad—but the door was already open.

Reclining in a leather recliner with his back to the door, Liam had a phone to his ear, his feet up on the window, and didn't bother to look over when Bev came in and dropped her bag next to him on the floor.

"Good morning, Liam."

He didn't move except to tilt the phone closer to his ear. "That's shit. We can't hold production that long."

Bev waited, knowing it was the first of many attempts to put her in her place. She looked at her watch. Maybe she could go get her coffee, fortify herself, buy some time.

"Tell him to call me before lunch or forget it." He leaned back and shoved the phone into his pocket. Chewing his lip, he frowned at the city.

"I was just going to get coffee," Bev said. "Would you like to join me?" Getting out of the building would help diffuse some of his cockiness. Get him off his home turf.

"Venti cappucino. I'll be in my office." He got up and walked out the door, Bev staring after him.

Then she laughed. So that's how he was going to play it.

She would go along for now, see how badly he wanted to fight her. She walked back out of the building to the café on the corner, added a ginger-spiced muffin for him, and returned to his office with a tray balanced in the crook of her arm. The door was closed, so she knocked. Waited, knocked again.

Finally, he shouted, "Come in!" and Bev went in, tray in hand.

There, sitting around the conference table at the far end, a large group of smirking, well-dressed people stared at her, at the dorky owner who had apparently been sent for coffee like an entry-level design flunky.

Only one person didn't look over. Liam, at the head of the table, was absorbed with an orange track jacket he was holding at arm's length.

Feeling her face get warm, Bev gripped the tray in her hands and made herself walk across the floor to him. She hadn't met most of these people yet, these cool-looking young women with perfect makeup and exposed, toned upper arms. Some of them looked away, lips pressed together, while others glued their eyes on Liam to see what he would do next. From the tension in the air, Bev figured they all knew who she was.

With each long, awkward step across the room, Bev tried to remember the details of all the mean-girl teen movies she'd seen over the years to decide her best next move. The hostility came in waves off one woman she'd met on the tour—Rachel, with the gray tape across her cubicle opening—and worse, shimmering with her enjoyment of Bev's situation. Two women at the opposite end gaped at her feet like they'd never seen Danskos before.

One woman began to laugh, barely trying to hide it. The sound of her amusement crawled up Bev's spine like a sleek, poisonous spider.

Bev wondered what Liam was planning next: the coffee wasn't right, artificial sweeteners were metabolically damaging, the muffin wasn't low-carb, there wasn't an available seat so could you please go get us a few more chairs?

She stopped walking, balanced the tray in one arm, and pulled out her cell phone with a shaking hand. She pretended to study it, pushed a button, then looked up. "Excuse me, everyone, but I'll have to delay our introduction a little longer," she said, forced a smile. "Liam, you can catch up with me later." Then she turned around on her heel and marched out of the room, still carrying the coffee in one hand and pretending to answer the phone in the other.

Instead of the elevator she hurried into the stairwell and ran up the stairs, the cardboard tray listing to one side, and reached her executive suite winded and shaking.

Maybe clogs weren't going to cut it in this business. She looked down. She was in another black suit, which that morning had felt like firm authority but now felt like suburban dentist. She went over to her desk and set down the tray, picked up her coffee, and gulped it down hot. She would not fight Liam head-on. She would not. There were better ways—quieter, gentler ways—of—of—

Of what? What was she doing?

She sat down. She was taking over the company. Not just playing around, she really wanted to do it. She would do it.

She reached over, picked up Liam's cappuccino, and sucked that one down too.

Now she could think. With her veins pumping caffeine and her nerves straining like rubber bands, Bev paced the office and worked through her options. First, she would not fire anyone. Secretly she thought that was why her grandfather had chosen her, because she would find a way for everyone to get along. Second, she would learn everything about everybody in the company and choose one of them as her right-hand woman. Or man, though she hadn't seen many of those. Which brought her to her third point: she would stop thinking about Liam.

No, first she would stop thinking about Liam.

She sat down and stared out at the vent pipes on the neighboring rooftops, thinking about Liam. About the way he'd looked, his hair slightly damp like he'd just come out of the shower. How his dress shirt fitted his shoulders. The hint of guilt in his eyes while he was trying to put her down, that he probably didn't think she could see.

With all the radioactive energy of two hundred milligrams of caffeine, she got up and went looking for HR. Let him think he could scare her into hiding. She'd quietly learn about the people laboring along at every level and figure out how to win them over. Whether they liked it or not.

Even him.

Chapter 8

TWO DAYS LATER Liam watched Wendi arrange the line into groups on the rolling rack next to his desk. "Did you bring Bev the binders?" he asked.

Wendi nodded and shoved her glasses up her nose. "What's she going to do with all that old stuff?" she asked, then added like the infant she was, "Some of those lines went back into the nineteen hundreds."

"She wants to learn as much as she can about the business." Which should keep her busy for a couple weeks, at least. That and the rolling racks of samples he'd had delivered to her office. "She has no background in apparel and doesn't want to screw things up with her ignorance."

"But the binders are just full of spec paperwork and production stuff that's totally out-of-date now. They're not even on the new database. And we don't source in half those countries anymore."

He continued to rearrange the line samples by delivery date, not interested in explaining himself to an entry-level assistant. Ever since he'd rescued Wendi from Ellen, she'd latched onto him without any of the subservient reserve he'd nurtured in the rest of the team. He missed it.

"And why is she making boards?" Wendi continued. "She asked me for her own glue sticks and foam core."

Liam turned his head away to hide his grin. "I suggested she sketch out a few ideas of her own. And share with us her first impressions at the line meeting on Monday."

"On Monday?" Wendi gaped at him. "When Darrin and Jennifer get back?"

"Maybe they'll find her fresh perspective useful."

Wendi snapped her mouth shut, her eyebrows flying high on her forehead, and Liam suspected she was imagining the same thing he was.

Bloodbath.

It would be an awkward but necessary experience to convince her she would be happiest owning the company from a distance. Orange County was only about six hundred miles away—an easy flight, once or twice a year. At the most. He'd made sure Wendi had told her all about her experiences as Ellen's assistant and left a stack of HR paperwork about the dozens of young, talented people who had quit under her thumb—some within a week. Bev wouldn't be selling to Ellen now, not with her determination to be nice.

But she would tire of being here in person.

In the meantime he'd keep her busy. For the rest of the week he kept her snowed under useless minutiae in the guise of "Training." She kept to Ed's suite and the business offices, far away from him and the product development team. By Friday, the staff had accepted his description of her as a temporary technicality and was getting optimistic about Ellen's lengthening absence.

Friday night he was so optimistic he left before seven, the first time in months, and even made it to the 24-hour Safeway before dark. He parked in his condo's basement garage, a luxury he never failed to appreciate, and took the elevator up to the twentieth floor, humming and smiling to himself.

But when he got to his door he paused, hand on the doorknob, and felt his mood turn black. The condo, with its expensive one-eighty view of the Bay he seldom got to appreciate, was now distinctly, unhappily occupied.

Though they sounded happy enough. He let the door slam behind him, dropped his keys onto the shelf by the kitchen, went to the fridge for a beer. *Not again.*

He strode across the carpeted hallway as loudly as he could, closing his eyes when he got to the bedroom door, which was open. "April."

He heard muffled exclamations and groans, bodies rolling across the mattress, and finally, feet on floor struggling into pants. "Uh," said a male voice.

"Oh, God," April groaned, sounding like an exasperated teenager, which she hadn't been for seven years. "He's just my brother. You don't have to go. "

"Yes, you do," Liam said. "No bed of your own?"

"You know I—" April began.

"I meant him." Liam leaned against the doorframe with his arms crossed and eyes still closed.

"I should go," the guy said. "Nice to meet you, uh—"

"Her name's April," Liam said.

"He knows my name!" April said, then sighed. "Right?"

Silence. Jeans zipping, one foot hopping on the floor as a shoe was pulled on the other. Hurried breathing, then his throat clearing.

"Right?" Liam asked him.

He skulked past him in the doorway. "Maybe I'll see you around." The guy fled down the hall and out the front door.

After a few long seconds, April stalked over to him. "You can open your eyes now."

"Handsome guy," Liam said. "Not too bright though."

Her face was torn between guilt and anger. "Couldn't you have waited a few minutes?"

"That's my bed. Thank God I didn't." He glared at her, not kidding anymore. "What's wrong with the couch? Where you sleep?"

She bit her lip and looked away. "He said he's got a bad back."

"I'm going to make us some dinner while you wash my sheets."

"But I told you, we were just getting—"

He held up his hand. "Stop, stop, stop. You want to ruin your life with some stupid loser with orthopedic problems, do it in your own home. Which means you'll have to get one first."

"That's not fair," April said. "I pay rent."

He tilted his head. "What?"

"Not, like, in cash," she said. "But I buy stuff for the place."

"Ah. Stuff."

She pointed down the hall towards the bathroom. "Toilet paper."

"It offends Paige," he said. "I had to put it away." Each square had a picture of Rush Limbaugh's face.

"Paige is a Nazi. Humanity offends her."

"I found it rather disturbing myself."

April, eager to push the conversation further away from her own culpability, jumped on the topic of his latest girlfriend. "Admit it, she's horrible."

"Don't change the subject." He looked down at her bare shoulders sticking out above his comforter she'd wrapped around herself and frowned. "Wash the duvet, too."

"You have gotten so gay, I swear." April turned around. "You were never like this before you started working in fashion." She sashayed over to the bed.

"Now who's offended by humanity?" Liam shut the door, walked to the kitchen, put down the beer, and wondered if he'd be better at his job if he were gay. People wouldn't doubt his career so much, he'd meet plenty of candidates for casual sex, and he wouldn't be thinking about what Bev Lewis would feel like under him naked.

"I can't believe I used 'gay' as an insult." April came back into the kitchen in jeans and a tight T-shirt that said *100% Natural* across her chest. Her curly brown hair was a messy cloud around her head. "I'm really disgusted with myself."

He frowned at her shirt. "Did you wash my sheets yet?"

"You are so anal." She walked past him and plucked a note off the fridge. "She called, by the way. *Das* girlfriend."

"What did she say?"

"To eat shit and die?" April got herself a beer. "What do you think she said? That you better call her back, or she's going to dump you. That you don't deserve her."

He reached down to get a pot out of the cabinet and filled it with water. "So if I don't call her back, she's going to dump me?" He was surprised to find he didn't feel too bad about that.

A small smile formed in the corner of April's mouth. She lifted the bottle to her lips. "That's right."

He put the pot on the stove and turned on the gas. "Was there any time limit on this offer?"

April burst out laughing and gave him a squeeze. "That's my bro. Mr. Commitment."

"It's not commitment that's the problem," he said.

"It's your taste in women?"

He saluted her with his beer. "I like my women."

"No, you don't. You just like to sleep with them."

"Pot, meet kettle," Liam said.

"You just sleep with the bitchy ones so you're not tempted to marry them. I'm on to you, bro."

"I almost wish you were right, April. Thing is, I like 'em bitchy. They turn me on." He raised an eyebrow. "Sure you want to hear more?"

April jabbed him in the chest. "Fine. Then marry one of them, if you like them so much. Poor Mom. That's all she talks about, you living alone."

He glared at her. "I wish."

"Seriously. What's your problem with getting hitched?"

"I don't want to suffer the side effects."

She lowered the bottle, sobering. "You mean children. So, just don't have them. Keep buying your condoms at Costco."

"I do not want to know my sister has been stealing my condoms," he muttered.

"As if even you could use them all up before the expiration. Anyway, just because you're afraid of being like Dad doesn't mean you can't date women who don't totally suck. Scratch that, who do suck, like in the right way—"

"April—"

"And you could never be like him. You're a total pushover. Can you imagine Dad letting Aunt Shirley sleep on *his* couch?"

He shook his head. "You've never seen me at work. I'm a demanding tyrant, just as bad as he was. Worse actually, because I've got more people to manage and higher stakes than my own reputation."

"I don't believe it."

"Believe it." He pulled open a drawer, looking for a spoon. "At least they're adults. I'd never risk lording that shit over a kid. Or the kid's mother."

"As if a woman like Paige would ever let you lord any shit over her."

"Which is why I date women like Paige," he said.

"I don't think bitchy women make you happy."

"You don't know what I'm really like, April. I do. I'm an arrogant pain in the ass, and any woman nice enough to put up with that for long would end up hurt, just like—" He stopped himself.

"Just like Mom," April said. He stared back at her, seeing he'd finally made his point. Their mother was everything sweet and light and wonderful and had deserved better than their domineering father, yet she'd loved him with her huge heart and still mourned him. April took another swig of her beer, dropped her gaze. "At least you're getting rid of Paige."

"Don't tell Mom yet. I think she kind of liked her."

"Are you kidding? Paige ordered veal."

"Ah, right. Of course."

"Then didn't touch it. Insult to injury."

He found a box of protein-rich pasta in the cabinet. "I don't think I ever did see her eat. We were too busy, you know, doing other things."

"Ugh, spare me. I refuse to believe a woman who doesn't eat could be any good in bed. Totally wrong personality profile."

Liam stared off into space, reflecting. He had no intention of telling his sister about the sordid details of his love life, even—or especially—when she was right. "Do you want any pasta?"

"So you're not even going to call her?"

"What, you're on her side now?"

"I'm on womankind's side." She came over and picked up the

box of pasta. "This stuff organic?"

He took it from her and waited for the water to boil. "I'll call her." But only to say goodbye. They'd been seeing each other for two months, which was longer than he'd expected. She'd liked his money and his job and his family's house in the Oakland Hills, but Liam?—not so much.

"Please wash my sheets. I'll grill you some portobellos."

She slapped her forehead. "Crap, I forgot. Mom invited us over tonight."

"Again?"

"Some lovesick guy went to Alaska and brought her a ton of halibut."

"So I have to scare away a guy who wants to sleep with my mother?" he said. "Again?" The women in his family were much too popular with men.

"No, he won't be there. Just the fish."

He looked down into the pot of tepid water. Alaskan halibut sounded pretty good. He wondered what Bev was doing tonight, all alone in Ed's empty house on Friday night. How had the rest of her week gone? Had Ellen changed the locks again?

He twisted off the burners. If he was thinking about Bev, his mother certainly was. And Trixie Johnson had already tagged her. Released her into the wild—for now—but standing by to recapture her for future and ongoing study. Perhaps over a slab of white fish.

Liam dumped the pot in the sink and went down the hallway to his sister. "Come on."

April was tearing the sheets off his bed. "You told me to put these in the wash."

"Forget it. Let's go."

"Make up your mind. Jeez."

With the Friday night traffic the drive over the Bay Bridge to Oakland took them almost an hour. A strange old Honda was in their mother's driveway, and when they walked in and saw the dining table was set and glowing with candles, Liam was afraid the lonely fisherman was lurking nearby.

But it was their brother Mark sitting there, eating a deviled egg off a napkin. "Hi, guys."

April ran over and threw her arms around him. "When did you get back? Mom said you wouldn't be able to visit this summer!"

Mark's light brown hair was shaggy and uncombed, his nose was sunburned and peeling and his ill-fitting khakis exposed orange and yellow argyle socks at his ankles. "Couple hours ago. Like the car? I just bought it. Got almost fifty miles to the gallon on the drive out. It's not a hybrid either. At least, not when I bought it. I did a few modifications."

Liam went over and squeezed his little brother's shoulder— though he was hardly little, just over six feet tall, and still had a few muscles left from Liam's reign as his personal trainer before he moved away a few years before. "Great to see you."

Trixie came into the dining room with a shit-eating grin. "He's staying. He's staying."

"Those kids in Milwaukee don't need you anymore?" Liam asked.

Mark opened his mouth, but his mother spoke. "He's applying for a job at Lawrence Hall of Science. Math camps and stuff," she said. "He's back to stay!"

"Dude, that's great." Liam smiled at him, curious to hear more, but his brother had a pained look in his eye that he recognized. "So, you watching the A's this year?"

Trixie came over and poked Liam in the arm. "Don't change

the subject. Ask him why."

"I'm sure he'll tell me when he feels like it," Liam said.

"He quit. He got sick of being so far from home, so he quit." Trixie snaked an arm around his waist and rested her cheek on Mark's broad shoulder.

Liam met Mark's eyes and raised an eyebrow. "Really?"

Trixie frowned at him. "Don't say it like that. Of course he did."

"I bet there was a girl," April said.

"I wish," Mark muttered, and they all laughed. Mark wasn't much of a ladies' man.

Letting out a deep, noisy sigh, Trixie squeezed Mark so hard he flinched. "I am bursting with joy. Bursting!"

Liam stepped towards the kitchen. "Man, I'm starving. Mind if I make myself an appetizer, Mom?"

"Don't you dare!" Trixie released Mark and ran after him. "You stay out there where you belong. It's bad enough Mark stole one of the eggs." She shoved Liam back into the dining room and disappeared into the kitchen.

Liam walked over and poured himself a glass of lemon-spiked ice water. "You're moving in here?" He cleared his throat. "With Mom?"

Mark eyed him over the rim of his glass, then kicked it back and drained it. "Just for a while. And don't. Just don't."

Liam was tempted to tease him about not being ready to survive in the wild, but that might drive him away again. Liam realized he was damn glad his only brother was back home. Trying to keep his face innocent, he asked, "What?"

Mark shook his head and looked at April. "What have you been up to? I hear you got a job with an insurance company in San Francisco?"

"Just temping, thank God," April said. "As if I'd want a career in insurance. I'd rather die."

"Tough hours, then, Ape?" Mark asked.

"Eight o'clock. In the morning. It's practically dark. I had to move in with Liam to get there on time."

Mark's pinched face softened into the sweet, open grin Liam remembered. "How long has she been crashing there?"

"Just a few weeks—" April said.

"Six months." He edged past her to put his arm around Mark. "You should see the losers she drags home."

"That's one way to get rid of her. Can't she live with one of them?" Mark said.

"I've tried, but none of them will keep her for long."

April kicked him in the shins and strode to the kitchen. "Just for that, I'm never moving out."

When their sister was gone Liam gave his brother a hard look in the eye. "Why are you really here?"

Mark's mouth dropped open to protest, but the fight drained out of him like air out of a bag. "Mom was right. I was lonely."

"Lonely? But you're—" he paused, trying to think of an unloaded term. Anti-social. A loner. Reclusive. "You're so independent."

"Not in Milwaukee apparently. I got home from school, ate, hung out online, went to bed. Never saw a living soul who wasn't part of my daily routine—work, shopping, whatever."

Liam couldn't hide his confusion. "How's that different from here?"

"I don't know. Just was."

"Huh. I didn't know you had it in you."

"I know. Maybe it's pushing thirty or something. I keep getting crazy ideas." Mark tapped his forehead with his knuckles.

"How about you?"

He felt his face get warm. "Not yet."

"Whoo-hoo," Mark said, grinning. "That's progress. Last time you mentioned pigs and hell. Who's the lucky lady?"

Liam stared at his brother, the man who had more experience with Legos than dating. "Let's hear more about how you're going to use Mom as some kind of practice wife."

"I know I don't want to be alone forever. I require skills I don't currently have. It makes perfect sense." He stuffed another egg into his mouth. "So, what's her name?"

Liam put his glass down on the table and shook his head. At least now their mother would be too busy to give Bev much attention. "I think I'll go see the dogs. Make sure they haven't been eaten. You want to come?"

"No. Thanks."

"Right." To avoid his mother and sister in the kitchen, Liam slipped out the front and walked around to the dog run along the side of the house, watching his step as best he could in the growing darkness. Inhaling the sharp evening breeze, he peered across the electronic fence line at Ed's—Bev's—house and wondered why it was so quiet. Where was she? It was past eight. To his knowledge she didn't know anyone other than Ellen in the Bay Area.

He was annoyed. She'd better not be still at Fite. That wouldn't be safe, even with the security guys, not for a woman who looked like she did. Like there was no way she was a man. Even walking to her car and driving to the Bay Bridge wouldn't be a good idea.

He'd have to talk to her about that.

But maybe he was overreacting and she was home, just conserving electricity. He walked back up the slope to peer over at the driveway, and was standing there in the dusk, casing the joint, just as her little RAV4 came around the bend, signaled, and turned into the driveway.

Liam jumped out of sight and reminded himself to go see the dogs. In the evenings they preferred to stay inside where their little bodies wouldn't catch a chill, but if company was coming over his mom kept them in an insulated porch off the kitchen. She'd installed a children's playhouse and carpeting and piped in their favorite bluegrass music, just so they wouldn't feel left out. He followed the sound of Ralph Stanley's banjo around the back.

His attention was behind him, however, on the house next door.

He heard her engine die and her car door slam. So why weren't any of the house lights coming on?

Biting the inside of his lip, he looked down at the quivering dogs. They looked like they would be happy to have a run around the yard, maybe check out any strange noises. In fact they were pressing their little bodies up against the door with desperation.

He jabbed the button on the screen door handle. Three of the quickest dogs jumped out and tumbled down the stairs, the rest following like geese in formation. They ran away from him and across the yard, their yapping building in volume and enthusiasm as they approached Ed's house.

Liam smiled and sauntered after them.

Chapter 9

WITHOUT PAUSING EVEN to pee, the dogs rushed to the top of the hill, immediately across the property line from Bev's car. Because of the electronic collars they wore, the dogs stopped in a row along the driveway and focused their energies on barking.

"What's the matter with you guys?" Liam said loudly, with as much irritation as he could muster. "Bev, are you there?"

Stepping into view, Bev had her keys in her hand and an exhausted, angry look on her face. "I'm here. Why are you?"

"The dogs got out again. My apologies." He tickled one dog behind an upright ear and walked over the boundary to Bev. "You all right?"

She didn't answer.

"Bev?"

She exhaled loudly. "The key doesn't work."

Knowing it was the wrong thing to do but unable to stop himself, he laughed.

"Oh, go away. Just go away." Her voice hitched and, waving him away, she turned back to the house.

"I'm sorry. It's just—" He followed her. "Let me see."

She swung around to face him and held up the keys. "It fits inside and turns. But the door won't budge."

Gently he took the keys from her and noticed how she jerked away from his touch. "Then it's probably nothing. Just sticky." He fitted the key in the hole, twisted, and the deadbolt slid open easily. Pressing the handle latch, he shoved. It opened a fraction of an inch then stopped. A chill prickled the back of his neck. "No problems with this yesterday?"

"None. It was all new. Nothing like this." Her voice shook.

"How about the side door?"

She buried her face in her hands.

"What?" He didn't like seeing her upset. "Stay here. I'll go see for myself."

Bev sank down to the stairs and sat there, forehead on her knees, while Liam strode around the house to the side door. This time the key wouldn't even go in the hole, as though something were wedged inside. He crouched down to peer at the lock, but it was too dim.

Strange. Very strange. He hiked down the slope and gazed up at the house from below, then made his way back up the flagstone path.

"I'll see if I can break in for you," he said. "I see a window open. It's not much of a climb."

"Break in?" She got to her feet. "Climb?" Her voice was quiet, but steady.

"That all right with you?"

"Just don't hurt yourself and sue me." She brushed off her pants and followed him back around the house. "This isn't your doing, then?"

He stopped, swung around, saw the exhaustion in her face. "No. This is not my doing."

"And I suppose the broken desk chair and deleted software and HR hassles weren't you, either?"

An unpleasant dread settled over him. "You've been having trouble this week?"

She narrowed her eyes. "Nothing I couldn't handle."

He didn't like the idea of people screwing around without his permission. "You should tell me everything that happened. Though it sounds pretty typical—the usual Fite FUBAR."

"It really wasn't you? You've been pretty direct about your other nastiness." She crossed her arms over her chest. "The binders —all seventy-three of them—were a nice touch. I especially liked your suggestion to design a spreadsheet outlining the selling history for every jogging short Fite had ever done."

"I hope you got a lot out of that."

To his surprise, she smiled sweetly. "I did, actually. Thank you."

"You're welcome."

"But the other stuff—not you?"

"No."

She nodded. "Well, that's some relief. I didn't want to have to fire you."

"Well, good news for both of us, then." If somebody was getting creative he'd have to put an end to it. Broken chairs and failing computers were common enough to be accidental, and he'd be suspicious if HR didn't have hassles for her; still, he'd have to look into it.

They hiked around the house until the deck was looming over their heads. He pointed up. "See that window on the south side? It's open, right?"

"Yes, but how can you get up there?"

"If I can jump high enough, no problem."

She crossed her arms over her chest. "Really."

"Really." Doubt his physical prowess, did she? He studied the deck over his head—about eight feet. He slapped his hands together, glancing at her.

She edged away. "Is this when you ask to use me as a step stool?"

"If I can't jump high enough, I'll be the step stool." He tilted his head back and gazed up. "But that might not be necessary." Tensing his muscles, Liam bent his knees, paused for a second and, with a massive groan, leapt into the air. The fingers on his right hand went over the edge, the nails scraping wood, but the left was short, and he came hurtling back down to the ground. He felt his ankle twist on the uneven ground.

"This is crazy," Bev said. "I'm trying the front door again. It's just stuck or something."

But Liam made another jump. This time he got both hands over the edge. Flooded with triumph, he swung by his hands to build momentum then hooked his right foot, then knee over the edge, and soon was hauling himself up over the railing. On his feet and panting, he peered down at Bev. "Oh ye of little faith."

"Sorry!" she called up. "Won't happen again."

Now he had to get around to the window. It wasn't over the deck but around the corner. He swung a leg over the railing to straddle it then got up on it like a balance beam. Reaching around the corner he found the open window with his fingers. "You see a screen on it?"

"No," she said. "In fact, that's what's so strange. I—"

Whatever she said he didn't hear because he was leaping through the air, praying his grip on the sill would hold. Once his second hand was secure he began to breathe again. His fingers burned with the strain. He kicked his foot up over his head into the open window, then his calf. Finally, he hauled the rest of himself up.

He fell, shoulder first, into the bathtub, striking his forehead against the edge.

"Aaach." He rubbed his head. Try to be a hero and fucking kill yourself.

Was that it? Was he trying to be a hero?

Bev was yelling. He staggered to his feet and stuck his throbbing head out the window.

"You made it!" Her teeth flashed in the dark.

Flooded with pride, he bit back a smile and waved. "Don't look so surprised." He pointed towards the front of the house and brought his head back in. He checked the mirror, glad to see there was no blood. Though that might earn him some points. Points for what, he didn't want to think about.

He walked through the house to the front door, then stopped cold and stared down at the floor.

Somebody had wedged the door shut. A black metal stapler, the old-fashioned, heavy kind, had been flipped open and worked under the door where it should swing open. A dozen pens were forced under as well, and when the gap became too small for pens, the intruder had shoved in a few pencils, scraping off the top layer of yellow paint.

Could Ellen have done this?

Breathing heavily, he worked all the obstructions loose and made a pile off to the side.

He stared at it a moment, feeling queasy, before he got up to open the door.

"Hurray!" She rushed in with a huge grin on her face and threw her arms around him. He felt soft roundness press against his chest, his pelvis, and under his hands as they came down, instinctively, to hold her against him. His heart had been pounding before, but now it stopped. Every inch of his body focused on the nearness of her, how she smelled, the breathy happy sounds she made in his ear.

Then she pulled away, eyes wide and cheeks flushed, not meeting his gaze.

Heart thudding, he gestured at the mess on the floor. "No reason to celebrate," he said, more roughly than he intended, angry with himself for the unexpected lust. He turned away. "Sure you want to stay here?"

"What do you mean? Of course—" she stopped and seemed to realize the significance of the office supplies. Her voice fell to a whisper. "Were these stuck under the door?"

He shut the door behind them and flicked on the rest of the lights. "Tell me what you said before about the bathroom window."

She stared at him in silent shock.

"Bev. The window."

"Give me a minute. I'm a little freaked out." She rubbed her forehead, shoulders drawn together, and he resisted the urge to put an arm around her. "I said I remember closing the window, because there was no screen. Last night I had flies."

He took a deep breath. "Wait here," he said, and stalked down the hall to the check out the rest of the house. He looked under beds and in closets and behind what little furniture there was, making sure nobody was hiding. He checked the side door off the laundry, disturbed to see the lock had been jammed with bobby pins from the inside. He went back and found Bev in the small bedroom she'd obviously been sleeping in, going through a suitcase thrown over the bed.

"Whoever it was could have climbed out the window," he said.

"Nothing was stolen." With shaky hands she unzipped a

compartment and pulled out a bag. "My iPod is still here. And cash and jewelry."

"Bev . . . "

She didn't look at him. Her suitcase overflowed with silky-looking girl things. Sexy things. Not seeing how he was transfixed by the sight of pink and black lace, Bev left the suitcase open and flopped down next to it and stared into space. "I wonder how she got in."

So, she wasn't going to deny the obvious. "Did you ever get the garage door opener?"

Bev lifted pained eyes to him. "No."

Liam turned and went to the kitchen to check the door to the garage. Unlocked. It would have been easy enough to come in, screw up the doors, open a window, and leave. Bev came up behind him.

"She really wants you gone," he said.

"She's not the only one."

He paused, then turned and met her gaze. "My motives are better."

"You both want the same thing," she said. "Same motive."

He liked the way her left eyebrow arched up into her forehead. Mocking but not hateful. He found himself making mental notes about the subtle differences between her and her aunt's features. "It's the same thing you want, babe," he said. "We're just counting on wanting it more than you. We've certainly had more practice."

"But I have the chance to bring my family together. I have the higher motives."

He threw his head back and laughed. "And if that were true you would apologize to Ellen. Take whatever she offered."

"She made that impossible. I was tempted but her terms

were . . . counterproductive. Taking all that money would have killed any good will."

"But taking the company didn't?"

She rubbed her temples. "There's still time. In a few months she'll calm down. I never wanted her to leave like that."

"I misjudged you at first, but not anymore." He strode through the house to the front door.

Bev was on his heels. "Just because all you guys care about is power—"

He bent down at the door and checked the lock. "As if you don't."

"Me?"

"You're in this for yourself. Just like the rest of us."

"Are you saying I don't want to help my family?"

He straightened and tugged down his shirt, noticing the way her eyes tracked the movement down his body with as much alarm as appreciation. "That's exactly what I'm saying."

"After all you've seen me do? I could have taken your money —"

"But you didn't, because I didn't offer any power. Like your aunt—and me," he leaned down until he could see flecks of gold in her blue eyes, "—that's what you crave."

It had been a wild shot, but it must have struck true. All the anger drained out of her face and she stared at him, blinking and frowning, until she looked away. "Damn it."

Her look was so stricken he felt a faint pang of remorse. He could have waited until Monday to point out she was no better than the rest of them, though to his credit he never would have suspected she knew so little about herself. Oddly uncomfortable, Liam cleared his throat. "As soon as I leave, make sure you lock all the doors and windows and disconnect the garage door opener.

Shove a wrench or something through the tracks. Nobody will be able to get in."

"You should go now. Your mom is probably getting worried."

Not if she assumed, rightly, that he'd come over to Bev's. No doubt she'd already named their future children; he'd have to tell her about the break-in before she started researching neighborhood school test scores. "I'll check on you before I go back to San Francisco."

"Please don't bother. I'll be fine."

"My mother must have given you her number, whether you wanted it or not. So you could call her if there's a problem."

"Exactly. So you can leave."

He stayed where he was, looking down at her guarded, unhappy face, missing the way she had flung herself at him. His hands twitched, remembering the feel of her. "Are you sure you're all right?"

She laughed without smiling. "You can drop the act, Liam. As you said, you're in this for yourself." She put her palm in the middle of his back and pushed him onto the front landing. "Just like the rest of us."

ðŸ‚¦

"You were stupid not to call the police," her mother said an hour later. At home with Bev's half-sister in Orange County, Gail had the truncated accents of a person laboring on an elliptical training machine. "I suppose you contaminated all the evidence?"

Bev sat on the floor with her back to the front door, one of the mangled pencils in her fingers, thinking about what Liam had said about her motives. It had grown full dark outside but she had on every light in the house, even the tiny bulb over the stove. The vast planes of glass facing the bay reflected the interior back at her, and she felt exposed.

Powerless.

"Mom, this is Oakland."

"So?"

"They've got their hands full with real crime. They're not going to go all CSI on a family squabble."

Gail sighed loudly. "I suppose I'll have to come up there now. Really, Bev. I wish you could show some backbone."

"I'm here, aren't I?" she snapped. She took a deep breath. "I'll be fine. Stay home. You don't want to come all the way up here." Having her mother around was the last thing she needed. She'd considered not telling her what had happened, but the house had felt big and exposed, and every year or two Bev had a deluded moment when she thought her mother would make her feel better.

"It certainly would be a hassle," Gail said. "I'm right in the middle of a cleanse."

"I'll have a security system installed." She thought of the neighbors. "Maybe get a dog."

"By the way, your cat hasn't moved since you left."

"She's like that."

"Kate tossed a load of laundry on top of her, and she didn't do a thing."

Sadly, Ball wouldn't be much help defending the house. But Bev missed her terribly. "She's getting old."

"Careful, or that's how you'll end up. A lump on the couch."

The digs were so common she barely noticed them anymore. "Is Kate done with her intervals yet?" Bev heard the machine groan as it shifted levels, and a distant sound of panting during a long pause. Kate, her twenty-two-year-old half-sister, was her best bet. Her closest friends would do anything for her, but quitting their jobs and leaving their husbands and toddlers seemed a bit much for a few office supplies jammed under a door. And Kate was family. She'd benefit from cleaning away the bad blood too.

"Hey," Kate said on the phone, breathing hard. "What's up?"

"Don't let Mom come up here and interfere." Kate was the baby and the favorite. She could finagle anything.

"She's kind of freaked about her sister trashing the house," Kate said.

Not so freaked about Bev being in the house while it happened, though. "You know, it's gorgeous up here. Feel like a change of scene?"

"To Oakland? Isn't it nasty?"

"God, not at all. It's beautiful. You wouldn't believe the view." Bev threw her mind around for something else tempting. Kate had just got her B.A., had no job, and as much as she was doted on by their mother, complained often of living at home. "The house is right next to a huge park. Lots of redwoods with running and hiking trails."

"Really?" Bev heard her pause to take a drink. "Any indoor equipment?"

"Oh, sure. There's a treadmill and a chin-up bar and all kinds of crap. And more at the office. Everything."

"Really? How's the weather?"

"Cool. Not so hot. Sunny in the afternoons, fog in the morning. You should see it roll in over the Golden Gate Bridge."

"I don't know," Kate said. "I was thinking about taking a few classes. Something marketable. Nobody's hiring."

"UC Berkeley is right down the street. They have an extension catalog." She paused. "If you think you could keep up. It is Berkeley, after all."

"Of course I could keep up. Just because I did two years of community college doesn't mean I'm not as smart as the boring dorks who didn't have any fun in high school."

"Like me?" Bev was smiling.

"You think you got me, don't you, with that Berkeley crack?'

Knowing she did, Bev laughed.

"Fine," Kate said. "Whatever."

"I'll pay for your gas," Bev said just as Kate hung up on her.

Now she just had to make it through tonight. Leaving on the lights she changed into sweats, made herself a quick ham sandwich, and turned on the TV.

After the third close-up on the clinically probed remains of a murdered brunette, she realized TV was a mistake. The room, the house, the neighborhood—all too quiet. She got up and checked the locks again, the windows, then feeling exposed with all the black windows staring at her, sank down and sat on the floor.

When the doorbell rang she jumped.

Then sighed in relief. She got up and hurried to the door, paused to compose her face, and pulled it open.

"You're just going to pop it open like that?" Liam stood in front of her, arms over his chest, glowering. "You didn't even wait to see if it was me?"

"I checked the peephole." She should have. But she'd known —known—it was him.

"You couldn't have. I ducked."

"Ducked? Why?"

"To see if you're being careful," he said. "Obviously not."

"You didn't seem so worried about me an hour ago." She meant to sound cynical, not petulant. But after breaking into the house for her—which had been a vision of male physical prowess that would probably resurface in her dreams—he'd just left her there alone.

His mouth twitched. "Need rescuing again?"

"If I did it would hardly be polite of you to rub my nose in it."

He bent down to pick up a cylindrical sack at his feet and pushed past her into the house. "Polite is overrated."

"What are you doing?"

He walked over to the sofa, reached into the sack, and pulled out a red sleeping bag, spreading it out over the cushions then sitting on top of it. The light material puffed up around him. While Bev stared, he began taking off his shoes. "Since somebody else wants you gone more than I do, I've decided to change tactics." With his shoes parked on the floor, he lifted his legs to stretch out on the couch.

She'd been too upset before to notice the jeans. Now she had to tear her thoughts away from muscled thighs encased in worn denim to hear him. "You're sleeping here?"

"If anything else happens, I want you to know it wasn't me. Even if something happens to you at Fite—big or small—it won't be me. I'm not saying I'll bend over to help you, and I'm still going to point out how much happier you'll be in L.A., but I'll be real obvious about it. Nothing sneaky."

She sat down on the edge of a chair. "Like, say, dumping a decade's worth of paperwork on my desk?"

"Not that it wouldn't be useful to go over past lines if you really were going to stick around as the owner of the company, but since you won't, I'll have to be patient. You'll become unhappy enough to leave without any help from me."

"And sleeping here will prove this?"

"At least I won't have to worry," he said. "You didn't have the sense to go get a hotel room, and though I sympathize about not going over to my mother's, I am related to the woman and have to obey her on occasion or I don't get my favorite dessert on my birthday."

"You don't have to stay. I know you're not the one trying to keep me out of the house."

"Ah, but you weren't so sure earlier. Part of you has some doubt. I should let you think I'm capable of such a thing, but I have my chivalrous side and can't bear the thought that you think I might do you harm. I guess I'm old-fashioned."

Bev was quite sure he could do her harm just by sitting there looking like that. He had a frayed hole over one knee, and she imagined touching the bare skin underneath. "If I thought you might hurt me, I wouldn't let you sleep right down the hall from me."

"Good. Then we're on the same page." He yawned, not seeming to notice her staring. "One reason I was such a strong competitor was that I always found the shortest distance between two points. Efficiency. Adjust my stroke, shave my hair, wear the new suit—whatever worked. To hell with convention or expectation or pride." He slid down onto his back and cupped the back of his head with his hands, exposing a sliver of bare abdomen above the jeans and a tantalizing peek of green underwear. Boxers. With white stripes. "Me sleeping on your couch is the most efficient solution to our dilemma."

She frowned. He could not sleep here. "No dilemma. I'll go to a motel." She turned to walk away.

"Too late now," he called after her. "I need you to give me a ride to BART in the morning."

She stopped. Turned around. "Where's your car?"

"My sister took it. Just a few minutes ago."

"I'll give you a ride now. BART runs late, right?"

He closed his eyes and sank lower onto his back. "No."

"No?"

"You don't mean it, anyway, or you'd be gone already. You're glad I'm here. You don't want to pay for a motel. You don't want to be at my mother's." Then he peeked up at her out of one eye. "And you don't want to be alone."

Chapter 10

THE WAY HE looked and spoke like he saw right through her made her stomach hurt. "And I don't want to be with you."

"Sure you do," he said. "Now you can turn off a few lights. Save the East Bay grid a few megawatts."

"I was just about to do that before you barged in."

"Liar. Nice girls don't lie so much."

Her body flooded with heat. "You come in here babbling about efficiency, and now you're calling me names—"

"Don't get upset. Upper-level managers need to control their tempers. Your aunt had such a problem with that. But then again, you two have so much in common."

She pointed a finger at him. "I am not upset. I am calmly instructing you to get your ass off my sofa and get the hell out of my house."

His grin widened, and she chided herself for falling into his trap.

"You talk like that in the preschool, Bev?" He had wriggled deeper into the couch and showed no sign of getting up. All those muscles would make him too heavy to lift.

"There's nothing efficient about you being here," she said. "It is, in fact, a waste of your time."

"No, actually, it is not, or believe me, I would be happily snoozing in my own bed instead of having to lie here thinking about my promiscuous, parasitic sister taking advantage of my clean sheets." He rolled to the side, pulled up his knees, and tugged a corner of the sleeping bag over his shoulder. "If I hadn't promised my mother I'd sleep on your couch tonight, she would have insisted on being here herself until you were forced to go back to her house and meet my brother, who, incidentally, is lonely."

"Lonely?" The way he had said it, and the unfocused look in his eye, suggested he was not entirely sober. "Unlike you?"

He laughed, not a cynical nasty laugh, but big and relaxed. "Very unlike. He might even be a—" he stopped himself and closed his eyes. "Never mind. But trust me. Not alike."

"And meeting him would have been inefficient? How?"

"Women make him nervous. If my mother took you in, he'd probably end up sleeping at my place. As if I want more company. This way, I suffer for one night and Mark can continue his studies at Mom U."

"Mom U—?"

"Any chance you have something figured out for tomorrow night?" He kicked at the sleeping bag and flipped onto his back. "Because this couch sucks."

"Good. I don't want you tempted to stay."

"I so know what you mean. I should buy it off you for my place. Maybe my sister will get the hint."

Bev stared at him, his eyes closed and his long legs draped over the cushions, and consoled herself that Kate would be driving up the next day. Turning off a few lights would be good. If bad guys broke in, they'd go for him first. She'd leave the lights on near the sofa to make sure they'd see him there.

"All right then," she said, finally relaxing enough to yawn. Her nerves had been frayed all week, and the shock of the break-in had charred her dwindling composure. Having him there did make her feel better. She walked over to retrieve the remains of her ham sandwich on the coffee table. "I guess I'll see you in the morning."

He cracked open an eyelid. "That's it? No more fight?"

She shook her head and yawned again. "I'm too tired. And you're right—I was afraid to be alone." The uneaten sandwich on her plate looked more appetizing than it had earlier. She picked it up to take a bite on her way to the kitchen.

"White bread has a higher glycemic index than pure table sugar, you know."

She had just been about to toss it in the garbage. Now she stopped and rotated in place to see him watching her. She lifted the sandwich to her mouth and slowly ate every bite, his eyes never leaving hers. "Mmm," she said, then licked her lips.

He didn't say anything but the contempt in his eyes transformed into something worse, something she'd endured her entire life in her Orange County enclave of exercise and fitness nuts—evangelical zeal. "I'll make you breakfast in the morning," he said. "Before you die of nutrient deprivation."

If there was one thing Bev knew about herself, it was that—unlike every woman in her family—she had never suffered from nutrient deprivation. Eating everything and anything would do that for you. Forgetting to be afraid of the shadows, she went around the house, turning off lights and trying not to peek at him sprawled on the couch, watching her.

He sat up. "You're wearing Fite."

She glanced down at her sweats then back up at him. "They were at T.J. Maxx."

His gaze dropped down to her thighs, down over her calves,

to her feet, slowly back up. "They fit you pretty well." Then he frowned. "You sleep in them?"

Smiling, she nodded. "Nice and stretchy."

"Never exercise, you said. Never?"

"Nope." She turned around to let him judge her big soft butt while she turned off a wall sconce on the way to her bedroom. "And never will."

Just as she walked out of sight she heard his low voice rumble out from the living room.

"We'll see about that."

ò.

She woke to the smell of vanilla. Her eyes popped open, expecting a sugar cookie on her pillow, only to see Liam standing next to her bed holding a beer stein as big as his shoe.

"I'm not thirsty," she said, though the sight of him and his tousled blond hair and his rumpled t-shirt did make her want a drink. Even his hands, wrapped around the brown mug, were sexy —not too hairy, not too skinny, just solid and clean and shapely.

Christ. I've lost it. She rolled her head back on her pillow and closed her eyes, the vision of long tapered fingers burned onto her retinas.

"It's a protein smoothie." He dropped the mug with a thunk on the nightstand. "I made one for both of us. Sorry to wake you but the ice is melting."

She cracked open an eye. "I had protein powder in my kitchen?" she asked. "Are you sure it wasn't bathroom cleaner?"

"I had to walk over to my mother's." His mouth flattened. "She says hello, by the way. I've assured her you are not dead."

She looked up at him from flat on her back, reluctant for him to see her sit up without a bra on. She pulled the covers up to her chin. "Very not dead. And yourself? How was the couch?"

"God-awful. Even my elbows are sore," he said, rubbing them. " How much do you want for it?"

Smiling, she looked over at her breakfast without picking it up. "Why the beer mug?"

"Only one big enough." He bent over, picked it up, and shoved it towards her. "Sit up and drink it before it loses its froth."

"Froth?"

"Best part." He nudged the rim of the cold, wet glass under her nose. It was going to leak onto her sheets unless she sat up.

Bravely deciding it was her duty to demonstrate how real breasts reacted to gravity, she wriggled upright and took the glass in both hands. "Thanks. I don't usually drink this stuff." As she feared, his eyes fell to her chest and stayed there.

He cleared his throat and to her surprise sat down on the edge of her bed, pulling the comforter taut over her lap. "Do you like it?"

Bev met his eyes over the glass, took a sip, and nodded. It was delicious.

"I put in a few of my mom's homegrown strawberries," he said. "And it's real milk, which I like, but I know some people—"

She wiped her lips. "It's good, thank you. Cold, but sweet." *Like you*, she thought, then felt a stabbing alarm that she was starting to like him. That she had always kind of liked him. But then she assured herself she should like her top VP—though not because he brought her high-protein beverages in bed and had gentle, intelligent eyes.

He slapped his thighs and got to his feet. "Drink all of it. It won't keep in the fridge. And from the looks of the groceries you've got around here, you need the sustenance." He strode out of the room, his old jeans hugging each firm buttock, and Bev wondered if he had slipped something into the smoothie because she felt herself getting hot and energetic.

Snap out of it.

She took another sip, her tongue getting used to the cold, and gulped down a thick mouthful. It wasn't waffles, but it was pretty good. Very good. It would have gone great with a cheeseburger and fries.

With a sigh, she leaned back on her pillows and listened to the sound of water running in the kitchen, thinking it gave the house a cozy feel it desperately needed. She didn't have to worry about break-ins or angry relatives—her executive vice president was on duty with big muscles and a sour disposition. She was safe.

When she had drank as much as she could, she got out of bed and called out to him. "It'll only take me a minute to get dressed, so I can give you a ride to BART."

He didn't answer so she took a few steps into the hallway and peeked into the kitchen. The clock radio over the microwave was playing Green Day while Liam rinsed out the blender in the sink, humming to himself with his back to her. The kitchen window faced south, picking up a low ray of morning sun that lit up his messy blond hair. He'd tied an apron around his waist, an ancient pink polka-dot thing trimmed with red gingham, and he was barefoot.

Like the kids in *Jurassic Park* facing the velociraptors, Bev froze where she was, terrified of being seen but mesmerized. She drank in the sight of his broad back framed in domestic bliss for a moment, then tip-toed backwards back to the bedroom, not breathing, as though disaster would strike if he saw her.

She closed and locked the door, letting out her breath in a whoosh. He was barefoot. Wearing an apron. In her kitchen.

It's true what they said about porn: *you know it when you see it.*

Grateful the mug was still chilled, she lifted it to her forehead and counted to ten. Her heart raced—not from happiness, but from panic.

She burned for him. Well, of course she did. Every woman would. But she had worked hard not to be every woman. Falling for a handsome face with muscles and vigor and cardiovascular superiority inspired women to shave their bikini lines and stop eating and forget themselves. He was the sort of guy Bev had vowed to never, ever want for herself. Again.

"Bev? You getting ready?"

She would have to keep the door locked until he left. If she opened it and saw him again she might show him how thankful she was he spent the night. With her mouth.

"Just getting dressed! Don't come in!"

He didn't answer so she thought he'd left until she heard his voice close at the door. "Pass me the glass so I can wash it."

"Don't worry about it. I'll get it."

He rattled the doorknob. "I promise I won't peek."

Her heart skipped and she went over to the mug, reaching out with an unsteady hand. "All right." She saw her hand pick up the mug and carry it over to the door. She watched her other hand turn the knob to pop the lock. His long fingers appeared in the opening, outstretched at chest level, and she imagined bumping into them to see what he would do.

She pushed the mug into his hand. "Thanks for making me breakfast."

His fingers brushed against hers as he wrapped them around the mug. She tensed, imagining she heard his breathing on the other side of the door until he finally said, "You're welcome," and drew back. "I'll make you another one some time." He returned to the kitchen.

Bev sat back down on the bed until her head cleared. He

didn't mean to imply anything. She was like a lonely eighth grader misinterpreting the cute boy's smile. Always overreacting.

After taking a quick, cold shower and putting on her favorite jeans and an old sweatshirt, Bev was ready to face him again. He stood out on the front deck, balancing his smoothie on the railing and gazing out over the bay.

"I'd ask my brother for a ride," he said, "but he's still asleep."

"No problem. Ready to go?"

He drained the rest of his drink and walked into the house. "When will your sister get here?"

She followed after, locking the sliding door behind them and sliding down a security bar. "Before dark, I'm sure."

"Lock all the windows too."

"I did."

"And the automatic garage door?"

"I'll be fine. I checked everything a million times last night, the first time you left."

He frowned down at her. "I shouldn't have left at all." How could she ever have thought his eyes were cold? They were too richly brown, the lashes too thick, the expression full of feeling—

"Let's go." She strode ahead of him. "I want time to get ready for my sister. Maybe buy some protein." She had to wait for him out at the car while he rechecked all the locks and even strode down the hill to rattle the side door and tap on windows.

"Is your sister soft and weak like you?" he asked, getting into the car next to her.

"She could kick your ass."

He grinned. "Look anything like you? I'd like to see that."

Jealous but polite, she backed up and pulled out into the hilly street. "She's very L.A.—blond and perfect. Kind of like you, but with more toned arms."

"More toned, huh?"

The car snaked its way down to the flat streets of the city while Bev kept her eyes on the road, secretly hoping he'd strip off his shirt to prove her wrong. But he just sighed and leaned back in the seat, saying nothing until several minutes had gone by and they were driving through the gourmet ghetto of Rockridge. "BART is near the freeway entrance, right?" she asked.

"Yeah, but—hold on. Right up there's an empty spot. Take it."

"Can't I just drop you off?"

"Slow down!" He pointed at the tiny stretch of visible curb ahead. "Pull over."

She braked. "You sure? Why?"

"Here."

Making the cars behind wait, Bev signaled and carefully backed up into the small spot, her arm stretched out along the back of Liam's seat while she craned around to look behind. When she turned around, her fingers brushed the back of his neck. She swallowed. "You can walk from here?"

"Follow me." He got out onto the sidewalk and put several coins in the meter while she watched with warring impulses. Sleeping on her couch had made him irresistibly rumpled. His jaw was unshaven, his t-shirt was wrinkled, and when he ran his hand through his unwashed hair it stuck up in a funny wave on one side. He came around to the driver's side and opened the door. "Come on."

She gripped the wheel and looked up at him. "Why?"

"Nothing bad. Promise."

The last thing she wanted was for him to suspect he made her nervous, so she got out and leaned against the car, buying time by reaching into her bag for an Altoid. He marched ahead to a small shop with faceless female mannequins in the window and—

She froze, the sharp peppermint stinging her tongue. "No."

He came back to her and grabbed her elbow. "Yes."

The skinny androids in the window were wearing Nike, Addidas, and Fite. "If you want to show me Fite, show me at work. I have to go home and get ready for my sister."

"You cannot own a fitnesswear company and never shop the stores. This is a boutique. Hardly our bread and butter, but it'll do."

"Forget it."

He propped his hands on his hips. "Coward."

"Please. I know what you're trying to do. You said it last night, but you should give up right now because stronger campaigns led by larger armies have been waged and lost." She wrenched her arm free. "I am not going to work out."

"Apparently not," he said. "Not here and not at Fite."

"That's not what—"

"Because refusing to walk into a store that sells our product out of some leftover childish resentment you have with your parents just shows you're not capable of holding a leadership position." He looked at his watch and glanced down the street at the BART tracks that crossed over College Avenue. "I'll try to catch the ten-sixteen. Guess I'll see you Monday."

"Nice try, Liam." She let him walk away. Then he kept walking. The shop was small and sandwiched between a used bookstore on one side and a taqueria on the other—nothing fancy. She wondered how they stayed in business, competing against the big box and department stores. *Damn.* "All right, Liam. Come back. All right!"

Without smiling, but with a funny tension around his mouth that suggested he'd like to, he nodded and walked directly to the door of the shop without waiting for her to catch up. He went inside with her on his heels, swearing under her breath, and nodded at the young saleswoman who was dusting a display of aromatherapy jars and vials along the far wall.

"Morning," the woman said. "I'm Kimmie if you need help."

"What size are you?" Liam asked Bev, pushing his way through a round rack stuffed with clothes.

"We're just browsing, thanks," Bev told Kimmie, nudging Liam with her hip to get him out of the way. Then she popped another Altoid and muttered to him, "Depends."

"Don't tell me you're shy," he said. "You don't seem the type."

"Female, you mean?" Not many women would want to blurt out their measurements to an Olympian with an attitude problem. "I guess a large—but most stuff doesn't fit me right. I have to try everything on."

He tilted his head and let his gaze drop down over her body, setting her nerves on fire. When his lips parted slightly as he stared at her breasts, she thought about pulling up her shirt and demanding to know if he'd seen enough. But the salesperson looked barely twenty, probably made minimum wage, and didn't deserve the drama.

"You have a very low waist-to-hip ratio. Not to mention waist-to-bust." He scowled.

"I have big breasts and a big butt. Nobody designs for me."

"You—" he stepped closer and lifted his hands around her waist, fingers outstretched in the air above her body as though measuring the space around her. "It's just that you're so small in the middle. Relatively speaking."

Heat and more heat. "Relatively."

Then he was touching her, with no gap between his hands and her body. She felt his large hands wrap around her waist. He barely touched her, but the contact burned. Then the pads of his fingers slid down over the curve of her hips. "Fascinating, really," he said, his voice like gravel.

Her chest felt tight. "Glad to be of interest."

He glanced up at her, withdrew his hands and stepped away. "Don't get upset. I'm just trying to figure out what you should try on first."

"I'm not upset," she said. She wasn't breathing right. His touch hadn't felt professional. The tension she saw tightening his jaw had not been professional tension. He was thinking about the exact same thing she was thinking about, and from the angry cloud darkening his face as he shoved shirts aside on the rack next to them, he didn't like it any more than she did.

"You won't be able to talk to Jennifer about fit problems unless you know for yourself how they feel," he said. "I'm obviously unable to judge for myself, and my mother and sister have given me their opinion. Now it's your turn." He pulled out several pair of dark pants bearing the Fite logo and a pair of t-shirts and thrust the pile at her.

Reluctantly she clutched them to her chest and made eye contact with Kimmie. "I guess I'd like a room." She walked over to a wall rack of sports bras, knowing he was right but annoyed he'd ambushed her. Since day one she had intended on dropping into Macy's—wonderfully impersonal Macy's—to see if she could wear any of the Fite line—but not in a Rockridge boutique with the help of a starved Amazon with buttocks like halved cantaloupes, and certainly not with him looking on.

"This one is totally the best for D cups. And up." Kimmie held up a white bra that looked more like a very small, thick, short, sleeveless t-shirt.

"That's quite a lot of coverage." Bev took it from her. "How do you get into it?"

"You just have to kind of pull like really, really hard. Over your head," she said. "I can help if you get stuck."

"That won't be necessary." Liam put his hand on Bev's shoulder and guided her towards the back of the store. "The changing rooms are over there."

Alarmed he was following so close, Bev said, "You can wait up at the front. Or better yet, go catch your train. No reason for you to be here."

"Oh, I think there is." The corner of his mouth twitched.

Kimmie scurried ahead to open one of the doors for her, smiled coyly at Liam, and stepped aside for Bev to walk in.

Bev slammed the door in Liam's face and locked it. The clothes hung on the chrome bar near the mirror.

She kicked off her shoes and turned away from the mirror to pull off her jeans. Perhaps the excessive reflective properties of the room were meant to inspire, but Bev felt goaded. The walls that weren't mirrored were covered with artistic, enlarged photographs of naked athletes in motion, just to drive home the message that you really, really weren't one of them.

Well, Bev wasn't falling for it; they wouldn't insult her into feeling bad about herself. She got her feet into the leg holes of a pair of pants and tugged them upward, then unhitched her bra and began the struggle to fit the compression top over her chest. At one point both breasts were shoved nearly down to her belly button like stretched water balloons, but she reached down and pulled them up into the high-tech embrace of the sixty-four dollar bra and felt fairly confident she would be able to remove it herself.

"You all right in there?" Liam 's voice was too close to the door for comfort. "I heard noises."

Just the sound of my breasts deflating. "I'm fine." She jerked a t-shirt off the hanger and pulled it over her head. With her breasts in captivity, the slippery shirt slid down over her chest without a fight, and, bracing for the worst, she turned to squint at herself in the mirror.

She groaned. Why did they put elastic bands all over the place? With waistbands so low on her hips they would give a Rodin sculpture fat rolls?

"I don't think so," she muttered, turning to look at her rear end. "Yikes." Butt cleavage was not a trend she was going to embrace, no matter how many apparel companies she inherited. The waist of her thong panties reached up above the pants several inches past the public school dress code limits. She turned back to the front, noting the yellowish-pink fabric of the top made her skin look cadaverous. She couldn't rip the shirt off fast enough.

Liam rattled the door. "Now how are you doing?"

Bev jumped and crossed her arms over her chest, glancing at the Fite shirt sitting in a heap on the floor. "It didn't do much for me."

"Let me in."

"No! I already took it off."

The doorknob turned. "Then put it back on, because I'm coming in."

The damn thing came unlocked. She threw her body against it. "Stay out there. What the hell do you think you're doing?"

"If you don't want me to see skin, then put something on. I'm coming in."

"Damn it." With one foot pushing the door closed, she craned across the dressing room to grab the next top and pull it on. It was as tight as the first, but only half as long. Her freakishly narrow waist--the one he had been fondling earlier—was exposed no matter how hard she pulled it down. "You gave me a kid's size!"

"They don't have kids' sizes here." And then he was standing in the open doorway. Big and looming and looking her over. "Interesting."

She stretched up to her full height and glared at him. "They need to fix the locks in this place."

He continued to stare. "Turn around."

"Liam—"

"If you want to be in apparel you'll have to get over this prissy self-consciousness."

"Prissy? Tell you what. You put this getup on. Then we'll see prissy." She pulled him all the way inside and shoved the door closed. At least the rest of the store didn't have to see her.

"It's horrible." He shook his head at her body.

"Yes. Thank you. Shall we buy it?"

"The rise is all wrong. Did you put them on backwards?"

She hooked her thumbs under the waistband and tugged upwards but the seams dug into her crotch and she had to wiggle to get comfortable. "The only problem is that I'm wearing them at all. Get out of here and I'll take them off."

To her horror he stepped right up behind her, stuck his finger under the waistband right at the flesh above her hip, and pulled the fabric away and over to read the tag. "And these are a large, too. They don't come in an XL."

"Yet another miscalculation. Not that extra width would do anything for me. They seem to have put all the fabric for the waist down at my ankles." Her feet were buried under the flared legs. "Am I supposed to wear heels with them while I'm doing my marathons? They seem a bit long."

"And you're hardly petite."

"Indeed."

Engrossed in the clothing on her body, he didn't lift his eyes to her face once as he continued his perusal. "And the top is a bit short on you too, isn't it?"

"Maybe it's a hat."

Again ignoring her personal space, he stuck his fingers under the bottom hem of the shirt and pulled. The rough tips of his fingertips brushed her ribcage and she shivered—not that he noticed. He stuck his hands up higher, to the bottom band of the compression bra underneath, and wiggled his finger under that elastic. "This bra is a best-seller. If we change it, even a little, we get complaints," he said, then abruptly pulled his fingers out and stepped back. "Jump."

Unnerved by the shock of his hands on her body, she blinked. "What?"

"Jump. Something high-impact. Don't worry, there's a hospital just down the street if you pass out or break something."

"I am not going to jump."

He narrowed his eyes. "Jump, or I tell the design team you've got the muscle tone of a Cabbage Patch Doll."

"I'd fire you."

"It would be worth it," he said. "Jump."

To hell with him. Just because she hated exercise didn't mean she was incapable. She bent her knees and sprung upwards, did it again just to show him she could, then stood with her hands on her surprised hips, glaring at him.

But he was smiling. And from the way he was pinching his lips, she saw he was on the verge of laughing. "Thank you. That was great."

She jabbed him in the shoulder. Hard as a rock, of course. "Now get out of here."

"Could you do it again? You moved so quickly—really, quite a blur—I didn't get to see if the bra worked on you."

"Out."

Shaking his head, he leaned over and took another pair of pants off the hook. "Now try these on."

"Face it, Liam, the company just doesn't make clothes for average women. They're not even close."

"That's what I'm afraid of. Though, let's be honest, Bev— you're hardly average." He thrust the pants into her arms. "We've been getting returns on these for being too big. Act like the businesswoman you're pretending to be and try them on please." Then he turned around and faced the door, crossing his arms over his chest.

"You aren't staying in here—"

He unhooked a hand and looked at his wrist. "I've only got another ten minutes."

She stared at his back. He thought he could intimidate her. Never dropping her gaze, she bent over and wriggled out of the pants.

No problem. They'd been trying to slide down by themselves since she put them on.

Stripped down to the cropped top and her thong panties, she waited for him to bolt, or make a joke, or apologize, or laugh— anything but stand there silently just over a foot away.

She thought of the cold breakfast in bed, of him stretching out on her couch, the way he'd scaled her house the night before to help her get in. "Liam," she said.

Her voice made his shoulders twitch. After a long second, he said, "Ready?"

She wanted to say yes. *Turn around and see me. You want to.* His sister had said she wasn't his type, but type or no, Bev was doing something to him. "Just a minute." She fumbled with the clips on the hanger, her hands starting to tremble. She held the pants up to her body and saw what the customers had complained about—the waistband was cut as wide as the hips.

"Now?" Liam asked.

"Cool it." Good advice for herself, too. Her face felt hot. She hesitated, looking at his broad shoulders, the clipped hair along the back his neck, and slipped her feet through the leg holes and pulled the stretchy knit over her hips.

And let the air she'd been holding out of her lungs. "All right, I'm decent."

He turned around. Neither one of them looked at the pants. "I didn't expect you to do it with me in the room."

She raised her chin. "I decided a long time ago not to be ashamed of my body."

As if she'd given him permission to judge the merits of her self-confidence, his gaze flickered downward, slowly and deliberately taking in each limb and curve. He looked back up into her eyes and took a step towards her.

Her heart began to pound high in her chest as though it were trying to climb out for air. She turned her back to him and tugged at the pants, pretending to study herself in the mirror. "What do you think?"

He was right behind her, warm and massive and now looking at her body reflected before them. With a shock of heat, she felt his hands come up around her waist and envelop bare, tender flesh. His lids fell, hiding the expression in his eyes while she held herself still, desperately afraid of what she wanted.

Still he didn't meet her eyes, but he edged closer, so close she could feel the rough denim of his jeans brush against her bottom. "They're falling off of you." His fingers tightened around her waist and slid down over her hips, taking the oversized fabric with them. The tiny black nylon triangle of her panties appeared between the span of his hands in the mirror.

He looked up then. Their darkening eyes were reflected side by side in the glass.

Chapter 11

FOR A MOMENT neither of them moved. Then, before Liam could claim it was a mistake and hide his desire with a joke or professional bravado, she sagged back against him and pressed her ass against his straining hard-on.

He inhaled sharply. *She wants it too.*

Her body was everything he had ever wanted, every feminine inch deliciously foreign and unlike himself. Soft, delicate, round, generous. Bundled contradictions. His fingers spread out over her hips to get a better grip. He caressed her in slow, curious circles.

He'd watched her that morning while she slept and hated himself for how close he'd come to touching her. Or pulling the covers down, just a few more inches, to gaze at her for as long as he wanted. He'd told himself that the uncomfortable couch was what had kept him awake long into the night, and his justifiable concern for her well-being—and hell, his own—but it was really this, this lust, that was driving him over the edge.

He dipped his head and drew her scent deep into his lungs, and his lips were so close to her temple he could feel her pulse. With an unsteady fingertip he brushed aside the curtain of hair covering her long, pale neck so he could get closer, and she was letting him, and inviting him, her head tilted to the side.

So close. He rubbed the strand of her hair between his fingers and ached to taste her, to feel her thrumming heartbeat with his kiss. But they were frozen, afraid, looking over the edge of their cliff and imagining how long they would fall before they would hit bottom and break.

From a distance, the chime of a bell. The front door of the store. Voices trailed back to them—Kimmie's and other women.

"Christ," Liam breathed, drawing back.

Bev twisted out of his grasp and pulled the pants up over her hips, looking at him in the mirror. She was high contrast, pale skin and dark hair and hot cheeks. He stared back, hands clenching into fists.

"I'm sorry," he said, and she dropped her gaze.

He should never have spent the night. Hands shaking, he fumbled with the doorknob and stepped outside.

She cleared her throat. "I bet."

He banged the door between them, walked out of the store, and strode down the sidewalk to his train before he screwed things up completely.

*

First thing Monday morning Liam called Darrin into his office. "We're delaying the line meeting."

As he expected, Darrin threw a fit, closing his eyes and flopping into a chair. "Then I want comp time for the weekend. I flew the redeye, on a Sunday, just to be here right now, here, for this meeting you're canceling. Through Denver. Fucking Bermuda Triangle, Denver, got laid over six extra hours. Then I got stuck in a row with an obese infant with some sort of digestive disorder, so I'm expensing my dry cleaning too," he said. "And for what? Why? Just yanking my chain again?"

"Bev isn't ready. She needs another day." Long enough to

forgive and forget what happened in that store. A humiliating meeting—orchestrated by himself last week—would be just the push she would need to fire him. If she hadn't decided to do it already.

"We'll have it without her. She's not important, is she?"

Liam's mind seized up at the question. He choked out a humorless laugh. "Not important?"

"Ellen told me all about her." He laughed and picked at his teeth. "Ugly Betty with big tits. Forget her."

"Hey. Watch the language."

"Why? Has she got the place bugged?" Darrin looked around. "Though I did see her headed this way just a minute ago, at least I assume it was her. Matched Ellen's description well enough, even the shoes. Holy shit—clogs?"

"Wait a minute. When did you talk to Ellen?"

"Came by the showroom to say goodbye."

"In New York? When?"

"Friday. Visiting her son all week, she said."

Ellen had been in New York last week? But—

"You canceled the meeting!" Bev was at the door looking just like she'd rolled out of bed. Back in the old Fite pants again— clearly soiled with something edible—and swamped by an insanely large sweatshirt. She looked adorable.

He sprung to his feet. "Bev, this is Darrin. The designer for Men's."

"Oh!" The furious panic on her face froze, then transformed into a soft, motherly smile. "I am so sorry to interrupt. Nice to meet you, Darrin. I'm Bev Lewis."

Darrin's sneer melted into a syrupy simper. "What a pleasure." He got to his feet and took her hand. "I hear you're giving us another day to get our line together."

Bev frowned at Liam. "I am?"

Liam gave her a level look. "You needed another day, Bev. To get ready." To get dressed, at least. Did she think wearing Fite would win them over? And he wasn't finished designing the boards for her to present.

His telepathy failed him. "No, I don't," she said, lifting her eyebrows at Darrin. "Am I the only reason for the delay?"

"So far as I know," Darrin said.

"And everyone else is ready?" she asked.

"Of course. My team worked through the weekend."

Liam wanted to smack him. And Bev was buying it, giving Darrin those big sympathetic eyes of hers.

"Then we have to have it today." She raised her eyebrows at Liam. "At ten, like you said last week."

"Darrin was just telling me how tired he is. One more day will —"

"I'm fine," Darrin said slowly, looking at Liam then back at Bev, measuring and calculating, the transparent weasel. "Whatever works for Bev works for me."

Bev gave him two thumbs up. "Great! See you then." And disappeared.

Liam picked at a thread on his sleeve, his remorse thickening. He had set her up. This was his idea. But that was last week, before —

Before. He ran his finger down the edge of his desk, remembering the feel of her impossibly soft skin under his palms. Whatever happened now was all his doing, and he'd have to live with it.

Smirking, Darrin got to his feet. "This should be good. I'll go alert the troops." He walked out of the office, obviously gleeful at having a new power structure to unbalance.

Liam felt queasy. He ran his hand down over his chest and rubbed his stomach, wondering if people still got ulcers from stress. Last week he hadn't known Bev was under attack from other forces. Last week he'd been convinced he was doing her a favor in the longterm by making her life at Fite so unpleasant she would go away.

Last week he hadn't liked her so much.

All Sunday he'd tried to call her but she didn't answer, and he didn't want to risk seeing her in person away from the office again. He got up and began clearing off his conference table for the meeting, a job he usually left to one of the assistants, then picked up his ball and began adding more dents to the walls. Thwack. Thwack. Thwack.

By nine fifty-five he sat at the head of his conference table chewing on his thumbnail. The design team was frantic, chatty, picking on each other and gluing last-minute bodies on the boards.

Bev didn't know what she was getting into. She didn't know what they were like. Two designers, each of their assistants, the merchandising coordinator, a couple of sales guys, himself—all gathered around the table to tear off heads and shit down necks.

Darrin sat at the opposite end of the table. "Let's get as much done today as we can. Even with the heiress."

The table was quiet until an assistant who ran with Liam on occasion during lunch, spoke up in the timid-but-eager voice of an underling looking for points. "I heard she lives in L.A."

"Has some kind of problem," another designer muttered. "Drugs or something."

"Meth, I think," somebody else said.

Liam sat up straight. "That is not true."

"Explains the hygiene. And convenient, too—God knows we

never sleep around here," Darrin said, not looking at him. The group around the table laughed. "Do you have my Barney's samples, Rachel?"

"Here." Rachel lifted up a shopping bag. "But I don't think it's meth. Nothing like that."

Liam nodded, relieved somebody in the building had some morals. Flabby though they were. "You shouldn't listen to Ellen," he said. "You know how she is."

"Oh, I didn't hear it from Ellen," Rachel said. "I'm pretty sure this is true. From somebody who would know."

"Heard what?" the other designer asked.

"How would anybody here know anything about her?" Liam asked, knowing he should keep himself out of it. He couldn't afford to look chummy with her; that was the point. She had to be the outsider. The satellite. The temp.

"Ellen mentioned she had problems," Darrin said. "So, Liam. Do an intervention yet?" and the gang laughed.

Liam gave him his coldest stare and everyone around the table stopped laughing, even Darrin. Two years ago, at the request of a young assistant's family, he had participated in an intervention. He'd been discreet, but word got around when she quit to go into rehab. "She's in no need of one. Whatever you've heard, it's crap. Ellen's crap."

Darrin regarded him, eyebrow raised. "Don't get excited. Some of the old-timers here could have heard about—Bev—over the years."

Liam dropped his voice to cold steel. "Her name is Beverly Lewis, she's in Ed's old office, and she is the new owner of this company. I suggest you all shut the hell up."

The room fell silent as the group stared at him over the table. Then, one by one, their heads dipped to avoid his glare and he was staring at the tops of a dozen expensive haircuts.

Just as Liam drew a breath to lecture them to behave during the meeting—to warn them that anyone who laughed or rolled their eyes would be processing the FedEx packages for a year—he heard the creak of the door swinging open.

"Hello?" said a cheerful voice behind him. "I'm Beverly Lewis. Mind if I come in?"

&

Liam considered bolting out to pull the fire alarm. He wanted her to be subtly discredited—not die a painful death while he watched.

Darrin struck first. With Bev's question hanging in the air, he turned his back to her and reached inside the Barney's shopping bag on the table. "Looks like she'll need your chair, Rachel," he said. "And since you'll be up you might as well get our visitor something to drink."

Snake, Liam thought. Darrin had managed to insult Bev and make Rachel resentful, with Bev to blame, at the same time. "Divide and conquer" was such an effective strategy at Fite it should have been screen-printed on their t-shirts.

Liam stepped aside and pulled out his chair. "She can have mine," he said, unavoidably triggering suspicions in the room that he'd already slept with the new owner. Instead of only trying to. "And I'll do a coffee run."

Rachel paused, mid-rise, giving Darrin a questioning look. Liam could see Darrin was about to override him and insist that Rachel get up when Bev came the rest of the way into the room and put her hand on Rachel's shoulder. "I don't need a chair." She smiled at everyone. "I just wanted to introduce myself. I brought treats." She looked over her shoulder to the door, where George— George, the Troll of the Back Door—was hovering with a wide, open box in his arms.

"On the table, Ms. Bev?" George asked, staggering over.

"If that's all right with you guys," she said to the surprised, speechless group. Unlike an hour ago, she was wearing a fitted pink sweater with dark designer jeans and heels, and looked adorably harmless and perfect and put-together. She caught Liam staring at her, and her smile faltered. "How about over here?" she said to George, gesturing to an uncluttered patch on the table.

George, who seemed to have strawberry jelly on his nose, nodded gratefully and dropped the box on the table. He gave Bev a goofy grin.

"Thanks so much, George. You're an angel."

"My pleasure, Ms. Bev," he said, and Liam felt light-headed. What the hell had she done to George?

Then people began to rise, their bottoms coming out of their chairs to peer inside whatever it was. One by one they broke into smiles.

"I'm sure this is all wrong for a fitness company," Bev said, "and I probably made too many. But what the hell."

Liam could smell the unmistakable aroma of freshly baked chocolate chip cookies from his side of the table, and saliva pooled in his mouth. One of the designers reached inside the box and froze, frowning. "Are they . . . warm?"

Bev nodded. "The third floor has an oven."

Every pair of eyes around the table grew wide. "You made them?" Rachel asked, now fully on her feet with her face in the box. "Oh, my God. Snickerdoodles."

"Hardly an ideal breakfast," Liam said, but nobody seemed to hear him. They were all on their feet reaching into the box and pulling out cookies and muffins, tubs of cream cheese and jam, plates, napkins, cups, Odwalla juice (several varieties), and miscellaneous paper bags.

An assistant held up a bag. "What are the marshmallows for?"

"There's hot chocolate in the thermos," Bev said.

"Fantastic," somebody whispered.

"No donuts?" Liam asked.

"In the white box," she said. "I didn't make those. They're from the place up the street."

"You got us Gerard's?" Darrin elbowed Rachel out of his way. "Oh, I love you. Their almond croissants are fatal."

"Which is not a good thing." Liam slumped back in his chair and crossed his arms. "Have anything with a lower sugar-to-nutrient level?"

Bev gave him a hard sideways look that said *please*, and he pressed his lips together in a hard line. Her dark hair was pulled back into a headband, exposing the shell curve of her ear and her creamy, soft neck, a hint of collarbone, the hollow of her cleavage under the vee of the sweater. Under his gaze, her face flushed as pink as the knit, and she looked away.

"Nice to see you again, Darrin," Bev said. Darrin was dressed in black cashmere and jeans that, combined with his black hair and pale skin, made him look like a gay, trendy vampire. Bev held out her hand. "I was just hearing about what amazing things you've done with the Kohl's buyer."

Clutching his almond croissant and the compliment, Darrin took her hand and smiled with genuine pleasure. "You heard about that?"

"Obviously I'm just a newbie," she said, "but anybody can see you've made the company a lot of money. We'll have to be very careful you don't get stolen away from us." To that last comment she added a raised eyebrow that froze Darrin mid-bite. As he sank into his chair, his eyes had the fixed, calculating gaze of a man pondering a larger apartment.

Next Bev turned to Jennifer. "I know that—since Ellen left—you're the designer for all of women's now. But everyone told me how, back when you were just out of school, you designed the top-selling Fite Foundations bra." She smiled. "Just this week I met a woman down the street who wanted me to thank you personally. She said it was obvious a woman was in charge of the Fite bras. She won't wear anything else, not even to work. I swear, she was about to hug me when I told her I was connected to the company."

Jennifer glowed. "It's the cups. No loaf."

"Really, she was so grateful for what you make here. I can't wait to watch you work." Bev touched her on the shoulder. "Make sure you get one of the treats before they're all gone."

Liam watched in awe as Jennifer, who in the eight years he'd known her had not once eaten anything other than raw vegetables, organic homemade yogurt, and refrigerated probiotic supplements, reached forward and withdrew a chocolate-glazed donut the size of her face. Not that she ate it, but she set it close to her then licked her fingers.

Bev was already moving on to her next victim, and her next. Liam watched her with growing admiration, amusement, and alarm. She was good. Very, very good. Somehow she knew everyone by name and immediately pinpointed the person's most valuable contribution to the company. She congratulated Wendi on her recent move to Men's as though it had been a promotion. She even came up with a compliment for Grace, an associate merchandiser in men's who he could vow had cost the company far more than she'd contributed, but had once stopped fifty dozen units of vertically-striped Fite the Man Tees from being sewn up horizontally, a fact that Bev pointed out as she offered Grace a second chocolate chip cookie.

"It was nothing." Grace cupped her hands to accept and cherish Bev's offering. "I just noticed the cut sheet was stapled sideways."

"But that's exactly the kind of unsung heroics the world needs," Bev said, as though a few hundred vertically-striped t-shirts would have led to global warming, political instability, and low test scores among inner-city youth.

Watch out for Rachel, Liam thought. Rachel had the brains to appear friendly, but after years of being passed over for promotions while doing all the work, she'd embraced evil as an inevitable tool to survival. It would take more than cookies and milk to warm up her charred soul.

"You work with all the designers?" Bev held on to Rachel's hand longer than she should have. Rachel liked her personal space and drew back as far as her arm would reach. "Is it true you've worked at Fite for over ten years?"

Liam cringed. The last thing Bev should do is remind Rachel she hadn't been promoted past Associate in all those years. He watched Rachel's smile tighten and her arm twitch as she tried to pull away.

"That's true," Rachel said.

Bev let her go and, unlike with the others, didn't gush with praise and promises. Instead, she just nodded and stepped away. "Come see me later today if you get a chance," she said. "I'm in my grandfather's old suite."

Rachel sat down, put the cookie she was holding down onto a napkin and stared at it. "Sure."

By the time Bev had worked her way around the rest of the table, half the box was empty, and the group was laughing and chatting together. Bev reached over to grab an orange juice for herself and saluted the table with the bottle. "Sorry again for the interruption, everyone." She walked towards the door. "Just thought I'd better say hi before you got down to business. I know how hard we push everyone, and maybe we don't remember to say it. So for what it's worth, from your new owner, such as I am, thanks." Her face split into a warm, genuine smile that made Liam's heart skip a beat. Then she walked out.

The people around the table stared at each other silently for ten seconds before bursting out in incredulous laughter.

Everyone but Rachel. Licking chocolate off her finger, she met Liam's gaze and frowned. "I could almost like her."

I know what you mean, he thought.

Chapter 12

BEV CLOSED THE door to her office and pressed her back against it. She'd been up since four that morning, cracking eggs and sifting flour, jumping to the bing of the egg timer as each batch came out of the kitchenette oven, then rushing out to collect the rest from local cafés and bakeries.

And though crashing the design cabal's meeting was stressful, it was nothing compared to the high anxiety of feeling Liam's hot gaze on her backside as she handed out cookies. What had he thought of her efforts to win people over? Were they laughing at her now, the goofy preschool teacher with the transparent bribes?

Was *he* laughing at her?

She marched over to her desk and sat down behind the stack of HR files she had stolen and been studying all weekend, even with her sister around. Memorizing. With the help of a couple of production patternmakers—a treasure house of gossip—Bev had worked up an unconventional org chart of the people at Fite in an effort to follow the first rule of back to school: *know their names.*

Liam's file sat on top of the others—a thin, old file that had nothing but his tax forms and benefit paperwork, a one-page hand-written note offering him the job years earlier and a newspaper clipping from the *Stanford Daily* heralding his gold medal win. Bev flipped open the file and took out the old newspaper, glancing at the door before she took plenty of time to gaze with admiration at the young Liam posing at the edge of the university pool, shirtless and dripping wet, a grinning, virile, triumphant specimen of masculine perfection.

Somebody tapped on the door. Slapping the file shut, she swept them all into the box under her desk and shoved it out of sight. "Come in!"

The door slid open, revealing Rachel's serious face. "You asked to see me."

Bev got to her feet and walked towards her, relieved it was only Rachel. She wasn't quite sure how to face Liam yet. "Great. Let's talk here." She gestured to the seating behind the exercise equipment. Rachel, clearly uncomfortable, sat on the couch closest to the door with her back straight.

One thing that had been obvious from looking at the files was that Rachel had been compensated well beyond her pay grade. However, unlike the other assistants, she had no performance reviews to justify it. In fact her file had been as empty as Liam's, except without the newspaper clipping about gold medals. She'd chatted with the patternmakers and assistants and memorized the highlights for her introductions this morning. In the interests of diplomacy she'd omitted the less flattering stories (such as the time Jennifer had apparently dropped a bolt of fuchsia Performance Blend out the fourth-floor window when it bled onto the white support lining during quality testing,) aiming instead to charm the group with compliments and bribes.

But Rachel was a mystery, and Bev had decided to talk to her privately. Universally liked—and pitied—Rachel had a reputation among the support staff as a workhorse, an ally, a cynic, a martyr, and a favorite drinking buddy. So when Bev looked through her file, she was confused to see no record of her climb up the ladder over her years at the company. Just the note of her salary, going up and up and up at six-month intervals.

And after seeing her in the meeting, Bev realized they had met once before, weeks earlier—in the bathroom. It was hard to reconcile the tough woman from that morning with the sobbing creature she'd tried to help on her first visit to Fite, but it was the same woman. She had a low, distinctive voice, the same short manicure.

Bev leaned back in the couch and smiled at her. "Thanks for coming to see me."

"Did I have a choice?"

"You could have put it off. Said you were busy."

"Not my style," Rachel said, holding her eyes.

Bev smiled. "It would be mine." She looked down at the hands in her lap. She might as well get to the point. "So, Rachel, what was the deal between you and my grandfather?"

Out of the corner of her eye, Bev saw Rachel's face jump with alarm, and the long thigh next to Bev's on the couch stiffened and pulled away. "What do you mean?"

"I've got the files," Bev said. "You were treated differently. Is there something I should know?"

Rachel drew back until there wasn't another inch on the couch she could have escaped into. "What are you implying?"

"Rachel. You make more money than your boss. You have four weeks of vacation time—"

"Which I never get to take."

"—and yet you were never officially promoted. And from what I've heard, you should have been years ago. I'd just like to know why."

"Got some special theory you want to share?"

Bev looked into her intelligent brown eyes and saw the fear hiding there. "I hear he seemed omniscient. Maybe that got harder as he got older. I can imagine how much he would appreciate having an insider—"

Rachel stared at her. "Insider?"

"You know, somebody he could talk to. About what was going on," Bev said, but saw immediately that was the wrong thing to say by the horrified amusement on Rachel's face.

"You think I was spying for him." She laughed bitterly and stood up.

"Wait—I don't think anything. I'm just asking."

"Nobody works as hard as I do," Rachel said. "Ask anyone."

"I have. That's why I want to promote you," Bev patted the seat next to her. "That's why I need to know if there's some reason I shouldn't."

That stopped her. "You want to promote me?"

"For reasons of my own."

"You just met me."

"Exactly," Bev said. "So, is there a reason you want to keep a job title that's beneath you?"

Rachel sank back down on the couch. "Not now."

"Will you tell me why there was before?"

Rachel hesitated. Then she shook her head no.

"Do you think you might tell me, some day?"

Shrugging, Rachel said, "Maybe."

That was as much as she could expect on the first try. Bev got up and went over to the kitchenette, where plates of extra cookies were piled up from that morning. "Help me eat some of these." She reached for the coffee pot. "Then we'll carry the rest down to the lunch room."

Rachel came over and propped a knee on a stool. "You really

baked those yourself."

"I'm big on bribes." Bev handed over a snickerdoodle.

Rachel took it. "Me too. It's the only way I can get my stuff done on time."

Bev poured her a cup of coffee and placed it in front of her, watching her chew and relax. Bev was just about ready to go in for the kill when—

"Rachel!" Liam stood at the door. "There you are."

Rachel jumped to her feet and abandoned the cookie. "I better get back to work."

Liam strode over. "How're you doing, Rachel?"

"We're still talking," Bev said, annoyed that Rachel was edging to the door. "Wait—at least finish your cookie."

Liam scowled at the counter. "Cookies again? How many of your preschoolers made it to kindergarten? Without diabetes?"

"Liam," Bev said. "Rachel and I hadn't finished."

"She doesn't have time." He slid a plate of the cookies out of the way to prop an elbow on the counter. "You don't realize how this place shuts down without her."

Bev bit into a cookie. "I was just offering her a promotion."

"A what?"

"Why is that such a surprise?" Bev asked. "You just told me the place shuts down without her."

"You just met her," Liam said. Rachel, who lingered in the doorway, nodded. "This is like what you did in the meeting this morning, isn't it? Just trying to get people to like you."

Bev saw Rachel's annoyance at the subtle insult. "Maybe I should give her your job," Bev said to him. "You can take over George's seat at the back door."

"I'd love it. When do I start?"

Bev turned to Rachel. "The promotion I'm offering might not

be what you want."

"I don't mind a title change."

"Nothing like putting 'Creative Director' on your email sig," Liam said.

Rachel grinned. "I do it anyway, with outside vendors and contractors. Nobody would have listened to me otherwise."

"I was thinking about making a whole new position for you," Bev said. "I need an assistant—"

Rachel's smile fell. "Assistant?"

"The way a vice president is an assistant." Bev paused for that to sink in. "To be more than a figurehead around here I'll need help. I need someone with your experience, Rachel. And popularity. Not many people around here are as well-respected as you are."

"They're just sucking up," Rachel said. But she was almost smiling.

"Darrin will hate it," Liam said. "Darrin will hate you."

"Can you do that?" Rachel asked. "Just hire me away like that?"

Liam's stare was making Bev uncomfortable. She remembered him sitting on the edge of her bed holding a sweet, frothy drink up to her lips. Staring at her in the dressing room. Sliding her pants down.

"Of course she can," Liam said expressionlessly. "She's the owner."

She swallowed and looked at Rachel. "What can I do to make it up to Darrin after I steal you away?"

"You can't think that way," Liam said. "You're the boss. If you apologize or give in to his demands you'll lose what little authority you have."

"You could move him to Women's." Rachel came back over to

the counter and picked up her unfinished cookie. "Ellen's couture stuff really bites. I know he hated it, too."

"Couture?" Bev asked.

"That's how we got asymmetrical armholes in the spring delivery," Rachel said.

Bev frowned. "Is there such a thing as couture fitness?"

"Only at Fite," Liam said. "Making ugly stuff nobody gets is our niche."

"And my grandfather didn't object?"

Rachel turned her back to her and began fussing with the plate of cookies, and Bev gave Liam a questioning look. He shrugged. "He would yell and throw things every once in a while —"

"The peekaboo tank," Rachel said.

"When things got a little extra creative, but for the most part he left the design decisions up to Ellen. He knew we had to find some way to break out of basics," he said. "And the overall profits were good."

"Thanks to Men's Fite the Man line," Rachel said. "All Liam's ideas."

"Really," Bev said.

Liam shook his head. "She's just sucking up. Darrin's good."

Interesting. She had no idea Liam was involved that deeply in design. "What was the 'peekaboo tank'?"

Rachel bit back a smile and looked at Liam, who was staring at Bev with more heat than was comfortable. His gaze flicked down to her chest then back up to her face. "I guess you could call it 'Jogbra meets Frederick's of Hollywood,'" he said.

He couldn't be serious. Bev looked at Rachel. "Just how 'peekaboo' are we talking?"

"There were no actual cut-outs," Liam said. "Technically, there was total coverage."

Rachel rolled her eyes. "The cups were a semi-metallic, elasticized, open-weave mesh. More gross than sexy. Made your nips look like little pink pancakes pushed against a screen door."

"Lovely," Bev said. "And whose idea was that? Ellen's?"

"She saw it in Paris," Rachel said. "Thought we could 'translate' it."

"Unfortunately the French have more words for that sort of thing than we do," Liam said. "Here in America it means 'trashy ho under arrest.'"

Rachel laughed, and Bev smiled weakly and leaned against the stool. The one goal she was becoming attached to as owner of the company was improving the women's line. How she could possibly tell experienced designers how to do their job?

"I didn't make enough cookies." She pressed her fingers into her temple. "So Darrin would be a better designer for Women's?"

"No," Liam said. "He may be a prick, but he's helped bring the men's line to the top of the heap. Whatever else you do, leave him in Men's."

"All right," Bev said, happy to let Liam deal with him. "But he'll need a new assistant. Or two."

"Who did you have in mind?" Rachel asked Bev, taking another bite. "I am kind of indispensable, you know. Went out of my way to get that way. Didn't realize it would also screw up my chances of getting promoted."

"Sorry about that," Liam said.

Rachel shrugged. "Ed made it up to me." She crammed the rest of the cookie in her mouth and glanced at her watch. "I really have to get back to my desk."

Running through potential candidates in her head, Bev led her to the door. "As soon as I line up a couple new people you'll come work for me. How about next Monday?"

"You won't find anyone by then, and I'll have to break them in. There's a lot. Two weeks, at least."

"We have plenty of great people here. How about next week you'll be half time with me, half in your old job."

"Plenty of great people? Here?"

Bev smiled and put her hand on her heart. "If people give you any trouble blame it on me."

Rachel shrugged. "You're the boss." Then she was gone.

Liam stayed, pacing around the treadmill in the middle of the room, glancing at her every other second.

Bev collapsed onto the sofa. "If you're going to run around like that, you might as well get on the treadmill." Were they going to talk about what happened? Her body suffused with heat, hoping to continue where they left off so abruptly two days earlier. "I won't get so dizzy watching you."

He stopped walking and, arms crossed over his chest, gazed out into the city behind her. Then he cleared his throat. "If you're going to fire me I'd like to know now. If that's all right with you."

"Because of what we did in the store, you mean?"

"What I did."

"We," she said. "Let's be honest."

He relaxed visibly. "All right. We."

"If I did fire you, you could sue, I bet."

"You know I wouldn't."

"Actually I don't," she said. "I don't know what you'd do to keep Fite."

"Not that." He made a disgusted sound. "Jesus. How humiliating."

Because they started something, or because they didn't finish? "I'm not going to fire you. Unless it's work related. And probably not even then, not that I should tell you that."

He walked over to the window. "I'd appreciate that."

Neither spoke for a long, awkward minute. She waited for him to promise it wouldn't happen again. Instead, he turned away from the window and sat on the opposite end of the sofa. His white dress shirt was rolled up to the elbows and unbuttoned at the neck, and it was impossible not to imagine touching him.

"It was cute how you charmed everyone," he said, "but cookies are not going to be enough. Darrin is only one of the people here eager to see you fail."

Cute. Apparently the worrisome personal chat was over. "Damn. And I'd just gone to Costco for more butter."

"It's not funny. They are not nice people."

"They're the same as any other people, Liam. Though first I need to bond a little bit."

"Perhaps if you wait until after dark you could score some smack on Mission Street. Get them really attached to you."

Bev was disappointed he had such a stick up his butt. "They're just treats. Like Cookie Monster says, 'Cookies are a sometimes food.' Sometimes doesn't mean never."

"You're quoting Cookie Monster?"

Bev stared at him. "Somebody has to."

His mouth fell open. Then he covered his face with his hands and broke out laughing, and the tension in the room popped like a balloon with a four-year-old.

"I wasn't kidding," she said, but he just laughed harder.

When his mirth finally drained out of him, he leaned his head back on the cushions and stared at the ceiling. "Ed left Fite to a couch potato who quotes Cookie Monster."

He was too close. She could smell his laundry detergent, something clean and faint. Edging her thigh away from his, she focused on the pedals of the elliptical machine so she wouldn't be tempted to stare at the way his veins snaked gracefully down his arm and over his wrists. "You're just like my family. Worrying and obsessing all the time about what you eat and don't eat, counting grams instead of tasting and living—"

"It's not food—it's fitness. Fitness is deep. Not the way you talk about it, like it's all superficial Hollywood bullshit—but in a spiritual, profound way. Listen, I'm not about looks. I've never been about looks." He tilted his head away, an odd flush creeping up his neck to his cheeks. "I wasn't the best-looking kid in the world, and everyone let me know it. I refuse to give a shit about how I look, but I do care how I feel."

Bev frowned, remembering the pictures he's seen of him at his mother's house. Big and blond, a junior Viking. "I thought you were a cute kid."

He glanced at her out of the corner of his eye, silent for a moment, then said, "You've only got one body, Bev—" He turned to face her and ran an intense gaze down her torso, down her legs, then back up to her face. "It's strong and . . . perfect. You should take care of what you have."

Heat flared in her belly. She pushed herself up and got to her feet, trying to think of something to say that wouldn't expose how vulnerable she was to what he thought. "You keep making it personal, and I'm just trying to do my job."

"Caring about physical health is part of your job. And the jobs of everyone here."

She shoved her hands in her pockets. "I can't pretend to be a fitness freak or a fashionista like the rest of you, but I can show them I can be liked and trusted. I'm trying to be a leader, and not by force. Flies and honey, you know?"

"Calling them fitness freaks is hardly the way to win them

over. But forget it. If you were a jock you might have a reason to stay here."

Sucking in her breath, she pointed a finger at him. "Admit it. They liked me."

"Don't depend on them liking you, Bev. It's not enough, and it never lasts."

"I thought you weren't going to fight me anymore."

"Is that what you think I'm doing?" He ran his hand through his hair. "I spent all of this morning and all day yesterday trying to save you. I tried to postpone the meeting. I bought some samples, made a few boards, sketched out a few ideas for you to present, but you barged ahead with—with—"

He spent all that time trying to help her? She put her hand on her chest, uneasy with how much that affected her. "Cookies," she said quietly.

"Which isn't going to help you where you need it most. But you don't want my help. I don't even want to give it. So I won't try."

"And where do you think I need help the most? It's true I don't know apparel, which is why I snatched up Rachel."

"Rachel won't be enough. What are you going to do when they find out you think exercise is for losers? Think they'll love you then?"

Bev took a step back. "I don't think exercise is—" She stopped herself. "It's just not for me."

"Then they'll wonder why you think owning Fite is." He walked out.

Chapter 13

FOR THE NEXT couple of weeks Liam stayed away from her, hearing through the unavoidable gossip that Rachel had announced her future move and Darrin would be gaining not just one, but two new assistants, which led Jennifer to throw a tantrum in the middle of Engineering until one of the patternmakers tapped her on the shoulder to share gossip she'd heard, about Jennifer getting not only a new assistant but a promotion to Creative Director, too.

Soon even George will be a VP.

He started hearing about meetings—not that Bev called them that, but they were meetings nonetheless—gatherings with Bev and designers and patternmakers and cutters and assistants at all levels where she didn't seem to do anything at all, but then paperwork was changed, and sketches revised, and color palettes tweaked.

Bev made her mark in her smiling, underhanded way, and Liam clenched his fists and watched. Waiting.

When a Saturday morning rolled around, Liam had made plans to get far, far away from his dilemma in San Francisco. Just after seven a.m., Liam slipped into his mother's house in Oakland to round up the last of his backpacking gear and drag his brother off for a much-needed jaunt in the fashion-free wilderness. The house was already alive with music and spinning blenders. Not a rolling rack in sight.

"Morning, Mom," he said to her, kissing her soft cheek while she played the theme to "Hill Street Blues" on the piano. The small, lopsided upright was shoved up against the picture window overlooking the bay. He paused to listen, letting the notes chip away at his worries. Then, as he often did, he leaned down to say in her ear, "Please let me buy you the grand, Crazy Lady. You're wasting yourself on this stack of kindling."

In reply, she switched from TV to Mendelssohn—the wedding march.

"Dad would have wanted you to get a new piano," he said, and she switched back to her original piece. Though he didn't know if that was true. His father had been a difficult man. A man who'd demanded unreasonable loyalty and had the power of personality to get it. "We can put this one in the corner or something. Not get rid of it."

Mark walked in with a pair of knotted boots hung over one shoulder. "Bad news, bro. Mice got into the attic and chewed up your backpack pretty bad. Frayed nylon and droppings are all over the place."

Trixie stopped playing and got to her feet. "Darn it. Just like last year. I'd better go see where they're coming in."

"No hurry," Mark said. "It's probably from the winter." But Trixie was already gone, eager to butt heads with nature again.

"How's your pack?" Liam was suspicious. Mark had never been much of an athlete, and hadn't been thrilled to hear about their weekend hiking plans.

"Mine's perfect." He smiled. "It was inside my college trunk."

"Why wasn't mine inside my college trunk?" He should have

brought it to the condo, cramped though it was, even if Oakland was a convenient stopover on the way to the Sierra.

"Probably because you've used yours since college." Mark sank into a recliner next to the piano and stretched out his legs. "Tough break. Guess we can't go this weekend after all."

"Nice try, you bum. I've got a rebate check at REI I've been meaning to use." He looked at his watch. Still a couple hours before the store opened. "I've packed all the food and got everything else ready. We'll load up the car and buy a new pack on the way. Even then we can still make the trailhead by midafternoon."

Mark sighed and lumbered to his feet. "Yes, Scout Leader."

"I'll back up the car." Liam walked outside. An unfamiliar late-model sedan was in Bev's driveway; after a second's hesitation he wandered closer to get a better look. He knew her sister had come up to stay with her, but with the break-in he didn't want to assume anything. The old Chevy didn't look like the kind of car a young L.A. girl would drive.

He moved closer and peeked through the passenger seat window, relieved to see a make-up bag, Diet Coke bottles, and an MP3 player strewn over the seat.

The blow to the back of his head threw him face forward over the hood of the car. Gasping, he rolled to the side and lifted his arms to defend himself from the next blow.

A woman's voice came from far away. "Kate! Stop! I know him!"

"Bev?" he asked. But the assailant kept at him, her second strike aimed at his groin. This one he deflected just in time and blinked away the stars from the first hit to focus on the short blonde in Fite's second delivery for spring of last year, balanced on the balls of her feet preparing to strike him again.

"Stop, Kate, damn it! That's Liam! From Fite!" Bev's voice was stronger now, but breathless, like she was running. Liam couldn't risk looking away from the psycho to see where she was exactly, but it sounded like down the street, not in the house.

"What the hell did you do to our house?" the psycho demanded, kicking him in the shins.

"Quit—hitting—me—!" He lunged forward and wrapped his arms around her in a bear hug, trying to disable her without hurting her. "Listen to your goddamn sister!"

But she slammed her head up into his chin, dropped several inches and tried to knee him in the balls again. Though he would have loved to return in kind, he grabbed her calf and held it tightly so she would have to focus on not falling over backwards instead of trying to unman him.

"Kate! Jeez!" Bev came up and grabbed her sister around the waist and jerked her backwards. "You can let go of her now. I've got her."

Liam eyed the hopping, violent female with skepticism. She was small but packed with muscles. "You must be the little sister." He didn't let go of her leg.

"You must be the loser who tried to scare us out of our house." She thrashed in his grip.

"Please, Liam. Let go of her leg."

"I want her to swear she won't try to hurt me again."

Kate pursed her lips, but stopped struggling. "For now."

"Good enough." He let go and braced himself.

"He is not the one screwing with the house," Bev said. "Why can't you believe me?"

Kate eyed him from head to toe then shifted her gaze and gave her sister the same once-over. "Because I know how you are with guys like him."

Curiously, Bev turned red.

"Guys like me?" He started to smile.

"He's totally like Rand," Kate said to her sister. "You lose all sense."

He had to admit he liked the idea of Bev losing sense over him. Though certainly not over some dork named Rand. "Is that so?"

"My sister is going inside." Bev, still holding Kate around the shoulders, tried to push her towards the house when Liam realized what she and her sister must have been doing when they came upon Liam looking into the car window.

Running. Bev had been running. "Nice shorts." He admired her round ass and felt dizzy. First her damn sister smacked him upside the head, now this. And they weren't Fite, either, which explained why they fit her so well.

"Now I get it," Kate was saying. "He's why you're jogging. I knew it couldn't be your job."

"He is my job," Bev said, glancing over at him. He smiled, and she stopped abruptly in alarm. "You're lip is bleeding!"

Liam ran his tongue along the corner of his mouth, tasting blood, and nodded. "So I am."

"You hurt him," Bev said to her sister. "You drew blood."

"He was spying."

"Go inside," she said to her, eyes flashing. "You're worse than a pit bull." She pointed at her house until Kate took a step in that direction, then she came over to Liam. She cupped his cheek and peered into his face with those big blue eyes. He looked down into them and felt dizzy again.

"He's swaying," Bev said, looking over at her sister. "Help me get him into the house."

Kate was sulking near the front door. "Bring him to his own

house. Where he should have stayed."

"Your family is charming." Liam lifted a finger to his lip that came away wet and red.

Bev hooked her arm in his and rotated him away from her sister. "Let's go to your mother's. I bet she has a first-aid kit." Then she peered up at him again, and he looked down and met her concerned gaze and wondered if it was the blood loss that made him feel light-headed.

"She's hunting right now," he said.

Frowning, Bev marched him down the yard. "Watch your step." She threaded through the shrubbery.

"How far did you go?" He slowed his stride, confident she wouldn't be able to propel him on her own, and studied the damp spots on her t-shirt. She was drenched. "Your sister pushed you too hard. I can tell just by looking at you. That's a terrible way to start an exercise program."

"We hardly got started," she said. "It was running up the hill to save your life that nearly killed me."

He pretended to stumble and sagged in her arm, making her hold him more tightly. "Thanks," he said, reveling in the feel of her soft hip digging into his, "but it's your sister whose life you saved. If she'd kept that up I really would've had to fight back."

But Bev didn't seem to believe him. She squeezed his arm and sighed. "Kate has anger issues. And too many years of kick aerobics."

"Really, Bev. I could have handled her."

"Of course you could," she said in that preschool teacher voice that made him want to go back to her psycho sister and beat the crap out of her. But Bev's body was an effective distraction. He lifted his arm out of her grasp and rested it across her shoulders so she was plastered up against his side, soft and strong and sweaty, and her steps faltered.

"Did she beat you up too?" Liam asked.

Bev chuckled, and the soft rumble tickled his senses and heightened his awareness of each inch of her next to his skin. "What were you doing in our driveway? Before eight on a Saturday morning?"

They were almost at his front door, and he didn't think he could slow his steps any further without looking pathetic. "Packing up for a backpacking trip with my brother. I saw the car and didn't think it looked right."

She stopped and looked up at him. "You were worried about me?"

Oh, boy. He had a shallow, tight feeling in his chest, probably from the strain of not peeling her wet t-shirt off of her. "I didn't want to have to sleep on your couch again." Then the image of him climbing into her bed struck him between the eyes, and he froze.

"Here you go." Bev extracted herself just enough to tap on the front door. She turned the handle and popped it open. "You'd better go first."

He didn't let go. It was insane but he couldn't, and Bev wasn't helping. She rotated in his arm and faced him, though not meeting his eyes. The side of one full breast brushed against his chest. And just like that he lost it. He reached past her, pulled the door shut, and backed her up against the side of the house. His heart thrashed in his chest.

Bev held still, eyes dark and blue, her body tense in his arms. He caught a strand of her hair in his fingers and pressed his thighs against hers.

The devil in his brain told him he'd already crossed the line once—the damage had been done; he might as well—

"You're hurt." She raised her hand to his mouth. The sight of blood on her fingers shocked him into sense, and he drew back.

"Sorry." Pressing his hand to his mouth, he broke away from her and went into the house, struggling to clear his head. What the hell was he doing?

"Where'd you go?" Mark barged across the living room with a pack over his shoulder. He pushed past Liam and ran right into Bev standing on the landing. "Oh!" he yelped, jumping back. "Excuse me."

Liam sighed. "Mark, this is Bev, your neighbor. Her sister just beat me up for no reason." True to form, Mark panicked at the sight of an unexpected female and blinked his eyes, saying nothing. "Bev, this is Mark, my brother. Show mercy and ignore him until he recovers."

"Nice to meet you, Mark." Her voice was unsteady but she waved a greeting. "There was a misunderstanding. My sister just has the wrong idea. Do you have a first-aid kit? I can't tell how bad it is, because of the blood—"

"Blood?" Mark asked weakly, swaying.

"Now you've done it." Liam grabbed his brother's arm and pushed him down onto a chair. "Head down. Just don't think about it."

Bev followed. "What happened?"

"Faints at the sight of blood," Liam said.

"Christ, you're dripping," Mark gasped.

"I'll get a washcloth." Bev ran off into the house.

"Faints at the sight of girls, more like it, you sissy." Liam said, rubbing Mark's back. "Chill. Just us menfolk now."

Mark bent over and put his head between his knees. "Fuck you. Vasovagal syncope has nothing whatsoever to do with my masculinity. Father was the same way."

Oh, Liam remembered. Years ago, Liam had smacked his head on the starter block climbing out of the pool, and the sight of blood had brought his father to his knees. The humiliation of passing out in a chlorinated puddle of water in front of dozens of strangers—even just during practice—had inspired his father to take away fifteen-year-old Liam's driver's permit until he was eighteen. Liam had almost wished he could go back in time to when he was a fat seven-year-old nobody, far beneath his father's notice.

"Here you go, you poor guy." Bev rushed in carrying a damp washcloth, but instead of coming to Liam she fell onto her knees at Mark's feet. "It's an awful feeling. I know. Just horrible."

Mark lifted his hand to take the washcloth while his pale cheeks flooded back with splotches of color. "Thanks, uh..."

"Bev. Don't exert yourself." She twisted around and looked up at Liam, who was pointedly bleeding down the side of his face. "Liam, go clean yourself up before your brother sees you again."

Liam stared at her hand resting on his brother's knee and felt an inexplicable rage bubble inside him. He could probably see right down her shirt from where he sat, the big faker. "Of course." He didn't pretend to hide his contempt. "If I faint from blood loss just leave me there. The mice can have my body."

He heard Bev mutter, "Such a baby" as he walked down the hall to the bathroom. While he waited for the water to run hot, Liam wiped away the congealing blood off his lip and realized he was clenching his teeth and fighting the urge to drive his fist through the mirror.

It was not that he was jealous. Bev was hot, and he wished he could take advantage of it, but Mark was his shy, geeky brother, and the trauma of having an outwardly sweet and stacked girl nursing him back to health was going to be too much for him.

Mark was probably already thinking he was in love.

He slammed the medicine cabinet shut and was peeling apart the Band-Aid when it occurred to him that Bev might have been trying to make him jealous. The thought should have made him angrier, given how protective he was of his little brother, but it did not. In fact, he had to wipe the grin off his face to fit the bandage over his split upper lip.

When he got back to the two lovebirds in the living room, his temper and his offending blood were out of sight. "Help me pack up the car, Mark," he said, "and we can be at the store right when they open."

"Store?" Mark stared at Bev next to him in a matching armchair.

"REI," Liam said. "My pack."

Not looking away from Bev, his darling brother said, "You can have mine. It's in great shape."

"Then you won't have a pack," Liam said.

"Oh, I'm not going."

Liam walked over and whacked him on the side of his head. "Fill up the water bottles while I check the tent. The mice only got into my pack, right?" He whacked him again. "Right?"

"Jeez." Mark got up and headed for the kitchen. "No need to get violent."

"Tell that to the neighbors. Kind of got me in the mood."

Bev stood up and came over to him. "How's the lip?"

"Oh, now you care."

Eyes bright, she bit back a smile and studied his lip. "Looks like you'll live."

He swallowed, feeling his pulse pick up again. Her hair was up in a pony tail, straggly and lopsided, and he had to dig his nails into his palms to stop himself from tearing the rubber band out and combing the long, black strands with his fingers. "Your sister will be disappointed."

"Nothing new there," Bev said. He liked the way her eyes could smile without the rest of her face moving.

Mark came back into the room. "How many Nalgene bottles are you bringing, anyway?" Then he looked at Bev standing close to Liam, and the slow social calculations on his face were visible from fifteen feet away.

"All of them," Liam said. "The creeks are dry this time of year."

"That'll be heavy," Mark said.

"Better to be tired than dehydrated."

Mark sighed and went back into the kitchen.

"He's sweet," Bev said, and Liam imagined shoving his brother off a cliff, which was all wrong. It was Bev who was trouble.

"Stay away from him."

"What?" Bev asked, incredulous.

"I mean, please stay away from him. He doesn't know you're not as nice as you look. You and your violent relatives."

She shook her head. "I think you should rest for a bit before you climb any mountains. Your brains are rattled."

Agreeing with her, he put an arm around her shoulders and led her to the door, annoyed at how badly he wanted her.

"See you at the office," he said, and suddenly wished it were Monday.

೩

He did see her at the office. Specifically, the office next door to his.

"I'm moving down here," she said Monday morning, while George and Rinaldo from the warehouse followed behind her with boxes and computer equipment and a rolling rack of samples.

"Whatever the hell for?"

She frowned at him. "That ivory tower wasn't working out. My grandfather's frat lounge, not practical."

"What are you talking about? It was a perfect way to don the mantle of power."

"Too cut off from the action. And I kept bumping into the foosball table." She walked past him, tore a paper towel off a roll in her hand, and began wiping off an old desk. "I've put the room to a much better use."

"Do you want the exercise ball chair?" Rachel wriggled past Liam to talk to Bev.

"God, no. You want it, you got it."

Rachel nodded. "It'll be awesome for my abs. And if anyone bothers me, I'll just throw it at them."

"Just lock the door to your office if people are bothering you." Bev smiled at her then turned her attention to Liam. "Oh dear, did you forget your sunscreen?"

Liam crossed his arms over his chest, well aware he had a white mask around his eyes. "Problem with the gear."

Rachel came over to stare at him, too. "It looks cool. Like Kung Fu Panda. Except the reverse."

"The sunscreen fell in a pit toilet." He'd never hike with his brother again. Thirty hours of continuous misery. When Mark wasn't dropping essential gear into latrines or whining about how tired or hot or cold he was, he was asking about Bev: *Is she married? Dating? Sleeping with you?*

Wanting to sleep with you?

"It's kind of cute." Bev was still staring. "Takes the edge off."

Liam scowled. "I don't want any edges off."

Rachel laughed. "I'd give you some foundation to cover it up, but I don't have quite that shade of lobster."

He gave her a cold look down his crimson proboscis then

strode back to his own office. Ever since Bev had shown up, he'd found his authority chipping away. Just that morning Carrie at the front desk had actually said hello to him.

Before he could sit down and get some work done, he heard activity in the empty office on the other side of him. "Damn it, Bev," he muttered, and went out to see Rachel rolling a cart stacked high with binders into the room. She looked up at him and grinned fearlessly.

"She's going to be our boss in a couple years," Bev said behind him.

Liam swung around. "You're taking both my offices?"

"*Your* offices? They were empty."

"For a reason."

She rolled her eyes. "For a jock, you're not much of a team player."

"For a couch potato, you're quite a busybody."

Laughing, she touched his arm. "Why, Liam—I think you're finally beginning to understand me."

He gave her his hardest glare, but she just smiled and walked away. With a limp. "You're injured."

"Now maybe you'll believe I'm not like designed like the rest of you. One little walk and I'm broken."

"Cut that out." He got ahead of her and grabbed her shoulders, making her face him. "You just dove in too fast."

She tensed under his grip and looked down at his hand on her shoulder. Suddenly it was like they were in the dressing room again and her body was pressing up against his. He softened his grip on her shoulders, feeling the heat of her body through her dress.

She wriggled free. "I went one block."

"It was the sprinting to interrupt a homicide that did it," he said, his voice rough. "If your sister hadn't assaulted me you would have been fine. Don't give up. It's great. Really."

"I knew you would gloat."

"This is gloating?" He drew back. "You want gloating, I'll give you gloating. I knew you couldn't do it. I knew all your bravado about hating exercise was just a lie. You're just too conceited."

Her mouth dropped open. "Conceited?"

"Can't be the best, won't do it." He shrugged and went over to carry Rachel's computer monitor for her. "You like to be on top of things. That power-thing again."

"That is not true."

"Put it off to the left," Rachel said, coming in and caressing the vast expanse of oak desktop with her palms. "This thing's bigger than my bed. I have room for two computers."

Liam looked at the desk with new eyes. *Bed*, he thought then frowned at Bev. There was no reason she should be wearing dresses again. The only people charmed by perfect, oversized breasts were straight men like him, and he was tired of the distraction. "What did you bake today?"

"No time for that. I bought BurnBars." She strode out. "Maybe that will shut you up."

The fantasy of her napping on the desk vanished. He hurried after her into her new office. "Who told you?"

She frowned. "Told me what?"

Her confusion stopped him. Smoothing his hand down the front of his shirt, he took a step back. "Never mind—my mother must have told you."

"Liam, I don't know what you're talking about." She gestured at a pile of small boxes on her desk. "If you don't like BurnBars, don't eat them. I had a coupon."

It was just a coincidence. For a moment he had thought

Darrin was making trouble, knowing how much he hated any reminders of his father. His overreaction embarrassed him. "Sorry. My dad invented the BurnBar. Back in the early eighties."

"Your father?"

"Sold it all to Kraft." So he could devote all his waking and sleeping hours to getting his son to the Olympics. "That's how we ended up living in a fancy house in the Oakland Hills next to Ed."

"Where did you live before that?"

"We had a duplex in the flats near the freeway."

Bev glanced over at her new desk, where the cases of BurnBars formed a small pyramid in one corner. "I kind of like them."

"So does everyone else." He went over and picked up a box. "I'll take some to Engineering for you. They'll love you even more."

She met his eyes, and they looked at each other for a moment. Then she smiled. "Wait until they see what else I have planned."

"I don't want to know."

"Yes, you do. Follow me."

He didn't have time. The red light on his phone was blinking, the cell in his pocket vibrated every five minutes with a phone mail reminder, he had a meeting ten minutes ago, and three days of email was still in unopened bold font in his in-box.

And Bev was wearing a dress. "What did you do now?" He sighed, following her into the hall, watching her hips sway, hearing the blood rush in his ears.

"Don't worry. You'll like it."

That's what I'm afraid of.

❧

Bev tightened the sash around her waist and tried to reach the elevator without limping. She felt his eyes on her back like radiation.

"Did you ice it?" Liam asked.

"I spent most of yesterday with my foot in a bucket."

"Good," he said. "But what about today? You should stay off of it."

"I'm fine."

"No, you control freak." He took her arm. "Lean on me. If you act macho you'll just take longer to heal."

Damn, he's big. She tested his strength by leaning heavily on him, and he didn't budge. The pain shooting up her heel was better than yesterday morning but still made it hard to walk normally. To her surprise, the two-inch mules her sister had picked out for her relieved some of the pressure. Then she had the dress to go with the shoes, and put the makeup on to go with the dress—

Did he even notice how totally hot she was?

"Something in Ed's suite?" He bent his knees and took more of her weight on his arm. "Let me guess—an all-you-can-eat donut buffet."

"You should share these good ideas of yours," she said. "Don't be shy."

They got into the elevator. She pressed the now-accessible button to her grandfather's floor.

Suddenly she became aware of the location of his hand holding her forearm—right under her left breast. He had to know where his fingers were, yet he wasn't making any effort to readjust his grip. The elevator door closed and the car rose. She stared straight ahead, not up into the warm brown eyes of her executive vice president who was touching her again.

The old elevator was slow. Her heel throbbed—but not badly enough to stumble sideways as she suddenly did, which forced him to put his arm around her waist and pull her closer.

His body tensed, his hand opening along the curve of her waist, showing her he'd come to the same conclusion. She kept reliving how he had almost kissed her on the front porch of his mother's house, the way his knee pushed between her legs when he pinned her against the door, and decided that dealing with this issue immediately was of professional value to both of them.

She reached forward and pressed the emergency stop button, freezing them between floors. "Liam—"

And then he was there. Trapping her face with his free hand, he dropped his head and covered her mouth with his, hard and fast. Just as her veins flooded with heat, he broke the kiss and his hold on her and stepped away.

She couldn't breathe, couldn't think. He looked furious, scowling at her and shaking his head like it was her fault.

Scowling back, she moved right up to him until her breasts brushed against his chest, slid her hand around the back of his neck, and pulled him down where she could reach him.

He came to life. His mouth opened over hers in a deep, angry kiss, and she stretched up against him, reveled in the feel of his hands in the valley of her back, the way he held her hips against his while his tongue slipped between her teeth and tangled with hers. His hands couldn't stay still; they slid up her ribs and up the sides of her breasts and down her spine and under the swell of her ass, all while his mouth devoured her. She forgot about everything but his touch.

He released her again, or maybe she pulled away to breathe. Her back thumped against the wall of the elevator, and they stared at each other, breathing heavily, open-mouthed and shocked.

In a rush, they came together again. After a long, deep kiss, he trailed his lips along her jaw and licked the curve of her ear.

A flare of heat made her gasp. Her knees weakened.

"Bev—"

"Don't—say it—"

They rotated, and she was the one pinning him against the wall, running her hands up his chest, measuring and savoring the planes of his body. He looked down at her with a stunned, ecstatic expression on his face, letting her break all the rules by herself until it seemed too much for him. He grabbed her around the waist and hauled her up to his mouth.

The elevator bell rang, but Bev tilted her head and sucked Liam's tongue, making him groan. His hold on her broke. She slid down his body until the tips of her toes hit the floor. When her heels landed a shock of pain shot through her leg, and she gasped into his mouth.

He tore his lips away. "You're hurt," he breathed.

She tried to hide it. Pressed herself against him.

But he gripped her shoulders and pushed her an arm's length away. "Let me see." He sank down to the floor and took her foot in his hands. His thumb rubbed the sore spot, just under the heel, while his hair brushed the outside of her bare leg. She was tormented with warring pleasures and pain.

Putting her hand on his shoulder for support, she struggled for air, wiggling her foot for his benefit. "I'm fine—just—forgot about it."

The high-pitched elevator alarm bell seemed to be getting louder. Soon somebody was going to call for help.

And not the help she needed. She released his shoulder and limped over to the elevator controls to release the car.

"Good idea." Liam stood up. "Don't want the attention." He reached out to take her arm again, but she drew back and held up a hand to stop him. He stared at her, chest heaving, then turned away.

They both began straightening their clothes. Bev didn't know her own thoughts, let alone his. In seconds, the elevator doors opened, and they stood on opposite sides of the car, not looking at each other. His face was flushed, but blank. She had no idea what to do next. What was he thinking? Casual sex had always been a disaster for her, but what else could this be? They were in a fucking elevator. Literally.

She stepped off the car in a daze, and he followed.

Seeming remarkably calm, he strode down the hall ahead of her. "You were going to show me something?"

She felt flushed. Ashamed of what she'd begun.

She'd known this might happen. He didn't need to see what she'd done to her grandfather's suite in person—he'd get the same email as everyone else. She'd just wanted to see his face when he found out she was going to open up an employee gym and lounge for everyone in the building—and had wanted to be alone with him again.

Hanging back to hold the elevator door, she let him walk ahead. "You go see for yourself," she said. "I need a minute."

He stopped and turned. Glanced down at her disheveled dress. "Right."

She backed up into the elevator and pushed the button to close the door between them. Anything to get away from him and think.

"Hold on." Liam stuck his arm in the door and gazed at her with dark, unblinking eyes. "My place."

"What?"

"My place. Tonight."

"Just like that?"

He closed his eyes for a second. "Let's hope so."

"What about your sister?"

"She won't be invited."

Her mind was annoyed with his tone, but her body began to thrum in anticipation. "I don't know where you live."

He nodded, glanced over his shoulder to make sure they were alone, and lowered his voice. "It's a high-rise on Beale, at Folsom. My building is the one with the purple guitar sculpture out front. I'll meet you there, near the sculpture, at seven," he said. "Can you remember that?"

She turned away, heart racing, and punched the elevator button again. "My memory isn't the problem."

Chapter 14

WHEN BEV CAME into view at the end of the street, casually dressed with a floppy leather purse slung over one shoulder, Liam let out the air he'd been holding in his lungs in a slow, steady exhale.

The breeze whipped her loose hair into the air around her head. The soft, dark waves exaggerated the fine bones of her face, her long neck, the generosity of her mouth. Was she as terrified as she looked? He strode forward to meet her halfway down the block, reached up and tucked a strand of her hair behind her ear as soon as she was close enough to touch.

She jerked her head away. "We need to talk."

First he had to shut up the voice in his head that was shouting, *She came!* and get a grip on the torrent of emotions tearing through his body. "Let's go up to my place."

"I'm not going inside. We can talk out here."

Stifling a howl of disappointment, he nodded and turned to walk at her side, determined not to scare her away. He wouldn't touch her again until they were in his condo. "I know what you're thinking, believe me," he said. "I never get personally involved at the office anymore. I even refuse lunch invitations from my own staff. Nobody knows anything about me outside of work they didn't learn from Ed or old newspaper clippings."

"This is supposed to impress me?"

"You think that getting involved with me—more involved, because let's face it, we've already crossed the line—is going to screw up your goals at the company. Am I right?"

She stopped and crossed her arms over her chest. The sexy dress was gone. Now she hid herself under a pea-green, shapeless sweater his brother might have picked out for himself. He knew what she was trying to do, but it was hopeless.

I can still imagine you naked, babe.

"You can't convince me it won't hurt our working relationship," she said.

"What working relationship? I've been trying to screw you over since you got here." She cracked a smile, and he took the opportunity to guide her another few feet closer to the entrance. "If anything, scratching this itch will probably help us get along better."

She started walking again. "Wonderful. You're comparing me to a rash."

Maybe he shouldn't wait until they got upstairs to remind her of her own desires. Cupping the back of her neck, he dipped his head down and brushed his lips against hers, inhaling the scent of her deep into his lungs. "I want you, Bev." He trailed kisses along her cheekbone to the hollow below her ear and felt her tremble.

Good. Now don't push her too fast.

He lifted his face a couple inches above hers. "I made dinner."

She didn't pull away. "Made? Or bought?"

"I buy the pasta, then boil it all by myself." He typed in the key-code at his building's front door. "You'll like it. Lots of carbs."

She sighed, annoyed again, and he congratulated himself on distracting her enough to follow him deeper inside. They got onto the elevator, and this time he kept his hands to himself.

The car rose twenty floors, and the doors slid apart.

"You didn't have to cook." She didn't move.

He put his hand in the door and smiled at her. She looked stricken, staring at him. Then she followed him into the carpeted hallway.

April had better not be there. If she hadn't gone out like he told her to, he'd hack into her blog and decimate her social life. But the condo was quiet and dim and filled with the smells of simmering garlic and tomatoes. He held the door open. "Here we are."

He heard her breathing the rich cooking smells, exhaling with a distinctly feminine groan of pleasure. He felt a surge of desire so intense he fisted his hands to stop him from pinning her against the front door and taking her right there.

Apparently unaware of his struggle, she studied the furniture. "Of course you have a real Winzler."

He admired the swell of her breasts, as much of them as he could see under the baggy fabric. "I'm going to burn that sweater." He hooked his arm around her waist and pulled her hard against him for another kiss.

After a painfully brief kiss, she shoved him away. "We talk. We eat. We do not—" she pointed at his mouth, "—do that."

For the first time he realized he may have been overconfident. Shoving his hands in his pockets, he leaned back in the doorway to the kitchen and kept his gaze fixed above her neck. "What would you like to drink—wine? A cocktail?"

"Water," she said. "Just water."

He sighed. "Make yourself comfortable." He should have just handed her a glass of wine the moment they walked in the door, and he shouldn't have kissed her like that. Something about Bev made him needy. Desperate. He readjusted his jeans.

From the kitchen he peeked around the breakfast counter into the living room, drank in the sight of her sitting in a narrow upright chair with her knees pressed together and fear in her eyes, then reached under the sink where he hid his best scotch. God knows his sister would never look for cleaning supplies.

"That's not water," she said when he handed her a glass of it.

He took a chair on the opposite side of the room, ten feet away. "Sure it is. Mostly." He kicked his own back and let the fire singe the fuzzy corners of his brain. "You want to talk, talk. I'm listening." He stared at her and had the blinding vision of kneeling at her feet with his head between her thighs.

Still sitting primly upright, she frowned at the glass resting on her knee. "If we—do this—everyone will know."

"If we don't people will think we did anyway." He took another gulp. Which was true. If they were going to pay, they might as well play. He looked at Bev over the rim of his glass.

She shifted uneasily in her chair, exaggerating the swell of her hips in the seat. Then she lifted the glass and drank.

Liam's heart, already racing, began to pound against his ribs. He tossed back the last of the scotch and got to his feet, not breaking eye contact with her. She took another swallow.

"I want you," he said, walking over to her.

She frowned. "Well, I find you repulsive."

Her mouth was rosy and glistening from the scotch. He leaned down, grinning, and licked it from one corner to the other while his hand slid around the back of her neck and dug into her thick, bewitching hair. The scotch had tasted good in the glass, but on her skin it was a narcotic. He had intended to guide her to her feet but found himself on his knees, kissing her while she sat on her chair, whimpering, moaning.

He trailed kisses down her neck, nibbling gently until he hit the thick acrylic knit. "I'm taking this off," he said in her ear, and tucked his fingers under her sweater and teased it up over her ribs.

She giggled then frowned, pushing him away half-heartedly. "It tickles."

His cock strained against the fly of his jeans. She sounded so young and sweet, but he knew better. He saw through her, how every act of niceness was carefully calculated and planned ahead. How she managed to disarm her enemies with charm. How she always seemed to get exactly what she wanted without ever seeming to fight for it.

"Tell me how you like it." He dipped his head lower to taste the naked skin of her belly. He licked her navel, and she jerked, sighed. He wrapped his arms around her body and pulled her soft flesh against his face. Her bottom came off the seat of the chair, and she clutched his shoulders for balance.

"I like it in bed." She pushed him away, stumbling to her feet, and rubbed her back. "Or somewhere padded."

He came after her and pulled her with him onto the sofa. He wanted her on top of him, to feel the full weight of her body along his, nothing held back. "Take off your clothes." Then he remembered how badly he wanted to finish what they had started in that store in Oakland the week before. "Wait. Come with me." He rolled aside and got to his feet.

She looked up at him, her hair strewn across the cushions, and raised an eyebrow.

"You'll like it." He held out his hand.

She took his hand—warm, smooth fingers—and followed him to the bedroom.

When he bent over to switch on the lamp on a side table, Bev came up behind him and wrapped her arms around his waist, slid her hands up his chest. He straightened, strung tight, pausing to enjoy the feel of her body pressed up against his. For two shapes with so little in common, their bodies fit together amazingly well. For a moment he forgot about the destination to savor the journey. The bodies enmeshed. No gaps. Just yielding flesh and muscle and bone.

Then Bev pulled his shirt up, slid her hand over his abs, and pinched his left nipple.

Electricity spiked through him. He spun around, captured her face in his hands to kiss her. Rich, sweet lips, open for him and wet and hungry. He rotated her in his arms and kicked the door shut, revealing the full-length mirror hung on the inside. Standing with their eyes locked on each other in the reflection, she lifted her arms over her head and wiggled her ass.

"Nice," he whispered, nibbling her neck. "I mean, naughty." He pulled the ugly sweater up and exposed a red lace bra that appeared two sizes too small. Groaning, he slipped the neckline over her head and buried his face in her hair, silently thanking her and fate and even Ed for contributing to the genetics of her glorious breasts spilling out of flimsy—he dipped a finger under the top swell of flesh until he felt her hardening nipple—"Silk."

A small moan rose up from her throat as she threw her head back. "Went shopping yesterday."

He withdrew his hand—soon, soon—and hurled the sweater across the room. Her hair fell down her back in a tousled curtain, black on white. Inhaling the scent of her scalp, he ran his hands down her body and met her eyes her in the mirror. "You are so damn beautiful."

She met his eyes, looking alarmed.

"What's the matter?" He pulled her closer and ground his hard cock through the jeans against her bottom, while his fingers teased her nipples through the lace.

Gasping, she shook her head and leaned into him. "You—terrify me."

"Serves you right." He brushed her hair aside so he could kiss the back of her neck, still searching for the source of the intoxicating citrus smell that followed her everywhere. It seemed to be everywhere on her skin, sweet and sharp and rich. He dropped kisses along her shoulder then dragged his tongue up the side of her neck to her ear and inside, tasting and breathing and whispering her name.

He watched her reaction in the mirror, surprised to see her staring at him with those stunning blue eyes. Below her face, the red bra with the full breasts spilling out of the cups snared his attention. He looked lower, to the curve of her bare abdomen, and down to the hint of red lace under the waistband of her jeans.

The jeans were as loose as her sweater had been, which she probably intended as a turn-off, but now, sagging low on her hips and exposing her panties, they reminded him of what delights he hadn't explored, delights he'd been obsessed with since that morning in the store's dressing room.

He opened his hands over the indentation of her waist and held them there, willing his body to be patient, go slow. They slid lower, his thumbs stroking her belly while his fingers dove under the gaping waistband.

She sucked in her breath, tensing her abs, and he squeezed the handful of woman in his hands and nibbled the side of her neck.

"No running away this time," she whispered, and he shook his head.

"Too late for that." He unbuttoned her jeans and slid his hand down over her pussy. "Don't even think about it."

Faintly, from the back of her throat, she whispered, "I meant you."

"I'd die first." She was hot under his palm. With a fingertip, he traced the elastic bands of her panties, his large hand a tight fit inside the jeans. Having his hand down her pants, and watching her aroused face in the mirror, he worried about losing his control.

He slid his hand away, pleased by her whimper of disappointment, and jerked the pants down over her hips to expose her glorious ass.

"You seemed to like the thong," she said, her voice rough. "In the dressing room."

Stunned with lust, Liam took a step back to get a better view of the narrow band of red silk slicing her perfectly round ass in two. Smiling at him, her fear draining away from her face, Bev kicked off her shoes and each leg of the jeans, jiggling her hips and breasts with each move. He closed his eyes to get a grip. The thunder of his heartbeat in his ears and drowned out what she said next.

"What?" he whispered.

Turning to face him, she slid her hands up his chest to the top button of his shirt and began unfastening. "Your turn."

He barely heard her the second time. The sight of her backside in the mirror, pinched by inadequate scraps of red lace, drove all the blood out of his brain to a presently more essential organ. Vaguely he was aware of Bev sliding his shirt apart and moving the fabric down his shoulders. While he swiftly unhooked her bra and bent over to feel the weight of her breasts on his face, she tugged the last of his shirt off his wrists.

She stepped around him to reverse their positions. Now she stood behind him, peering out from the side, her hands sliding up over his belly and chest, her pelvis grinding into his ass while they looked at each other in the mirror.

Except Bev wasn't keeping her eyes on his face. Embarrassingly enough for him she was caressing his chest and watching the muscles ripple under his skin.

"I thought you didn't like jocks," he said. Even after a decade exposing his body in public he didn't like to be stared at. Too much of the pudgy kid he used to be lingered in his soul. His mother had always loved him unconditionally, but not the other kids, the P.E. teachers, his father—

She flattened her palm over his abdomen, slid the tips of her fingers down the stripe of hair that led down under the waistband of his jeans, searching. "Like isn't the word," she said, then wrapped her fingers around him and squeezed.

With a groan he spun around, took her in his arms, and lifted her off the ground. "I know what you mean." He carried her over to the bed and dropped her onto her back.

She laughed up at him. "Glad you lift weights. No guy's ever picked me up before."

"Why do you think I do it?" He leaned over and jerked the panties off her hips in a single motion. He heard her gasp of surprise but didn't slow down until he saw all her dark curls and a hint of rosy flesh underneath. Her feet lifted off the bed, held together by the panties, and her thighs fell apart right under his gaze while she freed herself from the fabric. He shoved her knees wider and kissed his way up her sweet inner thighs until he had nowhere to go but down.

She thrashed under him. "Oh, God."

He lifted his head, slid his hands between her thighs to delicately work her folds apart. Savoring the sight, he dipped a finger inside her, drew the moisture up. "You are so beautiful," he said quietly. Then licked her.

She arched her back. "Oh—Liam!"

His mouth sucked, his fingers teased.

"Ah—" Bev's words melted into high, breathy sounds that drove him on. His jeans were killing him. He didn't know how much longer he would last—just so it was longer than her. She ran her fingers through his hair and pulled him closer. Such soft skin, so sweet—he licked and savored the taste of her, feeling her climb the steep slope to climax, pushing her higher—

"Not yet!" She pushed his head away. "I want you inside."

"Easy." He glanced up at her wild eyes, slid his fingers in and around, circled with his thumb. "Let it happen."

"But—not yet—"

He lowered his head and stroked her long and hard with his tongue, and she cried out and gave up the fight, throwing back her head, digging her heels into the mattress, abandoning herself entirely.

Liam barely stayed behind long enough to tear off his jeans and get a condom on. She fell back to earth, eyes unfocused, but then saw his cock hard in his hands and said, "Hurry."

"Coming," he said roughly. *Thank God.*

He climbed up her body, straddled her, and rubbed his cock against her belly, risking it just once because he couldn't help it, then bent down to kiss her while he took her with his hand and with one last, sweet agony, shoved himself deep inside her.

She cried out. He felt the surge of satisfaction at biting the forbidden fruit, claiming it at last, accepting the inevitable mistake.

The feel of her legs clamping around his hips shot him higher, and he thrilled in the sight of her giving in to him, not holding back, her voice gasping with hot, noisy pleasure, and when she raked her nails across his back, the pain drove him further into madness.

She was everywhere and everything, drowning him. He held on as long as he could, flying wildly with her to the limits of pleasure and pain, with this creature that was woman and girl and mysterious wild thing, until they both shattered.

"Bev," he gasped, not letting go, and they fell together.

Chapter 15

BEV STARED AT the ceiling through the strands of his blond hair. He was heavy and warm, his skin slick against hers, and as much as she wanted to stroke her hands down the muscles of his back and take more of him, the moment was fading. The fun was over and now it was time to pay. Any second now one of them would utter the lie, the lie that they hadn't just ruined something, that sex wouldn't change anything, that they would be able to do it again.

She slid her hands forward from their caressing perch on his broad shoulders and pushed him away.

"Sorry," he said, collapsing next to her. He kept his arm tight over her belly, buried his face in the thrumming pulse at her throat, tickled her with feather kisses.

Inside her chest a fist wrapped around her heart and squeezed. She closed her eyes, savoring another second of him.

This could not go on. She wiggled away, avoiding his gaze. "I need to go to the bathroom."

He held on to her waist while she sat up on the edge of the bed, and she heard him inhale sharply. "You are so beautiful," he said, tracing her spine with a fingertip. A large, gentle hand brushed her hair to the side, and suddenly his mouth was on her neck, below her ear, soft and hot.

She wasn't strong enough. His lips teased the nerves under her ear and around her hairline while his fingers caressed her shoulder. "Lemons," he whispered. "God, you smell so good."

He was like a shark mistaking the surfer for a seal, dragging her from shore, preparing to consume her whole in the second bite. Her mind flailed around for something to make him let go, let her stagger back to shore, maimed but alive.

She turned her head, closer to the mouth nibbling on her earlobe, and said, "I think I'm falling in love with you."

The kisses stopped. His hand stilled. After a long, tight moment he choked out, "Bev—"

"Gotcha." She pulled away—no resistance now—and walked to the bathroom where she could recover. She locked the door and dropped her face into her hands, light-headed from the effort of leaving his bed. The weak confusion of her heart was the old, familiar ache of mismatched needs. Like so many men—and lucky women too—Liam was capable of a sexual and emotional disconnect she had never mastered. Unlike those lucky people Bev's heart and mind and body were braided together like pigtails. Now when she looked at Liam, she imagined he felt the same way. She felt that he felt the same way.

And she was wrong.

"Bev?" He tapped on the door, sounding uncomfortable, and that just wouldn't do.

She splashed water on her face, dried herself in a towel—hesitating, because it was suffused with the smell of him—and went over to open the door with his towel wrapped around her. "I thought you were going to feed me dinner."

He had pulled his jeans on, which was telling. No belt, though. "Look, about—"

"Forget it, Liam. I was just—I don't know. Reminding both of us what we're screwing around with. Making a point."

He glanced down at her body in the towel. "I just broke up with somebody—"

God. Not the I'm-not-ready-yet defense. "And so did I. You don't have to go there. I'm going to get dressed, have a bite of whatever it is that I smelled when we walked in the door and go."

"But if we understand each other there's no reason for you to run off." He grinned and dipped a finger between her breasts, tugged at the towel. "What's done is done. We'll figure out how to keep it quiet at the office—millions do it every day."

She clutched the towel in her fist and stepped back. "In a minute, Liam. I'd like to clean up." And she shut the door again, screaming inwardly that only one of them understood the real problem.

She didn't want to eat spaghetti, but if she ran out of there like she wanted to do, he'd figure out how deeply she was sinking and look down on her.

As much as anyone else in the company, she needed to earn his respect. If he thought she'd weep into her pillow every night because they'd had a quick fuck, she'd never be able to take command in the office. Already she had George and Rachel and the patternmakers in her camp—she could not afford to lose him now.

She got dressed and found him in the kitchen. "Sure smells good."

He had pulled a t-shirt on but was barefoot. And no apron. "Hey there." He watched her carefully, spoon hovering over the pot.

"What is it? Farmer's market or Ragu?"

He hesitated, looking at her. "Too early for local tomatoes," he said. "But they were nice and ripe."

With a forced smile on her face, she dipped a finger in the sauce and tasted it. Hot, savory tomatoes filled her senses. "Nice kick to it."

He dropped the spoon, his eyes on her mouth. "Bev . . . " He stepped closer to her and brought a finger up to her lips. "You've got a little of it—right—on your—"

She jerked away before the warmth spreading out under her skin where he caressed her reached her brain. Dragging the back of her hand over her mouth, she turned away. "Where's that water pitcher of yours? I'm kind of thirsty."

Behind her, he was silent then banged something near the stove. She heard him exhale loudly. "It's in the fridge."

Now he was angry, which was a lot easier to resist than the sweet talk. She walked over to the five-foot-wide stainless steel gourmet refrigerator and jerked it open. Green vegetables washed and sorted into stacks of glass storage containers, cans of energy drinks, a flat of two dozen eggs, little tubs filled with exotic olives —none of it would have been found in her refrigerator. She pushed aside a wedge of $14 cheese to reach the pitcher, kicked the door shut, feeling surer than ever they were from different planets and hers was calling her home urgently.

"I hear my phone." She dropped the pitcher on the counter and strode from the room. She would tell him her sister needed her at home—for something—anything—

Liam followed her into the hall to her bag on the floor. "Bev, if you want to leave just say so."

"All right. I want to leave."

He frowned and moved closer. "Well, don't. The horse is out of the stable. We might as well enjoy—"

"We might as well admit it was a mistake," she said, while his hand slid up under her shirt and caressed the small of her back.

His lips traced her eyebrows. "We will." He kissed her temple. "Tomorrow."

She closed her eyes, felt her knees wobble. She remembered how he'd looked the first time she'd seen him, cold and forbidding, domineering, aloof.

"I have to go." She pushed away from his seductive mouth and hands to track down her shoes. When she hurried back towards the front door he was lounging back against it with his muscled arms over his chest.

"You're overreacting," he said.

You have no idea. "Thanks for the fuck," she said.

His mouth fell open.

"Excuse me." She reached around him to the door handle.

When she didn't back down he jerked away from the door. "My pleasure, Ms. Lewis." His voice was low and furious. "Glad to be of service."

She hoped he couldn't see her hands shaking. She opened the door and stepped into the hallway. "See you at the office."

The door slammed behind her.

ॐ

First thing in the morning, with her senses dull from a sleepless night, Bev met with Richard, the reinstated CFO. He was a skeletal man with curly red hair, an Amish-like beard, and a sad face. "Fite needs to cut back hard, one way or another," he said for the third time. "Or it's over."

"Your report was quite clear." She put her hands over the folder on her lap. "However, I'm uncomfortable about the lay-offs."

"Either lay off some now or lay off everyone later." Richard pinched his lower lip between his thumb and forefinger.

"But there are other cuts we could take. And of course, if we could get the revenues up, like say—" she pulled out a five-year graph, "—to a few years ago—"

"A few years ago we were all a lot richer," he said. "Including—or especially—our customers. We have to deal with reality."

She knew he was right, but the numbers made her sick to her stomach. "I can't do it," she said. "We have to find another way."

He shook his head, shoulders sinking. "One reason I came back was I didn't think my decision would last very long. I might as well have a job while I prepare for the next one."

"If that's what you're going to be doing, getting ready for a better job, you might as well go now."

Pursing his lips, he met her gaze with sad eyes. "I didn't say better, did I? I didn't leave here voluntarily. I love this company."

She sighed, remembering Kennedy at the preschool with her friend rock and gloomy attitude. "Everything is going to be fine. We just have to find a better way to cut costs. There must be lots of ways to get thrifty."

"Your grandfather was hardly known for his extravagance. Look around. The only reason we've lasted this long is we hang on a shoestring budget as it is. We haven't had the water coolers refilled in two years, the cleaning company is a lady and her disabled son who commute in from Fresno, and we unscrewed half the ceiling lights to reduce the PG&E," he said. "And, we've had a hiring freeze." He raised his eyebrows to indicate his awareness of her violation of that policy.

"Richard, we'll find a way. And I'd appreciate it if you didn't share your worst-case scenario with anyone else here at the company."

He sighed. "Other than Liam, you mean?"

"When did you talk with Liam?"

"When he called me to invite me back. I told him it was hopeless."

"And what did he say?"

Lifting his sad eyes to hers, Richard tried to smile. "Said everything would be different now with you in charge."

She swallowed. "He said that? Was he kidding?"

"How would I know?"

She clenched her teeth together and got up. "Of course. I'll ask him myself."

The thought of hunting Liam down so soon after last night made the butterflies in her stomach want to bend over and vomit.

It took her twenty minutes to find him. He was in her grandfather's old suite, standing on a stationary treadmill, staring out into the white sky over the city. His shoulders hunched with tension, and as she came up alongside him she saw that he had his arms braced over his chest, elbow-in-hand, like he was about to ram somebody.

"Hope you weren't gunning for a quickie," he said, stepping off the treadmill. "I've got a meeting in two minutes."

It was almost funny, the idea that she was using him for sex. She bit her lip, furious with herself for getting into bed with him. "I'm sorry about last night—"

"Which part?" He turned, eyes cold, and let his gaze sink down over her body with slow, clinical disinterest.

She straightened her spine. "I regret all of it, but I'm apologizing for the part when I was rude and walked out."

"Apology accepted."

She blinked, skeptical. "I was just talking to Richard. He says we're in deep trouble. We might not be able to make the payroll after next week."

"He's a pessimist," Liam said. "Even without the Target deal we'd have another month."

She stared at the way the light hit his irises, highlighting flecks of gold, and how the long brown lashes framed his eyes. How calm and remote he looked compared to the night before. Perfect.

He raised an eyebrow at her, noticing her stare, and she shook off her daze. "A Target deal?"

"They love the men's stuff, but they're just not excited yet about the women's line. Imagine that." He strode over to the weight bench, straddled it, and leaned onto his back under the bar. Long, lean thighs stretched out before her. "Think they'd like the Jogbra of Hollywood?"

She watched as he braced himself under the bar and pushed. His face clenched with the effort, the veins in his forearms visible under the skin, and then he dropped it down with a clatter.

She moved closer. "Shouldn't you have somebody spotting you?"

He looked up at her, face blank, then smirked. "There's no weight on the bar."

Ah. So there wasn't. She hadn't been looking way over there. "It could still hurt you, like if it fell on your neck."

He shook his head and sat up, eyes hard on hers. "You're worried about me getting hurt?"

"Turns out you're rather indispensable around here."

"But if I were a poser, you'd be glad to have me decapitated?" He slid out from under the bar and went over to a rack of round weights, slipped off a couple small ones, then returned to the bench. "Lie down, and I'll tell you all about the Target deal."

"I'm not—"

"It's two five-pound weights. Like lifting your cat." He crossed his arms over his chest. "Unless you'd rather look stupid when we go there next week. We need to do some magic on the women's line. They have this crazy idea we don't get their customer."

Her mouth fell open. "Next week?"

He rolled his eyes as though he were bored. "Lie down. I've only got a minute."

"You always say that."

"I didn't last night—you did," he said, and she flushed. He tapped the bar. "We have the chance to place more orders for a single delivery with one customer than we pulled in over all of last year. Want to hear more?"

"Fine." She threw a leg over the bench and lay on her back, conscious of her breasts jiggling sideways under her thin knit blouse. She grabbed the bar and shoved it upwards.

"Hold on, let me teach you some technique."

"One." She let it clang down. "Start talking."

He frowned at her hands on the bar. "Move both hands a couple inches to the left. You're not centered."

After a moment's hesitation, she did it. "Next week? Why didn't I see it on the calendar?"

"Because I didn't put it there." He put his hands over hers and readjusted her grip. "How does that feel?"

"Liam—"

He glanced down at her chest and slid his hands down her arms to her shoulders. "Get yourself grounded properly—I don't want you to blame me if you get hurt."

Her heart raced. Even upside down he was beautiful. "I won't get hurt," she said, teeth clenched. *I won't let myself.*

His hands tightened, then moved to her ribs, lightly brushing under her arms. He sank to his knees and whispered close to her ear, "No pain, no gain," and then his hands moved together and cupped her breasts.

She sucked in her breath. "You can't—" His fingers found

each nipple, and his mouth opened over the curve of her ear, inflaming her remaining nerves. One second of savoring, then she twisted roughly away and jumped to her feet. She glanced out into the hall. "If anybody saw you do that, I would—I would—"

Lazily, he strode over to her. "Fire me?"

"Kill you." She pointed a finger at his chest where his small, cold heart huddled. "You don't care."

"Oh, I care. I thought that was obvious." He adjusted his belt. "Come on, Ms. Lewis. Be realistic."

Cocky bastard. She hated all that self-confidence. "You were going to tell me about the Target deal."

"No deal yet." He hooked a hand around her waist and jerked her up against his hard body. "Working on that." He bent his head.

"No, no, no!" She pushed away from him and scurried over to the wall phone by the door. "I'm having Rachel join us so you stick to business."

"Rachel?" He followed her and stood too close. "Oh, good choice. She's been helping me get the Target groups together."

"What?" she cried. "You used my assistant—without my permission—" She clamped her mouth shut, upset Rachel had gone behind her back, with Liam, and over something so important, and they'd said nothing—

"You can't get any samples out of this place without her. Plus, she's good at keeping secrets." He trailed a fingertip up the side of her neck and along the curve of her ear, sending electricity down her spine. "Most of the time. You might not want to confide in her about your sexual obsessions, however."

"You're really going to make me regret last night, aren't you?"

His voice fell to a growl. "Why should you be the only one to suffer?"

"Well, I'm not going to play." She finished dialing Rachel's extension but got voice mail, and while Liam's fingertip edged lower to the neckline of her dress, she was too flustered to leave a coherent message, so just said, "It's Bev, find me," and hung up.

He dipped under the fabric and drew a line of fire along her bra strap. "Are you sure you don't want to wait until she gets back from L.A.?"

She swung around and scowled up at his wide-eyed face. Of course he hadn't forgotten Rachel's sourcing trip. Nothing big enough to distract his mind. She brushed his hand aside. "No, you may tell me now. On your way to that meeting you mentioned." With lots of people around.

"I'm checking out a new fit model for Women's." He was still standing less than a foot away. "I can't discuss anything with the patternmakers around. They take notes and sell them on eBay."

She slipped out from under him. "When were you going to tell me about the Target deal, anyway? The day before the meeting?"

"I wasn't ever going to tell you."

His handsome face, all smug and confident, reminded her of who she was dealing with. "You weren't ever going to tell me?"

"Nope."

He was still hiding critical business dealings from her. Or he was hiding things, until—

"You're telling me now because I slept with you." She clutched her forehead. "Jesus. I wish you'd told me what I was turning myself into, what price I could command for services rendered. I might have shown more restraint."

"Don't be silly—" His cell phone beeped, and he stopped, still smiling at her, to pull it out and read the screen. "They're waiting for me. Look, I could hardly keep on as I was, after, well, getting you naked."

"Chivalrous and bold, yet skanky."

His smirk disappeared. Eyes narrowing, he leaned closer. "Please. What would you say if you found out after last night, after I went down on you and had sex with you in my own bed, after I begged you to stay—what would you say if I didn't change how I treated you at work?" He nodded. "That's right. You'd think I was a total dick. And don't look like that—I know you don't think I'm as bad as all that, not really, or you wouldn't have slept with me."

She closed her eyes, angry because he was right. "All right." She looked at him. "You are now on my side. I suppose I can live with that." She looked past him, making sure they were alone. "So long as we both understand that was not why I did it. From now on we're just business partners with similar goals."

He grinned, eyes crafty. "Wonderful. My goal is to snag the deal myself and get all the credit and have sex with you again. So glad to hear you're cool with that."

"All the credit? You didn't tell any of the designers, either?"

"It's a back-channel meeting. Me and an old friend." He stepped back and smoothed his shirt down his chest in a gesture she was coming to recognize as self-protective. Her woman radar went off.

"An old girlfriend?"

His eyes flicked back to her, amused. "Jealous?"

"Relieved. Now maybe you'll leave me alone."

"You're still pretending last night was some kind of one-time binge." He slipped his cell back in his pocket and walked out the door. "When we both know it was just an appetizer."

Chapter 16

"WHAT SHOES ARE you wearing?" Liam frowned at the woman's feet crammed into five-inch platforms.

The aspiring model, a thin-hipped woman in her early twenties, kicked up her heel. "Aren't they profound?"

Liam had known instantly she was all wrong for what Fite needed for the woman's line. Still, she'd come all the way from Ukiah to interview for the fit model job, and he didn't want to hurt her feelings. "Very," he said. "Please take them off."

"But—they're Christian Louboutin."

Sally, the patternmaker waiting to check her measurements, patted her on the shoulder. "They mess up your posture for the fitting," she said. "Barefoot works. Flats are fine. Or tennis shoes."

"Tennis?"

From the depth of the disappointment on the woman's face, Liam decided she had purchased the designer shoes just for the interview. "Maybe you can return them," he said, and didn't say anything else until Sally took all her measurements. He thanked her for her time.

Jennifer ran in just as the model was heading for the elevator. "Liam, I'm sorry I'm late—Oh, it's over." She gave the woman a head-to-toe rundown before she disappeared behind the elevator doors. "What was the matter with this one?"

Liam threw down the sheet of the woman's recorded measurements. "Too tall, no butt, too short in the waist. And she's a six."

"I thought she looked great," Jennifer said, then cleared her throat. "But perhaps we do need to get someone a little more realistic."

Liam raised an eyebrow at her. "You met with Wendi's mother?"

Jennifer smiled tightly and crossed her arms over her chest. "I met with a number of women, including Wendi's mother, and wrote up a report. Didn't you get my email?"

"Summarize for me."

Her smile strained, Jennifer walked over to Sally's table and rifled through her piles of sketches and pattern pieces. Without looking up she said, "Nobody seems to like our fit. Nobody."

It wasn't really Jennifer's fault, being under Ellen's command until recently. At least she had the guts to admit it. "I'll read your report. Good work. Now we fix it."

"This chick just now was the last person I could find," Jennifer said. "Model agencies don't have women with average bodies. That's why they're *models*."

"What fit model does Levi's use? They've got a decent fit these days. It's not an athletic fit, but it's—" He held out his hands at butt level as though holding something round. "Feminine."

Sally edged between her desk and Jennifer, who was touching everything like it was hers. "They use an eight," Sally said, closing a binder, picking up her coffee mug. "You said you wanted a ten."

"It's more accurate in terms of the grading. To get closer to the average customer," he said.

Sally sighed. "I agree. I haven't been able to wear Fite since

Rachel was promoted."

He put a hand on the table. *Rachel*. "That's right. She started out here as a fit model, didn't she?"

"Right out of college."

"And it's not like she's gained weight since then," he said. "She's remarkably consistent."

Jennifer's eyes gleamed with the anticipation of trouble. "She will totally freak on you."

Sally looked between Jennifer and Liam, realized what they were suggesting, and shook her head. "She'd never agree to it. Never. Not even when we've been desperate for a quick fit to make an important meeting. After all these years, to poke and prod her like that, she'd find it humil—"

Liam gave her his sternest look, the one that used to command effortless authority, and she snapped her mouth shut. He let that sink in then said, "I'll talk to her."

Jennifer bit her lip. Sally nodded and said, "Of course, Mr. Johnson."

&.

In spite of what Liam had told Sally, he feared they were right about Rachel never agreeing to fit model again. He interviewed a few more candidates, even dragging Carrie from the front desk up to Engineering for measuring, but none had the specs they needed.

They were running out of time. He sat in the conference room, the long oblong table piled high with abandoned sketches and magazine tear sheets and swatches and sample trim, and worked through the Target dog and pony show in his mind. Jennifer thought it was just concept development for the main line, and he hadn't enlightened her, in part because he wanted a solo shot at the deal, and in part because he knew she'd be annoyed and snotty about expanding into Middle America. Expanding into expanding Middle America.

Behind him the racks on the walls were heavy with samples hung three to four deep, and whatever concept he'd been going for was as opaque as granite.

Something about action, he thought. Happy, rejuvenating action.

His mind kept wandering to the rejuvenating feeling of Beverly Lewis's breasts under his hands. He hadn't intended to do that. His plan, to treat her as shittily as she had him, only lasted— what, two minutes? Then as soon as she had some job crisis, he was back on his white horse. And then trying to get back on her.

Thanks for the fuck.

How dare she? They were having a perfectly nice time. Very, very nice. She didn't have to spoil it with a bitchy slap-down, as though he'd committed a crime by making love to her.

Needing to do something, he picked up the phone and called Jennifer, frustrated to get voice mail. "Get somebody over to clean up the first floor conference room. It's an embarrassment," he said and hung up. One second later, he dialed her again. "And don't ask Rachel—she's not your assistant anymore. Why not clean up after yourself for a change?" He tossed the receiver back into the cradle.

If they wanted touchy-feely they could talk to Bev.

Getting up so fast the chair skidded out behind him, Liam left the room and stalked down to his office, slowing his pace outside Bev's door. For some reason she had insisted on being the one to talk to Rachel about fit modeling for them, but Liam feared the fallout—Rachel carried grudges, one reason he'd never been aggressive about promoting her. If she didn't like a designer, their Fed Ex packages turned up missing at critical times. Design boards turned up with coffee ring stains. A sales guy from Reno who loved sexist jokes kept having his rental cars impounded.

Standing in the hallway, Liam reminded himself Bev was plenty bitchy enough to handle her. Hadn't he seen evidence of that?

Still, he lingered, unable to walk on to his office.

Thanks for the fuck.

He pushed through the partially ajar door into Bev's office just as Rachel was saying, as she reclined in a leather swivel chair, "Sure, Bev. It would be my pleasure."

Bev beamed and glanced up at Liam, who had frozen in place. They must have been talking about something else. "Morning."

Looking smug, Bev leaned back in her chair and waved. "Rachel's cool with trying on some stuff for us."

He looked at Rachel. "Great."

"She doesn't mind at all," Bev said.

"Really," he said. "Good."

Rachel bit her lip, not meeting his eyes, and he felt a chill down his spine. He sauntered over to lean on the desk, and stared at her until she began to fidget. "So, what was your price?"

Bev came around the desk and poked him in the shoulder. "Don't bully my Vice President of Trend. She's a miracle worker. In two hours she explained the workings of this business in a way that would have taken me years to learn myself. She's made me charts and graphs and diagrams—awesome. I love visuals. Of course she doesn't mind keeping the company afloat for a few more weeks."

"Ah, you gave her the full scoop."

"That we'd be dead without her perfect body? Yes."

Rachel gave her a half-smile. "I hope it'll work. I'm not quite as firm as I used to be."

Bev swung around and slapped her own behind, wiggling it

for emphasis. "You ain't got nothin', babe."

Liam gazed at her round ass and forgot what they were talking about.

Thanks for the—

He gritted his teeth and focused on Rachel. "Since you don't have a problem, none whatsoever, perhaps you could head up there right now," he said. "Have Jennifer and—whatshername, her new assistant—start checking out the entire Green Valley group, the Speed Demon group, and the rework of the fit on Core. Comfort and fit are key—don't take off your underwear to make it work. No ass cracks. No camel toes. No muffin tops. We need mass market appeal or we're dead."

Rachel's smile looked a bit forced, but she got up. "Sure."

"And don't let Jennifer boss you around," he added.

"Or what? You'll fire her?" Rachel asked, not laughing.

"I'd love to, but it's up to Bev."

They both looked at her hopefully.

"I'm not firing anybody! I thought I'd made that clear," Bev said.

"She said you were fat," Rachel said. "In case that changes your mind."

Liam choked, interested to see how Bev handled that bomb, but she just rolled her eyes and walked back around to her desk chair. "Don't be mean," she said to Rachel. "And thank you again for your heroic offer to play fit model temporarily."

Clearly disappointed, Rachel shrugged and left the room.

"Cool of you," he said to Bev. "Chilly, even."

"I've got Rachel's number. She's a lot like Annabelle Tucker, actually. A bit passive aggressive, but only when she's feeling unappreciated. Underneath the insecurity she's got a big heart."

He snorted. "I didn't know you were such an expert on teen

pop stars. I would have thought you'd be more of a Dora the Explorer fan."

Smiling, Bev pulled herself up to her computer. "Annabelle was one of my first students. Well, I wasn't the teacher yet, just in my first child psych class. Later, when she was older, I took care of her after school when her mom was working."

He froze and stared at her. "Annabelle Tucker? You were her *babysitter*?"

"I was desperate for the money. I did a lot of babysitting in those days."

Just yesterday he'd noticed the star's young beautiful face on four out of the five magazines in the checkout line at Safeway. Not only did she sing and dance—she climbed, kicked, flipped, swam, and skated her way through her hit musical-adventure show on the Disney Channel. Recently famous for getting into Princeton at fifteen, but deciding to wait a couple years to grow up first, Annabelle Tucker was the it-girl of the year.

"She was one of the first kids I really came to love." Her face clouded with pain, then anger. "Which I still don't think is a bad thing."

His mind raced with possibilities. "You know Annabelle Tucker."

"Don't look like that." She pointed a finger at him. "Just don't."

Feeling giddy, he braced his hands on the desk to look at her. "You know Annabelle Tucker."

The chair squeaked as Bev got to her feet to glare back. "Whatever's got you so excited, get it out of your mind."

"You know—"

"Yes, yes! Stop saying that!"

"Do you have any idea what kind of coup we would pull off to bring pictures of Annabelle Tucker wearing Fite to the Target buyers?" Laughing, he pounded on the desk, danced around it, grabbed her shoulders. "To hell with Target. If you can get Annabelle Tucker to wear Fite—just once where cameras catch her—we are totally made. With every retailer in the country. They'll be taking the first flight here to beg us to deliver."

Her face went wide with panic. "Stop it! I couldn't do that!" She jerked away and sat in her chair, pressing her hand to her forehead. "I don't use people."

"Oh, right," he said. He leaned down and whispered in her ear, "Ri-ight."

She shivered. "I shouldn't have mentioned her name. I should never have mentioned her—"

"This is it, Bev. The moment to face reality and be honest with yourself. Are you a woman or a mouse? Are you the timid, downtrodden preschool teacher, or the ruthless, triumphant leader of men and women desperate not to lose their jobs?"

She covered her ears. "Shut up!"

She was cute when she was in denial. He grabbed the arms of her chair and trapped her. "You know you want it." His breath came fast as he loomed over her. So close to her again, watching the impulses do combat across her adorable, creamy-cheeked face. His gaze dropped to her incredible mouth. For a moment he was paralyzed by the hint of gloss on her full bottom lip. "Admit it." He leaned down until their lips were so close he could taste the coffee on her breath.

"I don't do things like that," she whispered.

"Sure you do. That's why I like you so much." And he raised his fingers to her chin, tilted her face up, and before he could think about how shocked and angry and hurt he was at her for walking out on him when he'd begged her to stay, kissed her.

He didn't hurry this time, or push too hard, or lose himself in the heat that sparked when he touched her; he went slow, and gentle, savoring the moisture of her lips, the curiosity of her tongue, and the little noises she made in the back of her throat.

Slowly, gently, he kissed her, leading her where he wanted her to go only after he was invited, running his tongue along her teeth. When she tunneled her fingers through his hair and kissed him back, he almost lost the reins, but then he amused himself with the feel of her breast under his hand and the way she gasped at his teasing.

He drew back. Her eyes were closed, her mouth red and swollen, and she swayed closer for more.

That's more like it. He traced her bottom lip with his index finger, studied her face, the curve of her cheek, a freckle on her forehead, then released her. "See you tonight," he said. Breathing shallow, he strode towards the door while he still had the willpower.

He heard her sigh behind him. He grinned all the way back to his office, anticipating.

Chapter 17

"CAN YOU HELP me move this over by the window?" Bev bent over to pick up one end of the sofa.

"Put that down," Kate said. "I know you're stressed, but that's no way to work it out. It's Friday night. Sit down and make some of this tea for yourself. It's loaded with calming herbs. Then we'll go for a run."

"Forget it. I barely recovered from the last time."

"Which was all that tool's fault for trying to break into my car," she said. "I can't believe you haven't fired him yet."

Luckily for Bev's peace of mind, Kate was too self-absorbed to guess what Bev had done with the tool a few days earlier. She bent over to drag the sofa herself, but it slipped and thudded onto the floor at an asymmetrical angle. "Come on, just help me get it over there."

"You had it over there ten minutes ago. I'm not letting myself get pulled into some psychotic break." Kate sat on the sofa in question. "What happened to you, anyway?"

"Nothing. Get up."

"All week you've been hiding in your room, and now you're rearranging furniture. I'd say it was some guy, but it could hardly be that, this soon and with you working all the time. And what's the point with that? It's not like you can get fired."

Bev tried to tip her sister out of the sofa but gave up, plopping down at the other end. She stretched out her legs and used Kate's lap as a footrest. "I'm trying to keep Fite from going out of business." She leaned her head back and closed her eyes. "Thanks for your support."

Kate made a rude noise. "I'm here, aren't I? He hasn't broken in once since I got here."

Bev sighed. "He didn't even before you got here."

"Face it, Bev. You're stupid when it comes to really built guys. He's got means and motive. It's the only explanation."

"Aunt Ellen—"

"I'll let Mom explain why it isn't Ellen. You assumed it was her, which is one reason I can excuse you for falling for another Rand clone. He's even got the same beady little eyes. Like raisins."

Rand was the last good-looking guy she swore off. But he was easy to forget, not like—she gritted her teeth. "He's nothing like Rand. Nothing." Beady little eyes—hardly. Liam's were like deep pools of melted chocolate. Pushing aside that image, she sat upright with a start. "What do you mean, you'll let Mom explain?"

"When she gets here." Kate looked at her watch. "She left after the morning rush, so I'm guessing any minute we'll be seeing her sunny Botoxed face. And don't look like that. If I'd told you, imagine how stressed you would have been, and it wouldn't have done any good because she was totally coming, like it or not. Ever since Ellen called her last week she's been all freaking out about getting in touch with her youth and shit."

Mouth dry, Bev slipped her feet off her sister's lap and stood up. "Since Ellen called?" she asked. "Any minute? And you didn't tell me?"

"Well, look at you freaking out. Totally my point."

Bev sucked in a deep breath. At least she'd be too busy to think about Liam. "I have to clean the bathroom. No, the kitchen. You clean the bathroom and tell me everything Mom said about Ellen." Bev took Kate's mug out of her hands and jerked her to her feet. "The Bon Ami is under the sink with the sponge."

"I am so not getting between you and Mom and Ellen. If you want the gory details you can ask her when she gets here. Something about having a baby." Kate pulled her blond hair up on top of her head and slipped the rubber band around her wrist down to make a floppy ponytail while she walked into the bathroom. "Get us each a beer, why don't you? And crank up the tunes."

Baby? Bev followed Kate into the bathroom. "Who's having a baby?" Ellen was younger than Gail by a couple years, but was in her late forties. Still, stranger things had happened. "Ellen is having a baby?"

"Well, it's not me." Kate squatted down below the sink for the cleaning supplies. "Seriously though, get me a beer. Nobody should have their head in a toilet when they're sober."

Her mother would be there soon. She wasn't nice, but at least she was coherent. Giving up on Kate, she went into the kitchen, got her sister a beer—and after a second thought, one for herself —and tackled the pile of dishes in the sink.

While the water ran she sucked down two swallows of beer and squirted dish soap over the dishes. Where was her mother going to sleep? How the hell long was she going to stay? Kate came in, threw her empty bottle in the recycling can, and got another beer out of the fridge.

"I hear a car," she said. "Just thought you should know."

"This is good," Bev said. "Having Mom and Ellen talking to

each other is good. It's why I came up here in the first place."

"Keep telling yourself that." Kate washed her hands and opened a cupboard. "What's for dinner, anyway? Mom will want something when she gets here."

"Yet another reason you should have told me. Jesus." Bev looked at the bottle in her hand, imagined her mother's face when she learned there wasn't a gourmet meal waiting—let alone TiVo, Indonesian coffee beans, six-hundred-thread-count sheets, or Pilates machines—and decided to tackle the problem through the haze of fermented grains. She threw back her head and chugged the beer, reminding herself Gail Roche Lewis Torres wasn't a bad person—just a bad mother. To Gail, unconditional love was just lazy. To criticize was to care.

Sufficiently buzzed, Bev weaved through the house to the front door, stifled a giggle when she saw the misaligned couch, which made her think of Liam in his sleeping bag, who said he'd see her tonight, when her mother would be here.

She flung open the door, expecting a pretty fifty-year-old woman with Michelle Obama biceps, only to get the big, unpredictable hunk with chocolate eyes.

"Thank God!" She threw her arms around him and pressed her face against his chest. She inhaled his rich, manly smell. He hesitated for a second then put his arms around her and stroked her hair.

"Hi," he said. His sweater felt like cashmere under her cheek. She squeezed him harder, and he chuckled. "Easy, easy. My ribs are cracking."

Loosening her hold, she closed the front door to hide from her sister. The evening air was cold, but he was warm and had a way of touching her that soothed and excited her all at the same time. His mouth was so perfect, right there under his nose. She reached up and stroked his lower lip with her thumb, dipping it inside. "You have such cute teeth."

He rolled his eyes but gave an embarrassed, boyish smile, and she felt her heart swell in her chest. "You have cute teeth too," he said, and brushed his lips along hers. He slipped his tongue past the seam of her mouth and licked and twisted inside her, and she forgot about her heart and had dark, thoughtless thoughts that began low in her body and ended lower.

"Not here," he said, voice deep. He tried to move into the house, but she stopped him with another embrace, savoring the sound of his pounding heartbeat, wishing he were somebody else, somebody she could keep.

She sighed and looked past his shoulder. "You better go. My mother will be here any minute."

Liam buried his face in her hair. "Let's both ditch our mothers," he said. "Want to catch a movie?"

"You mean, like a date?"

He lowered his lips to her ear. "Too fast for you? We could have sex first, if you're not ready."

She slipped her hand down the outside of his jeans until she found the patch pocket and nestled her hand inside, enjoying the curve of his butt. Her head spun and her lips felt dry, so she licked them, noticing how his gaze tracked the motion of her tongue—

Her mother's white Lexus SUV pulled into the driveway, blasting three long, impatient honks.

"Oh, my God," Bev said, spinning out of Liam's arms. "Go. Go! Before she sees you."

"Too late," Liam said roughly. Chest heaving, he moved away from her another step, shoving his hands in his pockets. The driver's side door popped open, Beyoncé blaring, then the car fell silent. He said under his breath, "So what's our story? I came over for a cup of sugar?"

"I was kind of wondering that myself."

He ran his hand through his hair. "I'm your top VP. Make something up."

Gail walked around the hood, pale hair flowing back behind her head in the wind, and scowled, wrapping her arms around herself. "It's freezing!" Then, seeing Bev wasn't alone, she took in Liam's good looks with a slow, head-to-toe perusal and stopped dead. Bev felt her face turn red.

"Cup of sugar," Bev muttered. "I'll go get it."

"Wait. It gets worse." He jerked his head to the side. "Here comes another one."

She glanced over his shoulder and saw Trixie trotting over with a herd of her miniature dogs, waving both hands like windshield wipers in a downpour. "Ahoy there!"

Bev waved back and, unable to think of anything else to do, laughed.

"Really, Bev," Gail said, coming up the stairs while she smoothed down her hair. Her eyes shifted to Liam again, and her face adopted the toothy, enthusiastic, vaguely sexy expression she used whenever the lens cap came off a nearby camera. "Hello?"

"Mom, this is Liam Johnson, from Fite. His mother lives next door," Bev paused, covering her mouth to stifle a giggle. "Liam, this is Gail, my mother."

"Really, Bev." Gail studied Liam for another long moment before she held out her hand to him, fingers limp.

"Hello." Liam managed to take her hand in his and release it without making it obvious she had made him do all the work. "Pardon me, I was just leaving. Beverly, thank you for the signature." Then he patted his chest as though he had tucked an important contract inside.

Trixie led the dogs up onto the sidewalk and marched up the driveway, not hesitating as she maneuvered around the Lexus and trotted up the steps to the porch to join them. "How wonderful. More mouths to feed."

Bev heard a low, pained grunt coming from Liam's direction.

"Signature?" Gail asked. "For what? And why are we all standing out here in the cold? Is there another problem with the locks?"

Giving the dogs the pleasure of sniffing at everyone's ankles, Trixie came up to Liam's side and beamed at Bev's mother. "You must be Gail Roche. Here I told your daughter you were dead. Obviously not! My goodness, you look fifteen." She held up her hands to her neck and pinched the flap of skin under her chin. "I call this my turkey wattle. Without it I'd look twenty years younger, but still not as pretty as you. My goodness."

Liam's eyes were closed, and Bev saw the muscles in his jaw twitch. Gail, softened by the compliment, smiled at Trixie then grabbed the handle on the front door and pushed it open.

"Please excuse me," Gail said. "I've been on the road all day and my blood sugar is low. Beverly?"

"But that's why I came over," Trixie said. "I didn't know you were here, of course—that's quite a shock, actually, since in all these years I've never met you. But Liam disappeared again and I didn't want them to think I didn't know what was going on. Not that I'm going to make a fuss, but I hate secrets. Don't you, Gail? Such a waste of energy, and ultimately so destructive."

Twisting around in the doorway, Gail frowned, looking annoyed but uncomprehending. She smiled tightly and looked into the house. "Isn't Kate here? Kate!"

"We'll be going now." Liam took his mother's arm and tried to lead her down the steps.

"Not without insisting everyone comes over for dinner. Are you a vegetarian, Gail?"

"No, but—"

"Then you must come over for my famous chicken lasagna. Your daughter has become like family to us. Both of my sons are crazy about her, though of course I'm not supposed to talk about that sort of thing. Sorry, honey." She smiled at Bev.

"Oh, I'm fine," Bev assured her, feeling wobbly during her out-of-body experience.

Kate appeared in the doorway. "Oh, my God! Those are frickin' awesome dogs!" She fell down to the ground and held out her hands. "Are these the little guys I hear next door?"

"This must be your other daughter. What beautiful girls," Trixie said. Her smile grew crafty. "I've got more pups back at the house, and they love to make new friends."

Liam muttered something unintelligible under his breath, then, more loudly, "Mother, please. Let's leave them to their reunion in private."

"How do you handle so many dogs?" Kate asked.

"Oh, I work with a rescue group. I shouldn't have so many at once, but soon a few of them will have new homes."

"Oh, oh!" Kate said, eyes lighting up. "What do I have to do to get one?"

Gail stared at Liam as though she'd just realized who he was. "You're the Olympic swimmer. My father's protégé."

He paused. "Yes. I worked for your father for many years."

"And now for us," Gail said.

"Us?" Bev snorted, then swallowed it when her mother grabbed her arm and squeezed the tendons above her elbow.

Her smile not betraying the pain she was inflicting upon her child, Gail beamed at Trixie. "Fite has always been a family business. I'm very glad to meet your famous son—and so much sooner than I'd hoped."

"Can I come over and see the other puppies?" Kate asked.

Bev jumped in, alarm bells ringing. "Mom, you've been on the road all day, you must be tired—"

"Mark just came back to the nest for a while," Trixie said. "Which is why I made such a feast, but my boys don't eat like they used to, and I'd really appreciate your help—all of you—in helping us put it away."

"It would be our pleasure," Gail said. "We'll be over in a few minutes."

Bev and Liam's eyes met in shared pain.

Chapter 18

"HEADS UP, MARK." Liam strode into his brother's bedroom and flicked on the overhead light. He was plugged into a computer in the corner with his headphones on and bowl of neon-red Cheetos at his side, and blinked up at Liam like a child coming out of a dream.

"Was there an earthquake?" He took off his headphones.

"More like an invasion. Mom's invited the neighbors, and they're all female." Liam looked him over, shaking his head at the sight. "Thought I'd give you a chance to freshen up."

"Bev's coming over?"

The eagerness in his voice made Liam cringe, in part from recognition. Liam was just as pathetic, but better at hiding it. Glad Bev couldn't see him, Liam grabbed the bowl of Cheetos and scooped a handful into his mouth. "And her sister. And her mother." He peered down at an open suitcase on the floor overflowing with t-shirts and boxers and jeans. He was pretty sure the sour smell he was inhaling was coming from there. "Got anything to wear that doesn't stink? You'll spoil my dinner." Then again, he wouldn't have to worry about Bev finding him attractive.

"Sister?" he asked. "Is she as nice as Bev?"

Liam hesitated only for a moment before smiling. "Nicer,

even."

Mark clicked off his monitor and spun around in his seat. "Do I have time to shave?"

"Time before what?"

"Before they get here."

"Oh, they're already here, drinking the new Shiraz."

The visible anxiety in his brother's face never failed to amaze Liam. Mark was a good-looking guy, brilliant, and when he was relaxed, totally charming. But his self-confidence was crippled. Their father had given what little patience he had with children to Liam, and only then when he showed signs of paying him back for some of the effort, like a business investment. Mark had simply never paid out.

"I'll sit next to you if you want." Liam slapped Mark on the shoulder.

Mark bent over and picked a t-shirt out of the pile. Sniffed it, frowned, chose another. He tore off the shirt he was wearing and dropped it into the suitcase, then turned his attention to his pants. "Jeans okay?"

"They've got stains all down the front."

"It's just coffee."

"Still, a stickler might suggest a fresh pair."

"Ah." He unbuttoned the fly and let them drop.

Trixie flew into the room. "Liam! Where did you go?" Bev was right behind her. At least, until she saw Mark and ducked back into the hallway. "Oh, nice of you to change for dinner, honey," Trixie added.

"Mom!" Mark pulled his pants back up, his chest and face flushing red. He looked like he might be sick.

Trixie said, "I wanted Bev to see the fog rolling in. This room has the best view."

Liam frowned at her, suspicious. "Her house next door points in the same direction. I imagine she's seen it."

"No reason to be shy," Trixie told Mark in a stage whisper. "You have a lovely body."

Mark turned his anguished eyes on Liam, who felt a little guilty for laughing. "Go ahead," Liam said. "Lose the pants too. You're lovely."

"Trixie?" Bev called from the hallway. "Who made these monoprints? They're amazing!"

"Do you really think so?" Trixie left her sons and joined Bev in the hallway. "I made those ages ago at the—"

Liam strode over and pulled the door shut, slipped the lock he'd installed in high school, laughing. "You can count on Bev."

Mark was staring at him. "You've got a thing for her." He found an indistinguishable replacement t-shirt in the suitcase and pulled it over his head. "Don't you?"

Liam laughter trailed off. "Yes."

"Does she—forget it. Of course she does."

"I slept with her. I'm trying to repeat the experience."

Mark crossed his arms over his chest. "Do you love her?"

Liam laughed. "Jesus, Mark. I only met her a few weeks ago."

"That's long enough. I would know."

Unfortunately Mark fell in love as often as Liam fell in bed. "You need to protect yourself better."

"I don't understand you," Mark said. "The one thing I want and don't have a clue how to get, and you—you have to fight it off with a stick. Like it's a disease you don't want to catch."

"Not a disease. More like exposure to a virus that once you've got the antibodies, you test positive for the rest of your life. I'm just—delaying that particular inoculation."

"It's not fair," Mark said. He walked over to the mirror on the back of the closet door and scowled at himself, turning this way and that, licking his palm and smoothing down his hair. "I'm such a catch."

Liam walked over and tucked the label of his brother's t-shirt out of sight. Smiling, he rested his hands on his shoulders and squeezed. "Especially when you don't do your laundry for months. And spend all your time online. Chicks really dig that."

Mark jerked his elbow back to jab him in the ribs, then walked over to the door. "You said the sister's nice?"

"That's what I said." Liam followed him out into the hall, which his mother had already emptied to regroup for her next attack, and walked down the stairs thinking about viruses.

❧

Liam's mouth was at her ear. "Want another drink to deaden the pain?"

The feel of his breath made her jump. Beer, wine, Liam. She looked up into his warm brown eyes and held up her empty wine glass. "Just water this time, please." She glanced at her mother at the other end of the table next to Mark. "Your poor brother."

Liam frowned. "Don't worry about him."

"You do."

"I'm his brother. You can put him out of your mind."

She heard the jealous edge in his voice and laughed.

Kate walked in with an elfin dog in her hand and a huge grin on her face. "He likes me!"

Trixie smiled and looked over. "He's a she, sweetheart." She pointed a serving spoon at the little dog's underside. "No boy parts, see? All right, the chow's all here. Thank you so much for joining us tonight. I hope you don't mind if I've lit a little memorial candle for your father. We're not religious, but I did so appreciate what he did for Liam when my husband died. He was a difficult man—my husband I mean, though your father was no saint himself, as you know—and sadly for my kids, a much better husband than a father. So I was very grateful to Ed." She dug into the casserole, scooped up a mound of steaming tomato sauce and pasta, smiling at Gail. "Lasagna?"

Hiding her amusement at the sight of Gail's strained smile, Bev turned her head to see Mark return with a block of Parmesan. He was trying to get a good look at Kate, who had sat next to Bev and was still devoting every scrap of attention to the dog. "Hi," he said to her, then cleared his throat. "I'm Mark. Liam's brother."

Kate flicked her eyes over him once. "Sucks to be you," she said, returning her attention to the dog. Mark frowned and looked at Liam, who was up to something because he shrugged but looked amused in a bad way.

Gail reached forward and took a teaspoonful of lasagna, studying it in the deliberate way she did all her food so she could record the portions in her online calorie counter. "Thank you. It's funny we should meet so quickly. Ironically, I was just talking about your son—" she tilted her head at Liam but didn't look at him, "—with my sister. Have you met my sister Ellen?"

With both hands outstretched for the salad bowl, Bev froze. "You've been talking to Ellen about *Liam*?" Her voice came out too loud for the table.

"Really, Bev," Gail said, took a nibble of the lasagna, and smiled politely at Gail. "This is fabulous. Thank you. I knew it was too much to hope that Bev would prepare a decent meal. The only thing I've eaten all day is a BurnBar."

Trixie opened her mouth, then glanced at Liam and snapped it shut.

Liam passed her the Parmesan. "How's Ellen? Her departure was so . . . sudden."

"She is fantastic." Eyes bright, Gail brought her hand to her face and looked up at the ceiling. Sighing, she glanced at Bev. "Everything has changed. I told Kate all about it. Johnny's going to be a father—not married yet, but Ellen will take care of that." She smiled at Trixie. "Johnny is my nephew, Ellen's son. Bev, there is so much for us to talk about. You were right about so many things."

Bev was finding it difficult to swallow her mouthful of lettuce. "I was?"

"Ellen told me how you refused to leave the company to her unless we reunited as a family. She flew to L.A. just to tell me that. At first she just wanted me to get you back home, but then we got to talking and laughing and *crying*—" Gail glanced at Trixie again and rolled her eyes, "and then it was like we were fifteen again. Which is why I've come up now to let you off the hook." She glanced at Liam. "Both of you. Do you have any sisters, Trixie?"

"I'm afraid not," Trixie said.

A swirling, sinking whirlpool of dread formed in Bev's stomach. "I am not on a hook. And that's not what I—"

Gail put down her wine glass with a thump and caught Trixie's eye. "Ever since she was little, Bev wanted a different family. I think it's why she chose to work with children." She returned her gaze to Bev. "With me and Ellen here, you can go back to where you belong with a clear conscience."

Not now, Bev thought, shoving a forkful of lasagna into her mouth, frantically trying to think of how to extract herself and her mother from the table.

But Gail went on. "Now, Kate—Fite would be perfect for you. You're at a perfect point to start a new career." She slipped the fork into her mouth and shook her head. "My, this is delicious."

"I belong here," Bev said. "At Fite. Here. All of it."

"Really, Bev," her mother replied.

Teeth clenched, Bev looked around the table at the curious faces hanging on the exchange. Mark seemed unhappy and confused. Trixie was busy keeping the plates moving around the table, trying to communicate something to Liam, who had stopped pretending to eat and sat with both arms crossed over his chest.

"Leave me out of it," Kate said. "I've decided to work with dogs."

Gail reached over and squeezed her hand. "But you could do both. Oh—I've got it! Fite doesn't have a pet line yet, does it?"

"No, and there never will be," Liam said.

Gail turned and gave him an icy stare. "That's up to the owners to decide."

"No, it's up to the market," he said. "Dog clothes would ruin us."

"Management is going to have to think outside the box for a change," Gail said.

"Management is going to do a lot of things, none of them involving domesticated animals."

Kate tapped Bev on the shoulder. "By the way, I think Ball might be sick. Right before I came over here I noticed her spitting up her dinner."

Torn between concern for her elderly cat and the hostilities unfolding at the table, Bev nodded at her sister and tried to catch her mother's eye.

Gail was too busy staring at Liam to notice. "I'm sure you wouldn't want all your hard work to go to waste. That kind of old thinking has led the company into bankruptcy." Then she seemed to remember where she was, turning to Trixie with an apologetic smile. "So sorry to talk business. I'm sure we can continue this conversation at the office."

Bev's hands closed into fists. "At the office?"

"And who is Ball, honey?" Trixie asked, passing the green beans. "Some kind of pet?"

"My cat," Bev said, the whirlpool in her stomach churning faster. Her mother wanted to get involved with Fite. With Ellen. And swap Bev for Kate. But worse, her mother was insulting Liam and his work at Fite, a company she had loathed and avoided her entire life—in front of his own family.

Liam. He was arrogant and difficult and pig-headed and domineering, but—

She stood up so quickly the chair tipped over and clattered against the sideboard. Everyone, even the little dog, turned to stare. "Leave Liam alone. He's the best thing Fite's got."

Trixie's eyes got wide, watching her. Then slowly she reached for the pepper grinder. "Liam, do go get us another bottle of the Shiraz. We've run dry."

"And while I'm glad you're talking to Ellen," Bev went on, eyes fixed on her mother, "know that I'll do everything in my power to see to it she never sets foot at Fite again. We've just started to clean up the mess she left behind. And have you forgotten why Kate had to drive up here? I didn't sleep for two days after she broke into the house—"

"Really, Bev!" Gail gaped at her, not used to having Bev ever argue with her, let alone at a dinner table with strangers. "Sit down."

Liam caught Bev's gaze and held it, an intense look in his eyes she couldn't read. She wished she could touch him, have him touch her, make everyone else go away.

"Come help me pick out the wine." He pushed back his chair and stood up.

"You'd better take Norma back with you." Trixie pointed a finger at the handful of fur in Kate's lap. "Sorry, honey. People food gives her a rash."

Bev watched Liam pick up the dog and stride away, feeling the unsatisfied anger swirling in her gut. Without an apology to the table, she got up and went after him.

He was in the walled in porch off the back of the kitchen, surrounded by the little animals, bending over and petting palm-sized beige heads. Her heart clenched, seeing his everyday gentleness, but her temper was still flying high from the scene behind her.

"I could get used to this hero complex of yours," she said, "but it's probably too late. I've already spoiled the meal and I'll have to find a way to make it up to your mother somehow."

Before she could brace herself, he turned around and grabbed her. "I wasn't being a hero."

His mouth came down on hers, hungry and demanding, surprising her out of her anger. Heat flared in her body, already worked up from the tension at the table, and she met his kiss with fierce, urgent need of her own. He leaned back against the wall and her body stretched up against his, shoulder to belly to thigh, each inch where they touched coming alive.

"I'm the best thing, huh?" His voice was low and rough in her ear. His hand came up her back and around her waist to cup her breast. "Is that your professional opinion?" he asked, teasing her nipple into a hard point, "or just your hormones talking?"

She licked her way down his throat to his collarbone, worked his shirt apart with her teeth, kissing lower. "Purely professional, of course."

He groaned. "Oh, God. Keep doing that."

She took a strand of chest hair in her teeth and nibbled,

shocked by how she enjoyed the sound of his indrawn breath, how badly she wanted to get rough, jump him right there on the floor next to the dogs.

She pulled away. "I think I'm too angry to do this right now. I'm not myself."

He growled and bent lower. "Take out your anger on me. I like it." He slipped his hand down the front of her shirt and pushed it down, exposing her bra and the erect nipple beneath pressing through the nylon. "Bitchy women turn me on."

She clutched his shoulders, dug her fingernails in to hear him growl again, gasping when he sucked hard on the aching tip of her breast. He made no effort to hurry or take it easy; he was methodical and precise, undeterred by her small acts of violence.

"I always wanted to be a bitch." She threw her head back and forgot her mother. Now it was just him, his touch, what she wanted.

He licked his way up to her earlobe. "You have the funniest ideas about yourself. This nice girl thing. Funny."

"I'm—a preschool teacher." She gasped. "That's—about as nice—as you can get."

He breathed on the ticklish hollow under her ear. "Not a preschool teacher anymore."

Another thrill washed over her. "No."

He sighed and pulled her head to his chest, under his chin. "I snuck into your office and saw the Target line Jennifer has started to make for you." He slipped his hand under her shirt and caressed her back. "Rachel had the sample sewers make up an extra pair of the shorts, just for her to keep, because she doesn't want to wait for production." He kissed her hair. "Even the new private label tags look pretty good."

"Thanks." She was melting.

"You think it'll do the trick, don't you?"

She lifted her head and kissed the corner of his mouth, the half that was smiling. "I do, actually."

He looked into her eyes. "So do I." His hand cupped his cheek. "You're a natural, apparently. A fashion savant."

She grinned, suffused with happiness. He leaned down, rested his forehead on hers, and caressed her lower lip with his thumb. "Now we just have to get you training for your first marathon, and you've won the prize."

"What prize?"

His teeth flashed white in the dim porch. "That would be me, of course."

"I inherited *you*, too? I didn't see you listed in the will."

He smiled, but fell silent. She felt his muscles tense.

"We've been gone too long from the table." He gently pulled her shirt back up over her bra. "I shouldn't have given your mother any bad ideas, but I couldn't resist. You were sweet to defend me, but don't do it again or people will get suspicious."

"I said something. What was it?"

"Nothing. Sorry. We should get back."

"The will. It's because I mentioned the will." All the details she'd picked up over the past weeks flooded her mind—Liam knowing where Ed's water heater was, the extra set of keys, his unrivaled stature at the company, his mother lighting the memorial candle, his rude comments when they'd met. "You were supposed to be in the will."

He stroked her hair, tucking a loose strand behind her ear. "We should get back."

"My grandfather should have left you something. What did he promise you?" She swore under her breath. "If only he hadn't put everything into Fite, or passed some of it along to my mother,

I might be able to fulfill his promise. How much—not that it matters, since I'm still broke—"

"I don't want any money." He took a step back and his face closed up, cold and tight. "That's never what I wanted."

"Was it something in the house? We kept everything, Liam. Whatever it was, it's in storage. We can find it. I don't care if my mom objects, I'll—"

"Bev." His hard voice cut through her babbling. "Enough."

One of the dogs at his feet jerked his ears up and scurried off into a corner. Bev was hurt but didn't want to show it. "I was just trying to help."

"You were trying to be nice again. Don't bother."

"I'm the nurturing type." She reached her hand up to his face and smiled. "Let me nurture you a little bit."

He jerked his head away. "I've already got a mother."

Her jaw dropped open. To her horror she felt her eyes get warm. Grabbing on to her anger as a lifejacket, she dug her fingernails into her palms and tried to regain her breathing. "A better one than you deserve. Find me some wine and I'll bring it to her."

He closed his eyes for a moment. Shrugging, he pulled a bottle out of a case he didn't bother to read and followed her back through the kitchen to the dining room.

Her mother's face was probably disapproving, but Bev was careful not to look anywhere near it. Instead she turned all her attentions to Mark, sweet geeky Mark, and finished the meal exchanging teacher's secret methods of mixing common ingredients to make model volcanoes explode until she could excuse herself from the party to go check on her old, vomiting cat.

Chapter 19

"ELLEN IS THE only one who could've changed the locks," Bev said, reclining in the couch next to Ball and eating a bowl of Frosted Flakes. She was going over the argument with her mother for the sixth time since the dinner the night before. "I know it wasn't Liam. We discovered it together, and he was just as surprised as I was. Whoever did it had keys to the place."

Gail and Kate were already at work on the cardio machines they'd hauled in from the rear bedroom. Neither one would eat until they had accrued a large enough calorie deficit to cover their breakfast; they'd been at it for thirty minutes so far and had another half hour to go.

"Well, Ellen was in New York with Johnny when you called me about the break-in." Gail poked the buttons on her elliptical machine, making it hum into a new position. "That was the first thing I said to her, but she convinced me. She's totally innocent on that."

"Mom..." Bev began.

"You're just ashamed to admit this guy could have tricked you," her mother said.

Bev shook her head. "If you could have seen him—"

"I did see him." Gail raised her eyebrows. "All six feet more, blond, strapping inches of him. That's my point. It explains a lot."

She got up with her empty bowl and headed for the kitchen. "It wasn't him."

Gail bent over for her water bottle. "It doesn't matter what you believe. Ellen is family. Don't assume the worst."

Kate burst out laughing. "Weak argument, Mom. This is our family we're talking about."

Bev asked her mother, "Does she have an alibi for when the locks were changed too?"

"Alibi! You make her sound like a criminal."

"You were the one who wanted me to call the police."

"After the break-in! And you should have. The police should be involved when people—even tall, good-looking people—break into our houses to frighten us," Gail said.

"She doesn't have an alibi." Bev leaned closer. "It had to be her."

Gail scowled at the treadmill screen, face flushed and shiny, then swung her head to Bev. "She was overcome with grief. That's a fair explanation. You were a stranger to her, coming up to steal away her career and her home. Perhaps you should be grateful that was all she did."

Bev mouth dropped open. "You *knew*?"

"Not then, of course not." Gail slapped the machine, the pedals hummed and slowed, and she jumped off with a towel in her hand. "Last week she opened up about a lot of things. I admit I was suspicious of her, but that was before. I didn't feel right violating her confidence and sharing everything with you. Especially now that the sisterly relationship is so fragile."

Bev's feeling of triumph was short-lived. "She confessed to changing the locks, but she not to the break-in."

"It's impossible, Bev. Not that you'll ever believe me now—

you are so pigheaded. I knew you'd jump to conclusions." Her mother got up on tiptoes to read the screen display then marched off to the kitchen, wiping her forehead.

"Well?" Bev asked Kate.

She shrugged. "Who cares? Nothing's happened since." After a long gulp of water, she wiped her mouth on the back of her forearm and picked up her pace. "I kind of like the pet fashion idea, don't you? Or are you taking *his* side on that too?"

Fite had enough trouble with human beings. "I'm taking my side. And my side doesn't want any more family drama inside that building."

Kate gaped. "You can't mean *me*?"

"Yup."

"I came all the way up here, and you won't even let me in the stupid building of the family business?"

"You've never mentioned it before," Bev said.

"Well, it's not like I want to, but *jeez*. My grandpa too, you know?"

"You didn't even bother to go to the funeral."

"Not like he'd notice. Besides, Mom said I didn't have to."

"She told me the same thing. I went anyway," Bev said.

"That's because you're always trying to be better than everybody else."

What was it with the insults about her sincerity? "And you never think the rules apply to you because you're so special." Bev looked at her watch. "I'm going to work."

"It's Saturday!"

In less than a week she would be flying to Minneapolis with Liam. "As you pointed out, I've got to try to be better than everyone else."

Kate huffed and slapped the stop button on the treadmill. "If you're not going to let me help out at Fite, I might as well go home."

"Don't be that way."

"What? If you don't trust me to help out at Fite, why should I stay?"

"Because I'm going to convince Mom to go home tomorrow and I don't want to be here alone. We still don't know who broke in."

"Please. Not that he has to break anything now."

"What's that supposed to mean?"

"Why steal it if the cow's giving it out for free? Isn't it obvious? Gramps was pimping you out. He probably planned it this way all along."

Feeling a chill settle over her shoulders, Bev lowered her voice. "Maybe you *should* go home. Nobody's stopping you."

"I mean, all he has to do to take over Fite is take over you. And you're hardly playing hard to get. 'Oh, Liam! You're the best thing *evah*!'"

Bev's hands shook. "I'm going to finish getting ready for work. I'll be gone for the rest of the day. If you're serious about your threat to leave, now would be the time to follow through. Not that you follow through on anything."

Kate pointed a finger. "Just because I see right through him."

Gail came into the room peeling a low-fat string cheese from its wrapper. "Girls! Now don't *you* start. "

Kate gave Bev a narrow-eyed, daring, evil smile, and said nothing. "I've been dismissed, so I'm going home."

Gail's eyes went wide. "But I just got here!"

"Bev says there's no way in hell she'll let me work at Fite. Can you believe that?"

"Really, Bev!"

"Or you either, Mom," Bev said. "Sorry, but if that's why you're here, you'd better go with Kate."

Gail stared at her. "Excuse me?"

"Fite can't handle more people at the top steering it in different directions. There are great people there who can bring Fite around. It's my job to make sure they get the chance to do it."

"Now hold on there, Beverly Moon Lewis," Gail said, voice low. "I put up with that kind of talk last night, but no more." She pointed at the couch. "Both of you, *sit*."

"I won't change my mind," Bev said firmly.

"Oh, I think you will." She wiggled her finger.

Kate flung herself on the sofa, pretending not to care, but Bev stayed on her feet.

Her mother frowned at her, pursing her lips, but continued, "First of all, I think that doggie idea is wonderful, and so does Ellen. She said it was amazing nobody had thought of it yet."

"When did Ellen say that?" Bev asked.

"We spoke early this morning. New York hours. And that's not all she said, but we'll go over it when she gets here."

Bev pointed at her. "No. She is not getting involved. You are not getting involved."

Gail went over and stood next to Kate on the sofa. "I'm amazed that you continue to hold onto this crazy idea that you can stop Ellen from running her own company."

"It isn't hers. If Grandfather had left it to her, she would have sold it by now," Bev said. "She just wants the money."

Gail let out a deep breath. "Obviously I got here just in time. Listen to you. Some people are cut out for this business. Some people are not. The sooner you get back home to something not so stressful, where you can be yourself, the better."

"Enough!" Bev ran a hand through her hair. "You've never

understood me. You think I became a teacher because I didn't like *stress*? Have you ever been inside a classroom?" She threw up her hands. "Of course not. You haven't been inside a school since you were seventeen. Certainly none of *mine*."

Her mother's eyes went wide. "You'll thank me," she said finally, her voice rough. "You're obviously breaking under the stress. Stress floods your skin with free radicals. Do you want to lose your looks before you turn thirty?"

Bev marched over to the foyer. She didn't have time for this. "I turned thirty last December." She slung her purse over her shoulder. "Is that all you've got? Because I've got different values than you do. If I get prematurely saggy and gray, at least I'll have something I can be proud of that isn't reflected in a mirror."

That hit home. Gail sucked in her breath through her teeth. "Who do you think owns this house you're living in?"

Bev froze. She'd never rebelled as a teenager, too afraid to risk what little family she had.

Well, better late than never.

"Who do you think is sick of putting up with all your patronizing shit?" she said softly.

Gail's mouth fell open. She collapsed onto the sofa next to Kate. "Here I was feeling guilty about giving Ellen's son the house, and now I don't have to." She bit her lip, frowning through tears. "You don't want me, you can find somewhere else to live. Today."

Bev was too angry to give a damn about her mother's feelings. Later she might, but right then all she could think of was every dismissive comment her mother had ever made, a montage of put-downs that ran through her thoughts like a low-budget music video. "You're kicking me out," she said flatly.

"Not if you're reasonable."

"Which means having you, Ellen, and Kate take over?" Bev

snorted. "What do I do—run the daycare center?"

Gail shrugged. "That's an intriguing idea. Perhaps, down the line, if there's a need," she said. "But no. I figured you'd enjoy a little more time up here, enjoy some time off, travel and go home. Andy told me he could find you a temp job at the studio while you apply for teaching positions for next year."

Bev looked over at Kate, who was frowning but silent. "And how about you, Kate? That sounds like a good plan?"

Kate shrugged and took another sip from her water bottle. "Oh, sure. Now you want my support. As soon as you need something from me."

Bev glanced around the house then at her mother and sister's hostile faces. "I don't need anything from either one of you." She strode away from them to her bedroom and slammed the door.

She lifted her cat off the end of the bed and nuzzled her neck, fighting tears. "Change of plans, Ball," she said softly. "We're moving to San Francisco."

❧

When Liam heard the door swing open in the neighboring office, he jerked his head up from the sketches on his desk. Usually, he liked having his Saturdays to himself, but—

His pulse reacted to her presence even before she poked her pretty head into his office, offered a wave and a pinched smile, then disappeared, hauling a large plastic box.

He looked back down at the sketches and tried to regain his concentration. Running after her wouldn't look good. The first holiday delivery should have crops over the knee, almost to the ankles. Shorts would come back for the last November delivery, in basic colors to survive Christmas—

He pushed himself up from his desk and walked over to Bev's office, pausing in the doorway and leaning his hip on the jamb.

She was using a piece of red reflective piping as a headband and had resurrected the green sweater he'd vowed to destroy. He licked his lips, feeling hot. "Are you still angry at me?"

She continued flipping through the binder in front of her on the desk, chewing her lips. The motion caught his attention, and he lost himself in the vision of white teeth pressing up against pink, swollen flesh.

She finally glanced up. "And why would I be angry?"

He came into the room. "I broke the cardinal rule."

"Being an asshole?"

"No, you seem to like that."

She sighed and rested her cheek in her palm. "True enough."

"The rule I broke," he said, coming over and sitting across from her, out of groping distance, "was to mention my mother."

"I like your mother."

"So do I, actually. But at that moment I was making an unflattering comparison, and I'm sorry."

"You are?"

Liam fought the urge to pull her into his lap. "Yes."

"All right, then. I accept," she said. "I'm sorry too."

He didn't know why she would be but didn't want to argue, because then she might not let him touch her again, so he avoided her eyes and imagined her naked. Then clenched his jaw. That was not going to get them the account at Target.

He noticed a plastic box at her feet. "You brought your cat to work?"

She opened and closed her mouth, glanced at the carrier, and nodded. "She was lonely." The little door was open and tufts of fur stuck out through the slots.

"Spry little lady, isn't she?"

Bev leaned over to pet her cat, and the neckline of the baggy sweater flopped open, exposing hills of delicate, round, flesh and —black lace. His mouth went dry.

"She's old. Ancient, really." Then she sighed and went back to the papers on her desk. "There's so much to do. I don't know how I can pull it off. Between this Target deal and the financial nightmare that keeps getting worse, not to mention family squabbles, I'm beginning to wonder if they're right."

"Your mother after you again?"

"She got me, actually. She often does."

Liam hated to see her beaten down. "We could work together if you think that might help you fight off the demons," he said. "Pool our resources. Take over the lobby conference room."

Her eyes lit up. "Together?"

"We haven't tried that yet. Maybe we should."

"I thought you'd be mad," she said. "About me sneaking projects to Jennifer."

"So instead of talking to me about it, you went behind my back."

She bit her lip again, drawing his eyes. *Damn it.* "I didn't want to argue," she said.

"And you're pathologically non-confrontational."

"Fuck off," she said, grinning. "How was that?"

He smiled back, in spite of himself, and got to his feet. "Great. I'll meet you in the conference room with the three groups I'm working on and the latest sales figures."

"I've got some sample yardage I'd like you to see." She beamed. "But I don't know if it's a good vendor or not. Plus, it's narrow goods and might bring up the retail too high."

"Bring the tag, and we'll talk about it." He walked back to his office to gather all his stuff, strangely proud of the nursery school teacher with her hot fashion lingo. He knew he liked her too much, thought about her too much, wanted her too much—but she was doing a pretty good job with his company, had stood up to her family, and spending a Saturday afternoon talking shop with her wouldn't kill him.

He was hanging up his favorite samples on the conference room walls when she stumbled in, her arms full of binders and magazines and garments, invisible under the pile.

She dropped the armful on the table. "How did they sew up all this stuff so fast? I just asked them a couple days ago, and there's already a rack in my office—with all of it. I hope Jennifer didn't hurt anybody."

"Not physically, anyway." Liam picked up an armful and began hanging them on the opposite wall. Pants, shorts, crops, jackets, tees, support tanks. Thoughtful, he rearranged them, then moved them around again, then went back for another pile. Bev joined him and added more, saying nothing. When all the samples were up on the walls, each of them stepped back to study them.

"Oh, *God*," she said finally. "Say something."

"I told you. I snuck in during the week and thought it was good."

"But you haven't seen these yet." She walked over and ran her hand over the jacket that had immediately caught his eye—a charcoal gray hoodie with the identical red piping she wore in her hair.

Printed onto the sleeve was a new "Fite Gear" logo in metallic silver that reached from shoulder seam to wrist in bold block letters four inches tall.

He went over and tested the weight of the material between his thumb and forefinger. "These are the goods Jennifer was talking about."

She nodded. "If we order enough of it, we can afford it."

"Meaning, if we can sell enough of what we make out of it."

"Well?"

"Well, what?"

"Liam!" She sat down at the table, dropped her head in her hands, peered up at him through her fingers. "What do you *think*?"

He had no illusions about himself. He knew he was the type of man to enjoy having power over others, the power to praise or put down, correct or dismiss. Usually, his pleasure in this power wasn't on display, but Bev's looked so worried—

"Will you stop smiling at me like that!" she cried. "I can't tell if you're gloating because it sucks so bad, or because you think it's totally fantastic."

He gained control of his facial features and crossed his arms over his chest. "It's fine," he said. "Great. How's the fit?"

She sank down into her chair as the air left her lungs and looked up at the ceiling. "You said 'great.'"

"How's the fit? Or did Rachel refuse to—"

"No, she tried everything on. Not this latest stuff, but the core bottoms over there, and they're awesome. Those patternmakers and sewers are amazing. And Rachel's butt looked even more fabulous than usual." She got up and patted the samples. "I figure if we can sell a woman a decent pair of pants and make sure she knows our name, we can sell her another pair next time she comes in for paper towels and shampoo."

"That's the idea. But we have to be on spec. Consistently. Luckily that's one thing we can do. Ed was a stickler for QA. Our problem is that our women's specs have been consistently bad."

"But this is a chance to start over. What do you think of the new Fite Gear logo for them? Think Macy's will complain we've gone down-market?"

"We have no choice." He turned back to study the rest of the samples, glad his back was to her, because he was impressed. "I like the logo. I like the palette. I like the hippie global warming thing in that group, and the girlie flower thing in that one. It's good. Solid."

"But is it enough?"

He leaned back against the wall and shrugged. "How the hell would I know? I'm just a dumb jock."

She flopped back down into a chair. "Yeah, well, you're all I've got, so answer me anyway. What's your gut tell you?"

He gave her a long, steady look, and she flushed.

"Other than that!" she said.

Funny, he hadn't been thinking of sex. While his mind had been admiring the profit potential of a massive deal in the third quarter, his gut had been feeling grateful she hadn't gone back to Orange County just yet to teach fingerpainting. Which reminded him of a previous, interrupted conversation. "I think we'd nail it with a picture of Annabelle Tucker in that hoodie."

Her face froze. She swiveled away in her chair. "No."

"It would go great with her sporty, adolescent girl-power shtick." He squatted down to her eye level and gripped the arm of her chair. "Just one picture. She can email it to us."

"We'd be implying some kind of endorsement deal we don't have. No way."

"So just ask her to wear it on her next jog through the paparazzi. The size of that logo down the arm—nobody could miss it." He put his hand over hers. "What harm is there in asking? She's obviously not shy about selling out."

Bev pulled her hand away. "She is sixteen years old! You make her sound greedy when she's just a kid way over her head." Her beautiful eyes gazed into his, wide and distressed. "And it's all my fault."

Ah. "For introducing her to your father?"

"Yes! And now—you've seen the tabloids. She's never going to have a normal life. She'll probably get into drugs and sex and lose all her money to some parasite with a nice smile and it will be all over the news..." She squeezed her lips together and looked furious. More furious than sad.

"And what?"

"And Hilda will be right!"

Confused, Liam moved up into a chair next to her. "Who's Hilda?"

Bev slapped her hands on the table and began rifling through the sketches. "Forget it. We are not using Annabelle."

"She's a friend?" He saw the disgust ripple across Bev's face and guessed, "No, a co-worker." Remembering she'd been fired, he nodded his head. "Your boss. Your old boss."

"How the hell did you guess that?" She shook her head. "I don't care. What do you think of a hangtag advertising the contoured rise on the yoga pant?"

"You need to stop caring what people think of you." He reached out and rested his hand over her arm. "People who don't matter, anyway."

"She wasn't honest with me!" Bev said. "I worked for this woman for years and thought I was getting a promotion. I was going to buy a partnership with her with the Fite money. And she fired me because she thought I was too attached to the kids. 'Like a stage mom,' she said. That I manipulated them and sucked their natural life force out of them or something. Me! I loved them. I loved them, and I had to say goodbye to every one of them." Her eyes, glistening with tears, had turned a bright turquoise.

He brushed a tear off her cheekbone with his thumb. He had the urge to find this Hilda bitch and put her out of business. "She didn't get attached to the kids?"

She brushed his hand away. "She said it was our job to teach, not love."

"And people left their little kids with this lady?"

"We had dozens on the waitlist."

"Because of you, I bet. I wonder how long her waitlist is now that you're gone."

Through her tears, Bev's eyes warmed with mischief. "Not very, I hear." She patted her eyes. "The other teacher and I were friends. We email."

"So business is suffering without you." He tucked a strand of her hair behind her ear. "I can easily imagine that."

"I thought I was a power-hungry bitch. That's what you said."

"Power-hungry, yes. Bitch, not so much. Alas."

"Alas?"

"Otherwise you'd be constantly trying to manipulate me sexually." He shook his head. "Instead of fearing I was doing the same to you."

Her eyes got wide.

"Am I right?" He rolled his chair closer, so close he could smell the lemon—he ducked his head and drew her scent into his lungs—in her hair. *It must be her shampoo.*

Bev drew back a few inches. "I don't believe you're trying to manipulate me sexually. Half the time you ignore me."

"Only half?" He swiveled her chair so their knees were touching. In a swift, determined move he hauled her out of her seat and into his lap.

"Oh!" She struggled, but he wrapped his arms around her waist more tightly, savoring the pressure of her soft ass. "Stop it," she said. "All kinds of people are around today."

"I've decided to only ignore you a quarter of the time." He slid his hands up her belly to her breasts and cupped them, stroking and squeezing while his heart pounded against her back.

She wriggled, ripping a groan out of his throat. "I admit I find you very hard to resist, but—" she pried his fingers loose, "—use that twenty-five percent ignoring time now, because if we don't get this line figured out I won't be able to sleep at night."

He let her slip away, took a deep breath, and ran his hand through his hair. "You don't look like you're sleeping too well as it is."

"I just need to get through the next couple of weeks," she said. "Without letting Fite go out of business."

Taking a series of deep breaths with his eyes focused on the walls of the conference room instead of her flushed, aroused face, Liam waited for his body to calm down before he got up and went back to his chair on the opposite side of the table. "We won't let it," he said. "I won't let it."

The grief vanished, and her face broke into a wide, goofy grin that hit him across the table, grabbed his heart in a fist and squeezed.

"Good." She glowed at him.

He tried to swallow over the tension in his chest. Voice rough, he grumbled, "If you're so grateful, you can be the one to get the coffee."

Chapter 20

THE POTSTICKERS WERE cold but she ate them anyway, poking her plastic fork into the bottom of the waxy white box without looking away from Liam's sketches on the table. She blinked, trying to keep the black and white lines from going out of focus.

His fingers wrapped around her wrist.

"Hey, hands off." She pulled free. "If you wanted potstickers you should have ordered them for yourself, Mr. Broccoli Tofu."

"Bev."

She sighed and dropped the fork. "All right, go ahead. I'm too tired to eat." She looked up into his eyes and saw amusement and something else she didn't dare define as affection.

"Time to go home," he said. "You're delirious."

She yawned, slapped a hand over her mouth, yawned again. "We can't. We're not done." *And besides, I am home.* She'd already dragged her suitcase up to her grandfather's old suite. Thank God she'd never opened up the frat lounge to the rest of the company. Once the company was solvent again she could take a bigger salary, get her own apartment, make up with her mother at her own pace.

"Close enough." He got to his feet and gathered the papers

and binders on the table. "We can finish up Monday. We're both too tired to do anything else productive today."

She looked at her watch. "Tonight, you mean. It's past eight." A sense of well-being overtook her. All day they had worked together, side by side, putting the groups together and sharing their opinions like equals. Less formal than co-workers—more like . . . friends. Even though he had to explain why they couldn't manufacture what she wanted because their customer would never spend two hundred dollars on a t-shirt, he was never mean about it, and more than once had to educate her on the unavoidable realities of garment sourcing and manufacturing with a calm, sad smile.

"Damn, that's all?" He got to his feet and stretched his arms over his head, sighing. "I'm getting old."

Bev watched his t-shirt lift above the waistband of his jeans, exposing an Olympic stomach and the line of dark blond hair pointing south. "Do you miss swimming?" she asked dreamily, imagining him wet, slicing through the water.

She could see he recognized the admiration in her gaze, but instead of holding the pose for effect, he dropped his arms and tugged the shirt down, frowning, as though he didn't like her looking at his body.

"No." He turned around and moved the garments from the wall to a rolling rack.

"Does your shoulder still hurt?" she asked, watching him carry the clothes in large armfuls. "I mean, when you do other things?"

He glanced over at her, a faint, suggestive smile in the corner of his mouth. "What kind of things?"

"What if you just swim slowly? Or focus on kicking or something. Is there anything you can do?"

"It's not like my skin has become water soluble. I just can't do laps." He grimaced. "Thank God."

"Really?" She smiled. "You wouldn't want to do laps anymore?"

"No sane human being ever born on this earth *wants* to do laps. Granted, I knew lots of guys who did, which I submit as evidence of my theory since they were all crazy-ass bastards, much as I loved 'em."

"That's pretty ironic. Swimming is the one thing I do like. Even laps. Very relaxing."

He looked at her with interest. "Then you should do it more often. I might even reconsider my vow of lifetime lap-swimming abstinence if I get to see you in a bikini. Working on your strokes." He raised an eyebrow, eyes sparkling.

"You *never* liked to do laps?"

He met her incredulous gaze, sighed, and shook his head. "No."

"Then—" she hesitated, seeing his reluctance to talk, but too curious to stop. "Then why did you do it? It must have been years and years of training. The hours you must have spent in the pool —"

"You have no idea."

"And you didn't like it."

"Hated every minute." He shrugged. "Well, not all of it. I liked warming down in the hot tub. I liked my friends, traveling around the state, then the world." His mouth quirked. "The partying."

She knew she shouldn't laugh but couldn't help it. "I sure pegged you wrong," she said, slapping her hands together with delight. "What else are you hiding? Do you spend the weekends on the couch? Have a bag-a-day Cheetos habit?"

His eyebrows came together in the middle, but his lips fought a smile. "Don't dis Cheetos."

"So part of you can understand why I find—say, cardio machines—unbearable."

"Sure," he said. "So do I."

Surprise, surprise. "You do?"

"Yup. Never use them unless I'm desperate."

"Never?" She narrowed her eyes. "Define 'desperate.'"

"Raining, travel, injury—"

"Add 'hell or high water' and you've got me, too."

"We're practically the same person."

She smiled, feeling warm.

He grabbed the rolling rack and rearranged the samples. "Especially when you consider we agreed on almost every design question that came up today."

Neither spoke for a minute. The sound of San Francisco traffic filtered through the walls. "For the record I wish I didn't find exercise so boring. It probably would be good for me."

"You might as well say you find life boring. 'Exercise' is a massive overgeneralization."

"All right. All exercise I've ever tried is too boring to endure."

His smile fell. "If I could swim six hours straight outside in November with a head cold, then get up and do it again every day for ten more years, you can move your body for twenty minutes every once in a while." Then he tilted his head and let his gaze rake down over her torso, making her pulse skip.

Undecided about how to respond to the raw sexual interest in his eyes, she pushed to her feet and gathered a stack of binders to hold over her chest. "How could you have done all of that if you hated it?"

"I was a kid. I wasn't given a choice."

"But at some point you were old enough to rebel."

He wasn't looking at her anymore, and said nothing.

"What was driving you?"

Liam shoved the rack, heavy with samples, out the door. "Can you get the rest? I don't want the others seeing it until after we know how it goes over in Minneapolis."

Touched a nerve, did I? She grabbed more to add on to her stack of binders and sketches and hurried after him. "There must have been something about it that kept you going." She lengthened her stride to catch up. "You could have traveled and partied without working so hard all those years."

He kicked the door to his office wide open and rolled the rack inside. "Trying to psychoanalyze me, Bev?"

"No, I—" Pausing in the doorway, she rearranged the heavy stack of paper in her arms and waited for him to turn around and look at her. "Maybe a little. Was it something to do with your dad?"

The room fell silent. After a moment, he said flatly, "Did my mother tell you that?"

Surprised by the turn in his mood, she shook her head and continued walking into the room to set the things down on his desk. "Lucky guess. At dinner she mentioned he could be difficult."

"Yeah. Well." He moved over to the door. "Wait here while I go get the rest of the stuff so nobody sees it Monday and starts asking questions."

He was gone. She sank down into a chair, aching to know more but aware it had been a very long day. When he came back in with the rolls of fabric in his arms, she got to her feet. "I'm sorry. I shouldn't have pried. Go home and get some sleep."

He set down the fabric behind the door and came over to

where she stood at the desk, gaze sliding over her body from head to toe. Looking deep into her eyes, he brushed her cheek with the backs of his fingers, the corner of his mouth in a faint smile. "It's not that late."

Her throat tightened. For a moment she enjoyed the feel of his large, warm hand against her skin. "You're trying to distract me."

He moved closer, so that the hot length of him was flush against her body. "No shit."

"Why is it so hard to talk about your father?"

He dipped his head and breathed a kiss along her temple. "Why is it so hard for you to stop talking?"

She smiled. Melted against him. "How old were you when—"

His hand came up under her sweater and rested in the small of her back, holding her firmly and still against him. "If you kiss me I'll tell you all about it."

Trying to overcome the building desire low in her body, Bev tilted her head up and gave him a quick peck on the chin. "There. How old?"

Chuckling, he shook his head and shoved his knee between her legs while his hand kept her body hard against his. "Younger than I am now."

"Stop—" Her words faltered when his other hand went down over her ass and pulled her up along his hard thigh and the ridge of his erection through his jeans. "I'm guessing you were—early twenties—and Ed hired you—Oh!"

His hand unbuttoned her jeans, slid down the zipper, and then the denim was down at her knees. She felt cold air on her thighs and his fingers between her legs stroking, searching, and penetrating. His mouth came down hard on hers and then his tongue was there, demanding and hot in her mouth, skillfully teasing her lips apart while he bent her back over the desk.

Her eyes closed, and the black pool of desire swept her down, circling deeper with his touch, and she forgot what she was saying to enjoy the shimmering fire along her skin. Someone cried out.

"Hush," he said softly. "Don't want security to get curious."

She tensed. "Security?"

"Kidding," he said, kissing her neck. He trailed his fingers down her ribs and stroked the curve of her hip, his voice falling so low she could barely hear him. "You are so damn sexy. I can't stop thinking about you."

"Liam—" She tried to sit up, but he held her.

"All day, all night, all the time. I'm losing my mind." He nuzzled his head against hers.

"The door is open."

"There's nobody here, sweetheart. It's okay."

She pushed him away. "No."

His heavy-lidded gaze aimed downward, on her mouth, and lower, to her bare thighs. "Damn," he whispered, clenching his jaw and running his hand over his eyes. "I am such an idiot."

She wiggled away from him and pulled her pants up, her heart pounding. "I can't believe we almost did that here. With the door open." She hurried over and closed it, though the hallway was dark and silent.

Liam buttoned his jeans. "I've got no finesse around you. Ripping your pants off, kissing you, then mentioning security." Jaw clenched, he looked away from her to the rack of samples next to the desk, his chest visibly rising with each breath. He pulled his cell out of his pocket, glancing at her. "I'll call my sister and tell her to find somewhere else to sleep tonight."

He assumed—well, of course he did.

All he has to do to take over Fite is to take over you . . .

"No," she said. "Liam, I can't. I know it's reasonable for you to think I would, but no. I was tired and you have a way of getting to me and I really, no, I really can't."

An eyebrow went up. "You think I'm being reasonable?"

"To assume I'd finish what we just started. I should never have let you kiss me again. I'm sorry—"

He shoved his desk chair out of his way with his knee and walked over to her. "Let me kiss you?"

"Great. Now you're angry."

"Bev, just what do you think is going on here between us? Do you think I want this to happen?"

She stood up taller. Met his glare. "Obviously." But she felt herself sinking into a large gray area. She had no idea what he wanted, or why.

"You're my boss. Which would be bad enough, but you're a boss I had vowed to get rid of. Every minute I spend with you that might keep you here at Fite is a mistake. It takes me farther from what I want." He stared at her, calm and terrifying, transformed before her eyes back into the ice cube.

"What else do you want, Liam? You've still got your job, more power than ever, and the biggest paycheck around." She was determined not to add, *and my weak, stupid heart.* "What else is there?"

"What I deserve," he said. "I deserve more than this."

A clammy fear settled over her. She didn't know if he was talking about his job or their relationship.

They didn't have a relationship. That was the point.

He looked away from her. "I shouldn't have said anything. You want to know my deepest, darkest secrets, then get upset when you hear them." He shoved his hand through his hair again. "Yes, I wanted more than working for you. There's nothing insulting in that. I've been here over ten years—you've been here ten minutes. I don't care how smart or talented you are, I shouldn't have to work for you."

"You're just angry I didn't let you have sex with me."

"Oh, I'm the one. I'm the one who wants it, not you, of course not you. Not a nice girl like you."

She poked a finger into his chest, annoyed she was shaking. "While I appreciate your disappointment in your career and, apparently, your minor frustration at not getting laid at the office whenever you want, it is exactly why we are not ever going to touch each other again."

He glanced down at her finger. His voice fell. "I wouldn't classify my frustration as minor."

She pulled her hand back. "Sex with me can't be your consolation prize for having to work here. My body is not part of your benefits package."

He stared at her, eyes narrowing to slits. "*Your* body?"

"That's what I am to you, right? You were stuck with me and decided to make the best of the situation," she said. "Isn't that what you said? You're an efficient guy?"

"You keep leaving your decisions out of this scenario. You were an active participant in each stage of the game. So tell me, Bev, what did you get out of fucking the hired help? I doubt it was my charming conversation." He exhaled loudly and stalked over to the rolling rack, then shoved the samples back and forth, making the hangers squeal on the metal bar. "I see how you look at me. Your body's not in the benefits package—mine is."

Silence fell over the room. Bev's mouth went dry. Did he really think she would use him like that? Had other women made him feel like a piece of meat?

It was too ridiculous. Of course he was gorgeous, but the

world was full of gorgeous men. None were as brilliant, talented, and funny as he was. Tough but sweet.

Lovable.

"But you're right," he went on, "I was wrong to get involved with you. When Ed died, and he hadn't left Fite to me—not directly—I should have resigned immediately. To stay on and try to manipulate you was an act of sentimentality and fear. I admit it. I fooled around with you because I couldn't help myself. I can't. It annoys the hell out of me to think Ed is getting what he'd wanted all along, but I always admired the brilliant bastard, and he did usually get his way."

"What he wanted all along was for you to sleep with me?"

Liam stared at her, his brown eyes shining.

"I see," she gasped. *Not directly*. He'd never even met her. She put her hand over her mouth, ashamed of the fantasy of an old man having faith in her, feeling like an idiot. *He wouldn't have given Fite to the nicest person in the family if he thought she'd actually be crazy enough to keep it.*

"I've admitted my weaknesses. How about you?" He pushed the garment rack aside. "Are you ready to admit you just wanted a little fun with the gold medalist? Use him to advance your career? Save your pride? Or are you going to claim to be in love with me —like a really good girl would be?"

Chapter 21

LIAM DIDN'T THINK she would answer. But they were on a runaway train and, like it or not, they were going to say worse things than had already been said, tumble off the tracks, burst into flames, and fall apart.

Her eyes were turquoise again. The tears she'd been fighting highlighted the green under the blue. He swam in them, lost and angry, wishing they'd separated for the night hours ago before they got so tired they began telling the truth.

"I could love you, Liam." Bev crossed her arms over her chest. "That's the problem."

Definitely should have gone home hours ago.

He sighed. "I'm sorry, but I don't believe you."

"What?"

"That's just what you're telling yourself."

"You—you have no idea what I'm feeling."

"I think I do."

"The first moment I saw you I knew I had to be careful around you. That I'd get all stupid about you."

"Ah," he said. "The first moment you *saw* me. Emphasis on seeing. That's not love." He gave her a look. "It has a name, but nice girls wouldn't admit to it. It's too crude. Too shallow."

"You think I'm blinded by your good looks?"

"No, I think you're extremely aware of my good looks."

"You exaggerate your charms."

"We're only talking about how I look. If I believed you wanted the real me, the Liam who never deserved a gold medal or to be a fashion exec, then I'd—" he stopped himself, because the image of a long future with Bev in it flashed before his eyes, and he lost his breath.

"You'd what?"

Bev sleeping. Bev cooking. Bev jumping up and down. Bev laughing. Bev naked. Bev eating. Bev everything.

She frowned at him. "It's more than your looks," she said, but he was lost in the silent movie playing in his head, and her voice sounded far away.

It was funny that the first time he discovered he cared more about a woman than she did about him, it would be when he could do nothing about it. She was too smart to believe him. Too cautious—like he was. Used to be.

"What if I told you I wanted us to date, like normal people, and see what happened," he said slowly. "What would you say?"

Her eyes widened. While he waited, not breathing, a cloud of emotions drifted across her face—then settled on unwary. "But we work together."

"At the top of a privately held organization. Held by you, as a matter of fact."

She closed her eyes and rubbed the bridge of her nose. "Liam, it's late. We're both exhausted, we're under a lot of stress—"

"Is that a no?"

"To dating? You mean, openly? With everyone knowing?"

His temper was warring with his pride. "Yes."

"And then what?"

"Then what, when?"

"When—when we have problems everyone will know," she said. "It will be harder than it is already to manage people. To get things done."

A strange feeling came over him, like the nausea before a big meet. He could almost feel his toes curling over the starting block, waiting for the gun to pop, knowing his father was already cursing him out from the stands, that his mother was smiling and trying to rein in his father, that he didn't have to endure any of it if he had the guts.

If he had the guts he'd refuse to play the game he'd been shoved into. He could make his own rules. Find another way to win.

He looked into her big blue eyes and managed a smile, even though his stomach twisted. "If I didn't work here would you turn me down?" He stepped closer to her. "Knowing me as you do, with all my faults, would you want to see how far we could go with each other?"

She waved aside his question with a joke. "We've gone pretty far already."

"You know what I mean. You said you could love me, remember." He managed to keep his voice hard, but he'd never felt so soft in his life.

"It's more than just us, Liam. More than me. You can't leave Fite now—you're—you're essential."

"To Fite, or to you?"

She glanced away, then into his face, and smiled. "To me." Then, while his walls were down, she added, "I never would have survived this long here without you."

Insult to injury, he thought, chiding himself for being pathetic, for letting himself sink so deep, for still not being able to tell her off and walk away while he still had his pride.

"So if you had a choice between coming home with me tonight, and tomorrow night, and maybe the night after," he lifted his hand to her soft, creamy cheek, "versus only seeing me at work . . . you'd choose the latter?"

He thought he could feel her trembling. Her skin was red hot under his palm. She was blinking too much and he could hear each shallow breath pass her lips.

He knew the instant she decided: pity showed in her eyes, and he dropped his hand.

"It would be selfish of us, given the risk, how different we are . . . " She reached out to him. "I'm sorry—"

He spun away from her, not wanting her to see the pain that must be pathetically obvious on his face.

She was *sorry*.

He blinked, frowning, looking around his office—the only place, apparently, she really wanted him. It was an old, familiar pain, to be loved only in context, under condition, with services rendered, awards received, a performance-based compensation. For the first time he wondered if Ed had left him out of his will as a favor. To give him a choice.

Well, he'd made his choice. Too bad for him.

He swallowed, trying to suppress the violence in his chest.

"Liam?" she asked, touching his shoulder.

He jerked away. "Do you need a walk to BART?" His voice was rough.

"No—I've—got my car."

"So, you don't need me."

"Liam?"

"I think it's time you learned you can handle things by yourself." He walked over to his desk, pulled open the drawers, looked for anything he might want to keep. Unlike a month ago, he couldn't see a thing he cared about.

She dropped her face into her hands. "See? This is exactly what I'm talking about. Sex complicates everything."

"You are so right." He felt disgustingly complicated. He slammed the top desk drawer shut, pulled out the middle one, blindly shoved his hand through spare buttons and toggles and swatch cards, photos of line boards, tearsheets from *Lucky* and *WWD*, the first sell-through numbers for the Fite the Man shorts he'd designed. "I think we can both do without any more complications." He banged the drawer shut, decided not to even bother with the rest of them, and looked around for his jacket and running shoes.

"What are you doing? If you're threatening to leave again—"

"Not at all." He met her angry gaze with his own. "I'm informing you of my decision."

"But the meeting—"

"Is Thursday. I'm sure you'll do a great job."

"You don't mean that. You know I need you—"

"You don't." He pulled his lips back into a grimace. "And even if you did, too bad. You can't have me."

Her mouth dropped open. The mouth he'd never taste again. "You're quitting because I can't date you? Don't you think that's a bit childish? Or worse?"

"Worse than childish?" He raised his eyebrow at her. "That's pretty bad coming from a preschool teacher." He sneered. "Excuse me. An *ex*-preschool teacher. I'm sure you'll never settle for that life again."

"I might have to, if you walk out of here now."

"So I should stay just for you?"

"For the company. The one you love."

Love. Same word, different thing. "I do love this place," he said. "Problem is, it doesn't love me back."

"Well, it needs you. Every day I get emails from Richard about some new horrible red ink that's going to swallow us up, and the sales guys complain the accounts aren't getting paid, and the returns are eating away our profits, that we're lucky if Marshall's takes our September deliveries for a three-percent markup—"

"What does any of this have to do with me?"

"You shouldn't take out your anger on Fite. Hate me, fine, but if you leave me alone right now, it's the entire company that's going to suffer—"

"If you really believe that, why don't you go home to L.A.? Hire someone qualified?"

That got her. Eyes bright, she took a step back, staring at him. "Maybe I will," she said through her teeth.

"Great. Awesome. Maybe I'll apply for a job then, after you're gone." And with his running shoes under his arm and his jacket over his shoulder, he left Bev and his office and Fite and walked out into the cold San Francisco summer night.

❧

"Where's Liam?" Rachel asked late Tuesday morning. She had a box cutter in one hand and Chinese takeout in the other. "His office is all locked up."

In the two days since Liam had walked out, Bev had convinced herself she'd done the right thing. She would never have control of the company with that kind of extortion coming from her top employee. *Date me or I'm leaving. Sleep with me or I quit.* Where would it end? *Give me a blow job in the marker room or I won't ship the second spring delivery to Kohl's?*

He said wanted to date like "normal" people—but they were the two most powerful, visible figures of a fragile organization that revolved around them. She was already having enough trouble winning people's respect—even her own family doubted her. Sleeping with the handsome, alpha VP would subtly, perhaps permanently, undermine her authority. She'd become the boss's girlfriend, not the boss.

And, of course, the relationship itself would be doomed from the start. Fighting, screwing, arguing, kissing, hurting—all that drama wasn't healthy. They'd burn out in a couple months—the breakup painfully visible to everyone in the building. They would be like unhappy parents driving the family into divorce.

No. She'd known if she got stupid about him it would ruin everything. She had already started to care too much—so much she'd almost believed he was devastated by her rejection. But then he left. Just like that.

She'd done the right thing. Thank God, because otherwise she'd be miserable. Sleeping on the couch in an industrial office building over the weekend, crying and angry and heartbroken—that was bad enough, but to think it was unnecessary, that she'd made some kind of mistake—well, that would crush what little hope she had left.

With the thick smell of soy sauce and peanut oil wafting over from where Rachel stood across from her, Bev took a deep breath and slid her keyboard away from her on the desk, knowing she couldn't put it off forever. She'd have to tell people. Not everyone, and not today, but she had to start somewhere.

"He might not be coming back," Bev said. "He—he says he has some things to figure out."

Eyes wide, Rachel dropped into a chair. "Not coming back?"

"Probably not." She tried to smile.

Rachel's eyes widened further. "You figured it out, didn't you? About your grandfather's sick little plan for you guys?"

A hollow pit gaped open inside Bev's stomach. "Little plan?" She didn't want to hear this. Her voice dropped. "What plan?"

"Only one way to keep it in the family and put Liam in charge. He was totally obsessed with keeping it in the family. Not like he could set him up with Ellen—not that she'd mind being with a younger man, but they always hated each other. I bet he would have made it a condition of the will if that had been legal." Rachel's mouth curved up on one side.

Bev swallowed over the lump in her throat. Kate and Rachel both thought the same thing—

"I didn't think Liam would do it, going after you and all, but I guess he really, really loved his job," Rachel said.

That was too much. Bev stood up. "You should go eat your lunch and get back to work."

Rachel snapped her mouth shut, looked down at the white and red plastic bag of takeout in her lap. "But what are you going to do?"

Bev smiled tightly. "Do?"

"Without him. How will you keep it together?"

"He wasn't that indispensable. Nobody is."

"Liam was. You must be totally freaking out."

For the first time she wondered if she'd made the right choice in her right-hand woman. "We'll be fine. Everyone needs to have a little faith—in themselves most of all." She got to her feet and walked across the office to the door.

Rachel followed. "No, their faith in you is what matters."

"Then you better start singing my praises." *Whether you believe them or not.* Rachel might not love her, but at least she did an excellent job helping Bev fake it with everyone else. "Start with Engineering. They're the source of all the gossip around here. Maybe I can win over the sales guys after the Target deal."

"That's still on?"

"Damn, it better be. We'll be dead with out it," Bev said. "What are you doing?"

Rachel put her lunch down on the floor outside Liam's office and rattled the doorknob. "We better get in there and finish the presentation, don't you think? Where's your key?"

"I was just about to do that." She had been putting it off, loathe to make Liam's absence official. "Go have your lunch. I'd rather do this by myself."

Rachel hesitated, her hand still on the knob. "You sure? If it's as big a deal as you said—"

"Just for now. Let's meet at five and get it into boxes for tomorrow. That too late?"

"Five? I wish. I haven't been out of here before six in years."

"You should work on that."

"Gee, thanks, boss." Rachel picked up her lunch, rolled her eyes, and disappeared into her office.

Bev stared after her for a moment wondering why her family's most annoying characteristics seem to have been institutionalized at Fite. When Kate and her mother had watched her drive away from the Oakland house, their faces had looked exactly like that. The same wounded-but-disgusted expression.

She retrieved the master key from her purse and went back to open Liam's door, trying not to get emotional about it but getting emotional about it.

"It even smells like you," she muttered into the dark. Not wanting to deal with Rachel's moody scrutiny, she closed the door behind her and patted the wall to find the switch. She turned and looked at Liam's desk just as the delayed overhead lighting illuminated the disaster.

"Oh my God," she whispered.

His office had been torn apart.

Tattered clothing sagged off their hangers on the wall, torn sketches covered the chairs, and zigzagging piles of white foam core boards littered the floor. Bev turned around slowly, checked the unforced door latch and locked it. She went over to the desk on quiet feet, listening for any hint of another occupant but deciding she was alone.

She took a deep breath and forced herself to keep it together. In spite of the shocking mess all over the room, most of his desk was untouched. The computer, the cup of pens and pinking shears, the hangtag gun and strands of tape measure—all neat and tidy in the corner of his desk, just like Saturday night.

But the presentation—every garment and board and sketch and swatch—had been ruined.

He wouldn't do this.

A knock of the door made her heart jump into her throat. She pressed a hand over her chest and tried to breathe.

But who would? Could Ellen have slipped in without being noticed?

Her own mother?

The mere possibility filled her with raw, confused pain. In a daze, Bev walked slowly over to the door but didn't open it. "Yes?" Her voice sounded calm and far away.

"Bev?" Rachel asked.

Eager to commiserate, she reached to unlock the door—and stopped herself. For some reason she couldn't articulate to herself, she didn't want to let Rachel see the destruction. It would be horrible for morale, and the temptation for Rachel to gossip would be too great.

"Yes?" Bev let her hand drop to her side.

Silence. Then, "I'm done with lunch. I could meet now if you want."

"No. Five is still better for me."

After another long pause, Rachel said, "All right," and there was silence again.

Bev took a deep breath, grateful she didn't have to soothe Rachel as well as herself. She put her palm on the door and closed her eyes.

Think.

All she'd done since Liam had left was think. Nobody was left to talk to—she'd alienated her aunt, her mother, her sister, and now Liam.

She turned back around and stared at the carnage, jaw clenched. If not Liam or her family, then who would do this?

Who wants me to fail?

Her foot caught on a balled-up sweatshirt on the floor. She picked it up. It was the charcoal hoodie Liam had wanted Annabelle to wear, marked up with the dusty wheel-marks of an office chair.

Her first design, and he'd liked it.

She sank down in Liam's chair, picked up the plastic hangtag gun on the edge of the desk and pointed it at the door where she'd last seen him.

Unsatisfied with her target, she pointed it at her own head, the small metal needle poking her in the temple, and squeezed the trigger.

"Pow," she said.

Chapter 22

"LIAM, IT'S FOR you."

It was late Tuesday afternoon. April stood in the doorway waving the phone while Liam scraped the last stripes of peeling paint off his bedroom dresser. "I'm busy."

"You haven't slept in days. Take a break already. Lord."

"Who is it?"

"Not *her*. Unfortunately."

Warily Liam put down the scraper and wiped the sweat off his forehead with his wrist, studying April's face for any hint of matchmaking. Since Sunday she'd been the All Bev, All the Time channel, as though she'd never seen him have trouble getting over a woman before and suddenly was obsessed with uniting him with his one true soul mate.

He took off his gloves and snatched the phone out of her hands. "You just want the condo to yourself," he muttered, then into the phone he asked, "Hello?"

"Hi, Liam," came a depressed, familiar voice. Kimberly Jaeger, his ex, now at Target. She sounded even unhappier than usual.

"Hey, good thing you called," he said. "Change of plans."

"Oh, thank God," Kimberly sighed. "I was feeling guilty."

He closed his eyes. "Don't say it."

"I can't do it. If it was just you and me, unofficially chatting, you know, catching up—"

"You can still do that. Just do that with Bev."

The phone went quiet. "I can't."

"There's no difference. It's the same product line. Just I won't be there."

"Why do you care? You quit." She paused. "What happened—did she get too serious? I thought that was why you never fooled around at work anymore."

Liam frowned. "Who told you—?" he cut himself off and stared at the roll of blue masking tape on the floor. "Come to think of it, who told you anything? How did you know I left?"

"I used to work there, big guy. Things get around."

"Not to Minneapolis." He paced his room, kicking aside lumpy drop clothes and wishing he had a different way of working through depression than starting major home renovations. "Who, Kimberly?" His heart was starting to pound. "Other shit happened, weird shit. I need to know."

"It's nothing like that, I shouldn't have—"

"Was it Ellen? You know she—"

"I would never talk to that bitch. Are you kidding?"

"Who, then?"

"I won't tell you. She's—it's an old friend."

"Jennifer."

"No, I told you, I'm not squealing."

He took a deep breath. Time to try a new tactic. "You never were much of a squealer," he said, loading his voice with innuendo.

"Very funny."

But he could tell she was smiling. "Whoever it is, it's nobody you liked more than me. Right?"

"I didn't like anyone more than you. That was the problem."

"And now?"

"Now I'm cured," she said. "Now I can cancel meetings with you without any qualms whatsoever."

"You said you felt guilty."

"No more than I'd feel for any old friend."

"Then it wouldn't have anything to do with jealousy? Like, say, if you were feeling insecure about my feelings for Ed's granddaughter—who, by the way, you'd love to meet. You always said there wasn't a woman alive who could resist me when I turned on the charm."

"Only because you hoard it and then use it all at once. Very unfair."

"Well," he said, "Bev Lewis managed to deflect it. And me."

Kimberly laughed. "No kidding."

Liam had wanted her to be amused, but he himself wasn't in the slightest. "Aren't you curious to meet such a woman?"

"I am, actually," she said, and Liam felt hopeful, but she added, "but I can't. Zack would bust my ass. You, an old friend, the gold medal and all that, he'd forgive. Ed Roche's granddaughter—no."

He let out the breath he'd been holding. "We've busted our asses for you, Kimberley."

"I know. I'm sorry."

"Just one hour. Give her an hour. You might have something strong enough to pass on to Zack."

"What do you care? You quit."

He didn't want to care, but he couldn't just let Bev go under like this. No guilt could land on his head. "It's the principle," he said. "Most of the designs are mine. Lots of hard work went into them. I like to know they're put to use."

"Funny, you never seemed to get too attached to your ideas

when we worked together. That was your strength. You never got personal."

He snorted. "Yeah. Well. People change."

"Apparently. You really like this girl."

"Unfortunately."

"You really, really like her."

"Everyone does, whether they want to or not. Even George hand-delivers her packages."

She paused. "No."

"Really."

"What a nightmare." She laughed softly. "Good thing I'm not at Fite anymore. I would probably hate her."

"You'd want to, but then she'd bring you a Meyer lemon tart from Gerard's and you'd be her bitch forever."

"*Oh*," she moaned. "I *love* those."

"That's what I'm talking about. She'd know," he said. "In fact I'm surprised she hasn't sent you any yet. Like, Fed Ex or something."

"If she promised to bring me—" she stopped herself. "No, damn it, no. I called you because I had some weird old guilt, but I'm over it. If you're ever in the frozen north, give me a ring. Hey, you looking for a job? Because—"

"No." But he wondered. Beggars couldn't be choosers. And getting thousands of miles away from Bev had its appeal. "At least, not yet. I'm taking a little time off."

"Don't wait too long. People will forget about you."

Liam had the sick feeling one of the people forgetting him might be Bev. He dropped the phone on his unmade bed, went over to the window and stared out at the Bay Bridge, over the monochromatic grays of water and steel and fog, towards Oakland.

Not now, she wouldn't. Not if Fite went under because of him.

He scowled at his face reflected back at him in the glass, noticing the streak of paint in his hair. He touched it, trying to wipe it off, and his fingers came away sticky and red.

Not my problem. He turned away from the window and walked across the room to find a clean rag and finish what he'd started.

                                             ❧

To Bev's surprise, Rachel didn't show for their five o'clock meeting Tuesday evening.

"Nasty UTI," Rachel said when she called at six, just as Bev was giving up on her. "Sorry I couldn't call, but it was a bitch. I will totally be there first thing in the morning. The antibiotics should kick in by then."

"Don't worry about it," Bev said. "You need your rest."

But Bev wasn't happy about Rachel's defection. She had spent all day trying to resurrect the Target presentation, printing sketches off the design database and mocking up miniature boards out of new, compact foam core, using new swatches she pasted up herself, imitating as best she could. But it didn't look nearly as good.

They could only do their best, but hers might not be good enough.

Once the building had emptied out, she dragged her cat and her laptop and a stack of financial records upstairs with her, jogging up the stairwell so any stragglers didn't see her get off the elevator on her grandfather's old floor.

Locked up in her suite, she settled Ball next to her on the sofa, wrapped both of them up in the thick purple fleece she'd lifted from the sample yardage room and lost herself in the last two year's financial documents she'd printed out from the databases. Back at UCLA, to satisfy her father, she'd taken a series of business classes. She wasn't quite sure what she was looking for but kept turning pages, eventually catching on to Richard's accounting style.

Being in the Fite building after hours, pouring over sell-through numbers and fluctuating profits and enjoying it, Bev decided she wasn't angry with Hilda anymore. If she hadn't been so impossible, Bev would be there instead of here—and as crazy as Fite was, with its dysfunction and gossip, its unpredictable schedules and unreliable profitability and temperamental employees, she had to admit that she rather, sort of, kind of, totally *loved it.*

Or could have. She missed Liam. Fite wasn't the same without him.

I could have loved him.

She was an idiot. She already loved him. He'd wanted her and she'd chosen Fite and now she'd have neither.

Ball rose up in a stretch and padded up into her lap, a gesture of affection that had Bev fighting tears.

You're just tired. She hadn't slept well in weeks. Exhausted and lonely, of course she would start doubting herself, getting emotional, wanting the impossible.

She would never, ever let Liam have the chance to come and work at Fite again because he had given up and run.

Maybe you'll apply for a job when I'm gone, my ass, she thought, falling asleep where she lay with Ball in her arms, purple fleece between them and the cold night.

Just as the sun was coming up through the haze of fog Wednesday morning, her cell phone chirped and vibrated under the couch cushion, waking her from a fitful dream about dancing clothes—like *Fantasia* with supermodels.

Ball meowed and resettled herself facing the other direction, tail under Bev's nose. Bev wriggled to a sitting position, unearthed her phone, squinted at the unfamiliar area code before answering with a yawn.

"Oh, shoot—I woke you," a woman said. "I swore I'd never do that when I moved back east, but I didn't get a chance to call you yesterday and didn't want to put it off any longer."

Something about the woman's voice cut through Bev's sleep-dulled brain. She sat up straighter. "Who is this?"

The woman sighed. "I'm Kimberly Jaeger, from Target. I'm afraid I have to cancel the little meeting Liam may have mentioned."

Bev's throat went dry. "What?"

"It was never an official thing anyway, but as a courtesy I wanted to inform you and your staff of the changes needed due to the circumstances. I'm sure you understand."

"The circumstances—"

"With Liam no longer an employee."

"But—the designs are the same—you have to—"

"It would be a waste of our mutual resources," Kimberly said.

"Hey, don't worry about my end. They're already wasted. Might as well—"

"No. But I hope we get the chance to meet some day." She sounded like she meant it. "Best of luck to you."

"Just a few minutes—"

The phone clicked, decapitating her hope.

Her hand sunk down to her lap, thumb over the power button on her phone. She wasn't sleepy anymore.

Could Liam have called his old girlfriend out of spite—

No, she couldn't believe he would do that. Not without

telling Bev first, to rub her nose in it and teach her a lesson.

No, not even then.

Ball was still sleeping on the edge of the sofa. Bev ran her hand down her back, savoring her warmth, grateful she wasn't entirely alone. "Go ahead and sleep in, lazy butt." Bev tucked the fleece sample yardage around her. "I've got to take a shower and have a nervous breakdown."

She went out for a bagel before facing the tragedy in her office. She didn't know what was worse—that she'd recreated the best designs and somehow managed to display them on foam core in a semi-professional way and it was all for nothing, or that she was relieved she didn't have to show her efforts to anyone else. For all her work and pride at how far she had come, it probably wasn't good enough to land a big deal.

And now she didn't have to tell Rachel that the original presentation was sabotaged. She'd just hide it all away in a closet and tell her the meeting was canceled, and they'd find another source of capital—from somewhere—until the standard accounts signed their orders and money was flowing again.

Everything will be fine.

After leaving Rachel a message on her voice mail, she made her way across town to her car in the discount lot and drove west until Geary Street ended at the Pacific and the sky was a blinding white panorama of fog.

Parked in front of the Cliff House, squinting at the sea lions and the gulls squatting on the rocks, Bev sucked in an enormous breath and dialed her father's number.

"I was wondering if you'd call," he said.

"Hi, Dad. How are you?"

"Save your breath. What do you need?"

That got her. She pushed open the car door and stepped

outside into the cold, gasping as the hard wind blew her hair sideways across her face. "A little emotional support, first of all. Is that too much to ask?"

"I hear your mother's up there. Pushed all your buttons again, didn't she?"

She squeezed the phone in her hand, tempted to throw it over the concrete retaining wall to the rocky shore below.

"I need to ask you a favor," she said.

He chuckled. "Here we go. Lay it on me, sweetheart."

"Fite is having a short-term cash-flow problem—"

"Oh, Bev."

"Don't say it!" She picked up a pebble from the wall along the sidewalk and hurled it as hard as she could into the ocean. It was too small to see where it landed, if it even reached the water. "I'm hanging by a thread here. I'm so close. The last thing I need is another person who claims to love me putting me down and doubting my abilities."

"I was just going to say—"

"I know, I know. You told me not to try and I ignored you, and here I am crawling back to you for help. But I'm almost there, Dad. I'm working my ass off and I'm good at it. All I need is one little thing from you and I refuse to listen to all the reasons you think I'm going to fail." She sucked in a deep breath and bent over to the cracked sidewalk to find a bigger stone to throw.

He paused. "Your mother must have really done a number on you."

"Not just her. Kate. Ellen. You and Andy. Each one of you tells me what I can't do, why I'm not good enough, tough enough, whatever. Just because I'm not like you." She threw another rock, grunting with the effort and feeling a strain her shoulder. "I'm sick of it! Just help me out, all right?"

A gust of wind kicked up and whistled across the mouthpiece of her phone, deafening the line. If her father said anything she couldn't hear it. Feeling drained, she brushed the hair out of her eyes, sucking in another breath of ocean air, and got back in the car.

The phone was quiet. She pulled it away from her ear to read the display, see if he'd hung up.

He hadn't. She heard him clear his throat.

"First of all, let me apologize," he said finally.

Closing her eyes, she sank back into her seat and rubbed her shoulder. "It's okay. I shouldn't have lost my temper—"

"Hold on. You've had your say. Let me have mine."

She swallowed. "Sure. Go ahead."

"Thank you." He cleared his throat again. "First of all, I apologize for my bad taste in choosing your mother. I bear primary responsibility for that. She's never been the nurturing type and since I'm not either, you've been left holding the shit end of the stick."

"But—"

"Let me finish."

She bit her lip. "Sorry."

"However," he continued, "as much as I hate to admit it, you wouldn't be the terrific person you are without her DNA. And since there's nothing we can do about changing the past anyway, you'll just have to accept my condolences for your unlucky break in the mother department and move on."

Terrific person?

"Now, about this crazy idea you have that I think you're going to fail."

"It's not crazy. You practically said just that when we had lunch that day. Andy too."

"You misunderstood us. You'd never worked in a struggling corporation, people depending on you, lacking the resources to make it work. We were afraid you didn't realize what you were getting into. That you'd be unhappy." He paused. "Like us."

Her breath caught. She'd never thought he was unhappy with his work—just life in general. "You're unhappy?"

"Not always. But often. I see Andy falling into the same trap and it would kill me to watch you make the same mistake. No family, working a hundred hours a week, pissing your life away. And for what? I've made a mess of a couple marriages, but one thing I'll never regret is having you and Andy. The best thing that ever happened to me."

Bev wiped her eyes. "Oh, Dad."

"And it kills me that you think I'd want to rub your nose in your mistakes. If I've ever done that before, I'm sorry. My own father was like that and I never forgave him. Dead almost thirty years and I'm still shouting at him in my sleep."

She didn't know what to say. He'd never spoken about his father, never hinted at any unresolved pain. Her tears threatened to wash away her contacts; she dug into her purse for a tissue. "I always wondered about him."

"He wasn't easy but he provided for us. That was a man's job back then," he said roughly. "Can't live in the past, but I don't want to repeat it either. You've got to know I love you."

She smiled. "I know."

"And that I'm proud of you. Always have been. If I criticized your job it's just because I thought you deserved better. You do deserve better," he said. "This company of your grandfather's— they're lucky to have you."

She closed her eyes and felt the tears escape down her face. "Thank you," she whispered. "That means so much."

"And whatever I can do to help you out, I'm honored to do it. I wish I hadn't screwed up, driving you to wait this long to ask for my assistance," he said. "Andy feels the same way. He's chomping at the bit to fly up there and support you, but I told him we had to wait for an invitation. Out of respect."

She had to put the phone down to blow her nose. After she could speak, she lifted it back to her face. "Thank you, Dad."

He didn't respond right away. "I love you, sweetheart." He cleared his throat roughly. "So, now that that little Oprah moment is out of the way, what can I do for you?"

She watched a sea lion, balancing on the edge of a large rock in the surf, roll onto its back and wave its flippers like a child making a snow angel.

Then she looked at herself in the rearview mirror, into her bright, red-rimmed eyes, and felt a surge of power, love, and hope.

"I need Annabelle Tucker's direct phone number," she said, and smiled.

Chapter 23

WHEN BEV WALKED into Richard's office, he was combing his hair and staring off into space. She had to tap on the doorframe to get his attention. "Morning."

Clutching the comb in his palm, he glanced down at his desk, slapped a book shut, and frowned up at her. "You're early."

"I had to move up another meeting." She smiled and took a seat across from him, pretending not to stare at the Tom Clancy hardcover he had under his elbows. Nice to know somebody had a little extra time. "I got your message." First the Target call, then her dad, now Richard. Bad day to use the telephone.

"You need to make a decision today," he said. "Payroll's next Friday."

She looked into his droopy face. At first she had felt sorry for him getting fired and rehired and having so little respect among the other management, if Liam was any judge. But now she knew better. "I'm not going to lay off two dozen people just because you say so."

He frowned down at his desk "You got rid of everyone else who knew anything."

"I didn't get rid of anyone."

"Ellen would disagree."

"You don't work for her anymore." She looked down at the stack of spreadsheets in her lap, flipped through them until she found the worst one. "I have a question about some of your numbers."

His eyes darted up to her face. He didn't take the paper she held out to him. "Oh?"

"In fact, I have a question about one number in particular. One kind of big number. From June."

Richard's lower lip, shiny with spit, began to quiver. He closed his eyes. "I shouldn't have come back."

His confession wasn't as heartfelt as she'd wanted, but it would do. "You could have told me," she said. "I know how ... forceful ... my aunt can be."

"It was my idea," he said. "All these years, and then he left it to a stranger. It just didn't seem right."

"She wasn't the owner. You had no authority."

"One little bonus. She would pay you off, then come back. Full circle. I saw it as a Fite-related business expense." He pinched the bridge of his nose. "But then you didn't take it, and, well ... "

"She fired you. That must have been a shock."

"And she kept the money. Your grandfather had already taken out quite a bit of cash earlier this year." He dropped his head into his hands. "Fite just doesn't have the legs to pull through."

Bev took out another stack of spreadsheets, barely controlling the urge to shake him. "It might if you stop paying executives who don't work here anymore. Can you give me one good reason why you keep sending checks—very large checks—to Ellen's home address?"

"It's her salary."

"She quit!"

He glanced away. "Nobody filled out the paperwork."

Inside her, Bev felt the last strands of patience snap. She slammed her hands on the desk and leaned over it into Richard's face. "Drop the bullshit, Richard. I'm your boss. Me. Not her."

His face turned red. Then, eyes shining, he leaned under his desk, pulled out a briefcase, and flipped it open as he swiveled it around to her. "See? Just my lunch and the paper. You can walk me to the door."

"Hold on. Just hold on."

"Aren't you firing me?"

"Sit." She pointed at the chair. "There's more I need to know." She wanted to fire him—right after she'd impaled him with his Clancy hardcover—but she had to think of Fite first. If he left now, like this, with payroll hanging by a thread—

"I'm getting a lawyer," he said.

And they could not afford a lawsuit right now. She leaned closer to him. "You might not need one, Richard, if you help me."

He hovered over his chair, bracing his hands on the desk, and shook his head. "Right."

"You know I'm desperate."

His eyes fixed on her, unblinking. "Fite really is in trouble."

"I believe it. But is it as bad as you've been saying?"

"We can't go on like this indefinitely. If we lay off the numbers I told you, the rest of us should be good for another year," he said. "Ellen said you'd be gone by then."

Don't kill him. Later, maybe. Just not yet. "I've given up too much to walk away now." Her nose was only inches from his. "Or even a year from now. I've alienated my mother, my sister, given up my apartment, been kicked out of my house, turned away—" she closed her eyes and thought of Liam's hands sliding over her hips, "—money, more money I've ever had in my life—and after all that I still don't regret a thing. Even keeping you around is going to turn out to be good—for both of us."

He stared at her. "You're not going to fire me?"

"Not even if you want me to."

"You should. What I did was very unethical."

"I believe in second chances. Fite just needs a little time to get its mojo back." She pointed a finger at him. "Without any layoffs. If Liam says you can work miracles I believe it. He's not the type to throw around compliments."

"Liam said that?"

"He did."

Richard pursed his lips, squeezed them between his fingers, and sighed through his nose. "I can buy you another two months," he said. "After that you can include me in the two dozen."

&

It took her three days to reach the teen pop star she'd first met as an incontinent, hyperactive five-year-old.

"Oh, I totally got it, Bev," Annabelle said that Saturday morning, sounding short of breath. From the sound of the music and the humming machines in the background, Bev guessed she was at the gym. "Don't stress about a thing."

Bev was on a long walk through Golden Gate Park, sucking in as much fresh, foggy air as she could after a week of living and sleeping in the Fite building. For once getting her heart rate up felt really, really good. Nobody needed to know she was wearing a Fite bra and Power Panties, or that her new crosstrainers made her want to break into a run. Liam couldn't nag or tease or pressure her to do anything anymore, because he was gone.

Because he left.

After she'd rejected him.

Bev massaged her temples. "Whatever you do, I need to know it's okay with your mother."

"My mom? Please. She wants me to accidentally release a sex tape on my eighteenth birthday."

"No!" Bev remembered Tina Tucker as being a bit . . . ambitious . . . about her daughter, but wow.

"It's something I was going to do anyway. I'll just make sure to wear Fite when I do it," Annabelle said, laughing when Bev squealed in protest. "Not the sex tape. Something else. Anything in particular you're marketing right now?"

Bev shoved aside her memory of Annabelle gluing macaroni to empty toilet paper rolls, feeling ancient at thirty. "Something not too sexy. Something other girls could wear, not just a pop star."

"No, you've got it all wrong, Bev. I am the pop star. That's why they'll want it."

Bev smiled, grateful but uneasy. "I'll mail you something new we're working on. Just a hooded sweatshirt, but it's got a huge Fite logo that will stand out in pictures."

"Send me more than that," Annabelle said. "I'll improvise."

"You don't have to go crazy—"

"Leave it to me, Bev. I'm really good at this stuff." Then the machine in the background came to a sudden stop, and Bev could hear her gulping down water. "I was ready to take the Annabelle brand to the next level anyway."

"Promise me you'll show your mother first."

"Bev, she so doesn't care."

"Humor me."

"Tell you what. Send me extra Fite merch, and she'll place them herself. She loves underground marketing. Since I fired her as my manager she's been kinda bored."

Poor Tina. "I'll send a truckload." Bev thanked her again and hung up to get to work. She swung around so fast she nearly collided with a trio of cyclists coming up behind her. One of the guys screamed, careening off the road while his friends laughed and weaved around her, Lycra-butts pumping. She watched them ride off around a grove of eucalyptus, mentally screen-printing Fite logos on each skinny ass.

She had to get back to Fite to write up the cut sheets and sample requests so they could start working first thing Monday morning. If she was fast enough, she thought, breaking into a jog, she could find enough new stuff lying around the showroom to make it into the Saturday afternoon mail.

Liam wouldn't see that she ran east through the rest of the park, all the way down the panhandle and up and down through the lower Haight, across town and south of Market Street. Liam wouldn't see anything.

Because Liam had *left*.

❧

One week without Fite and Liam was restless, disoriented, cranky, and bored out of his mind.

After two weeks he started seeing things. Hallucinating, like a shipwreck victim on a raft in the middle of the ocean, seeing bottles of water and ten-course meals everywhere. Except what he saw, while he washed the dishes and painted the trim in his bathroom and replaced the garbage disposal, was Bev standing next to him, sharing in his chores, in his life. Sometimes—all right, often—she was naked, which was some consolation.

The third week, things got scary. On this Monday evening drive over to Oakland he could see Bev sitting next to him in the passenger seat, disturbingly with no skin showing, because going to have weekly dinner at Mom's was just the sort of thing people did together. Committed, boring, married people.

"Thank God somebody's going to feed me," April said. It was

his sister, not Bev, who sat next to him as they passed onto the eastern span of the bridge. "I've been starving since you tore up the kitchen."

"Property comes with responsibilities," he said. "I've been putting maintenance projects off too long."

"Replacing the tile countertops with hand-crafted concrete was hardly necessary."

"You don't like it, get your own place."

She sighed. "I wish you'd just call her."

When they pulled up the road to his mother's house, he only glanced at Bev's house, determined to be relieved if her RAV4 wasn't in the driveway.

But it wasn't in the driveway, and when the dogs burst out of the house and ran across the yard to nibble on his legs, Liam wasn't relieved. He hadn't been breathing well since they pulled off on Broadway, and now, realizing he wouldn't see her today—

His mother waded through the wriggling puppies and put her arm around his waist.

"He still hasn't called her," April said.

Trixie said, "He will," and for once left it at that.

When they went into the house, Mark was sitting at the kitchen table surrounded by Legos and a laptop, drinking beer and wearing an apron. "I'm making Mom a new napkin holder. Robotic." He grinned. "I've programmed it to dispense on voice commands."

Liam patted him on the back. "To think you almost didn't get into MIT. What a waste that would have been."

"Blow me," Mark said, and the machine in his hands beeped and raised a lever. "I hear you're unemployed too."

"And me too!" April popped a stuffed olive in her mouth, looking at their mother. "Don't worry. Liam hates being a bum.

You'll only have two losers to support soon." She reached over the kitchen table and hit the button on the flat screen TV mounted to the wall.

"I don't mind," Trixie said. "It gives us more time together." She squeezed Liam again and sat next to Mark and the Legos. "Plus, Mark is an excellent cook."

Liam opened his mouth to make a joke, insult him in his loving, brotherly way, but he didn't have it in him. So he got himself a beer instead, and when the TV seemed too loud and the kitchen too crowded for his mood, he wandered back to the porch to see the dogs and remember the last time he'd been there.

Bev had rejected him, but—it hadn't been easy. He saw how she'd looked at him, as if he'd come fresh from Gerard's bakery in a warm paper bag. It had hurt him at the time, thinking she only wanted his body—

"I'm such a sissy," he muttered.

"Shut up," April said, coming up behind him. "It had to happen eventually."

"Becoming a sissy?"

"No, you big homophobe. A human being." Then, to his shock, April threw her arms around his chest and smiled up at him. "I'm so happy for you."

"I want to kill myself, and you're happy."

"You're just afraid she doesn't love you back. But she might. She gave you that look."

"Look?"

April opened her eyes wide, dropped her mouth open, and panted.

Liam frowned at her. "I'm in love with a zombie?"

Her face broke into a smile and she squeezed him so hard his ribs creaked. "I'm so happy for you."

He sighed through the pain. "I'm going to have to go back."

"But we just got here," April said. "I am not leaving before we eat."

"No, I mean to Fite."

"Yay!" she said, squeezed him one more time until he cried out.

"Just until I can get another big deal back on track. So I don't have to feel guilty." *And she can see what she's missing.* He sucked in his gut and ran his hands through his hair. She could gaze and yearn.

"New shirt?" April asked. "Kind of tight, isn't it?"

"Is it?" He frowned down at himself before he noticed she was smiling. "Cut that out."

"You're so insecure." She tilted her head and studied him. "Mom says it's because you were a fat kid."

He could feel the blood rush to his face. After all these years, to have phantom buttons wired to unwanted nerves. He rolled his eyes. "No, it's because my father didn't love me enough."

"Sorry, that's my excuse. You were his favorite."

"Only after I started breaking records," he said. "I was always one meet away from being thrown aside."

"That's not true."

"He used to taunt me, threatening to train Mark to swim instead—"

April laughed. "Mark sinks."

"—and when I didn't take that seriously, he enrolled him in chess camp. He was going to be the next Bobby Fischer, and to hell with me."

Her voice got soft. "I remember that. He went away all summer."

"Poor Mark. You were right. I had it good." He sipped his

beer. "He was such a shitty father."

She bit her lip and frowned into her glass. "I hate to hear you say it. He can't defend himself." She sighed. "He was okay to me, I guess. I was just, you know, *there*."

Liam tousled her hair. "You're never just 'there,' April, but you were a girl and you were the baby," he said. "I used to wish Mom would dump him and marry someone else so you and Mark could have a new dad. By then I knew I was stuck with him. He'd invested too much in me to give up, but I wished I could do something for you guys."

"He's gone, Liam. Put him out of your mind."

Liam finished his beer. "Actually he's not the one on my mind these days."

"Great. Keep thinking about her."

As if I could stop. He was still afraid of turning into his father, of bullying a theoretical wife and their theoretical children, but— who was he kidding? He wanted her with an ache that had spread into every corner of his body. If anyone could look out for herself and the little people around them, it was Bev. She'd already proven that.

He put his arm around his sister and guided her back towards the kitchen. "You better sleep here tonight. I tore up the condo's guest bathroom before we left."

"And she's next door," April said.

Hopefully.

Mark was standing, pot in hand, by the kitchen table. "The macaroni and cheese is ready."

"Like, from a box?" April asked, crestfallen.

"That's my boy." Liam slapped Mark on the back just as he noticed the images flashing across the TV. He froze with one hand resting on Mark's shoulder.

"Hey," April said. "Isn't that Annabelle Tucker? What is that thing she's—sorta—wearing?"

Liam stared at the screen, stepped closer. Then he smiled, happiness swelling up in his chest. "Fite," he said. "The Bev version."

Trixie whistled. "Holy moly."

"Nice," Mark said, staring at the TV, blushing.

That's my girl. Licking his lips, Liam reached into his pocket. "Time to chat with my friends at Target again."

Chapter 24

THAT SAME EVENING, on the other side of the San Francisco Bay, Bev toasted Rachel with a flute of champagne. "Here's to Fite. I couldn't have done it without you." It had been a long couple of weeks, but Annabelle had outdone herself. Fite wasn't going out of business for a while.

Rachel tapped her glass against Bev's and sipped, eyes on the laptop propped open on the conference room table. The TMZ headline read: "A-TUCK FITES THE POWER."

"I never imagined wearing a hoodie quite that way," Rachel said.

Bev clicked on the photo to enlarge.

To make the headlines they needed, Annabelle had worn a small Fite sweatshirt zipped up around her hips like a skirt, lavender hiking boots, a navel ring, a Fite bra—and nothing else.

Rachel poured herself another glass. "Is she wearing underwear?"

"Yes," Bev said. "See? Right there. Plenty of underwear." I have not corrupted an innocent sixteen-year-old. Her idea. Her idea.

"Oh, got it. Same purple as the boots." Rachel looked dazed. "You told her to do that?"

"I asked her to wear Fite. She—improvised."

Rachel sucked down her second glass of champagne. "Damn. Just—damn." She slammed the glass down on the table. "You're not what I expected."

Bev wasn't surprised Rachel was depressed, just that she wasn't trying to hide it anymore. She got out the shopping bag under her chair and took out her package. "I got you something." The frame was two by three feet, wrapped in heavy brown paper and bubble wrap. "To show my gratitude."

Rachel stopped in the middle of pouring a third glass and frowned. "You got me something?"

"I know you didn't like being the fit model, but you did it anyway. I'm convinced it made a difference—"

"Not the way 'A-Tuck' wears it."

"—and it will make a difference," Bev continued, "now that Target and Macy's and Sports Authority and whoever is coming to us. We're ready for them."

Glass in one hand, Rachel picked at the tape holding the package together. Bev handed her a pair of scissors and set down her own glass to watch.

"It's a picture?" Rachel banged her glass on the table, hand shaking, to tear the paper off the glass more quickly. When the image was exposed, her face, flushed from the champagne, faded to gray. "Where did you find this?"

Bev leaned forward to study the enlarged photograph. "He looks so happy. I wish I had known that side of him. Or any side, really."

Rachel threw her an enraged look over her shoulder. "Where? Where did you get this?"

"Here," Bev said. Rachel scanned the walls of the conference room for clues, but Bev said, "No, here in the building. In his rooms upstairs."

Rachel glared at her then turned her attention back to the photograph. "Of course. Your building." She pushed the frame towards Bev, tears in her eyes. "This is your property."

Bev didn't move. "No, that's a gift. I'm sure you'd like to keep it." She looked down at her grandfather and Rachel embracing and happy in a living room she didn't recognize. "I know you loved him. You don't have to pretend anymore. All right? You don't have to pretend."

Rachel gazed down at the photograph with a tiny smile forming in the corner of her mouth.

Then she looked at Bev, the smile gone.

"Go to hell," she said.

☙

"What do you mean, she's not here?" Liam asked.

Blocking the doorway of Ed's old house, Kate chewed gum and glared.

"She has to be." He looked at his watch. "It's past eight. When did she go out? She's not answering her cell."

Kate snapped her gum, narrowing her eyes. "Are you fucking with me?"

"Not at the moment."

"That explains the broken window." Her upper lip curled. "You didn't know she'd left. Well, nice try, but we're not afraid of you. Or anything else."

She started to close the door, but Liam stuck his foot inside and braced it open. "Broken window? Left when?"

Kate tried to kick him, but he was prepared. Within a second, Kate was hopping on one leg with the opposite foot in Liam's calm grip.

"It wasn't me, but I know who it is." Kimberly had been thrilled to hear from him, tell him about her calls from Rachel, grovel for Bev to come to Minneapolis.

"Oh, right." Kate thrust her leg towards his groin.

He lifted her foot higher and unbalanced her. "Listen to me, you nut. It's her assistant at Fite. I'll give you her address. Go kick *her*."

She buckled her knee, fell onto the floor, flipped onto her back, and twisted around to kick him with her free leg. "Let go of me!"

He maneuvered out of range but kept her foot in the air. "Bev —might be—in trouble!" he said in between thrashings. "She's not answering her phone—and now you say she's not here—will you just fucking listen to me?"

Kate landed a hard kick in his shins, grunted, "There!" then relaxed. "One minute," she said, panting on her back, "then your ass is grass."

He flung her leg away and strode into the house. A moment of nostalgia crept over him, remembering Bev prancing around the house in her Fite pajamas, eating her Wonder bread, looking damn adorable . . .

"Tell me about the window." He held up a hand to stop her eye-rolling indignation. "I don't know why Rachel has lost it, but I assure you she's your winner."

Kate frowned at him but seemed to consider it. "I admit I was surprised about the window. Since you seemed to like keeping Bev around."

To his annoyance he felt his face grow warm. "When did you notice the window?"

"In fact, I was starting to think you were getting kind of stupid about her. Your mom talks about her constantly."

"The window?"

She flopped next to him on the couch. "Last week. I had

meant to be gone by then and my mom, too, but—well, since Mom kicked Bev out she didn't want to leave the house empty."

He sat up straighter. "Your mom what?"

"We assumed she was at your place," she said. "She isn't at your mom's. I checked."

"Very sisterly of you." He knew where she had to be, and he didn't like it. He was on the wrong side of the bay.

Kate crossed her arms over her chest and narrowed her eyes. "Funny she didn't tell you about it."

"I have to talk to her." He started to get up but Kate stretched her leg out and put her foot on his chest.

"Why would her assistant break windows and shit?"

He stared at her foot until she withdrew it. "Bev made her a vice president, but she seems to be carrying a grudge. She was quite close to your grandfather."

She wrinkled her nose. "How old is this chick?"

"Twenty-eight?" He thought back to her last birthday party. "Something like that."

"Go, Gramps. Yuck, that is so gross."

"I could be wrong. But there were rumors."

"Grandfather sure had a sick sense of humor, on top of being a horndog." She scooted over and slapped him on the knee. "Well, I am glad you weren't the one. I didn't really think it was you, not after I saw the way you looked at her."

He gave her a cold look and stood up. "You just like an excuse to hurt people. Unlike your sister."

"That's not true, I—"

Liam was already across the room opening the front door. "Rachel still thinks Bev lives here, so lock up."

She came after him. "I can take her. What does she look like?"

"Just lock up."

"I better come with you. You have a few good moves, but you don't have a killer instinct. This chick plays dirty."

"Stay here and tell your mother—"

Just then a white SUV pulled into the driveway and blinded him. He held up his arm to shield his eyes.

Kate waved. "Hi Mom!"

Shit.

Kate skipped past him and tapped on the driver's side glass. "He's looking for Bev! She's not with him!"

Gail left the engine and lights on and got out of the car. He didn't move, so she came over. "Where is she?"

"I'm trying to find out."

"If she ran out on you, I'm not helping you find her," Gail said.

"I haven't seen her in weeks. When I left Fite."

Gail's eyes went wide. "But she's been staying at your place. She must have been."

"No."

Kate ran over to the house, locked the front door, and came back. "We'll take the Lexus."

Gail gripped his arm. "But where can she be? She'd never pay for a hotel."

Gratified she was concerned about her kid, Liam reached for his keys. "I'll call you as soon as I find her."

Gail blocked him. "We'll go together."

He looked into her face, so unlike Bev's—except for the eyes. She had Bev's eyes. Sooner or later he'd have to learn how to get along with all of her crazy relatives.

Later would be better. "I'll call you when I find her," he said, stepping into the dirt to get around her.

In front of him, the SUV's passenger door swung open, and a thin brunette climbed out.

"Hello, Liam," Ellen said.

Startled, he froze, shoes in the flowerbed, and saw amusement flicker across her face. "Ellen," he said. He turned to jump over the bushes into his mother's driveway.

"I hear you've adopted little Beverly," Ellen called after him. "Interesting strategy. I didn't think you had it in you."

Gail strode over and ushered Kate into the car. "She hasn't been with him. We're going to find her now."

"No, I am." Liam pulled out his keys. "I promise I'll call."

"What's the hurry?" Ellen tugged the lapels of her jacket closer to her chin. "Let's see the house so I can send pictures to Johnny."

"What do you mean, what's the hurry?" Gail said, her voice rising to a squeak. "Kate was sure she was with Liam, enjoying herself for once, but instead..." She bit her lip and looked past the house at the San Francisco skyline.

Camera in hand, Ellen took off the lens cap and aimed past them to the sunset over the Golden Gate. "That view will get them," she said. "But I'll have to do the interior shots tomorrow. It's too dark now."

Gail spun around to face her sister. "We are having a crisis here!"

Liam opened the door to his car. "Don't worry. What's your number, Gail? I'll call as soon as I find her."

She frowned at him. "You seem to know where she is."

"Of course he does," Ellen said. "He's not an idiot."

"Are you calling me an idiot?" Gail demanded.

"Just use your brain. Where did Daddy hide out when he wanted to get away?"

Gail touched her forehead. "You think she's at Fite?"

Ellen aimed the camera at the house and clicked this way and that. "Duh."

"You can stop taking pictures, you heartless bitch," Gail said. "There is no way in hell I'm giving my house to any child of yours."

As eager as Liam was to find Bev, he found himself unwilling to leave just yet.

Ellen turned away and took another picture. "Such a drama queen."

Hands balled into fists, Gail swung around, headed for her car. "Too bad the locks were changed or you might be able to go inside." She got in, slammed the door, and kicked the engine into reverse.

Ellen looked over her shoulder. "Damn it!" She shoved the camera in her pocket. "Don't you dare—!" Arms waving, she ran down the driveway after the departing car. Gail screeched out into the road, blasting the horn, and was gone.

Realizing he shouldn't have lingered, Liam hopped inside his own car and started the engine. But Ellen, now stranded, stood at the end of his mother's driveway staring at him through the rearview mirror.

She didn't move until he gave up, leaned over, and pushed open the passenger door for her to join him.

ॐ

Liam would've been proud of her.

She could've had Richard fire Rachel and spare herself the discomfort; instead, the new, tough, managerial Bev had arranged a private confrontation, determined to see it through.

Big mistake.

"Why is it so hard to admit you loved him?" Bev said. "Lots of people did."

"Not like me," Rachel said.

Bev studied her face under the copper-colored bob, healthy and young and miserable. "How long—when did you, the two of you—"

"What?"

"Were you together a long time?"

"You think—" she shook her head, shuddering with disgust. "That was the worst part about keeping it a secret. People are so sick."

Bev stared at her, feeling stupid. Then, finally, she understood. "You're related to him. To us."

Rachel snorted. "You are such a genius."

It was all there—the bitterness, the intelligence, even the shape of her upper lip. Bev held up her glass for another toast. "So, we're what—cousins?"

"No!" Rachel shook her head. "He was my *father*."

For a second Bev imagined her slicing her hand off and throwing her into the bowels of the Death Star. "An aunt. I should have seen the resemblance."

"We are nothing alike," Rachel said. "You've been nothing but bubbles and sunshine since you got here, and I can't stand it. Cookies, smiles, puke."

"I meant your resemblance to Ellen. It's uncanny. Well, all right, what do you want? Or, actually, what do you think you want? What did you think would happen? The company runs out of money, I leave, and . . . ? You step in?"

"Yeah."

"And how did you plan on doing that? Waving your birth certificate?"

"I have something better—cold, hard cash."

"Ah," Bev said. "He gave you money."

"You bet he did."

"You're rich, but you resent me for getting the company?"

"He loved me!"

"Be grateful for that. He barely knew my name."

"I know! I could have killed you!"

Bev shuddered, looked down at her grandfather's smiling face under Rachel's hand. "You can see how much he cared about you right there in the picture."

"But I wanted Fite. He knew that."

"Tell me, Rachel, did my grandfather strike you as a particularly enlightened man? When it came to women?"

Rachel's thumb traced the corner of the frame. "He was getting better. I'm hardly a girly girl, and I proved myself, slaved for him—"

"And forgive me, but your last name really is Farley, isn't it?" Not Roche.

Her blue eyes flashed. "He knew my mom had to give me my stepfather's name."

For a moment Bev wished she had confronted Rachel during the day. When other people were around. Rachel had a wild, unhinged look that was making her palms sweat. "But who did he promote to be executive vice president?" she asked softly.

Rachel slammed the picture down on the table. Bev jumped back, clutching her heart, darting her gaze between Rachel's twisted face and the diagonal crack that had appeared across the framed glass. "That dick was supposed to marry me. That was the plan. Late nights wiggling my ass in his face—hah! I told Daddy he had to be gay because he never slept with any of the women at work, let alone me. But Daddy just told me I wasn't his type, and sure enough, you waddle in here with your big boobs and your Roche name and bam! Suddenly Liam pretends he's in love." She picked up a glass of Champagne and drained it. "But you saw through that. Now it's just us."

Bev clasped her hands together to stop their visible shaking. "Your father planned for you and Liam to get together?" She nudged the frame and its broken glass away from the edge of the table. Perhaps she was glad she'd never met the old man.

"It was my idea, but Daddy liked it. I promised him I'd name our kids Roche, and nothing would ever have to change."

"Lovely," Bev said, swallowing over the lump in her throat.

"At first I was pissed you slept with him, but now I'm grateful because you drove him away." Rachel leaned back, smiled. "You'll be happy to take my money. Anything to save the company, right?"

"Not anything."

"Come on, you were never going to stick around. The only reason you didn't sell out to Ellen was because one, she's a bitch, and two, you met Liam and were like, get me some of that. Well, they're both gone, and I'm here and totally loaded." She pinched a shard of broken glass in the frame between her thumb and index finger and poked it into the print underneath.

Bev stood up. "I don't want your money. You'll need it when you leave here."

"You won't fire me. It will take months for the A-Tuck money to flow in," she said, pouring herself another glass of Champagne. "Besides, we're family. You're too nice to get rid of me."

Her conviction was so strong, so disgusted, and so unfounded, Bev couldn't help but laugh—just as Liam burst into the room. Laughter dying, Bev swayed on her feet and gripped the table for balance.

His eyes found hers. They stared at each other across the room, everything else falling away, even Rachel's smug malevolence.

It felt so good to see him she smiled, dumb and happy, before she remembered he had abandoned her in her time of need and was probably showing up now to gloat about using Annabelle Tucker.

She sank back down into her chair, looked down into her empty glass. "What are you doing here?"

"Your assistant has been screwing with you."

"I know." Bev picked up a scrap of black Lycra-cotton blend and began wiping away the condensation on the table from the champagne bottles. "Turns out she's family. Explains everything. She's my aunt, can you believe that? My aunt."

He nodded. "She told you?"

"You knew?" She could see he did. "All this time, and you—"

"Ellen told me just now." He looked over his shoulder just as her aunt appeared in the doorway.

"You're going to believe him?" she asked Bev. "I'd be a little more suspicious if I were you."

"Don't worry, sis," Rachel said into her glass between swallows. "She's got him all figured out." She sounded drunk.

Liam gazed at Bev from across the room with a melting, hungry expression that took the air out of her lungs.

He hadn't shaved in a while, and his hair was messy and flopped unevenly over his left eye. He wore jeans—not designer Casual Friday jeans, but faded, torn, paint-stained Levi's. Above that he wore a royal blue dress shirt, the one he used to wear to work, but was now wrinkled and unbuttoned and failed to cover a plain white undershirt.

She saw his big heart in his eyes, and realized she'd made a horrible mistake.

"Of course I believe him," she said, never taking her eyes off of him. "I thought she was my grandfather's girlfriend."

Rachel made a disgusted sound that Liam ignored. "Me too," he said, smiling at her, warm and warmer, and she felt her heart beat faster with each breath.

Ellen picked up a bottle, grimaced at the label, and dropped it back on the table. "Don't be a sucker. Father told him everything else, why not that?" She looked at Bev. "Get ready for him to suddenly want to get serious. Now you're the only one standing between him and the one thing he really wants."

"Don't listen to her," Liam said.

He'd already suggested they get serious, and she'd doubted him, insulted him, pushed him away. "Is that true, Liam? You want to get serious about me?"

He didn't hesitate. "Yes."

Her breathing, already fast, became tight and uneven, a conscious struggle. "Oh?"

Gail burst into the room. "You're all right!"

"Mom?" Then her sister popped up behind her. "Kate? What are you doing here?"

Gail rushed over and grabbed Bev's shoulders. "You were supposed to be with him. Liam. I thought you were with Liam."

Bev stared at the black circles under her mother's eyes. "Were you crying?"

Gail grabbed her face in her cold hands. "Have you really been sleeping here? In this old building? *Alone?*"

Stuck in her mother's grip, stunned by her mother's visible worry, Bev said, "You wouldn't back down. I had nowhere else to go."

Gail closed her eyes. Mascara clumped unevenly near her nose on one side. "I never thought you would leave because of anything I said." Her eyes popped open. "Since when have you ever listened to anything I say?"

"I always listen."

"But you're so independent. It used to drive me crazy that you wouldn't wear the clothes I picked out, make friends with the girls I liked, do anything with your hair." Gail released one cheek to stroke Bev's hair, then glanced around the room.

The others were staring at them.

"Well, she's all right," Gail said, waving at them. "Everyone can go now. My daughter will come home with me." She put an arm around Bev's shoulders.

"Not right now, Mom, but thank you." She put an arm around her waist and gave her a squeeze before she wiggled herself free. "How did you get in, by the way? The doors should be locked."

Kate pushed past them and walked over to Rachel. "This the ho?"

Rachel rose unsteadily to her feet. "He was my father. My father. Who the hell are you?"

"Rachel, meet your other niece, Kate," Liam said. He pushed Kate closer and moved over to Bev. "Does she kick women, too?"

Bev's mouth went dry. *Don't think about him now.* She caught a hint of cologne and leaned into him. *And for God's sake, don't smell him.*

Kate put her hand on Rachel's shoulder. "So, you're the bitch who broke into our house."

Rachel slapped her hand away. "That's Aunt Bitch to you."

One swift kick, and Rachel was down. Bev tried to stop her sister, but Liam put an arm around her, trapping her against his body, and she could only watch as Kate got violent with the woman who had caused so much trouble.

Knee pressed into Rachel's throat, Kate said, "If it weren't for you I'd be home right now, Aunt Bitch."

Bev broke away from Liam. "Let her up, Kate!"

"This person claims to be—" Gail swung around to Ellen. "Is it true?"

Ellen shrugged. "Look at her. What do you think?"

Gail scowled at Rachel. "I think she looks like Grandma Roche."

"That's what I thought," Ellen said.

"You didn't tell me," Gail said.

"You hated my guts."

Gail looked at her. "You hated mine."

Ellen raised an eyebrow. "Only because you left. I was fifteen, Gail. You left."

"Dad kicked me out."

"You could have written."

Gail laughed unsteadily. "I could have written," she said. "You have no idea what I was going through."

"When you left," Ellen said, "so did Dad. I didn't see him for six months."

"But—where—who stayed with you?"

Ellen's face was cold. "Mom was dead. You ran away. Dad—" She cleared her throat. "I finally found him here. I don't know what he did at first, before the kitchen and bathroom were installed, but when I tracked him down he seemed pretty damn happy. Had everything he needed." She turned around, her back to the room.

Gail was the first to speak. "So you were alone?" She went over to her sister. "But you were—didn't anyone—"

Ellen shrugged. "At first I had trouble with things like groceries and permission slips and bills, but Dad left the checkbook and kept the account loaded. Once I got good at forging his signature, I was fine. I'm tough. I survived."

"Oh, Ellen." Gail's voice shook. She hesitated then put her hand on Ellen's shoulder.

"He never did come back," Ellen said. "And neither did you."

Gail burst into tears.

Bev felt Liam moving closer to her, and looked at him to see the concern in his eyes. She realized her cheeks were wet.

"Damn," Kate said, distracted by the scene.

"Get off of me." Rachel rolled out of range, kicked her, and staggered to her feet. Eyes wild, she looked at Bev. "Tell her to leave me alone."

Bev was still staring at Ellen's back. "Tell her yourself."

Rachel, shaking, held her finger up, pointing at each of them in the room in rotation like the spinner in Chutes and Ladders. "All of you, do you hear that? Leave me alone!"

"That will be easier when you actually leave," Bev said. "And when you stop driving over to Oakland to break things."

"You will never have his money," Rachel said. "Not one of you."

Ellen turned around. "What money?" Her cheeks were splotchy.

"You thought I wanted to be part of the family," Rachel spat out. "As if that was some kind of fucking prize."

Ellen's voice dropped. "What money?"

Bev leaned over to pick up the framed photograph and got to her feet. "She got some money."

"What money?" Gail stood shoulder to shoulder with Ellen.

"He told me he gave it to charity. Putting a down payment on his immortal soul," Ellen said. "You didn't let on a thing."

"He found out he was dying before Christmas. He wanted to look out for me," Rachel said.

"And so he did." Bev tilted the picture up, careful not to tip out the broken glass, and bent the back out to release the photo, which she carried over to Rachel. "It's time for you to go," she said, taking Rachel's arm tightly in her hand.

"But who is she?" Gail asked. "Is she our sister?"

After a moment Ellen laughed. Her voice surprisingly gentle, she said, "I'll explain everything later."

Bev forced Rachel out into the hall, and she went easily, probably because Kate was assuming another fighting position. When they were ten feet out of the room in the dim corridor and alone, Bev said, "One year from now, you are welcome to come back here." She loosened her grip on Rachel's arm. "We'll go out for coffee. We'll talk. I won't give you a job, but I promise to listen."

"Sure you'll be here? Any of you?" Rachel pulled her arm free and rubbed it. "You think it'll be easy to keep this place running without me? Without my money?"

"Without you breaking windows and ripping up samples?"

She pinched her lips together, looked away. "I wanted to believe you were for real. I did, for a while."

"I am real."

"You started screwing Liam. And then, the fit modeling. I really, really hate fit modeling."

"Noted." Bev shoved the picture at her. "You'll never do it again."

"Nothing works here without me making it work."

Bev nodded towards the exit behind her. "Maybe nothing will break, either." She turned and saw Liam watching the exchange from the conference room doorway, back lit and huge and unreadable.

Did he come back for Fite, or for her?

Rachel was still standing there in the semi-darkness. "I hated

—what I did to the Target presentation—that just about killed me." She burst out with a noise that was a laugh or a sob. "All that work. It was horrible."

"You need a break, Rachel. Book a trip somewhere, bring a friend. Get away from this place for long enough to make a difference." Bev sighed. "And if anything weird happens around here or at the Oakland house, to Liam or to anyone in my—our—family, I'm calling up your mother in Borrego Springs and telling her everything. She worked here for twenty years, right? I don't think she'd like to know what you've been up to."

Rachel gasped. "How—"

"Do you understand?"

The hallway went quiet. Bev could see the conference room light reflected in Rachel's eyes.

"Yes," Rachel said.

Bev said, "See you when you get back."

Chapter 25

STANDING IN THE hallway, watching Bev stride back towards the conference room, Liam longed to haul her up into his arms.

Not yet. She still had the rest of her family to deal with.

Eyes locked with his, she stopped a few feet in front of him. The shadowy hallway swallowed up her dark hair, emphasizing her pale face like an actor on stage. He stared back at her.

"Nicely done," he said finally, smiling.

She gave him a warm, tentative smile that made his throat ache. Then she shrugged a shoulder, laughing off his compliment. "Thanks. It got a little messy."

"You were great."

She stared at him, glanced past him into the conference room. "Will you wait for me?"

He reached out and caressed her hair, watching her lips part while he stroked the cool silk. "That's what I'm doing," he said softly.

She leaned into him, eyes heavy with desire.

He dropped her hair and cleared his throat. "Go on. Get rid of them. I'll be right here." He strode off towards the lobby before he could succumb to temptation and drag her into a quiet corner.

First he wanted to have a few words with Rachel. She was just walking past Carrie's desk, heading for the street. "Hold up!"

Rachel shot him a look and kept going.

Liam jogged over and stood in front of the front door, more pissed than ever. "You're going to listen to me."

"Get out of my way."

He straightened up to his full height. "You're in no position to demand anything."

Rachel rolled her eyes. "Before, I wasn't. I am now. What are you going to do—fire me?"

"Here's the deal. You're never coming back into this building."

"Bev—my *niece*—thinks differently."

"Let her. It helps her sleep at night." He leaned closer. "My needs are different. My needs are to issue a restraining order if I ever see you here again, because as a manager here, I have a responsibility to act on the sixteen documented cases of co-workers complaining about your erratic and violent behavior."

Her mouth dropped open. "You do not."

"I accept the inevitability of you popping up every once in a while over the years in Bev's family's life," he said. "Just so you understand, I'll be there watching, and these touching reunions will never happen anywhere near Fite. Or anywhere we live."

She choked out a laugh. "We?"

"Me and Bev."

"You cocky bastard," Rachel said. "She'll never forgive you for taking off when she was in trouble. Not that she really needed you —she got a teenage slut to fix everything. She won't even give you your job back."

He smiled and pushed the door open for her. "Remember what I said."

"Kiss my ass." She walked out with the large photo flapping at her side.

We'll spend the holidays with my family. He locked the door and watched her disappear down the sidewalk.

"Let her have the house, Mom," Bev was saying when he got back to the conference room. "All she really wants is to have Johnny live nearby, and her future grandbaby, right, Aunt Ellen? And if I let you get involved with Fite—"

"Not me," Gail said. "Kate."

"If I let Kate get involved with Fite—"

Gail leaned forward. "Not just involved. A real career."

"—then you'd be willing to give the house to Johnny?"

Kate threw the t-shirt she was holding onto a chair. "This people stuff isn't my thing. It would have to be something where I could really get creative."

Bev shot her an icy look that reminded Liam of her aunt. Both of them.

"Help me out here, sis," Bev said. "We can work out your job description later."

Kate shook her head. "No way. I'm too young to sell out. I need to know I'm signing on to something I can believe in."

"How about you, Liam?" Ellen asked. "Are you too young to sell out?"

Liam met her gaze. Looked over at Bev, who frowned.

"Leave him out of this," Bev said.

Ellen put her hand over her heart. "Goodness. How romantic."

He didn't care what Ellen thought. It was the wariness in Bev's eyes that bothered him. "Bev and I need to talk. In private."

"There's no reason for you to be here," Bev said to him. "I'm sure you've got better things to do than worry about me and my family."

"No, I don't."

Distress flickered across her face. "Please. Just go. You wanted out of here, go ahead."

"I made a mistake." He caught Ellen's eye. "And no, I'm not feeling too young."

"Now you want to sell out?" Bev asked. "Is that what Ellen meant? You're willing to do anything to have Fite back?"

She wanted to force this here, in front of everyone? Fine. "Quite the opposite." He walked over to her. "I'm willing to do anything to get *you* back."

He saw the shock in her face, the fear, and wished he could relish it after the weeks of his own suffering, but all it did was stab him with more pain. He lifted his hand to her cheek. "I was wrong to leave. I didn't give you a chance."

She swallowed. "To call Annabelle?"

"To love me," he said. "But now I've decided I can do all the loving for a while. Until you catch up."

Bev's eyes, wide and bright, shifted to turquoise. "Oh," she whispered. She gazed at him with such open disbelief, such hope, he was able to tamp down his own panic.

"I wish I could say I'd work here without any pressure, that just being around you would be enough," he said, "but I'd be lying. I'd never be satisfied. I wasn't before, when it was just your body I wanted. Now—forget it."

She rested her cheek in his palm. "What parts do you want now?"

He gave her a lopsided grin.

"Don't believe him," Ellen said. "It's just another way of getting on top."

Bev frowned at her aunt then back at him. A smile crept across her face. "That doesn't sound so bad."

His body raged with heat. "I'm glad to hear that."

"Would you feel used if I asked you to come back to Fite?"

"Depends how you pay me."

She slid her hand up his chest. "You won't sue for sexual harassment?"

"Not if you marry me," he said, and Gail gasped. But Bev didn't recoil so he went on. "We can date first if you'd like."

She flung herself at him so suddenly he fell back against the table. Soft, warm limbs wrapped around him, firm and strong, smelling like her, tasting like her, everything he wanted.

"Oh, for God's sake," Ellen said. "Can't that wait?"

No. Liam buried his face in Bev's neck, inhaling her scent, feeling her skin, making her tremble in his arms. "I love you," he growled.

Her mouth tickled his ear. "I love you too," she said, and he felt the last of the brick inside him crumble.

Kate kicked a rolling rack with her foot and knocked it into the table. "Sorry to interrupt," she said, "but the rest of us are still here."

Liam grabbed the rolling rack, wrenching it away from Kate's foot, and shoved it across the room. "Nobody's keeping you."

"We aren't leaving until you promise Kate a job," Gail said.

Kate glared. "I don't want a job."

"Apple, meet tree," Ellen said.

Gail turned on her. "You shut up. No job for Kate, no house for Johnny."

Ellen shrugged. "So much for family." She walked to the door.

"No!" Bev cried. "You've come so close. You can't just leave like that after all these years!"

He couldn't believe what he was about to do, and Ed's crazed ghost would haunt him in the corridors at night for as long as he lived, but he'd make Kate the CFO if it would get him alone with

Bev, warm and naked, *right now*.

"Two words," he said loudly, and everyone looked at him. "Fite Dog."

Kate's face lit up, but Bev gripped his arm in concern. "You'd do that for her?"

He smiled down at her. "I'd do it for you," he said, savoring the way she glowed at him.

Kate aimed a finger at him. "You think it would suck, but you're wrong. It'll be the biggest money-maker Fite has ever seen."

"Whatever you say." He kissed the corner of Bev's eyebrow, just below a freckle.

Far away he heard Kate say, "You are going to eat your words, buddy. Just you wait."

"Oh, honey." Gail scurried over and put an arm around Kate's waist, bouncing their hips together. "It's a wonderful idea. If it's what you want I'll sacrifice my father's drafty old mausoleum to a man who can't even get married without his mommy telling him to do it."

Ellen got to her feet and held out her hand. "I'll need the keys."

Gail looked at Kate under her arm then dragged her over to Bev's side, pulled her away from Liam and hugged her on the other side. "This is how it should be. Me and my girls."

Bev hugged her briefly. "Ellen, if you find a way to get along with my mother—and Rachel, actually—not just for a week, but long term, lasting, sincere getting-along, then you can come back to Fite," she said. "You'd have to put up with me and Liam calling the shots, but Grandfather seemed to like having you around, and this is his company, and if he'd wanted to fire you he would have done it years ago."

Liam froze. No, not Ellen. After all this. Ellen *and* Fite Dog?

Ellen was staring at Bev, not moving. "And the house?"

"Yours," Bev said. "You just have to keep the peace. Each year you two are making progress in your relationship, as determined by me, I'll—I'll distribute a share of the profits at Fite." She glanced at Liam. "Can I do that?"

"How about we pay them all to go away?"

Bev laughed, catching herself just as Ellen was saying, "What if I don't want to come back to Fite?"

The room fell quiet.

"Don't you?" Bev asked.

"Not particularly. Not anymore." She got up and walked over to Gail. "And I don't need to be paid to talk to my own damn sister."

The two women stared at each other.

"Oh, Ellen, I am so sorry," Gail said, and burst into tears.

Face expressionless, Ellen opened her arms, and the two women embraced.

"This is why I like dogs," Kate said. "No drama."

"Really, Kate." Gail pulled away from Ellen and wiped her eyes. "Let's leave these two lovebirds." She reached into her pocket and pulled out a keychain. "Here, Ellen. To the house."

Ellen waved it away. "I can wait. Johnny won't be out here for months."

"But you should be able to go in whenever you want," Gail said. "We are family."

"Can we go, please? You two had dinner, but I'm starving," Kate said.

"I'll need a ride, too," Ellen said. "Good night, Liam. Bev."

"Bye." Liam was staring at the tender inner crease of Bev's elbows, realizing he'd never kissed them before. She looked up and saw him staring, saw the heat in his face, and turned pink.

"Now, please." Ellen walked out the door.

Kate followed. "Before they start up again."

Gail lingered for a moment in the doorway, frowning and wiping her wet cheeks. "Liam," she said, and he looked up. "Don't let her sleep here again tonight."

He met her gaze and nodded while Bev sighed in frustration. "I am right here. Don't start talking to me through him. I know he's big and manly and all that—"

"See you later, Liam." Gail blew him a kiss and left.

Liam ran his hand down his chest to smooth his shirt. "I bet you need a home-cooked meal. I'm making you a home-cooked meal. You never did eat my marinara."

"That's a big step." She pressed her chest up against him, pinning his hand over his heart. "How about sex first?"

His vision went dark. In one swift move he slipped his free hand around the back of her neck and kissed her.

❧

She broke the kiss to nibble on his ear. "Did you know that couch upstairs is a sofa bed?" She arched into him. "Took me a week to figure that out."

His fingers found the hem of her shirt, slipped underneath, and roamed over her back. "Did you know my condo is five minutes away?"

"What about—" she gasped as he unhooked her bra. "—April?"

He palmed her breasts, his eyes going out of focus. "What's with you always wanting to invite my sister?" Then he shoved her shirt and bra up to her chin and sucked the tip of her left nipple hard into his mouth.

Bev cried out. Tunneled her fingers through his hair. "We are not doing this in the conference room." She stroked the blond hair in her fingers, gazing up at the popcorn ceiling panels. "Oh!"

His teeth found the other nipple. "She's stranded at my mother's." His laughter tickled her tender flesh. "I'm taking you home with me." His hands dipped under the waistband of her slacks, slipping down over each round cheek, pulling her against him. "Eventually."

She pushed him away to look into his face. "This isn't fair."

Kissing and stroking, he moved his hand around her hips to the front. She felt him grin against her neck. "You can go first."

"I mean to you." She started to laugh, but her breath caught in her mouth as his finger slipped inside her. Whatever she was trying to say got scrambled in her bloodless brain. For a moment she gave herself up to it, but her worries wouldn't melt along with her muscles. "You'll always be wondering—"

"If you'll ever stop talking?" He added a finger and she gasped.

With self-discipline she didn't know she possessed, she wriggled away. "If I love you as much as you love me."

"No, I won't."

"Yes—"

"I know you don't. But that's okay."

She took another step back. "See? And you think *I'm* competitive."

He laughed. "All right, I give up. You love me the most." He went after her, eyes dark and fixed on her mouth.

"Now you're just saying that."

"No shit. Come here."

Her heel caught on the protruding wheel of an office chair as she ducked out of reach and bolted for the door. Her purse was in her office, and she made a run for it.

"Bev!" He appeared in the doorway of her office just as she lifted Ball off a chair and into her arms. With the fur at her chin she twirled around to face him.

His frustrated scowl broke into a mocking smile. "Give me the cat and nobody gets hurt."

She could feel her pulse in her throat. If he would just let her think. She needed a minute before she got swept up in everything he was promising, before she took everything she wanted, before it was too late to set the stage for a future that would stick.

She looked down at Ball, a silky lump of fluff in her arms. "That's it," she said softly. "I'll give it to you."

"Kidding. The cat's yours." He strode into the office. "Though I assumed you were a package deal."

With Ball still in her arms, she jogged past him and out the door. "My stuff is all upstairs."

He let out a frustrated sigh and followed her down the hall and up the stairwell, but by the time they reached her soon-to-be-vacated sleeping quarters he was looking cheerfully predatory. "Good idea. First we make the earth move, then you move into my place."

Heart skipping around in her chest, she smiled at him. "You mentioned that before and I didn't believe you." She took in the sight of him, from golden head to broad shoulder to long, strong legs, then back up to the loving, patient look in his eyes. "You gave me a choice—personal or professional, not both—"

"Forget it." He was there, taking Ball out of her arms. "I was an idiot."

"I chose wrong." She held up her hands to keep him from sweeping her away again. "So you left. You chose me over Fite. I'll never, ever doubt you again."

His hand hooked around her waist and pulled her hard against his body. "Excellent." He buried his face in her neck.

"But you—"

His lips nibbled the pulse under her jaw.

She inhaled deeply, lost her thoughts briefly in the rich scent of him. "—you'll always wonder."

"Nah." His tongue traced the path of her racing pulse up to her ear while his hands slipped up her body, touching everywhere, under her clothes, hot fingers on her skin.

"And so," she gasped and sank into him, "I'll—do—the same."

"Sure you will." He led her over to the sofa, pushed her back onto it, and climbed on top of her, heavy and everywhere. His hands dragged the hem of her shirt up to her bra and he dipped his head. Firm lips found her nipple through the nylon, and sparks of painful lust shot through her body while she stared at the blurry half-moon out the window over his shoulder and decided he was more than a fair trade. He could have Fite, she could have him.

She smiled and closed her eyes. He didn't believe her, but she'd show him.

He lifted himself up on one arm and frowned down at her. "This thing pulls out into a bed?"

She nodded, imagining how happy Engineering would be to have him back. Bev never did get a handle on all that garment construction stuff. And the sales guys would throw him a party.

"Well, come on." He lifted her up to her feet. He tore off the cushions, found the handle to the mattress frame and tugged it out, never taking his eyes off of her.

"Hi," she said shyly. He'd unhooked her bra, and she could feel her breasts heavy under her shirt. His eyelids fell, and she saw the humor drain out of him, the facade of mockery gone, leaving in its place hard, raw desire. For her.

She glanced past him at the bed, very glad she'd splurged on the expensive cotton sheets, the down comforter, extra pillows; he wouldn't know she'd been curling up every night under a scrap of fleece that had failed its pill and color transfer testing.

He held out a hand. His eyes, nearly black, searched her face, then dropped down over her body.

She lifted her shirt over her head, taking the unfastened bra with it, and dropped it on the floor. With eyes locked with his she slid her pants over her hips, slowly, shifting to one side to show him the curve of her ass.

He tore off his own shirt and shoes and pants and boxers and socks before she had worked her ankles free. He was very ready. She stared down at him, her heart beating too fast, and she fell on top of him on the thin, squeaking mattress. His mouth whispered love in her ear and his hands roaming over her body like a gale. She lifted her knees to straddle him, interrupted by his fingers slipping under her panties and between her legs, everywhere. She traced his collarbone, the hard curve of his shoulder, and swiveled her hips hungrily to meet his, his erection sliding along the cleft of her bottom.

He groaned and pushed out from under her, pinned her to the bed. "Not yet, sweetheart." Locks of his hair tickled her belly as he leaned down to remove her panties. She arched her back to help, and he got distracted, staring at her breasts, then fell on top of her to suck and lick and tease until the desire in her belly wound tighter and tighter and she pounded on his back to ease the torment.

"Now!" she gasped.

But he laughed silently, mouth wet on another part of her, sucking her fingers, licking her, bending her back and over and around with maddening, impossible need. She met his passion with hard need of her own, and blind hunger, and love, and he slid inside of her just at the moment she needed him most. She cried out and spun out of herself, just right, with him.

&

They made love a second time in the elevator, with poor Ball tucked into her carrier in the corner. Liam was glad only he knew about the security camera, though Bev gave him a suspicious look when he hung his shirt over the box in the ceiling before hitting the emergency stop button.

He didn't care about the million-dollar parking ticket, or the cat vomiting on the seat, just that he got Bev to his torn-up condo as soon as possible—not just for a third go, but to ease his mind and close the deal. Once her suitcase and cat were at his place, and that damn bachelor pad's of Ed's was safely converted to cubicles, he could relax and believe he was really going to get what he wanted.

"What happened?" Bev asked when she saw his decimated kitchen.

He came up behind her and hooked his hands around her waist. "I thought I'd lost you, so I had to keep busy." Then he swore, remembering the bathroom. The drop cloths over his bedroom floor. He'd have to keep her so distracted in bed she didn't notice.

"I kind of did the same thing. I would've done anything to keep Fite up and running. Since it was all I had left."

"You did amazingly well," he said. "Your grandfather wasn't crazy after all. I should have trusted him."

Bev gazed into his eyes. "Do you really believe that?"

"Unfortunately. His evil plan for me to seduce you turned out to be just the thing." He rested his chin on the top of her head. "You're not a bad boss and you're very creative with the bennies."

She tensed. "But that's all over."

He turned her around in his arms. "Bev . . . "

"Being the boss, I mean." She rolled her eyes. "See? This is what I'm talking about. I haven't convinced you of diddly squat."

He let out his breath. Pulled her close. "Just keep telling me. It'll sink in eventually."

"I love you, I love you, I love you."

He smiled. Felt her up. "Good."

"No, you're just being polite. That's why I made you choose. So you'd know, in your bones."

He pressed his hips against her. "Oh, my bones know."

"I'll work a few more weeks. Then it'll be yours again." She pulled out of his arms and ran a hand through her tangled hair, frowning. "You got a working shower in this place? I'd really like to—"

He snorted. "A few more weeks. Right."

"So you know I'd rather have you than Fite." She went over and stuck her head in the fridge. "I wonder if I can get a job at Levi's or something. I can't imagine going back to teaching now."

He shook his head, smiling, and captured her from behind again. "You do whatever you like. Buy a doughnut shop. Teach molecular biology at Cal. Hang out in my bed, naked, while I bring home the bacon—"

"Bacon is right, you sexist pig."

He sighed, enjoyed the feel of her, the fit of her. "I can dream."

She turned in his arms, beer in hand, and went up on her toes to kiss his chin. "You don't believe me. About proving my love."

He smiled into her eyes. "I know you, Bev. You want to look like you're doing the right thing, but there's no way you'd give up Fite now. At the end of the day—" he gave her a deep, sweet kiss, "—you're looking out for Numero Uno."

"Oh, yeah?"

"Yeah."

She bit her lip, trying to scowl, but her face split into a wide, adoring grin. "And you don't have a problem with that?"

"Nope."

"Because you're the same way." Her eyes sparkled. "Admit it."

He tilted his head and looked at her. "You bet I am," he said seriously. "At the end of the day, I'm looking out for you too."

Then he began a kiss that was so sweet, so deep, and lasted so long, Bev didn't notice his bedroom was painted three different colors until the next morning.

Epilogue

IT WAS ALMOST ten-thirty when Bev walked through Fite's front door. She wore an outfit from the first Fite Gear delivery, dark purple sweats with a long, stretchy jacket tied around her waist with a Fite logo on her butt—like three other women on the BART train with her that afternoon.

She didn't walk up right away to Carrie, who was on the phone, turned slightly to the side. Bev needed a minute to compose herself. Catch her breath.

"Bev!" Carrie slammed down the phone. "Why didn't you tell me you were here?" She ran around the desk and came over, arms wide.

Bev accepted the warm impact with a smile and tried not to lose it. Lately all she did was cry. "You looked busy."

"I am. Liam is promoting me to Trim Buyer."

"That's perfect for you."

Carrie drew back. "You look fantastic."

"Thanks. Is that a new design?" She pointed at the green pendant around Carrie's neck.

She nodded brightly. "My best-seller." She lowered her voice. "Liam doesn't mind me selling on Etsy as long as I don't mention Fite."

"Good for you," Bev said. "So, where is he?"

"Office. He's been holed up all day, throwing that ball against the wall, driving everyone crazy."

Annoyed, Bev looked at her watch. "He promised to be waiting for me out here." She did not want to go into any enclosed, private spaces with him. No matter how many times he promised to keep his hands to himself, next time he saw an opening he'd be on her like spit on lipstick. "Will you please tell him I'm here?"

"Hey there, Ms. Bev. Long time no see." George came up behind her dragging a dolly into the lobby. He was trying to frown and grin at the same time.

"How's your wife doing?" she asked him. "Any luck with the chiropractor?"

"Those quacks got her wrapped around their greedy little fingers. All in her head. And my wallet." He dumped his package in front of Carrie, waved, and went back the way he came, the ghost of a smile on his lips.

Carrie shook her head at Bev, the phone at her ear. "It went straight to voicemail. He must be on the line."

She refused to wait for him. Being at Fite again was harder than she'd expected. "I'll go find him." She pushed the door open and went down the hall to his office, surprised to see new carpeting, bright lighting, fresh paint. Guess the money was flowing in. He was doing fine. Without her.

His door was closed, which was more of the 'too much,' so she walked in without knocking and tried to keep her pulse steady when she took in the sight of him leaning back on his chair with his stocking-feet up on the desk.

"You look busy," she said, closing the door behind her.

He frowned at her between the gap in his feet, his handsome

face framed by wiggling toes. "What are you doing here?" He dropped his feet to the floor, muttered something into the receiver and hung up the phone. "You promised to let me take care of things on my own."

"It's Tuesday afternoon." She walked in and sank into a chair. Her feet were killing her. Really, Fite needed to work on their walking shoes. "We had a deal."

"Not—" He tilted his head and stared at her. "Still?"

"Hey, you're the one who said I had to set a good example."

He came around the desk. Smiled slowly. "Too late." He dropped to his knees and slid his hand over her rounded belly. As always, his touch set her nerves on fire. "Letting the staff knock you up is hardly setting a good example." His mouth found the hollow between her breasts and trailed kisses down her shirt.

She pushed her knee into his ribs. "This is why we meet in the lobby, remember?"

"I thought you'd love the excuse to stay on the couch." He drew back and frowned, his brown eyes intense. "Which is where you should be. Or in bed."

"Dr. Jane said I could still walk with you once a week, as long as I didn't feel contractions."

"She doesn't know you hiked through SOMA to get to that walk."

Bev kissed the tip of his nose. "She worries too much. And so do you."

"I'd airlift you home if I could." He gripped her shoulders and pushed them apart. "Now I have to call a cab."

"As if I'd let you."

"Oh, bossy again, are we?" He raised an eyebrow. "Nice try, but as of yesterday at eight a.m., I am the boss of this here establishment until you and Baby Fite come back to work."

"Yeah, well, I still own this here establishment."

"Community property state, babe. Fifty-fifty."

She exhaled in frustration and slumped back in the chair, feet sticking out. "More fine print," she said. "I swear, from now on I'm not signing anything."

He laughed and held out his hand. "Come on, I'll carry you to the sofa upstairs."

She lumbered to her feet. "Forget it. You may be cute but I've learned my lesson. Four months of bed rest. You have no idea what I'm going through. From now on you may admire me from a respectable distance."

He hooked an arm around her waist and pulled her tight. "This is about right," he said, eyes full of love, and kissed her gently on the lips. "It's selfish of me, but I'm glad you came."

She buried her smile in his neck. Inhaled his scent, practiced her love bites. "Better make it worth my while."

He growled and moved his mouth over hers, kissing her like a man who knew she was going to let him carry her wherever he wanted.

Just one more time.

**Read how Liam's brother Mark finds his own happy
ending in…**

This Time Next Door (Oakland Hills #2)
by Gretchen Galway

Readers first met Mark Johnson in *Love Handles* as Liam's
brilliant but awkward younger brother. In *This Time Next Door*,
Mark the software engineer decides to break away from his
computer and get a life, starting with the petite woman who's
moved in next door. But when he meets her large, blond
housemate, Rose, he starts to dream…bigger.

Twenty-six-year-old Rose Devlin may shop in the plus-size
department, but she's never had a problem attracting men—
with disastrous consequences. Recovering from her latest
mistake, Rose has sworn off casual flings and moved to
California to grow up, help her best friend, and make
something of herself.

When Rose asks the cute-but-geeky Mark to help her land a
job in high tech, she never expects to unearth his quiet
strength, stunning accomplishments—and hidden talents.
With a secret in her own past, Rose tries to keep her distance,
but she finds that nerdy Mark isn't so nerdy when the lights go
out. And that maybe, just maybe, she's not too grown up to
risk one more disaster…

About the Author

GRETCHEN GALWAY is a *USA Today* bestselling author who writes romantic comedies because love is too painful to survive without laughing. Raised in the American Midwest, she now lives in California with her husband and two kids.

Sign up for her newsletter at www.gretchengalway.com to hear about new books, sales, and special goodies!

CPSIA information can be obtained at www.ICGtesting.com
Printed in the USA
LVOW06s0046111215

466308LV00004B/422/P